If the Stars Align

If The Stars Align is a refreshing and remarkable debut by Nathalie Theodore. Told through interwoven timelines, we follow the lives of Dex and Sunny as their friendship and love is tested over decades. An emotional and unforgettable love story about opportune timing and fate. One of my favorite literary couples ever created. I thoroughly was immersed from start to finish!

KAYLA NEGOHOSIAN, GOODREADS REVIEWER

If The Stars Align is a heartfelt romance novel that takes readers on an emotional journey through the intertwined lives of Dex and Sunny. Written from both of their perspectives, the story spans their friendship from high school to college and into adulthood, keeping readers guessing whether their love is truly meant to be. The dual narrative is a refreshing glimpse into both sides of a love story. With its blend of humor, emotion, and relatable characters, this book is perfect for romance enthusiasts or anyone looking for an engaging escape into a beautiful tale of connection and destiny.

PARISSA ANDIDEH, GOODREADS REVIEWER

If the Stars Align is a sweet romance with a heavy side of spice! This is a great beach read that will have you rooting for both Dex and Sunny! I was captivated from beginning to end. While this book is a love story it also deals with a handful of heavier topics that everyone can relate to (single parent, mental health, generational trauma) thus adding some great substance underlying the story. The author did a great job with character development. I can't wait for the sequel!

SARAH KOOPERMAN, GOODREADS REVIEWER

If the Stars Align is a captivating romance story about Sunny and Dex, two lovable characters for whom you're rooting to find love. The writing is authentic and draws you into their love story, leaving you unable to put the book down. You feel as if you're right there with the characters. The author does a wonderful job weaving the two perspectives of Sunny and Dex into the book as they both navigate relationships, family, careers and growing up. I love the integration of mental health, its stigma and struggles into the book as well. This steamy, heartwarming romance will not disappoint!

EMILY GIGER, GOODREADS REVIEWER

DRAMATIC HEARTS CLUB
BOOK ONE

If the Stars Align

NATHALIE THEODORE

If the Stars Align

WRITTEN IN THE STARS PRESS

Cover and Interior Design by We Got You Covered Book Design

WWW.WEGOTYOUCOVEREDBOOKDESIGN.COM

ISBN: 978-1-966472-00-1

TO MY HUSBAND, DOMINIQUE,
FOR ALWAYS BELIEVING IN ME.

one

SUNNY
SPRING OF 1998

I want you to know that I have always loved you.

The words are written in Bic blue ink, on lined paper freshly ripped out of my AP English notebook. Words that I've been dying to say *out loud* for years now…but I haven't managed to yet. Turns out, it's not so easy telling your best friend that you've been in love with him for as long as you can remember. Especially when that friend is Oliver Dexter, known to his myriad friends and admirers simply as "Dex," whose popularity borders on celebrity in suburban Beachwood, Ohio, where we live. But even when we're alone, I can't seem to muster the courage to tell him how I feel. Every time I've tried, I get tongue-tied. I'm much better at expressing my thoughts in writing anyway. So a letter will have to do.

But my feelings for Dex aren't the only secret I've been keeping. While my love letter burns a hole in the right back pocket of my jeans, hidden in the left pocket is an acceptance from UCLA. And if all goes according to plan tonight—if Dex tells me he feels the same way—we'll go to college there together in the fall. He'll study acting, and I'll study creative writing.

No one knows I applied there, not even Dex, because I decided to surprise him. He's the only person I've told about my dream of writing novels, romance novels in particular, and from the moment I confessed to him, he's encouraged me to follow my passion. Unlike my workaholic mother, who would surely laugh in my face if I told her. As far as she knows, I'm dead set on studying pre-law at Northwestern. If Dex *does* reciprocate my feelings, it'll be a full-on battle to get her on board with me going to UCLA. But I'll cross that bridge when I get there. *If* I get there. First, I have a love letter to deliver.

It's opening night of the senior class play, *Romeo & Juliet*, and literally everyone and their mother is here. It's true—even my own mom who, somewhat unbelievably, switched her hospital shift with another surgeon for probably the second time in her entire career so she could accompany me. Normally, I would have discouraged her from going to the trouble, but I figured it might not be a bad idea to have a trauma doctor on hand in case my declaration of love takes a catastrophic turn. And to be perfectly honest, I'm not feeling very well. The boxed macaroni I made my mom and me for dinner tonight feels like it's sitting in my chest, and my hands are clammy, and my throat feels tight, and—

I'm panicking.

I don't know why I chose tonight of all nights to tell Dex I'm in love with him. Maybe it's because everyone who's here this evening is here to see *him* starring in the lead role. For the first time in our school's history, tickets sold out in advance for every show. On my way into the auditorium earlier, I walked past a group of freshmen who were fangirling so hard they were literally crying. As if Dex weren't already hot enough without any help from Shakespeare's most swoonworthy hero, the anticipation of Dex as *Romeo* set off a chain reaction of hormone surges that spread across Beachwood like wildfire. Rumor has it, there are girls from other schools who snuck in tonight just to see him. And now everyone will know what I've known all along.

That Oliver Dexter is special.

And it's not solely because he was blessed with movie-star good looks and the talent to match. It's true—whenever we went to the mall as kids, talent scouts would hand Mrs. Dexter their business cards and ask if her son had done any acting or modeling. It's because he's smart. Sensitive. Thoughtful. He has the biggest heart. And he's the best friend anyone could ask for. I miss the days when it was just me and him playing in the treehouse in his backyard. He used to be all mine, but now he's slipping through my fingers like the sand we built castles with when we were kids.

And I'm terrified.

The auditorium lights come up for intermission. That's my cue.

"I'm going to the bathroom," I tell my mom as I'm already hastily stepping over her to get to the aisle, but she's busy reading the program and only nods. I weave my way through throngs of students, and parents, and teachers, and—yup, those girls definitely do *not* go to this school—and I finally make my way out of the auditorium.

Then, out of nowhere, someone comes barreling right into me.

"Hey, Sunny!" my friend Mia says, enveloping me in a very tight squeeze. She's barely five feet tall, but curiously strong.

Once I get over the shock of her startling me, I heave a sigh of relief. After Dex, Mia is my closest friend, and I could really use a dose of her sweet, bubbly optimism right now. She's like a walking advertisement for energy drinks, even though she's never had a drop of caffeine in her life. I shudder to think what would happen if she did.

"I didn't see you in the auditorium!" she continues, unwrapping her arms from around me. "Where are you sitting?"

"I'm actually here with my mom. We're in the back row because she got tied up doing paperwork, so we were running late." I roll my eyes. "It's so typical—she took the day off from the hospital and *still* managed to work twelve hours straight."

Mia looks shocked. "No way, your *mom* is here? I'd love to meet her! I mean—of course I've *seen* her before, like from a distance… but I don't think I've ever really talked to her, you know?"

It speaks volumes that one of my closest friends, whom I've known for *seven years*, has never had an actual conversation with my mom.

"Anyway—now I know why I couldn't find you!" Mia goes on. "I figured you'd be in the front row with Dex's parents."

Under normal circumstances, I would be here with the Dexters—I practically grew up in their home, after all. A few weeks after I met Dex—known as "Ollie," then—Mrs. Dexter offered to start picking me up from school so I could play at their house instead of waiting for my mom's shift to end in the company of my gray-haired nanny. Thanks to the Dexters, I got what I'd always wanted—what I'd always needed. A family.

And the fear of losing them paralyzes me. Which is why I've waited so long to tell Dex how I feel. Because not only do I stand to lose him—but his wonderful parents as well. It was too big a gamble to take before now, when they've played such an integral role in my life. But we're collegebound and leaving Beachwood soon.

"Okay, well, I'm going to head back in! I can't wait to see the rest of the show. Dex is *amazing*!" Mia squeals. "You coming?"

The blood rushes to my face. As close as Mia and I are, I've never confided in her about my feelings for Dex. In all these years, I've never told a soul and, as far as I know, there's only one person who's ever guessed—Asher Abadie, way back in middle school, at Laura Levine's bat mitzvah party.

A transfer student, he was kind but awkward: the tallest kid in seventh grade by far, and thin as a rake, with wire-rim glasses that took up the bulk of his face. Asher said he'd noticed me stealing glances at Dex as girl after girl asked him to dance, and wanted to make sure I was alright. It was sweet, albeit mortifying. He wasn't one for gossip, so I didn't worry too much that he'd divulge my secret. But I can't say I wasn't relieved when his family moved again the following year.

Apart from astute Asher Abadie, no one else has confronted me. Mia *has* hinted several times over the years that she thinks Dex and I would make a cute couple, but I've insisted I only see him as a friend. Mia has no poker face—it's one of the things I love about her—and if she knew the truth, there's no way she wouldn't be weird around Dex.

And I can't even fathom how she'd react if she knew that her straight-laced best friend secretly devours steamy novels, and dreams of being a romance writer instead of a lawyer. As student government president and valedictorian, I have a certain image to uphold.

I can't say I don't feel guilty, though. Mia tells me everything, which is what best friends *should* do, but even with her, I'm a closed book. The only person I feel truly comfortable with is Dex. It's just different with him.

"I'm going to make a quick pit stop first," I lie. "I'll see you after the show and introduce you to my mom."

"Perfect!" Mia says with a bounce in her step as she turns to walk away.

When she's out of sight, I reach into the back pocket of my jeans and pull out my letter, hands shaking. I unfold it carefully and read the first lines, even though they're all etched into my mind. I put the words on paper mere hours ago—but they've been living in my heart and soul for over a decade.

I loved you when you walked into Mrs. Delmonico's kindergarten classroom on the first day of school, a bright-eyed little boy with your oversized blue backpack and scabbed knees.

It was 1985. I was standing alone in a quiet corner watching the other kids run around the room. I felt lonely and out of place—very much the "new girl," even though we were all new.

Until Ollie walked through the door and stood right next to me.

"I have a pet turtle at home," he said to me. "Wanna see?"

"I love turtles," I said, not knowing if that was true. But it didn't matter. As of that day we were instant best friends—inseparable.

I loved you then, and I love you now, and every single moment in between. Like when we were nine, and you convinced my mom to let me go hiking with you for the first time.

Worrying is my mother's love language, and she loves me tremendously. As a trauma surgeon, she spends her days troubleshooting life's worst-case scenarios, and she shut me down mid-sentence when I asked for permission to go. Ollie decided to take matters into his own hands. At school the next morning, he marched right up to her and told her that I was a lot stronger than she gave me credit for. My mom stared at him icily. And that's when Ollie flashed his irresistible grin. It was like magic—watching my mom's pursed lips break into a smile as she conceded. Even back then, he had a way of charming people.

I loved you when we played spin the bottle at Evan Chen's house in sixth grade, and you kissed me, even though the bottle was arguably pointing at Katie Klein.

Everything seemed to go in slow motion as Ollie crawled over to where I sat cross-legged on the lime green shag carpet, his perfect face approaching mine, which blazed with heat. I closed my eyes, and his lips landed on mine. He tasted like Orange Crush.

Afterward, I had this picture in my head of how things would be from then on. Me and Ollie on the tire swings, holding hands and sneaking kisses when no one was around.

But nothing changed in the slightest. I was so embarrassed, I couldn't look him in the eye for weeks.

I even loved you when you had your first girlfriend. And I've spent every moment since then wondering if you'll ever kiss me again.

Her name was Lisa Tucker—and even *before* she dated Dex, I was always envious of her because she was the first girl in our class to get boobs (whereas, at eighteen, I can probably still fit into my old training bras). Dex *never* talks about other girls with me, but rumor had it he felt Lisa up in a dark corner of the roller rink at Mark Dunn's fourteenth birthday party. I don't know for sure, because I wasn't invited. That was the first party Dex got invited to that I didn't. But no matter how popular he gets, he doesn't let the fame go to his head. He may walk the halls of our high school like he owns the place—all high fives and head nods—but he's still my best friend. The kids at school even have a nickname for us—"Sunny D"—like the beloved orange drink we used to chug when we were eleven.

It's sweet, yet bitter as well. Because, like a total cliché, I'm pining for the most popular boy in school. And while he's out enjoying house parties and going on dates, I'm usually home alone, reading the latest addition to my stash of romance novels and trying not to think about which girl-du-jour Dex is kissing…and why the hell it isn't me.

Maybe it doesn't make sense—to tell you now, or to tell you like this. But I can't keep denying what I know in my heart is true.

Oliver Dexter…I'm truly, madly, deeply in love with you.

Yes, the last line was inspired by Savage Garden. But that song perfectly captures how I feel. Because if there's one thing I know for certain, it's that I loved Oliver Dexter the moment I met him. And I love him more with every single breath I've taken since then.

I just haven't had the courage to tell him until now.

That's right—it's showtime.

I carefully re-fold the letter along its original creases and return it to my back pocket because my hands are getting sweaty, and I don't want to give my heart to Dex on a soggy piece of notebook paper. I dart across the hall and make my way to the door that leads backstage. The intermission is fifteen minutes long, and I've spent more than half of it talking to Mia, re-reading my letter, and wondering if anyone has ever died from unrequited love because, what if he rejects me? What if he laughs in my face? What if his eyes crinkle with pity, and he says he doesn't feel the same way? What if—

"Five more minutes, guys! Make your way back to the auditorium please!" the drama teacher, Ms. Mack, yells from across the hall.

Dammit. Okay, this is it. I'm going in.

I fling open the backstage door and run up the steps before I have a chance to question myself again. Right away, I see Dex in the wings offstage. He smiles, and a wave of calm washes over me.

But the moment of calm is fleeting. Because when I realize what Dex is smiling at—or *whom*, to be exact—a colossal surge of anxiety snatches my serenity in one fell swoop, like a riptide.

He's smiling at Jenna Andersen.

Perfect Jenna Andersen. The Homecoming Queen. The Head Cheerleader. The Most Popular Girl in School.

He doesn't see me standing at the top of the steps. His eyes are fixed on *her*. Jenna's back is turned to me, but I can hear her giggle as she flips her flawless hair—glossy and straight and obnoxiously obedient, unlike my curls, which have a mind of their own. Since she moved to Beachwood in sixth grade, I haven't stopped comparing myself to her. She's the perfectly proportioned, all-American, girl next door. And I am…not.

As I watch her stand on her tiptoes, my own feet begin to tingle, and when she wraps her arms around his neck, I lose all feeling in my hands. My brain is struggling to catch up, but my gut knows exactly what's about to happen next.

She kisses him.

I can't believe this. She beat me to the punch.

Hot tears sting my eyes. I cover my mouth so Dex can't hear me sob.

I race down the steps and take a moment to collect myself. My hands go to my back pockets, and my first instinct is to take my love letter and rip it to shreds.

But I can't.

So I reach for my UCLA acceptance instead. I tear it to pieces and shove it back in my jeans so no one finds it.

Looks like I'll be going to Northwestern after all.

I hear Jenna giggle again from up the stairs and take a few seconds to wipe my cheeks before opening the door to the hall. I have a choice to make, and I need to make it quickly. I can either accept the fact that I quite possibly just lost the love of my life to the prettiest girl I've ever seen…

Or I can do what I always do when Dex starts dating someone new—pretend it isn't happening. Because until he tells me himself that he's in a real relationship, I can choose to believe it's nothing serious.

I take a deep breath and step into the hall. Almost everyone is back in the auditorium now, and as I hurriedly make my way there, I spot my mom walking toward me.

"You okay, sweetheart? The second half of the show is about to start."

"I'm fine," I say as convincingly as I can. "The mac and cheese just isn't sitting well."

"I'm sure I have some antacids in my purse," my mom offers. "Or do you want to go home, instead?"

"No, I'll be alright. I want to see the rest of the show."

"Oh, good. Because I have to say…Dex's portrayal of Romeo is probably one of the best I've seen," my mom admits, her eyebrows raised like she can't believe she's saying it herself.

I can't help but smile. Although she hasn't come out and said it, ever since Dex and I started high school, I've been getting the sense that she isn't his biggest fan, despite his charm. So hearing her acknowledge how talented he is feels validating. "Isn't he incredible?" I say as we walk back into the auditorium together.

"I bet that boy's going to be famous one day," my mom says as we take our seats. She squeezes my knee. "And you can say you knew him when."

The lights go down just in time to hide my tears as they begin to fall again.

two

SUNNY

SUMMER OF 1998

The doorbell rings at 8:00 p.m. Normally I'd fly down the stairs to meet Dex, but tonight is different. My heart is heavy and my gaze wistful as I stand in the doorway of the room I grew up in, no longer familiar and cozy, but foreign territory. The walls are bare. My things are in boxes. My suitcases are packed. Summer flew by, which is always the case. And I'll be leaving for Northwestern in two days.

I got it in my head that I wanted to go there when I was eleven. I was telling ghost stories with the Dexters around their firepit one chilly autumn evening, and Mr. Dexter lent me his NU Law sweatshirt. He's an attorney with a successful solo practice doing immigration law. Later that night, he squeezed my shoulder and said, "That sweatshirt looks great on you, darling! I think we've got a future Wildcat here!"

That's when I decided to follow in his footsteps. But five years later, one of my mom's patients gave her a copy of Nicholas Sparks' *The Notebook*, and everything changed. My mom's jaded heart can't handle romance, so she tossed the book onto her Goodwill donation pile. Bored and curious, I rescued it. I stayed up the entire night reading it cover to cover, and from that day on, I was hooked.

The more love stories I read, the more I feel the urge to write my own. What could be better than crafting a tale about two imperfect people who are perfect for each other? I posed that very question in one of the personal essays I wrote for UCLA. I wasn't sure if being honest about my romance writing dreams on a college application was clever or risky, but either way, it worked. And when Dex received his acceptance letter too, it felt like fate.

Everything would have fallen into place, if only he hadn't been kissing Jenna backstage. I would have given him my love letter, and we'd both be going to Los Angeles, where I'd be writing our happily ever after.

But instead, tonight is our last night together.

Every step I take is leaden as I make my way downstairs to answer the door.

"Hey, you," he says, wrapping his arms around me when I step out onto the porch.

"Hi," I say on a long exhale, my cheek resting on his shoulder. If I could freeze one moment in time, it would be this. I never, ever, want to let go of him.

"What do you wanna do tonight?" he asks when we finally pull away from each other.

I sigh. "Can we pretend it's like any other night…and just drive?"

Dex gives me a half-smile. "Yeah," he says, nodding slowly. "I like that plan."

He's sad—I can tell. I'd like to think he's sad about leaving me but, honestly, he could be sad about saying goodbye to Jenna, for all I know. After she kissed him on the opening night of *Romeo and Juliet,* for the rest of the school year, I had to listen to her gush about him to her friends in the locker room every morning before PE. But school's been out for a couple of months, and I have no idea if they're still together.

I tend not to ask questions when I don't think I'll like the answers.

Dex tosses me his keys, and I take the driver's seat of Mr. Dexter's car while Dex gets in on the passenger side. I buckle up and start to reverse out of the driveway. And when I'm on the road and picking up speed, the freedom I feel behind the wheel is so exhilarating, so intoxicating, I feel myself smiling despite the anguish that's staked a claim on my heart.

"See?" Dex says, noticing my grin. "I knew you'd love driving."

My mom had actual panic attacks at the thought of me getting behind the wheel, which didn't make her a very good teacher. Every time I practiced with her, she'd nearly give me a heart attack by repeatedly shouting "CAREFUL!" apropos of absolutely nothing. It was so stressful that, even though I managed to pass my driving test and get my license, I had no desire to drive ever again. But Dex wouldn't hear of it. The day after graduation, he insisted I start driving with him.

I was incredibly nervous at first. I didn't want to embarrass myself. But with cool, calm, Dex by my side, I got comfortable behind the wheel pretty fast.

"I couldn't have done this without you," I say, my eyes on the road but the corners of my mouth upturned. "Thank you so much."

"The pleasure was all mine," Dex says quietly before clearing his throat. At a stop sign, I turn toward him, but he's looking out the window.

When we're moving again, he turns up the volume on the radio. "Bittersweet Symphony," by The Verve, is playing and, before long, we're both singing at the top of our lungs as I drive with the windows down, the fresh summer air cooling our skin. I catch a glimpse of my reflection in the rear-view mirror, and I'm beaming. I don't think I ever look happier than when I'm with him. If only things could stay like this. But by this time tomorrow, Dex will be living in LA. It's unfathomable, really. I mean, we've been inseparable since we were five years old. I hardly know who I am without him.

I stop at a red light and steal a glance in his direction. He looks over at me—still singing—and as soon as our eyes meet, he breaks into that movie star grin of his and, right away, my heart melts.

I'm hopelessly in love.

And it's not only because he's gorgeous. It's the way he's always been there for me. Like when I had chickenpox in third grade, and I was quarantined in my bedroom. He'd never had it himself, so he was susceptible, but he insisted on coming over and keeping me company. He brought a stack of his favorite movies on VHS and made my mom set up her TV/VCR in my room. He curled up next to me in my bed, his head on my shoulder, and we watched movies until I laughed and forgot how badly I was itching. Until bright red spots appeared on his face.

"Green light," Dex says, yanking me back to the present. I laugh at myself as I step on the gas. Dex chuckles too. "Penny for your thoughts?"

My face is on fire. "Just taking a trip down memory lane, I guess. But you know what? I changed my mind. I don't want to just drive around tonight."

Dex smiles as I make a quick U-turn. "You're the boss. Where are we going?"

"It's a surprise," I say, grinning.

Ten minutes later, I'm turning onto Dex's street.

"You're taking me home?" There's a tinge of disappointment in his voice, which makes me feel a little bit guilty—but also a little bit giddy.

"Not quite," I tease as I roll right past his driveway. "Be patient, we're almost there."

I coast to the end of the street, make a right turn, then left, and park on the side of the road. As I pull the keys out of the ignition, I see Dex's signature half-smile take shape. As quickly as I can, I unbuckle and get out of the car. "Race you to the swing set!" I yell before I slam the driver's side door shut and dash onto the grassy field.

"You're cheating! No head starts!" I hear him say as he races after me. And instantly, it's like we're kids again.

"You've got longer legs!" I shout as I beat him by just a fraction of a second. I turn around, take hold of the iron chains, and hop onto my swing as Dex settles onto his.

"Gosh, when was the last time we were here?" he asks as his eyes shift from right to left across our favorite childhood playground.

I shrug as I catch my breath. "Maybe middle school?" And then I laugh. "Seventh grade, I think. The year you told everyone at school to start calling you Dex."

Because Ollie was a kid's name, and Oliver wasn't cool enough, I guess. It was inconvenient for me because I'd already written Mrs. Oliver Dexter all over my Lisa Frank spiral notebooks—and that had a much better ring to it than Mrs. Dex. But I digress.

"No, it was more recent than that," Dex says, shaking his head. "It was—the summer you got braces," he says after a beat. "Right before we started high school. You made us wait here for the ice cream truck every day for a week because your teeth hurt, and you said the only thing that helped were push-pops."

I chuckle. "How could I forget? Yeah, my teeth only hurt the first couple of days…I was definitely milking it after that."

"I know," he says.

I look at him and smile. We're both swinging slowly, letting the light summer breeze do most of the work.

"By the way, it was pretty cool of you to come over this morning just to say goodbye to my parents," Dex tells me with a tender look in his eyes.

"Of *course*—I wouldn't dream of leaving for college without saying goodbye to them." I kick at the woodchips beneath my feet. "With my mom's schedule being so unpredictable, the time I spent with your mom and dad was my stability. And as busy as your dad was, he never missed a family dinner. I know he wanted to be there for you, of course—"

"Sunny, he knew how important those dinners were to you too." The absolute sincerity in Dex's expression brings tears to my eyes.

Mr. Dexter is the closest thing to a dad I've ever had. My mom spent years in an on-again, off-again relationship that turned off permanently when she found out she was pregnant with me. I used to ask her questions about my biological father when I was a kid, but she downright refused to talk about him. After a while, I just stopped asking. I guess the fact that he chose not to be involved is all I really need to know.

I try my best not to cry. "I just hope your parents know how grateful I am. And how important they are to me."

"Of course they know," Dex replies. "Believe me, they feel the same way about you." And because he anticipates that I'll shrug it off, he adds with emphasis, *It's true*, just as I begin to dismissively shake my head.

I laugh. "You know me so well. And…thank you."

"Anytime." Dex's grin turns wistful as he takes his gaze up to the velvety night sky and sighs. "I can't believe this is it. Our last night together in Beachwood. For now."

I sigh. "I know. It's gonna be weird, being so far away."

Dex shakes his head. "I'm kicking myself for not applying to Northwestern." He winks at me, which makes me think he's kidding…but I'm not entirely sure. Then he looks down at his lap. "It'll be okay. We'll talk every day, and we'll see each other over breaks. And before we know it, it'll be summer again."

"Do you promise?" I ask, my words emerging as a near-whisper. "That we'll talk every day?"

Dex holds out his hand. "Pinky swear."

We hook our fingers and swing back and forth together.

"Will you promise *me* something?" he asks after a minute

of silence. "Don't stop writing. I know you want to go to law school, but there's nothing stopping you from being a lawyer who writes romance novels."

I laugh. "All I write are poems. Writing a novel is a pipe dream, Dex." I pull my pinky away from his.

"Not for you, Sunny. You have the talent and the passion to make it happen. I just don't want you to give up on your dream."

"Okay," is all I say. He has no idea I gave up *all* my dreams when I declined my offer from UCLA.

"Good," he says, though he seems dissatisfied. He knows me better than to believe me.

"Dex…I'm scared," I say so quietly I wonder if he can hear me.

He looks at me, his eyebrows knit together. "Scared of what?"

I bite my lower lip. "What if I don't make friends at school?"

Dex scoffs. "Are you kidding me? Everyone loves you."

I roll my eyes, but mostly to keep more tears from falling. "I think it's *you* they love. And they're only friends with me…by association."

Dex digs his shoes into the woodchips to stop his swing and gently grabs hold of my chain, turning me toward him. "Sunny, you don't really think that, do you?"

I don't know what to think. It's not always easy being the leading man's sidekick.

It's not that people don't like me—quite the contrary. Pretty much everyone likes me, because I'm nice, and quiet, and unassuming. But does anyone really *want* to be the nice, quiet, unassuming girl? Not me. I don't necessarily crave being the center of attention either—but maybe somewhere in between.

I attempt a deep breath, but my chest only tightens. "It's just a fear of mine, I guess."

Dex looks crestfallen. "It kills me that you don't know how amazing you are."

The intensity of his gaze causes my heart to beat so quickly that I have to turn away. When I do, he lets go of my chain, and I start swinging slowly again.

"You are so smart, and thoughtful, and generous, and kind. You're going to have more friends at Northwestern than you'll know what to do with," he continues. "They'll be lining up—taking numbers—to hang out with you." I chuckle as Dex looks down at his lap pensively and his half-smile goes flat. "Not to mention, the guys…"

I snort. "The *guys*? Dex, in case you haven't noticed, there are *zero* guys lining up to date me."

Which is why I ended up going to prom with a group of my girlfriends—while Dex went with Jenna. I know he's only trying to be nice, but I can't help but feel ashamed of my non-existent love life. I want to get asked out on dates. To get noticed by boys. Well, *one* boy, in particular. But mostly, I feel invisible.

There was one time I thought my luck might change. It was at Laura Levine's bat mitzvah party, *after* Asher Abadie had outed me. I was at the refreshment table, feeding my misery with Cheez Balls, when the DJ announced the final song—"Save the Best for Last," by Vanessa Williams. I made a beeline for the door to spare myself the heartache of having to watch Dex dance with yet another girl. That's when I felt a gentle tap on my shoulder. It was him.

I tried to play it cool, but my heart threatened to leap from my chest. Dex had saved his last dance for *me*. Just like the song, he'd "Saved the Best for Last." I laid my head on his shoulder as we swayed from side to side. From across the room, an amused Asher winked at me, then smiled as he shook his head.

I was sure Dex would kiss me again that night.

But he didn't.

"Just wait and you'll see," Dex says from his swing, his eyes still shifted away from me. "You're going to have your pick of boyfriends soon."

I shake my head. "I really don't think that's true, judging by my experience in high school."

"Sunny, most guys in high school just wanna fuck around," Dex tells me. "And honestly?" I look over at him. "I think they know better than to waste your time. You're too mature for them now but trust me—you're the type of girl they want to marry one day."

I search Dex's face for any hint of levity but there is absolutely nothing light-hearted about the way his eyes are fixed on me right now. He looks dead serious.

And I'm speechless.

My mind is racing, trying to come up with some sort of response, when the first few droplets of rain fall from the billowy clouds overhead. I look up. "Oh no, I think it's about to—"

I'm cut off by an earsplitting crack of thunder that parts the heavens and unleashes a spectacular, unexpected summer storm.

Whatever moment we were beginning to find ourselves in is immediately washed away. Dex and I look up at the sky, then turn to look at each other through dripping wet eyelashes, the corners of our mouths upturned in stunned amusement as we get more and more drenched with each passing second.

"Race you back to the car!" Dex yells with a grin as he starts jogging backward. When I'm about to catch up to him, he picks up speed and starts to turn around.

"Oh no you don't!" I shout over another earth-shattering clap of thunder. I reach out and grab his shirt to turn him back toward me, but he hooks his arms around my waist, and we end up in a heap on the wet grass, with me on top of him. We're laughing so hard there are tears streaming down our cheeks—or maybe raindrops, it's hard to tell.

"All those times we raced to the swings when we were kids… you were letting me win, weren't you?" I ask between giggles.

Dex grins. "A gentleman never tells."

As our laughter dies down and we begin to catch our breath, I become more aware of the rhythm of his heart beating against mine, of our chests rising and falling at the exact same time. Of the closeness of our lips—the closest our lips have been since our first and only kiss.

Dex tucks a strand of wet hair behind my ear. "I'm gonna miss you so damn much, Sunny."

"Me too," I answer back instantly.

As the rain continues to crash down on us, Dex looks at me in a way he's never looked at me before and, for the first time, the possibility of something new hangs in the electric air between us. And it doesn't feel awkward at all, even for the several seconds we're both silent and gazing into each other's eyes. It feels so normal, in fact, that it takes an actual effort to keep my lips from landing on his—like I'm resisting a magnetic pull—and I wonder if I should even bother trying to fight it.

But before I get the chance to decide, a bolt of lightning illuminates the sky, accompanied by another roar of thunder so loud it sets off a nearby car alarm.

"We should get home," Dex says as he rolls us over. He pulls me up and keeps my hand in his as we run the rest of the short distance to his dad's car.

Shivering in my soaking wet tank top and shorts, I crank up the heat and turn to face Dex as soon as he slides into the passenger seat. "Maybe you should drive back," I yell over the heavy splats of rain pounding on the car so loudly, you'd swear it was raining pennies.

Dex considers, but shakes his head. "You're going to have to drive in weather like this at some point anyway, and I'm right here, so don't worry. Just drive more slowly than you normally would, and give yourself extra room to stop in case the roads are slick."

I nod and start driving us back to my house. If it weren't for the weather and having to concentrate so hard on what I'm doing, I'm sure my mind would be going a hundred miles an hour, desperately trying to make sense of what just happened. But right now, my singular focus is getting us home safely. And thankfully, I do.

"Well played," Dex says when I pull over. As usual, I park a block away from my house, and Dex and I switch seats on the off-chance my mom is home from work and waiting up for me.

"Are you ever going to tell your mom you started driving again? You can't keep it a secret forever," he says as he adjusts the rear-view mirror and starts rolling forward.

I shake my head vehemently. "Not unless she has a lobotomy. You know how much she worries. I mean, you have to admit… she *is* a little nuts."

Dex laughs as he pulls into my driveway. The lights are off, which means she's still at work. "Your mom isn't nuts," he says. Then his smile fades as he reaches for my hand. "She just loves you, Sunny."

I glance down at our interlaced fingers and, without warning, tears start to fall from my eyes, like the sudden summer rain that has us both sopping wet.

"I don't wanna say goodbye, Dex."

There's so much more I want to say…but it feels like the timing isn't right. So I settle for only that.

"Good," he says quietly. "Because neither do I." His eyes are glistening. "This is a night like any other, remember?"

I nod, and we wrap our arms around each other like we always do and, before I get out of the car, he says, "I'll call you tomorrow," like he always does, and we pretend that tomorrow is an ordinary day—and that, when he calls me, he'll be calling from the house we both grew up in.

Not from a dorm room halfway across the country.

three

DEX

I back out of Sunny's driveway. I make the short trip back to my house. But as soon as I get through the door, it starts happening. My chest is tight. My throat is closing.

I race to the kitchen and down a glass of ice cold water. It doesn't help.

God, I'm so fucking mad at myself.

I wasted the perfect chance. The *girl of my dreams* was lying on top of me. And the way she looked at me, it was different this time. It felt like love. It was all I could do not to tell her the truth.

But what would Sunny think if I told her I loved her and, "Oh by the way, last night I had sex with someone else?"

Fuck!

I didn't plan to sleep with Jenna, it just happened. It was her first time.

And mine too.

I'd had other opportunities—I just really wanted to hold out for Sunny. But she's so hard to read. And we're about to leave for different colleges. How long could I possibly wait?

I'm such a goddamn idiot.

My heart races. I gasp for breath.

I try again to ground myself.

I find a picture of us on the side of the fridge and reach for it, my hands trembling. We're sitting on the tire swings that used to be in my backyard. We'd only just met, but we look like we'd been friends forever.

I'll never forget the first time I saw her. I remember exactly what she looked like in her yellow dress. I didn't even know her name was Sunny yet, but I knew right away she was the brightest light I'd ever seen. What a relief to find that light after weeks and weeks of darkness.

Months earlier, I found out I was finally going to be a big brother. After I was born, my mom had three miscarriages. So when this baby girl finally came along and stuck, my parents were ecstatic.

But our happiness was short-lived. One day, my mom went to the hospital. And she didn't come back for days.

And days and days and days.

My heart ached—I remember that. I was convinced I'd never see her again. Never smell the sweet perfume on her skin. Never feel the warmth of her arms around me. Never hear her say how much she thanked her lucky stars for me.

But eventually she did come home, with a smaller belly and no baby. She walked straight up the stairs, went straight to her room, and got straight into bed. And she stayed there for weeks.

When I asked my dad what happened, his bottom lip

quivered. He couldn't find the words. He suggested we go to the pet store and said I could get anything I wanted. I chose a turtle, of all things. For a few weeks, I regretted my decision. But then, everything became clear to me. Because, you know who really loved turtles? Sunny. That turtle is the reason she agreed to come over and play with me.

And when Sunny started coming over, my house felt alive for the first time in months. The sound of laughter echoed in the halls. My mom opened the blinds to let the light in. *Finally*, she was herself again. Sunny didn't know it, but she filled a giant hole in the heart of my family. We had needed her as much as she'd needed us.

We needed her.

I need her.

My hands are numb. *Dammit.*

This picture isn't helping at all.

Everything in this house reminds me of Sunny. That usually makes me happy, but tonight it only reminds me that I royally fucked up.

I'm tempted to head back outside…

But a bolt of lightning pierces the sky.

The rain's still coming down like crazy.

I'm trapped in here. My vision's hazy—

Shit…I'm doing it again…

When I panic, I tend to rhyme in my head.

It helps slow down my racing mind.

If only it would *fucking* work this time!

People take one look at me and think my life is perfect.

They have no damn clue what goes on beneath the surface.

But what if I start rhyming out loud one day?

Will people laugh at me? Judge me? Call me insane?

Don't go there, Ollie. You're spiraling.

I rush up the stairs and head toward my bedroom. But my squeaky door hinge is so goddamn loud, my parents start stirring. "Is that you, Dex?"

"Yup, sorry to wake you! Just going to sleep." I sound cool, calm, and confident.

I really am a pro at this act.

But I *hate* these fucking panic attacks.

They started months after my mom came home from the hospital. I never felt anxious when Sunny was over, but when she was gone? Now that was another story. I refused to leave my mom's side. If she left my sight, I was scared to death. One or two nights a week, I'd wake up screaming.

One night I dreamed that a ghost stole the baby from my arms. When my mom came in to comfort me, I asked where my sister was.

"I like to think she's a star in the sky, watching over us. And maybe when we see a flicker, we'll know she's there."

A star in the sky. I liked that idea. But for some reason I started to sob.

My parents took me to see a psychologist. I remember drawing pictures. Mom with a big belly, smiling. Mom with a smaller belly, sleeping. Me, alone and crying, my tears pooling in a puddle of blue crayon at my feet. Bright, beautiful Sunny in her yellow dress.

I overheard my parents talking about my therapy sessions one night when I was supposed to be sleeping. I didn't understand most of what they said, but the phrase "separation anxiety" became embedded in my head because they repeated it so many times.

But with Sunny, I was carefree. A normal, happy kid. We rode our bikes, and played hopscotch and hide and seek, and I never, not once, felt a tinge of anxiety. We went camping together under the stars, and it was the soundest I ever slept, with Sunny by my side.

My heart rate's slowing down.

I put my hand on my stomach and take a deep breath. Maybe this panic attack is over. I get off the floor and look outside my window. The rain's coming down even harder than before.

It's like the heavens are crying because I had sex with Jenna.

I made such a stupid mistake last night.

It's starting again—my chest is tight.

The room is spinning. I sit on my bed.

I dig through a box that's near my nightstand.

I find my old journal and flip through each page.

Find the stars Sunny drew me in fifth—no, sixth grade.

Sixth fucking grade. That's the year I was bullied. It started on a Monday, in the boys' locker room. Tommy Giannetti approached me with his minions. He called me a pretty boy and spat in my face. Then he pushed me into a wall while everyone laughed. The next day it happened all over again.

The fourteenth time he cornered me, Tommy and I were alone. He had his hands around my neck, and I thought he was gonna choke me. But he planted his lips on mine instead. If I snitched to anyone, he swore he'd fucking kill me.

Tommy never kissed me again because we were never alone together again. But he bullied me plenty more times. And I never told anyone. Not a soul. Not even Sunny.

I started having bad dreams again, though, almost nightly. But I didn't yell out for my mom anymore. I was too old for that. Instead I sat up in the dark, sweating and panting, my heart racing, my fingers trembling. Sometimes I'd wring my hands to try to keep them from shaking. It was hell on Earth. I was afraid I was dying each and every time.

But I spent every minute of the summer after sixth grade with Sunny. And for three perfect months, I had zero worries. I also had a massive growth spurt. I was taller than Tommy when we went back to school in the fall.

I wasn't scared of the locker room that day. I waited for the boys with an actual grin on my face.

"What the hell are you smiling at, Ollie?" Tommy said with his menacing glare. But his expression changed the second he realized I wasn't only taller than him—I looked a lot stronger now too.

"It's not Ollie anymore," I retorted. "Call me Dex."

And Dex punched Tommy square in the stomach, while the Ollie inside me did a happy dance. Tommy doubled over, groaning, as the boys surrounding us whooped and hollered in disbelief. From that day forward, his crew followed *me*.

"If you tell, I tell," I whispered in Tommy's ear.

Tommy clutched his stomach. "Got it, Dex."

Yup, I was Dex now.

Dex was cool, calm, confident.

He was popular and adored.

He was an act.

A performance I put on for survival. To deal with the anxious little kid inside me.

Yes, Ollie's still here beneath the façade. I wish he weren't. But these are the cards I was dealt.

The only time I'm ever my true self is when I'm with Sunny. Whether I'm Ollie or Dex, it doesn't matter, I don't even have to think about it then. When I'm with her, I'm free. God, I love making her happy. The way her cheeks go rosy and her eyes light up. The way I feel her joy, like warmth, in my own body.

Sunny is everything. My entire world. But I've never had the nerve to tell her the truth.

God, I wish I'd been more bold.

But wasn't I bold when I kissed her at Evan Chen's house? It had been *my* idea to play spin the bottle. I'd lost hours that week practice-spinning. But when it was my turn to play, my hands were shaking—and the bottle didn't spin as fast as I anticipated. It pointed to Sunny's left, it was obvious. But I kissed her anyway. If you ask me, I'd say that's pretty damn courageous. I figured now she'd *have* to know how I felt about her.

But nothing changed. I was devastated.

Then at Laura Levine's bat mitzvah party, Sunny spent the entire night being chatted up by Asher. I don't know why I was surprised. Of course other guys were interested in Sunny—how could they *not* be? I couldn't wait any longer to tell her how I felt. If I didn't act fast, I was going to lose her. That's when I walked up and asked her to dance.

Sunny smiled coolly and gave a little nod. It wasn't much, but it was enough. I grinned so wide when she walked into my arms. We'd hugged thousands of times, but to be able to hold her and not let go…

It was heaven.

I closed my eyes and swayed with her, and breathed in the scent of her hair, sweet, like strawberries. And maybe a little powdered cheese, if I wasn't mistaken. I loved the smell of powdered cheese. And I loved her. So much.

And finally—*finally*—I was going to tell her.

But as soon as I opened my eyes, I caught Sunny smiling at *Asher.*

I thought Sunny and I were soulmates. But clearly she wasn't interested in me.

Still, when Lisa Tucker asked me to be her date to Mark Dunn's party, I couldn't help but wonder if it would have an effect on Sunny. She wouldn't be there, anyway—Sunny was wise beyond her years and much too cool for a lot of these things. She would've much rather stayed home reading *Pride and Prejudice* than hang out with a bunch of kids at a roller rink. So I agreed to go with Lisa. But I didn't have the first clue how to act on a date. I got sweaty from head to toe just thinking about it. So I got advice from my cousin Ben. That's how Dex became a ladies' man.

It was all a part of the act.

During our freshman year of high school, I took a drama

class, and it came as no surprise to me that I did so well. My teacher, Ms. Mack, was floored by my ability to transform into a different person. *Well, I've definitely had a lot of practice*, I said to myself.

"You have what it takes to be a star, Dex," she told me. "Would you consider pursuing acting? I have a close connection at UCLA, so keep that in mind down the road."

It made sense. I'm a lot more comfortable living as Dex, so I applied to UCLA.

But here's a secret I never shared—I actually applied to Northwestern too. I thought maybe, on the off chance that Sunny had feelings for me, we could end up going to the same school. I didn't tell her, to save myself the embarrassment in case I didn't get in. And, sure enough, that's exactly what happened.

It put a whole lot in perspective for me. Just like I feared—I wasn't good enough for Sunny. So even though I wanted to tell her how I felt, that goddamn rejection letter killed my confidence.

And when Jenna asked me to prom, I heard myself saying yes. We were messing around, just for fun. Our relationship wasn't serious.

I still can't believe we slept together.

And afterward, Jenna told me she *loves* me. Other than prom, and hooking up at her house when her parents were out, we've never even been on a date. I had absolutely no clue how to respond. I started to panic. So I asked myself, what would Dex say? Then I looked in her eyes with a confident smile and told her, "I love you, too."

But—*fuck.* I *don't* love Jenna. My heart belongs to Sunny. And now I've messed everything up.

I don't know how I'll cope without her.

When the stars align, one day, we'll be together.

It's the only thought that brings me comfort.

I have to believe it if I'm gonna move forward.

…

The storm has passed. I lie down in bed, relieved but exhausted. In less than twelve hours, I'll be leaving for LA. I close my eyes and try to sleep—I'll sure as hell need it to keep up this act. If I can't be with Sunny, I can't be myself.

So starting tomorrow, there's only Dex.

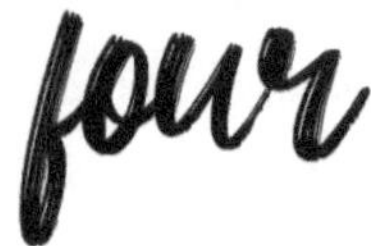

SUNNY

SUMMER OF 1999

Mia's freshman year ended weeks before mine, and she's been bored out of her mind back home in Beachwood, so she offers to pick me up from the airport. I leave the freezing cold terminal and let the hot summer air melt the chill from my skin. I look up at the clear blue sky and enjoy the warmth of the sun on my hair. I have one year of college under my belt, and now I'm home. I've always loved summers in Beachwood. But summers in Beachwood were always synonymous with Dex. And it's been months since I last talked to him.

Mia pulls up to the curb, and I do my best to ignore the anxiety that's bubbling up inside me. "Sunny!" she squeals as soon as I get in the car. She gives me a huge (slightly painful) hug and, when she lets go, her eyes are wide. "I almost didn't recognize you!"

I bite my lip and smile, aware that I look very different now than I did when we graduated from high school a year ago. I was a late bloomer, but it was worth the wait.

"You have the curves you always dreamed of!" Mia continues, awestruck. I laugh, remembering all the times I'd lamented to her about my flat chest. "And your hair looks gorgeous!"

"Thanks," I say, my cheeks getting warmer by the second. I get a lot more attention these days than I did back in high school—but I'm still not used to it. "I made a friend in my dorm with similar hair, and she taught me how to style it."

I guess that's the one thing I do know about my biological father—I must have gotten my curls from him, because my mom's hair is stick-straight. When I was a kid, she pulled my wild mane into a ponytail because she had no clue what else to do with it. I always felt like I stood out like a sore thumb in our small Midwestern suburb, where the standard of beauty can be boiled down to one lucky girl: Jenna Andersen. With her silky blonde hair and green eyes, she could be on the cover of *Seventeen*. Meanwhile, I rarely see models who look like me: big brown eyes, olive skin, and chocolate-hued curls with a hint of auburn (my redheaded mother's only contribution).

But thanks to my new friend at school, at least now my curls are frizz-free and cascade down my back in pretty ringlets. My roommate says I have "princess hair." And for the first time in my life, I actually don't hate it. I might even love it.

"Well, you look *hot*!" Mia says as she pulls away from the curb. "Everyone's going to be shocked when they see you at the party tonight."

"What party?" I ask her, confused, as she changes lanes and starts to pick up speed.

"Oh—you probably haven't checked your email yet. Seth

Arden's parents are out of town, and he invited everyone from our class to his house. You have to come! It's going to be amazing," Mia goes on, talking a mile a minute. "I'm sure Dex will be there. You must be so excited. When was the last time you guys saw each other?"

My heart lurches, and it isn't only because Mia takes corners like a NASCAR driver. With one hand braced against the dashboard, I answer, "Not since Thanksgiving."

And Thanksgiving was a total disaster. My mom and I had dinner at noon before she had to be at the hospital. Even though it was only the two of us, she ordered a whole turkey and all the trimmings from her favorite five-star restaurant. We started the meal seated at our barely used dining room table but, within minutes, my mom got a phone call from a frazzled surgery resident and ate standing in the kitchen while I took my plate to the couch.

After my mom left for work, Dex picked me up so I could have a real Thanksgiving dinner at his house. Mrs. Dexter made everything from scratch, and I was so happy to be with them again—but Dex had this terrible cold and didn't want to get too close. There I was hoping we could pick up where we left off on our last night before college, when we almost kissed in the rain. At least I *thought* we almost kissed. I don't know, now. Maybe I was imagining things.

Or maybe I was losing Dex. Maybe he had a gorgeous girlfriend in LA he hadn't mentioned yet. I knew he wasn't still involved with Jenna, because he'd casually mentioned in conversation that she was dating someone she met in school. But maybe he was seeing someone else. So back at Northwestern, I conducted an experiment: if I didn't call him first, how long would it take for him to call me? The results were exactly what I feared. I didn't hear from him for weeks. I didn't even bother going home for spring break. My mom would be working anyway, so I accepted my roommate's invitation to her family's lake house in Michigan.

"Oh my gosh, so you guys haven't seen in each other in, like…six months? That's crazy! You should definitely come to the party then! I can pick you up. How's nine o'clock?" Mia asks eagerly.

I sigh. "I don't know, Mia. I had to wake up early this morning to finish packing, and I'm pretty exhausted. I'll probably just stay in tonight."

Mia frowns. "Are you sure?" she asks without waiting for my reply. "Well, if you change your mind, you can always call me," she says as she passes a truck that has to be going ninety miles an hour.

"I will," I say, relieved that she doesn't press me any further. Truthfully, I got more than enough sleep last night, but I'm not sure I want to see Dex for the first time in six months at a house party full of kids from our high school.

"So what are your plans for the summer?" Mia goes on to ask.

"Not a whole lot. Babysitting. Hanging out. In a few weeks, I'll be going to Chicago." I pause for just a second, considering whether I want to continue. "To visit my boyfriend."

"Hold up!" Mia shrieks, slamming on the brakes at a red light. I jolt forward in my seat. "You have a boyfriend?!"

"Mia, you have *got* to drive more slowly. You're going to get us killed! And you're making me motion-sick," I say, crinkling my nose.

"Oh my god, I'm so sorry," Mia says with a grimace. "Me and my lead foot—I promise I'll slow down."

When the light turns green, she creeps forward, going about fifteen miles per hour. The car behind us starts honking impatiently, and I burst out laughing. "Not *that* slow, Grandma!"

Mia giggles, her face flushed, and accelerates to a reasonable pace. "Sorry! You know I only have one speed, Sunny! You love this about me!"

"I do love this about you," I reply, smiling. "*Not* when it comes to driving—but, in general, your boundless energy is inspiring."

Mia smiles. "Thank you. And you're right…I should definitely pay more attention to the speed limit. Now, let's please rewind so you can explain why you have a boyfriend I know nothing about? I swear, Sunny, you are the most secretive person on the planet."

I crank up the air conditioning, my face warm. "Well…I wanted to tell you in person. It's not the same over the phone, you know?" It's a lame excuse, but hopefully she accepts it.

Mia nods. "Okay, so tell me about him!"

"His name is Chris Jenkins," I begin. "He's a rising sophomore too. We met waiting in line to get into a frat party. He was standing behind me and overheard me tell my friends that I was freezing and wanted to leave, so he offered me some of the hot chocolate mixed with peppermint Schnapps he was carrying in a thermos."

"Love it," Mia says approvingly.

"It was delicious…but I was still chilled to the bone, so Chris suggested we try another activity to get warm. That's when I kissed him—right there in line. A couple of weeks later, he asked me to be his girlfriend."

Mia gasps excitedly. "I can't believe you kissed him in front of everyone! That's not like you at all!"

"I know," I say with a little chuckle. "I guess I'm becoming a new Sunny." It was a bold move, and definitely out of character. But I hadn't heard from Dex in weeks, and…

I needed the distraction.

The next time Dex called me, I told him I had a boyfriend. I don't think I would have if Chris hadn't walked into my room just as I'd picked up my phone. Dex overheard him say, "Hey, babe," and I had no choice but to explain. Dex sounded really happy for me and told me to enjoy my night with Chris.

And that was the last time I heard from him. Dex was my best friend for thirteen years—how could he stop talking to me? Maybe I'm naïve…but I thought we'd always be "Sunny D." I guess that's what happens when you're miles apart. I just never thought it would happen to us.

"Well, I like this new Sunny, and clearly Chris does too!" Mia exclaims as I take a deep breath and refocus on the present. "I'm not surprised he wanted to lock you down, considering how smoking hot you are."

I laugh but, in a way, she's right. I can tell that Chris is very attracted to me—and it feels so good to be wanted like that. Finally. Although, he did once make a comment about my curls. When we were kissing one night, he said, "I wish I could run my fingers through your hair."

To be honest, it hurt my feelings. But I kept that to myself.

"So have you guys…" Mia looks at me out of the corner of her eye and grins. "You know…slept together?"

All I can muster is a sheepish smile.

Three weeks into dating, I told Chris I was ready to have sex. I surprised myself—I always thought I'd wait until I was in love. But I was curious. Plus I never dated in high school and felt like I had some catching up to do. Maybe I wanted to catch up to Dex, I'm not sure. We've never talked about it, but I assume he's *not* a virgin.

I doubt it was Chris's first time, either. As soon as I gave him the green light, he grabbed a condom from the back pocket of his jeans, like he'd been waiting expectantly the whole time.

"Sunny, that's so exciting!" Mia says, turning toward me at a stop sign. "How's the sex? Is he good in bed? Oh my god, I shouldn't even be asking you that, I'm sorry—you don't have to tell me. Only if you want to!" She attempts to suppress a squeal.

"It's great," I say with a bashful grin.

But I'm lying.

It's not what I imagined at all. It hurt a bit at first—I was prepared for that—but I thought that, with time, it would start to feel good.

It didn't. It still hasn't.

Although he's a great kisser, sex with Chris is quick and anticlimactic, for me at least. I keep *trying* to enjoy it. But the pleasure never comes…

And neither do I.

So I fake it. Because Chris is a nice guy. And he's into me, and—the sex *has* to get better at some point, right?

"Well, I'm extremely happy for you," Mia says as she pulls

into my mom's driveway. The lights are on, which is strange because my mom told me she'd be at work.

"You deserve a great boyfriend, Sunny. I know you've wanted one for a long time," Mia continues softly with a tilt of her head.

I smile and look down at my lap, then back up at her again. "How are things with you and Evan? Still good?"

Mia's been dating Evan Chen (whose house was the setting of the infamous spin-the-bottle party) since freshman year of high school. They're madly in love and adorable together.

She smiles. "Better than ever. Thank god we're both at OSU. He's in Hong Kong right now visiting family, but he'll be back soon."

"You two are the cutest," I tell her.

"Well, let me know if you change your mind about the party tonight," Mia says, giving me one of her extra-tight squeezes.

"Will do. Thanks again." I get out of her car, grab my things, and head to the front porch while Mia drives away. As I'm searching my purse for my keys, my mom opens the door.

"Hey, Mom! Weren't you supposed to be working today?" I give her a hug. "I thought that's why you couldn't pick me up at the airport."

"I just got home, maybe ten minutes before you," she explains as she grabs my suitcase and we make our way inside. "You know how unpredictable my schedule is."

I let out a small grunt of acknowledgment as I lock the door behind us and let my heavy backpack fall from my shoulders onto the tiled floor.

"Ice cream?" my mom asks as she makes a beeline for the freezer.

"Rocky road, please—thanks," I yell from the foyer as I kick off my shoes.

"So how do you think you did on your exams?" she asks when I join her in the kitchen a minute later. "Did poli sci go okay?"

She's busy scooping and doesn't see me shake my head. I'm not surprised she's interrogating me about my finals within minutes of my arrival, but that doesn't mean I'm not disappointed. I'd bet good money that the Dexters aren't grilling their son about his grades right now. They're probably grilling a delicious chicken dinner in their backyard.

I sigh before I answer. "I think I did well. I studied hard and felt prepared." I take a seat and, when she sets our bowls on the table, I immediately dig into a mound of gooey marshmallow.

"Oh, good," my mom says with a relieved smile. "When will you have your grades back?"

"In the next few days. Don't worry, I'll let you know as soon as I get them," I say before swallowing a huge spoonful of ice cream. I squeeze my eyes shut. Brain freeze.

"I know you will, sweetie," she replies, but I can tell she's already onto her next thought. And unlike me, she's barely touched her ice cream. "It's just that Northwestern Law is so competitive, so we need to make sure your application stands out. Shouldn't you be doing something besides babysitting this summer? It's probably too late to get an internship, but maybe you can volunteer somewhere..."

The truth is, I plan to spend my free time this summer catching up on all the romance novels I didn't have time to read during the school year, and maybe even writing something that *doesn't* involve political theory. But I don't tell my mother that.

"I'll be fine, Mom. My schedule will be even more demanding next year, so I'd really like to take this summer to relax."

Her eyebrows go up like she's surprised I've expressed a boundary with her. Come to think of it, I'm a little surprised too. A year away at college must have done me some good.

"Well, what are your plans for next week?" she asks. "I suppose you'll want to see Dex?" Her tone is nonchalant, but she avoids eye contact.

"Of course," I say without elaborating.

"Does Chris know? About your plans?" I look up from my bowl to see my mom pursing her lips as she works to excise a plump black cherry from layers of vanilla ice cream with true surgical precision.

My heart starts pumping faster. I'm irritated, partly because she wouldn't even know about Chris if it weren't for my roommate, who spilled the beans when my mom visited me on campus for my birthday. It was a rare weekend she happened to have off from work. "What's there to know?" I say with a scowl that only ever appears in the presence of my mother.

She takes a moment to swallow her bite, then shrugs. "Well, Chris is a nice boy, that's all. And I don't think he'd be too happy if he knew his girlfriend was planning to spend the entire summer with her high school crush."

"High school *crush*?" I stammer, nearly dropping my spoon. "What are you—"

"Oh sweetie, you don't have to pretend. I mean, who wouldn't have a crush on Dex, right? He's gorgeous. But he's not a serious boy—"

"What are you even talking about?" I ask, my eyes narrowed and my nostrils flared. "Don't you remember how amazing he was in the senior play? You said it yourself—he'll probably be famous one day. He is supremely talented, and smart, and *very* serious about acting—"

"Well, that's not a serious career now, is it?" My mom stands up from the table and takes her bowl of half-eaten ice cream to the sink. "Chris, on the other hand, has his entire future planned out. Do you know how hard it is to get into the seven-year medical program at Northwestern? He's a bright boy, Sunny. He's good for you."

"Mom, you've never even met Chris! You only think he's good for me because you'd love to have a doctor son-in-law to patch me up whenever disaster strikes—"

"Well disaster does strike, when you least expect it," she says, her back still turned to me as she scrubs her dish.

My mom never talks about losing her parents in a car accident when she was seventeen, so I typically don't mention it. I've never confronted her about her anxiety either. But something has to change. Neither of us benefit from her constant worrying.

"It's awful how your parents died," I say. "And becoming a surgeon so you could spare other people that pain…that's admirable. Helping people is something you *can* control. But there are certain things you can't. And living in fear won't change that. Worrying won't keep me safe."

She still hasn't turned around, so I have no idea what she's thinking. How she's feeling. But I guess I'm setting another boundary. I'm not quite sure what's gotten into me. Maybe I'm gearing up so I can talk to Dex. I want to know why he stopped talking to me. I want to know if we're still friends.

"Let's not make this about me, Sunny," she says at last. "I had a really long night at the hospital, and I'm exhausted." She tucks her hair behind her ear and finally faces me. "All I'm saying is, you need to be careful not to fall into old patterns. A lot has changed since high school. You have a boyfriend now. So if you're planning to hang out with Dex, you should probably mention it to Chris. You wouldn't want him to hear from someone else and get the wrong idea. Doesn't that Rogers boy down the street go to Northwestern?"

I don't know a boy named Rogers, nor am I aware of anyone on our street who goes to Northwestern, but my mom doesn't wait for me to answer. She plants a kiss on the top of my head and says, "I'm going upstairs to get some rest."

I stay seated at the kitchen table for a few minutes in stunned silence before I grab my things from the foyer and head upstairs to my room. I plop down on my bed, my head spinning. These conversations with my mom suck all the life out of me.

It's exhausting trying to be what someone *else* wants you to be.

There's only one person I want to talk to right now. The one person I've always been myself with. My heart sinks, wondering if I should reach out to him.

A minute later, the phone line in my room rings.

But it's not the person I want it to be. It's Chris.

"Hello?" I answer.

"You made it home!" he says with a smile in his voice.

"Yup…" I reply with a heavy sigh.

"Well, *that* doesn't sound good. What's the matter?"

"My mom," I say. "I've been home for half an hour and we're already butting heads."

"Wow, that was quick. What were you arguing about?"

I shrug, even though he can't see it. "Just stupid stuff. Nothing important. How was your drive home?"

"All thirty minutes of it?" he says with a chuckle. "It was fine. But…I really miss you. I can't wait for you to come visit next month."

"I miss you too," I say as I open up my laptop and navigate to my email browser.

"I don't know how I'm going to last twenty-eight whole days without you in my bed," he tells me.

My eyes widen and a knot forms in my stomach. And in that moment, I realize I'm actually relieved to have a break from faking orgasms.

"Yeah…me too," I say after a long exhale.

"So what are your plans for next week?" he asks.

"Um, I'm not sure yet. Probably just seeing old friends. Maybe hanging out with Dex." I'm not sure if I'm being courteous, as my mom suggested—or if I'm sabotaging myself.

"*Dex?*" Chris asks with a note of surprise in his voice. "I thought you weren't talking to him anymore."

I swallow. "Well, we were both busy with school, and we stopped talking as much…but that doesn't mean we're not friends."

I hope.

Chris scoffs. "*Okay…*"

"Okay, *what?*" I ask him with a bit more sass than I intended.

That conversation with my mom really got to me.

"I don't know, Sunny. You had pictures of that guy all over your dorm room—"

"Oh my god, Chris, I had like *two* pictures of us when we were *kids*—"

"You definitely had more than two pictures of him. And one of them was from your high school graduation, and he had his arm around you, and..." Chris pauses. "He's a good-looking guy, Sunny. I'm not an idiot—"

"What's that supposed to mean?"

"Every time you talk about him, you blush. Admit it—you like him. I mean, how could you not?"

"I don't know what you're talking about. Dex and I have never been more than just friends."

Chris is silent for several seconds. "So, what...you're just gonna spend your whole summer with him? Like old times?"

"Chris, you can't tell me whom I can and can't hang out with," I say decisively.

"No. But I *can* break up with you."

There are tears streaming down my face now. I'm just not sure why. "Is that really what you want?"

"I guess Kim was right all along. You're really *not* that into me."

I snort. "Oh—you mean Kim from down the hall who has a *massive* crush on you?"

Kim with the silky straight hair guys can run their fingers through.

"She doesn't have a crush on me," he says unconvincingly. "But regardless, she's right. I'm *way* more into you than you're into me. I can tell, Sunny. When we're, like, messing around in bed, and stuff. I just feel like…your mind is somewhere else. Thinking about Dex, I guess."

A stabbing pain pierces my chest.

Everything Chris is saying is true. I just figured I could keep those feelings buried in my subconscious. I had no idea my affection for Dex was that obvious.

I sniffle. "I don't know what to say, Chris…I'm…I'm really sorry I made you feel that way."

"Yeah, well, shit happens," he says, followed by a lengthy exhale. "I'm gonna go."

"Yeah." I nod. "Okay."

"Have a nice summer, Sunny."

It sounds more like, *Have a nice life.*

I choke back more tears. "You too, Chris," I say before I hang up.

I'm sobbing now. And I know it's not because Chris and I just broke up.

It's because I've spent the last three hundred days with a heartache that I've been trying so hard, and apparently unsuccessfully, to hide.

It's because I've missed Oliver Dexter so much I can hardly breathe. Like I've been missing a part of me I need so I can feel…like *me.*

I've been so many different versions of Sunny since I started at Northwestern. All I want is to feel like *myself* again.

And I'm never more myself than when I'm with Dex. I know that sounds woefully co-dependent. But I can't help it. Maybe this is what happens when you fall for the guy who's been your best friend since kindergarten.

When my tears slow down to a trickle, I wipe my eyes and scroll through emails on my laptop. I stop when I find Seth Arden's party invitation.

And that's when I call Mia.

five

SUNNY

Mia parks across the street from the Ardens' house, which is practically vibrating with the booming bass of the hip hop songs we listened to in middle school. The anticipation of seeing Dex is nerve-wracking enough on its own, but add in the thumping throwback tunes and the drunk jocks on the porch howling at the moon, and now I'm a total wreck. I flip down the sun visor and check my reflection in the mirror to make sure I haven't reverted back to thirteen-year-old Sunny.

I was pretty quiet on the car ride over, but hopefully Mia chalked it up to the fact that I'd just been dumped. I didn't want to tell her. It was so embarrassing to admit, mere hours after I'd told her about Chris. But I didn't want her mentioning to anyone at the party that I'm in a relationship.

I don't have the audacity to expect that anything will happen between me and Dex tonight. I'll be happy just to know he's still my friend.

But I'd like to keep my options open.

Of course I didn't tell Mia that Chris broke up with me

because I have feelings for Dex. I told her he dumped me for Kim from down the hall. It's not far-fetched. I'll bet anything they'll be hooking up before long.

"You okay, Sunny?" Mia asks me. That's when I realize I've just been staring across the street.

I paste on a hopefully convincing smile. "It's been a long day, but I'm fine."

Mia nods and gazes down at her lap for several seconds. "Look, Sunny," she says when her eyes are back on me. "I probably shouldn't even bring this up…I know you and Chris *just* broke up, but…"

She hesitates again. Mia never hesitates. It's making me nervous.

"What, Mia?" I ask with more urgency in my voice than I intended.

"Well—why the *heck* did you and Dex never date in high school?" she blurts out.

I scoff. "Me and Dex? What are you—"

"Oh come on, Sunny. You're perfect for each other. You can pretend all you want, but I'm done biting my tongue. I can tell the two of you are in love."

I'm stunned. "Are you saying…do you *really* think Dex has feelings for me?"

Mia smiles. "I've seen the way he looks at you when he thinks no one's watching. It's just like me and Evan. I know true love when I see it. And you act like you couldn't care less who he's dating but, when he slow danced with Jenna on prom night… you cried."

I suck in a breath. "How did you—"

Mia bites her lip. "I followed you into the bathroom. I heard you sobbing in a stall. And I honestly didn't know whether you'd want me to help you. I mean, you're my best friend, Sunny, but sometimes I feel like I hardly know you. It even took months for you to tell me you had a boyfriend!"

She's right. I avoided telling her about Chris because I was afraid she'd call me out. She'd ask me, "What about Dex?" and the image I've been trying so hard to uphold would fall apart. I can feel it happening now.

"I'm sorry, Mia. You're my best friend, and I want to tell you everything…but being an open book doesn't come naturally to everyone."

The idea of showing people who I am terrifies me. If they don't like what they see, will they leave me? With no family in the picture besides my mom, I can hardly afford to find out.

"If you'd told me about Dex, I could have been there for you, Sunny."

"Mia, there's nothing to tell! Dex and I are friends, and that's all we'll ever be. He's dated plenty of girls in our class. If he really wanted to, he could have dated me."

It's the most honest thing I've said in a long time.

"Sunny, have you noticed that Dex has never asked a girl out himself? He says yes when they ask, probably because he doesn't want to hurt their feelings, but he's *never* the one to initiate. And the girls who ask him out never get past a few dates." Mia tilts her head. "Why do you think that is?"

Of course I've noticed. I just never let myself read into it. If Mia has a theory, I'd like to hear her say it. "Why do *you* think that is?" I ask, my gaze shying away from hers.

"Because he's been waiting for *you*, silly!" she says, laughing.

I look into her eyes. "You don't know that. Do you?"

Mia's grin fades when she shakes her head. "I've never talked to him about it, I swear. I know you wouldn't want me to. But I think *you* should. Maybe tonight's too soon after your breakup, but…it's just something to think about."

"I've really missed him, Mia," I confess. "We lost touch over the past few months, and I want him back in my life. No matter what that looks like."

Mia takes hold of my hands. "Well, let's get in there," she says, nodding across the street. "And just remember, I'm here if you need me."

When we're out of the car, Mia looks me up and down. Despite my nerves, I feel confident that I picked a really good outfit. I'm wearing a black, form-fitting shirt and a short floral skirt.

Mia grins. "Dex is gonna *die* when he sees you."

As we make our way inside, Mia gets pulled into a game of "Never Have I Ever," but not before making sure I'll be okay without her. I set her free and, before she runs off, she winks at me. On my own, I take a minute to survey the room. The house is crowded as hell, and pretty dark too, but it doesn't surprise me that the first face I register belongs to Oliver Dexter.

He's standing in the middle of a crowd, telling a story. All eyes are on him and—I can tell—he's loving every second of it. He looks so confident, so at ease, so *happy*, he's practically glowing. When he delivers the punchline, everyone bursts into laughter. I turn away, my pulse racing, my throat dry, wondering if coming to this party was a big mistake.

Dex seems to be doing perfectly fine without me in his life.

My eyes dart to the front door. *If I leave now, he'll never even know I was here.*

I spot Mia across the room, laughing among a group of girls that includes Jenna Andersen's three best friends but, to my relief, Jenna isn't with them. I'm about to tell Mia that I developed a migraine and need to call a cab, when I feel someone's hand on my waist.

"Sunny? Is that you?"

I know immediately who's behind me. It's like time stops when he touches me.

I spin around. "Dex," I whisper. And when I see the way his eyes light up as he looks at me, the tightness in my chest eases. I can breathe.

"God, I missed you," he says, pulling me into his arms. The world around us fades, and we're the only two people in the room now.

I bury my face in the crook between his neck and shoulder. "We were supposed to talk every day," I say, my eyes stinging.

Dex pulls back to look at me, but keeps his hands on my waist. "I know. I'm so sorry, Sunny, I have no idea what I was thinking. I guess I figured I should give you some space. You told me you were dating someone, and I didn't want to get in the way—"

Despite myself, I laugh.

Dex's brow furrows. "What?" he asks.

"Nothing, it's just…it's a moot point now. That relationship is over."

Dex half-smiles. *God*, I missed that.

"It's really hard being so far away," I say.

"I know." Dex pulls me in close again, one hand around my waist, the other cradling the back of my head. "It's okay. We're home now."

I smile as Dex takes my hand and leads me to the kitchen to get a beer. "Okay," he says when we both have drinks. "Tell me everything I've missed."

We only talk to each other the rest of the night. On a soft suede couch in the living room, we sip Natty Lights in red Solo cups and talk about the highlights of freshman year. About drinking games, and late night mac and cheese cooked in illicit crockpots. About open mic nights, and acing pop quizzes on three hours of sleep. About frat parties and fragmented memories of spring break. I tell Dex about the fake IDs my friends and I made with packing tape and hotel keycards, and he laughs and makes me show him mine.

"There is absolutely *no* way that you actually got into a bar in Chicago with this thing," he says, still laughing and flicking the card for emphasis.

"I did! You have to believe me!" I insist, playfully squeezing his shoulder, then letting my hand travel down the length of his arm. He curls his fingertips around mine for a few seconds before letting go.

"Well, this is the worst fake I've ever seen, so I'm guessing they let you in because you're pretty," he says, looking down at his cup.

I feel a smile start to creep onto my lips, and I quickly take a sip of my drink in an attempt to hide the gigantic grin that's looming behind it. This is the first time Dex has ever called me pretty.

Just then, Mia swoops in. "Hey, Dex!"

"What's up, Mia," he says with a smile. He stands to give her a hug, and when he sits back down again, he rests his arm on the back of the couch—around me.

"I think I'm going to head out," Mia tells Dex. "Did you drive? Would you mind giving Sunny a ride home?" Then she turns toward me. "Is that okay?" The way she looks me in the eye, I *know* she's leaving early on purpose. And I absolutely love her for it.

"Of course," Dex and I both say at the exact same time. Then we look at each other and smile.

"Perfect! I know you guys have a lot of catching up to do. Call me tomorrow, Sunny!" Mia yells as she zips through the crowd toward the door.

Dex tilts his head toward mine so he doesn't have to shout above the drunken squeals behind us. "It's really loud down here," he says. "Do you want to go upstairs?"

I smile and nod. And when I do, he looks at me with those eyes—the same eyes I saw him give Jenna at prom, during the last slow dance. The ones that made me cry alone in a stall.

But his eyes are fixed on me now. My face is so hot I feel feverish.

And then we're in the guest room, sitting on the bed. The door is locked.

Dex's gaze travels from my eyes down to my lips. He looks like he wants to devour me. My blood pulses in all the places I'm desperate for him to touch me.

He leans in slowly, and he kisses me so softly, I'm almost convinced I imagined it. But when I touch my hand to his face, he's there, and he's real, and I smile, and he kisses me harder this time, and I kiss him back, and for the first time in a long time, I feel like I'm exactly where I'm meant to be.

"Wow," Dex says breathlessly, barely tearing his lips away from mine. "You're a really good kisser."

"You too," I say with a smile before we continue making out. After a minute or two, he pulls away and looks at me, his thumb sweeping across my cheek.

"They're happy tears," I say.

A part of me wonders if I should feel embarrassed—but I'm honestly too fucking ecstatic to care. Dex kisses me again, then moves his mouth to my neck, and just the touch of his lips on my skin is already infinitely more pleasurable than a hundred nights I spent with Chris.

I straddle Dex's lap and peel off my shirt, grateful that I decided to wear my good bra tonight. He leans back, and his gaze falls from my eyes, to my chest, and down to my waist.

He shakes his head. "My *god*, you're sexy."

"I have boobs now," I tell him with a giggle.

Dex lets out a breathy laugh as his eyebrows lift. "I see that."

When his gaze meets mine again, we stop laughing, and his expression shifts, like suddenly he remembers I'm *Sunny*. His childhood best friend—just a more grownup version.

And that's when he closes his eyes and kisses the space on my chest where my heart lies, beating for him, and only him.

My hands move up his muscular arms and over his broad shoulders and up the nape of his neck until my fingers are in his hair, and he wraps his arms tight around me and we kiss like it's something we've done a million times before.

Then, with one hand still wrapped around my waist, he moves his other hand up my thigh and under my skirt. "Can I touch you?" he asks me softly.

I bite my lip and nod my consent. And when he touches me, the pleasure I see in his eyes is just as intense as the pleasure I feel with every stroke of his fingers. I've imagined this moment so many times, but it's real now, and he's touching me exactly the way I like to touch myself, like somehow he's privy to my innermost thoughts and deepest desires, and I can hardly catch my breath because, *Oh my god, Oliver Dexter is touching me*, and within a few minutes, I'm almost to the point of unraveling.

"Wait," I tell him breathlessly. "I want you."

Dex leans back and locks eyes with me, his chest rising and falling in rhythm with mine. "Are you sure?"

I nod. "Yes. I'm sure."

"You only had that one beer, right?" he asks, his brow furrowed.

I laugh. "Yes—and I didn't even finish it. Don't worry, Dex. I really want this," I assure him. "I want *you*."

With his arms still tight around me, he lays me down on the bed. He takes off what's left of my clothes, and then I help him strip off his. He pulls a condom out of his wallet and puts it on.

"Have you done this before?" he asks when he's on top of me.

Have I had sex before? Yes. Have I had sex with someone I'm madly in love with? Never. I honestly don't know how to answer. "Does it matter?" I ask him.

"No, I just…I don't want to hurt you," he whispers.

"You won't hurt me, Dex. Trust me, I've never been this

turned on in my life."

He responds by pressing his lips to mine. For a minute or two we kiss, and then he pulls back to look at me again. I nod, and he continues to watch me as he pushes inside me, and when he's in all the way, my eyes flutter closed, and I arch my back and sigh, and Dex makes this delicious sound I've never heard him make before, and we move together so effortlessly—a dance between lovers—and if he were to ask me again if I've ever done this, I now know the answer would be a resounding no—no, never in my life have I ever felt anything like this.

I had no idea it could be this fucking good.

six

SUNNY

I had sex with Oliver Dexter last night.

It's the first thought in my head when I wake up the next morning. I rub the sleep from my eyes and sit up, my entire body still buzzing with excitement—so much so that I hop out of bed and run to my full-length mirror to see if I look any different.

I touch my smiling lips, which are still swollen pink from kissing him. I tilt my head and spot the faintest hint of a mark on my neck where he sucked on my skin.

This really happened. It wasn't a dream.

He made me come. I'm no stranger to self-love and have enjoyed many orgasms by myself before last night, but this was on another level. Feeling the warmth of his skin on mine, inhaling his clean, soapy scent mixed with the salty taste of his sweat, and hearing the pleasure in his sighs—and that look of unfettered desire in his eyes—all my senses heightened as I surrendered myself completely. Like the sun-kissed ocean surrenders to a summer breeze. Warm waves of ecstasy rippling inside me.

It was extraordinary. And I can't wait to do it again.

While I'm still admiring my post-sex-with-Dex glow in the mirror, my phone line rings. It's him.

"Hey," I say, not even trying to hide how happy I am that he's calling me.

"What are you up to?" he asks with a sexy rasp in his voice that causes my heart to pound as wildly as if he'd been talking dirty to me.

I grin at my flushed reflection in the mirror and start fanning my face with my hand. "Nothing really…I just woke up."

"Me too. Want me to pick you up? My parents are at work. We can hang out here."

"Yeah," I say with a smile so wide my cheeks hurt. "That sounds good."

But it feels different being with him in the daytime, with the bright summer sun streaming in through his window, completely exposing me to him. And I find myself worrying that Dex—with his perfect abs, and pecs, and delts, and, hell, even his traps are amazing—will *really* see me now, in the light of day, and whatever spell he was under last night will break. And that fear becomes more and more real with each passing second, as his mouth travels from my lips to my neck, then around my nipples and past my bellybutton, his body shifting further down the bed, where he starts kissing my inner thighs, then looks up to me for permission.

My heart is hammering. "No one's ever done that before," I admit.

"Do you want me to?" he asks.

My mind is going a mile a minute. I *do* want him to. *So*

much. But I'm scared. We've already had sex but, somehow, this particular act seems even more intimate.

Dex can read the ambivalence on my face. He smiles. "Well, I like doing it. And I'm good at it," he adds, not so humbly.

I already know this because I overheard Jenna talking about it in the locker room, post-prom. But of course I don't tell Dex that. Instead, I allow my curiosity to take the lead, lean back, and say, "Okay. Show me."

And—*holy shit*—he does.

"Wow," I say breathlessly afterward, a blissful smile emerging on my face. "You weren't lying. You *are* really good at that." I let out a little laugh and stretch out on Dex's bed, my skin still warm, my heart still fluttering. He lies on his side and kisses my shoulder.

"Well, you can thank Ben the next time you see him," he says with a laugh.

"Your cousin?" I ask, confused.

"Yeah. He always wanted a little brother, so he kinda took me under his wing," Dex explains. "I used to call him up for advice before dates. He taught me everything I know."

"Well, thank you, Ben," I say with a giggle. Then the thought of Dex with other girls enters my head, and my smile starts to fade. I wonder how many he's had in his bed. How many he's made feel this way. But I quickly push the images out of my mind. The past doesn't matter. He's with me now.

"Okay, lie down," I playfully demand. "Time for me to show you what *I* know."

I don't know much at all. With Chris, things progressed quickly from kissing to sex, no foreplay, which I now understand is the reason I never enjoyed it. And I don't have an older cousin to call up for sex advice, but I *do* have a friend at school who told me about a technique she'd learned from a book called *Sex Tips for Straight Women from a Gay Man.* So I reciprocate. And it turns out I'm pretty damn good at it too.

So good that Dex has to stop me.

"Sunny, wait. This feels amazing, but I want to make you come again," he says. "I love watching you let go like that."

My cheeks are red hot as he reaches into his nightstand for a condom. "Actually…I'm on the pill," I tell him. "So we don't need to use a condom if you don't want to."

I got on birth control as an added measure of protection when Chris and I started sleeping together, but we still used condoms every time. It's different with Dex, though.

I'm in love with him.

Dex smiles and pulls me on top of him. "I've never done this before," he says. "Without a condom, I mean."

"Me neither," I say, smiling back.

We may not have been each other's firsts, but sharing this particular first with Dex feels significant. I guide him inside me and move my hips, the mid-afternoon sun casting its glow on me like a spotlight.

"You're a goddess," he says to me—and I feel like one too, with my long hair draped over my shoulders, framing my breasts, and my lover's admiring eyes soaking in every bare inch of me.

I don't feel self-conscious at all anymore. In fact, I've never felt more beautiful.

When we're done, Dex pulls me close and we lie on his bed

together, catching our breath and staring at the ceiling. I've been in this space nearly as much as my own bedroom, but never like this. Naked in Dex's arms. It feels surreal. To think of the hours I spent here, hoping against all odds that he would look up from whatever play he was reading and *kiss* me—a mere kiss would have been enough back then—but now, here I am, my wildest dreams come true.

He takes my hand and holds it over his heart. "I feel like I died and went to heaven," he says.

"La petite mort," I answer, a smile blooming across my face. "It's what the French call an orgasm, but the literal translation is *little death*. I've always liked that idea. I just never knew what it felt like until now."

Dex turns to face me and props himself on his elbow. He coils a strand of my hair around his fingertip and looks into my eyes. "I want to die a thousand deaths with you," he says.

Later that night, when I'm back home and getting ready for bed, Mia calls me. I can tell right away that it's not the first time she's tried to reach me today.

"Sunny! Oh my god, woman!" she exclaims.

I smile, but what else is new. I haven't stopped smiling all day. "I know," I answer sheepishly. "I was supposed to call you, I'm sorry."

"It's okay. As long as you have a good excuse," she says more calmly.

"I have the *best* excuse," I tell her. "I was with Dex."

"Oh my god, I freakin' knew it!" she screams. I have to pull the phone away from my ear. "What happened last night? Tell me everything! Only if you want to, of course."

I giggle and lie back on my bed. I close my eyes, my grin still wide. "Mia...he kissed me," I nearly whisper.

I hear a high-pitched squeal followed by a clattering sound and some static. "Sorry, I dropped the phone," Mia says so fast, it almost sounds like one word. "So *he* made the first move, right? I told you he's in love with you! Did you guys talk? Did you tell him how you feel about him? How did this happen?"

I start answering her questions before she hyperventilates. "He told me he was giving me space because I had a boyfriend. And I told him it was over between me and Chris, and then... we just talked. Not about feelings, specifically. We caught up. But things felt different between us. The way he was looking at me...I knew he wanted to kiss me."

Rip off my clothes and ravage me. It was like a scene out of one of my favorite romance novels.

Mia heaves an enormous sigh. "This is *so* exciting. So you guys are, like, together now? Dating?"

I shrug. "I mean, it's only been a day. I don't think we need to put a label on it yet." My heart rate picks up.

Mia giggles. "No, of course not. I'm getting ahead of myself. You know me! So, was it just a kiss? Or more? You don't have to tell me. Unless you want to!"

"We...made out," I say. "A lot."

I'm proud of myself for confiding in Mia, but I also don't feel the need to give her every detail.

Mia inhales like she's trying very hard not to spontaneously combust. "Okay," she says as she breathes out. "I won't tell anyone, I promise. Not even Evan. Not until you're ready. But when you are, let me know. We can plan a double date! Can you imagine? Oh my god, so fun! Okay, I'll stop now."

She's getting ahead of herself again, but the idea of me and Dex hanging out with Mia and Evan as a pair of couples makes me giddy. I used to daydream about that in high school. And now, just maybe, my dreams are coming true.

"Goodnight, Mia," I say, still grinning.

It's the best summer of my life. Me and Dex, and lazy afternoons on the beach, the smell of Banana Boat sunscreen baked into our skin. Air-conditioned matinées on scorching hot days, followed by long walks with ice cream. In the evenings we have dinner with his parents, just like we always did. And it's even sweeter this time, because I'd been so afraid of losing them too—when I thought that I'd lost him. But all is right with the world. I'm part of their family again.

We play a lot and work very little—me babysitting sporadically for my neighbor's twins, and Dex teaching swim lessons a few times a week at the community center. If Mia and Evan were in town, I'm sure we'd be hanging out with them too. But Evan's aunt and uncle encouraged him to stay at their home in Hong Kong for the entire summer, and they were kind enough to invite Mia to join him. I miss her, but I'm definitely enjoying all this time alone with Dex. On our free days, while his parents are at work, we spend hours and hours in his bed.

But soon, this blissful summer will come to an end. And although Dex and I have had sex countless times (I lost track after twenty, and that was only two weeks in), neither of us has initiated a conversation about actual feelings, much less defining our relationship. Is Dex my boyfriend? I have no idea. And what happens when we go back to college in a couple of weeks? I don't know the answer to that either. I'm not sure I want to.

Because, deep down, this all feels too good to be true. And I don't want to rock the boat, so I decide to leave well enough alone. I choose uncertainty because, if I ask Dex for answers, I run the risk of losing him.

But as the summer dwindles, I find it harder to keep my angst at bay.

It's a rainy Monday morning, and Dex is teaching swim lessons, so I take slow sips of coffee at the kitchen table and poke at my cereal while wondering how I'll make it through another school year without him. Just when I'm starting to spiral, I hear my mom come in through the front door. She sighs as she makes her way into the kitchen.

"Hey, Mom. You're home…early? Or late maybe?"

"Late," she says while stifling a yawn. "Ruptured spleen. He's fine now, although it was touch and go there for a while, because—"

"I'm glad he's okay," I chime in quickly before she gives me the gory details. Sometimes when my mom's especially tired, she forgets that I can only handle the CliffsNotes version of her workday. And right now, she looks exhausted. But instead of heading upstairs to lie down, she grabs a yogurt from the fridge and sits across from me. It's such a rare occasion when we eat breakfast together, it feels completely unnatural. We take a few bites in silence, and I glance over at the clock on the stove, willing time to speed up so I can be back in Dex's arms, where I belong.

"Are you okay, sweetie?" my mom asks as she haphazardly stirs her yogurt. "You seem pensive."

I shrug as though I have no clue what she's talking about, then shake my head. "I'm fine."

My mom stirs a bit more determinedly, even though the fruit on the bottom of her cup of yogurt is clearly well-distributed at this point. "I hear that you and Dex have been spending a lot of time together this summer," she says without looking up at me, which is a very good thing because, if she *were* to look at me, she'd know right away that I'm in acute distress. Flushed cheeks, shallow breathing, beads of sweat on my brow. Her specialty is trauma—these are the kinds of things she notices.

I take a deep breath and try my hardest not to sound panicked. "How would you happen to know that, Mom? You've barely been home the entire summer," I say, keeping my eyes on the soggy flakes swimming in my bowl.

I hear my mom exhale. "I ran into John Dexter at the hospital the other day. He was visiting a colleague. He told me they've been seeing a lot of you at their house lately. Just like old times." When I look up, her bloodshot eyes are fixed on me. "He's thrilled, of course."

I can't help but smile despite the weighty displeasure that's causing my mom's brow to furrow and the corners of her mouth to turn down. "Well, I love spending time with them. You know that."

"Hmm," my mom grumbles as she stabs at that poor, defenseless cup of yogurt. "I just want to make sure you're focusing on what's important. Getting into Northwestern Law won't be easy, Sunny. You need to keep your eyes on the prize. Maybe there are some books you can read to get a head start for next year."

I let out a heaving sigh. "Mom, I honestly don't know what you're worried about. I worked really hard last year and got As in all my classes. My eyes *are* on the prize. But it's summer, and if I don't take a break from studying, I'll burn out. And as far as Dex goes…we're catching up. That's all."

I try hard to sound nonchalant but, on the inside, I'm freaking out. My mom's been at work since yesterday evening, right? Is there any way she could have found out that Dex drove us to our high school last night, and we snuck in through the back door of the gym? That we ended up having *sex* in our library's small (but stellar) poetry section? He was reading me his favorite Neruda poem…and it was the way he looked at me when he said "sunbeam" that did me in.

I'm being ridiculous. There's no way she could possibly know that. Is there?

"Just don't get too attached," she demands, her eyes burning holes straight through me.

I get up from the table and pour myself more coffee, which is a terrible idea because it will only make me more jittery. "Attached?" I attempt to say as coolly as possible despite my shaking hands.

"Look, sweetheart. We've talked about this before. Dex is handsome and charming—no one can blame you for having a crush. But I hope a crush is *all* it is. Because you'll never be able to hold onto a man like him. Trust me."

It's the cruelest thing anyone's ever said to me. I wonder if she can see it in my eyes when I sit back down and sip my coffee—how much she just hurt me.

"I don't only mean *you*, sweetie, of course not. You're smart, and beautiful, and *any* man would be lucky to have you. But Dex is not the kind of guy who's ever going to settle down. I mean, he wants to be an actor, for Chrissake. And with *his* good looks? He'll have women throwing themselves at him left and right. I'm sure he already does. And is that *really* what you want, Sunny? To live in a man's shadow like that? To abandon your own dreams and follow him around like a lovesick puppy? And hope, against all odds, that he'll come home to you every night?"

I stand up from the table and take my still-full coffee mug and bowl of soggy flakes to the sink. "You're being absurd," I say in my most convincing voice. "Dex and I are just friends."

I make it out of the kitchen, up the stairs, and into the bathroom just seconds before I throw up.

It's Labor Day weekend. The unofficial end of summer.

Dex suggested we go on a camping trip, which we haven't done since junior year of high school. And for the first time ever, it'll be only the two of us. I'm so excited, despite the looming cloud that's been over my head ever since the morning my mom roasted Dex during breakfast. I didn't even consider telling her the actual truth about where I was going this weekend. I lied and said my roommate invited me to her family's lake house in Michigan again. Not that my mom can stop me from going on an unchaperoned camping trip with Dex—I'm a grown woman—but I don't want to give her another opportunity to slander him. I'm already having a hard enough time getting her malignant words out of my head.

You'll never be able to hold onto a man like him.

But whenever I'm with Dex, and he's kissing me, and touching me, and his arms are wrapped tightly around me, all my worries disappear. And when he looks into my eyes the way he's looking at me right now, like he truly, deeply knows me…that's when I know in my heart that everything's going to be okay.

"You have the biggest smile on your face," he says to me with a laugh in between kisses. We're lying on a blanket under a sky full of stars, in a secluded spot at our favorite childhood campsite, and I'm so giddy, I can't help but giggle. And maybe it's the two beers I downed with the brats we made for dinner, but I'm feeling a little more bold than usual tonight. So this time, I tell him exactly what I'm thinking.

"It's just so crazy. I mean, we used to come here all the time as kids. And now, here we are…kissing." I giggle again, and Dex's lips land on mine, both of us smiling.

"I used to think about this all the time," he whispers in my ear before he starts to kiss the skin right beneath it.

If Dex thought I looked happy a minute ago, he should see me now. But he's busy kissing his way across my collarbone. "Oh, yeah?" I say as my hands travel down to unzip his pants. "Did you used to think about me touching you like this?"

His chuckle quickly turns into a groan. "You have no idea, Sunny."

"*Trust* me, I do," I tell him with an airy laugh. "I used to think about us too."

Dex raises his eyebrows as he smiles. "Is that right," he says as he pulls off my shirt.

I bite my lip and nod as his hand moves under my bra. "And it was always good in my dreams, Dex…but this is *so* much better than I ever could have imagined."

Neither of us is laughing anymore. We kiss and touch each other with a new sense of wonder now that this truth has been unveiled. Now that I know he's wanted me, and he knows I've wanted him.

"Sunny," he says quietly after several minutes of kissing. "When you told me you were dating someone back in February, it really wrecked me. I'm not telling you because I want you to feel bad. I just want you to understand. Why I stopped calling you."

I search his eyes, confused. "But you sounded…thrilled. You said you were happy for me—"

"I was acting, Sunny. I'm an actor, remember?"

I frown. "Do you act when we're together?"

"Not normally," Dex tells me. "But I wanted you to be happy."

I smile. "I'm happy now."

We kiss, and when our eyes meet again, Dex smiles and

shakes his head.

"What is it?" I ask him.

"I just can't believe how lucky I am. To be with you."

My gaze slinks away from his. "No…*I'm* the lucky one," I tell him.

"Sunny," Dex says. He waits until I look at him. "Do you have any idea how beautiful you are?" He wraps one of my curls around his finger. "For starters, you have the prettiest hair I've ever seen in my entire life. It was the first thing I noticed about you—"

"Because it's different from everyone else's. I used to feel so out of place as a kid." I sigh. "Like I never fit in."

"Who says you have to fit in? Sunny, when I spotted you at Seth's party, you were halfway across the room—you weren't even facing me—but as soon as I saw your hair, I knew it was you. Even though your clothes were different. And you'd changed so much since the last time I'd seen you," he says, his fingers slowly tracing the curve of my waist and gripping my hip.

His touch makes it nearly impossible for me to focus on anything besides the heat building between us, but somehow I manage to. And boy, am I glad.

"I *love* that about you," he continues. "Nobody looks like you because you are so uniquely beautiful. And it's not only your hair. You have the most beautiful, glowing skin. The most gorgeous, big brown eyes I can get lost in. The most perfect pink lips—"

Now I've heard all I need to hear.

I press my mouth against his and wrap my legs around his waist. I want him, and he knows it.

But before he gives himself to me, he takes my face in his

hands and says, "Sunny, you're the most amazing person I've ever met."

And any fear I had about us, at least for now, is put to rest.

When we lie looking at the stars again, Dex reaches for my hand. "I wonder what Mrs. Delmonico would think of all this," he says.

I whip my head to face him, and we burst out laughing. I imagine the look of shock on our kindergarten teacher's face if she somehow caught wind of what Dex and I were just doing.

"Gross," I say when I catch my breath. "But…what about your parents?" I ask, propping myself on my elbow. "You haven't told them, have you?"

He shakes his head. "I wouldn't say anything without talking to you first. But honestly, I think they'd be cool with it."

I smile. "Yeah…I think so too."

"Your mom wouldn't be happy, though," Dex says with a sigh. "I don't think she's my biggest fan."

My heart aches when I see the look on his face. "Dex, this is my mom we're talking about. She hardly likes anyone." I reach out to rub his arm.

He contemplates my answer. "Maybe. But sometimes it feels more targeted than that."

I shake my head. "I think she's jealous because of how close I am to you and your parents. It's totally irrational…I mean, the reason I spent so much time at your house was because of *her* busy schedule. But feelings don't always make sense, I guess."

Dex nods. "You're right. That's probably what it is."

I sigh. "Let's not talk about my mom tonight. The sky is too beautiful." I roll onto my back again and gaze at the heavens, letting my eyes lose focus so the stars bleed into one another like a giant glowing canopy overhead.

"This was my favorite part of camping growing up," Dex says as he laces his fingers through mine again. "Getting lost in the stars with you."

"Your favorite stars were the twinkling ones. You'd get so excited whenever you saw a flicker. You'd call your mom over to our blanket every time so she could see it too," I recall with a smile.

Dex squeezes my hand, but he's quiet, so I turn back to look at him.

"Before we started kindergarten, my mom was pregnant with a baby girl," he says. "But we lost her. When I asked about my sister, Mom said she was a star in the sky, watching over us."

I blink back tears. "Oh, Dex, I'm so sorry. I had no idea—"

"There's no way you could've known. We never talked about it. I think mostly because, once you came into our lives, the clouds parted. And finally, it was…Sunny."

I match his smile, but I'm crying. I can hardly say a word. "Thank you," I whisper eventually. "That's the most beautiful thing anyone's ever said to me."

Dex wipes my tears and we kiss for so long, I lose track of time. The sky is velvety black, and I'd give anything for it to stay like this. But soon it'll be morning, and tonight will be another memory. It guts me. *Every moment in time is so goddamn fleeting.* Like this summer, which burned bright in its prime, but is already fading away.

"You okay?" Dex asks me.

I realize I'm sniffling again. "Being here with you is a dream come true," I tell him, my voice shaky. "But it kills me to think that soon *this* will be also be a memory. I just…I wish I could freeze time and stay here with you."

"Hey, come here," Dex says as he takes me in his arms. I inhale his soapy scent, and the heaviness in my heart lifts a bit. "I know it's hard being apart. But this isn't the end for us, Sunny. I promise. It's only the beginning."

seven

DEX
SPRING OF 2000

It's approaching ten o'clock and I'm still sitting onstage listening to the director give incredibly detailed notes to every cast member. He's only about halfway done. I'm desperate to get back to my dorm and call Sunny, but we're an "ecosystem" now, as our director likes to say, so his feedback applies to everyone. I agree it'll probably make me a better actor in the long run. Plus I don't want to piss him off. He cast me in the starring role on the spot, without bothering to see the roomful of actors who showed up after me. Since we started rehearsing, he's taken me on as his protégé, sharing everything he's learned from his twenty years in the industry.

I still can't believe I got the lead in *A Streetcar Named Desire.* And as a sophomore no less. The seniors I went up against were really fucking pissed.

I glance at my watch again. It's a quarter past ten, which means past midnight in Evanston. I realize my leg is shaking and hope no one notices how anxious I'm getting. Rehearsals have been running ridiculously late this week. Last night, Sunny stayed up until one in the morning, her time, just so she could say goodnight. It's lucky that her roommate's always at her boyfriend's, so at least we don't have to worry about waking her. I feel awful that Sunny waits up for me, but at the same time, I'm grateful. If I don't catch her before bed, I won't get a good night's sleep.

Finally, the director wraps up. I grab my backpack and am heading for the exit when the actress playing Stella runs up to me.

"Dex, wait up!" Her face is flushed when she reaches me. She smiles at a few castmates on their way out the door and waits until they've left before she continues.

"So, I've been thinking, since we play a married couple in the show, we should get to know each other better. Like…more *intimately?*" She bats her eyelashes and bites her lip.

If Sunny knew how often things like this happen to me…

My first instinct is to turn around and run. But I'll be working with this actress for weeks, so I can't make things awkward between us.

Instead, I half-smile and look down before my eyes meet hers again. I tilt my head. "I have a girlfriend," I say, holding her gaze.

My performance was subtle, but I can tell it came across exactly like I intended. I'd paused just long enough before I answered to make her *think* I was tempted.

"Lucky girl," she replies with a flirtatious smile. "Well, if you change your mind…"

She walks past me, making sure her chest grazes my arm on her way out.

Now the actor playing Mitch is walking up. "Dude, please tell me you're hitting that. She's so fucking sexy."

I shake my head. "I am *not.*"

"But she wants to, right? Jesus, what I wouldn't give to look like you." He sighs as he walks past me.

It's almost ten-thirty now. Fuck.

I run back to my dorm room and dial Sunny's number. "I'm so sorry," I say as soon as she answers.

"It's okay," she replies sweetly, stifling a yawn.

All at once, the stress of being Dex leaves my body. Just hearing her voice does that to me.

"How was your day?" I ask, settling onto my bed. My roommate's with his girlfriend too, so it's just me and Sunny. It's the first time all day I've felt genuinely happy.

She heaves a deep sigh. "Well…I slept through my alarm and missed my poli sci exam this morning. But it's not a big deal! My professor's letting me take a make-up test."

My muscles tense again. "The make-up tests are always harder, Sunny. Is he docking points from you too?"

"Maybe…" she replies, her voice rising like it's a question. "Just a few."

My heart sinks. "Jesus," I say after an exasperated exhale. "I'm so sorry, Sunny. This is my fault. If it weren't for my rehearsals running late, you wouldn't be waiting up for me to call—"

"Dex, *I'm* the one who decided to stay up the night before an exam, and *I'm* the one who slept through my alarm. You can't blame yourself."

I suck in a breath. "I don't know, Sunny. I think maybe we

should scale back on the phone calls." The thought of talking to her less is terrifying. These phone calls are my lifeline. "Just until my play is done," I add quickly.

"So, I make one stupid mistake and now we can't talk anymore? That hardly seems fair," she says.

She's trying her best not to cry. I don't have to see her to know there are tears in her eyes. It kills me. But there's no way I'll let myself be a burden on her.

"Look, I know how serious you are about getting into Northwestern Law. You've gotten an A in every poli sci class you've taken so far. I can't be the reason your grades start slipping."

She only sniffles.

"Just hear me out, okay? We'll talk on the weekends. And during the week, we'll email. It'll be fine. I promise." I'm trying to convince *myself* more than her.

"Fine," she concedes after several seconds. "We'll email."

"And talk on the weekends," I remind her. "And before you know it, it'll be summer, and you can do everything you said you wanted to do to me when you called me drunk the other night."

She laughs. "Promise?"

"Are you kidding? I'm counting the days."

"Okay," she says.

She's smiling now, I can hear it in her voice. I close my eyes and picture her in her bed, her long hair splayed out on her pillow. Her rosy cheeks glowing. She's absolutely gorgeous.

No one could ever compare.

eight

SUNNY

The Cleveland airport is bustling, and as I weave my way through the terminal, I feel like a fish swimming upstream. While I'm on my way home for spring break, everyone else appears to be leaving. Everywhere I look, there are groups of college kids in their university gear on their way to Cancun, or Palm Springs. Sullen teenagers with their parents, probably traveling to look at universities. Families with young children heading to Disney, their toddlers already sporting mouse ears.

I've never been to Disney World. When I was in second grade, the Dexters offered to take me with them on their family vacation, but my mom said no, of course. She tried to comfort me with some cautionary tale about her colleague's stepsister, who had briefly lost sight of her kid at Sea World twenty years earlier. My mom recalled the tale as if reliving her own trauma, and was genuinely shocked when I said her story did *not* make me feel better.

But none of that matters now. One day, I'll right my mom's wrong. I'll take my own children to Disney World. And experiencing the magic through their eyes—knowing that *I* made it happen for them—will be a greater joy than I can imagine.

When I finally make it outside, Mia's pulling up, already smiling.

"Thanks so much for picking me up…*again*," I say with a chuckle as I get in her car. "You know I can just take a cab—"

"Oh, stop it," Mia insists as she nearly squeezes the life out of me. "That's what friends are for! Besides, I love our drives home from the airport. This is when I find out all the juicy details about your life that you won't tell me over the phone!"

I sigh as she pulls away from the curb. "I wish I had juicy details to share, but Dex and I still haven't seen each other since winter break. It's torture," I whine with an exaggerated pout.

"I'm sorry," Mia sympathizes. "What did you say he was doing for spring break again? Some guys' trip?"

"Yeah, his cousin Ben is getting married this summer and wanted to go hiking with his groomsmen in Montana."

"Sounds…rustic," Mia says scrunching her nose.

I laugh at her reaction—Mia's not outdoorsy at all. "They'll have fun," I say. "I just miss Dex so much. This year's been really tough."

Mia frowns. "I can imagine."

She's *so lucky* she gets to go to school with Evan.

"Seems like you guys have been doing pretty well with the distance, though. I mean, you talk all the time, right?" Mia adds, trying to focus on the positive as always.

"We *were* talking every night, until I slept through my poli sci exam a few weeks ago," I say, rolling my eyes. "I'm so mad at myself. I stayed up late the night before the test waiting for Dex to call. His rehearsal ran late, so he thinks it's his fault." I look down at my lap. "He even said we should scale back on phone calls until his play is over."

"When will that be?" Mia asks as she races down the expressway at a speed that falls just short of where I'd have to ask her to slow down.

I sigh. "Next month. The worst part is I'm dying to see him perform, but I can't afford my own plane ticket. And I obviously can't ask my mom for help."

"I can't believe you still haven't told her you and Dex are together. He's your *boyfriend*, Sunny! You guys love each other. What are you gonna do when he proposes? Secretly elope without your mom there? Actually—I can totally see you doing that," Mia says with a furrowed brow.

I giggle despite the knots in my stomach. Mia assumes that Dex and I are "boyfriend" and "girlfriend," and that we've already said, "I love you," and I haven't corrected her. But the truth is, we still haven't defined our relationship. I'm definitely not doing it now, though, when Dex is tied up with his play and we've been talking less and less. I'm worried if I bring it up he'll say the distance is too hard and call it all off. I'd rather just ride things out until this summer. Being together will make everything better.

"I'll tell my mom, eventually," I reply as Mia pulls into my mom's driveway. She's not home yet, and I'm relieved. I'm not in the mood to be interrogated about my grades. I don't intend to tell her about the points I lost on my poli sci exam, but it's a lot easier to lie to her over the phone than it is in person. She'd make a damn good detective if she weren't such a damn good surgeon.

I give Mia a hug, and I'm just about to say goodbye (and congratulate her for driving much more responsibly this time) when I notice a band on her finger. Her *ring* finger. I take her hand in mine and see a small but sparkly diamond.

"Oh my god, Mia! Is this what I think it is?" I ask her, my heart palpitating.

Mia's cheeks turn bright pink. "We're not engaged—not yet. It's a promise ring. Evan gave it to me for my birthday."

"That's so sweet! And so exciting! I can't believe you're already talking about marriage! Why didn't you tell me?" The tables have turned. I'm the one bombarding her with questions this time. I can't help it, I'm just so…surprised.

Mia's eyes shift to her lap. I can tell she's embarrassed. "I felt kinda bad bringing it up after you told me how hard the distance has been for you and Dex."

"Oh my god, Mia, please don't feel bad! I'm really happy for you!" I'm talking so loudly I'm afraid it borders on shrill.

But Mia doesn't seem to notice. She breathes a sigh of relief. "Okay, good, because I've been dying to tell you! Evan and I would get married tomorrow if we could, but our parents would kill us if we don't at least graduate first." She smiles with a dreamy look in her eyes. "It's so hard waiting though. I just love him so much. I want us to have a home together, and a family—the whole nine yards."

"That sounds amazing," I tell her.

It does. I want all of that too, with Dex. But *he* wants to be a famous actor. How could we build the kind of life I want together?

"I wish I didn't have to drive back to school tomorrow. It sucks that our spring breaks aren't lined up. I know I'm jumping ahead, but I thought it might be fun to look at wedding dresses," Mia says, her eyes bugging out as if to say, *Oh my god, can you believe this is happening?*

I can't.

"Oh well, maybe we can go this summer," she continues with a shrug. "Anyway, you're gonna come to Evan's birthday dinner tonight, right? The new Italian place? Eight o'clock?"

"Wouldn't miss it!" I say as Mia wraps her arms tightly around me. When she releases her grip, I turn to get out of the car. I need to move fast. I can only hold back my tears for so long.

I wave goodbye as she backs out of the driveway, then practically run up the porch steps to our front door. When I'm in the house with the door locked behind me, I have to stop and take a deep breath.

I shouldn't be crying. I feel like an awful friend.

I'm happy for Mia, I am. But there's a sinking feeling in my gut.

If I looked in the front hall mirror right now, I bet I'd be green with envy.

Somehow, I've nearly made it through spring quarter. In just seven short days, I'll be home for the summer and, most importantly, with Dex. But first, I have finals to study for. It's a Saturday night and my friends are out partying, finals be damned. But my poli sci grade is teetering between a high B and a low A, and if I want to tip the balance, I need to ace this test.

No pressure.

I get back to my dorm room after a quick dinner at the student center, and I'm about to buckle down when I see the flashing red light on the base of my phone. I have two new voicemails. I perk up immediately. I bet at least one of them is from Dex.

This might be the first time I've smiled all week. I've been in such a funk since spring break. I spent most of it at home alone, reading romance novels and eating TV dinners on the couch. Meanwhile, Dex was having the time of his life with Ben and his friends in Montana. I wondered if this was a glimpse into my future with him. He'd be jet-setting all over the world, a famous actor, and I'd be lonely, and missing him.

The only time I went out over spring break was for Evan's birthday dinner. And watching him and Mia together—how he sat with his arm around her all night, and the way they gazed into each other's eyes, and whispered "love you, babe" with mirrored grins—it was both heartwarming and *unbearably* triggering.

If I was insecure about my relationship with Dex before that night, now I'm a complete disaster. Anyone can see that Mia and Evan are meant to be, but what about me and Dex? I don't even know if he's committed to me, and I'm still too afraid to ask him. Although his play is over and it was a major success (a local theater critic called his performance "stunningly flawless"), he's been so busy catching up on schoolwork that our calls are still few and far between.

An encouraging message from him is exactly what I need to get me through this last week.

I pick up the phone and listen with a giddy grin that falls flat almost instantly. The first message is from my mom, not Dex. She's calling to wish me good luck with finals—but it sounds more like a threat than anything else.

The second message is from Mia, asking me what I think of purple for bridesmaids dresses.

I put down the phone and massage my temples. I feel a headache coming on. I open my poli sci book, but I can't concentrate at all. After about fifteen minutes, I give up and head to the student lounge to read. I'm disheartened that it's empty—the sight of diligent students always kicks me into high gear. Half an hour later, I feel like I'm going to jump out of my skin. Luckily, that's exactly when another student walks into the room.

I give her a little smile and she whispers, "Hey," breathlessly as she plops her things onto the table across from me. She's wearing a cropped tank top and a long flowy skirt with sandals. She has a nose stud, and her hair is up in double buns with pretty wisps framing her face. I don't know why, but my first thought is how different her style is from Mia's, which is mostly Abercrombie, with the occasional purchase from Gap. The only similarity they share is the shade of their hair, a very dark brown that's nearly black.

I watch as my unwitting study buddy sits and swings her legs onto the chair facing hers. She reaches for one of the books in her stack. Nietzsche, by the looks of it. *This is good.* She seems very focused, and I'm hoping her studiousness will rub off on me. With renewed energy, I turn back to my poli sci book. But a few minutes later, she breaks the silence.

"So," she says, waiting for me to look up. "What's your story?"

I tilt my head. "What do you mean?"

"I've seen you around. I feel like you have an intense aura about you," she says, squinting as if to bring my aura into better focus.

"You could say that, yeah," I admit with a wry laugh.

She raises her eyebrows and leans forward onto her elbows with a smile, as if to say, "Tell me more."

"It's just…there's this guy I can't stop thinking about," I blurt out.

The truth is, I've been dying to talk to someone about my undefined relationship with Dex. I obviously can't ask Mia for advice—she'd never understand. Her relationship with Evan has always been so easy and uncomplicated. And frankly, she'd be appalled if she knew I was too scared to have a mature conversation with Dex about where I stand. I know exactly what Mia would say: "Sunny, are you kidding me? Put on your big-girl pants and do it already!" I can hear her voice clear as day in my head.

I've kept my Northwestern friends in the dark as well. As far as they're concerned, Dex is my boyfriend. At a certain point, I caved and started referring to him as such because it was easier to lie than admit I have no clue if we're in a committed relationship.

But keeping up this charade is driving me insane. I've been so distracted this school year, and I know it's because I've kept my concerns about Dex to myself instead of confiding in my friends. And now, it would seem, I'm at a breaking point.

So I tell this stranger *everything*. The unfiltered truth. And it feels so good, being completely honest for once. Like a huge weight has lifted off me.

"So, let me get this straight," she says, her brow furrowed. "You're in a de facto long-distance relationship with a guy who may or may not be your boyfriend, but you're too afraid to ask because you've been in love with him your entire life, and you don't want to risk losing him forever if he doesn't feel the same way about you?"

I wince. "Pretty much."

She nods in silence for several seconds. "I bet he's really hot. Am I right?"

I groan. "So *ridiculously* hot. How did you guess?"

"I've found from personal experience that there's a positive correlation between how hot the guy is and how cloudy my judgment gets."

I laugh. "Sounds about right. I did try, once…to tell him I love him. It was our senior year of high school, and I wrote him this letter, and I was on my way to give it to him when I found him kissing someone else. The prettiest, most popular girl in school. And it devastated me. And that was *before* I'd ever slept with him. And now…" I trail off, wiping tears from my eyes.

My new friend gets up and gives me a hug, then sits in the chair right next to me. "It must be hard meeting the love of your life when you're a kid. I mean, you've loved him for years, but you're only twenty, and you still have to get through school, and start your career, and figure out who you are. And so does he—"

"There are so many moving parts." I sigh. "It feels like the odds are stacked against us."

"That's why you want to hold onto him as long as you can," she says, reading my mind.

I nod, grateful that she understands. This new friend, whose name I don't even know. "I'm Sunny, by the way," I say between sniffles.

She smiles. "Samira. But everyone calls me Sam."

"Thanks for listening, Sam."

She sits forward in her chair to give me another hug, then leans back again. "Okay," she says emphatically, slapping the table with her palms. "I *have* to see a picture of this gorgeous guy."

I let out a much-needed giggle. "I have a bunch in my room. It's just a few doors down." I guess poli sci will have to wait until tomorrow. I need this more.

Sam glances down at her open book, then slams it shut. "Fuck it," she says. "Let's go—it's not like I was going to read this anyway."

We pack up our things and head to my room. I motion for Sam to take a seat on my bed, then pull a photo album from my bookshelf and find my favorite picture of me and Dex. Ben took it last summer. He was in town with his girlfriend, now fiancée, and the four of us had gone to the beach together. Dex and I are standing in front of the water, our toes in the sand. He's shirtless, wearing navy board shorts. He has his arm around my waist, and I'm looking up at him and laughing. It's windy and I have to hold back my long hair, but my curls look beautiful floating behind me. I'm wearing a pink two-piece with strings that tie around my back and behind my neck. I love that swimsuit.

Dex loves taking it off.

"Okay, here," I say, removing the picture from its plastic sleeve and handing it over to Sam.

Her eyes widen instantly. "Holy *fucking* shit, are you serious? He looks like a goddamn supermodel! No wonder you can't stop thinking about him!"

I nod, my face suddenly hot as hell. I'm used to this reaction—Dex turns heads wherever we go. I just can't help but feel like there's an implication behind it. Like, how did someone like *you* manage to snag someone like *him*?

As if reading my mind again, Sam continues.

"I mean, you're gorgeous too, so it's no surprise he likes you. You guys look really good together."

"Thanks," I say, still embarrassed. Sam hands me back the photo and I take another look at myself in it. I look happy, I know that. But gorgeous? The only time I feel gorgeous is when Dex is looking at me. If only I could see what he sees. I guess growing up alongside him wasn't exactly great for my self-esteem. He got so much attention that I felt mostly invisible. It's like he's divine, and the rest of us, merely human.

I think Sam can tell that my mind is spinning, so she switches gears to lighten the mood. "So, tell me about the sex," she says, laughing.

"How much time have you got?" I joke as I plop down beside her on the bed.

It's funny that I can speak so freely with someone I only just met.

nine

SUNNY

SUMMER OF 2000

I take a cab home from the Cleveland airport this time. I told Mia that my mom had the day off and was picking me up. I feel awful for lying.

It's not that I don't want to see her. I just want to see Dex first. I've been waiting for this moment for five fucking months, and I don't want anything to ruin it. I don't want to talk to Mia about how hard the distance is, or how I'll survive another two years of this. I don't want to hear about her wedding plans, or schedule a time to go look at dresses.

All I want is Dex.

His flight lands two hours after mine, so I have just enough time to shower and change. I'm slipping on a short summer dress over my sexy new underwear when I hear a car honk twice from the driveway.

I run downstairs and, when I open the front door, I see him leaning against the hood of his car like the dreamy heartthrob in some '80's movie, and when he locks eyes with me and smiles, I swear he's ten times more handsome than I remember.

"Hey, you," he says, like he always does. I wrap my arms around his neck and he smells like the exact same soap, but this time mixed with CK One, and it's everything I can do not to kiss him right here, but I have no idea when my mom will be home.

Dex gives me a soft peck on the cheek, then nods toward the new Volvo parked in the driveway. "Did your mom get a new car?"

I shake my head. "My mom's at work. That one's mine."

He laughs. "You told her you started driving again, and she bought you a car. See? I told you she'd be okay with it."

I smirk. "She was *not* okay with it. She was worried sick that I'd buy a clunker with my babysitting money and end up dead in a ditch. Those were her exact words."

Dex half-smiles. "Sounds like her. But you know your mom. She only worries like that because—"

"I know, I know. Because she loves me," I tell him.

Dex cups my face in his palms and nods, his smiling eyes sending chills up my spine. *God, I want him.* But just as my mind starts wandering to thoughts of us naked, his forehead creases.

"How'd you do on your poli sci exam?" he asks me.

I bite my lip and make him sweat for a few seconds. "I aced it," I say finally.

"Phew," he sighs with a smile, wiping imaginary sweat from his brow.

I giggle. "You weren't really that worried, were you?"

"Nah," he says, pulling me back into him. "You're the smartest person I know."

I squeeze him tighter, and the urge to kiss him threatens to take over again, but this time it's even harder to fight. "Let's get outta here," I whisper in his ear.

Dex takes my hand and leads me to the passenger side of his car. "My parents are home, so I was thinking we could drive to the lake," he says as he opens the door for me.

When we get there, he parks in an empty lot. It's a perfect summer night, and we'd been driving with the windows down, listening to Radiohead, but now he rolls them up and turns the music low, even though he's checked several times to make sure there's no one else around.

We start kissing, our first kisses in five whole months, and they're soft and slow. He's taking his time with me. Savoring me. Toying with me, because he knows how desperately I need him inside me. I let out a tortured sigh and he smiles, enjoying the effect he has on me.

"Back seat?" he finally suggests.

"I thought you'd never ask."

Dex climbs back first, then helps me onto his lap. We kiss and strip off our clothes—everything except my new sheer black bra, which leaves little to the imagination. He leans against the seat and brings one hand to the back of his head as his eyes wash over me.

"You get sexier every time I see you, you know that?" he says, his voice gritty with desire. He pulls the thin straps off my shoulders one at a time, softly kissing every inch of my neck. He kisses my collarbone, then moves down, brushing his lips over the mesh covering my nipples. I reach back to unclasp my bra and let it fall, giving him unfettered access to me. He takes my nipple in his mouth and circles it with his tongue. At the same time, his fingers find their way between my thighs, and the pleasure is so intense, I arch my back and moan, my hand on the car ceiling.

"God I missed that sound," Dex says, his lips meeting the space between my breasts as I run my fingers up his neck and into his hair. Then our mouths find our way back to each other, and his hands are massaging my thighs, and I take his bottom lip between my teeth and bite until I feel him smile.

I pull back and lock eyes with him, and the way he's looking at me makes me feel wildly alive in a way I haven't felt in months. In a way I only ever feel when I'm with him.

"I need you," I whisper, almost pleading, and when I lift my hips he pushes into me, and I let out that moan he likes again without even thinking. He clasps his arms tight around me and says, "Isn't it insane how we fit together so perfectly?" I nod and kiss him eagerly, my hands moving up his body, every part of us touching, even our eyelashes fluttering against each other's as we move together. He feels so damn good, I never want this to end. But eventually our bodies give in, and we surrender. And we're smiling, and sweaty, and breathless.

Another little death.

"Jesus," Dex says into my neck. "That was incredible."

"I know," I say with a satisfied sigh. "Although…I'm pretty sure I bonked my head on the ceiling once or twice."

"Come here," he says, and I tilt my head to let him kiss the spot I'd just been rubbing. "Next time we'll do it in my bed."

"I can't wait," I whisper before I kiss him again.

"How about tomorrow night?" he says, his mouth traveling

back to my nipples. "My parents are going out."

"Your mom and dad…they still don't know about us?" I ask.

Dex looks up from my breasts and shakes his head.

I bite my lip. "What if we told them? I mean, my house isn't an option for obvious reasons, but we can probably be honest with your parents, right? It'd be nice not to have to sneak around so much."

Dex's eyes shift back and forth a couple of times.

He's *thinking* about it. My heart sinks.

Eventually, he shakes his head. "It's risky, Sunny. I mean, you don't want your mom to know about us—and I get that. But what if one of my parents lets it slip somehow? You know how chatty my dad gets. Remember last summer, when he saw your mom at the hospital and told her you were practically living at my house?"

I let out a puff of air. "Yeah. That did kind of suck. No… you're right. Better safe than sorry."

He *does* have a point. But I still feel uneasy.

I'm not good enough for him. What if he's ashamed of me?

"Shit," he says, leaning back and running a hand over his hair. "I forgot I told Seth I'd hang out with him tomorrow night." He groans. "Maybe I can reschedule."

"Don't worry about it," I say with a casual shrug that I hope masks my disappointment. "I'll come over on Monday while your parents are at work."

But it turns out, it's not that simple.

The next day, Dex's dad offers me an internship I simply can't refuse. I mean, I could—I have plenty of opportunities to babysit again this summer. But if my mom were to find out that I'd rather hang out with toddlers than get firsthand experience in a law office, she'd disown me. At least this way I can spend quality time with Mr. Dexter, and my mom can't complain because it'll look great on my law school application.

I actually learned something interesting about Dex's dad when he offered me the internship. We were talking about his first law job, and I asked if he'd always wanted to be a lawyer. I was sure he'd say yes, so imagine my surprise when he told me he once dreamed of being a writer. He said he'd "written it off" (pun intended) as too impractical.

It was like he stuck a pin in my hopeful heart and it deflated. Mr. Dexter is one of the most reasonable people I know, and I've always trusted his judgment. If *he* didn't think he could manage a successful writing career, it surely doesn't make sense for me to hold onto that dream.

I've all but let it go at this point anyway. Outside of my schoolwork, I have very little time for reading or writing. I'd been thinking about taking a fiction writing course in the fall—just for fun—but after chatting with Mr. Dexter, I think a law seminar would be more sensible.

A few days after I start my internship, Dex lands the role of Lysander in a community theater production of *A Midsummer Night's Dream*. He told me the director was in tears during his audition. While I'm thrilled for him, of course, his rehearsals run late into the night again, which means we need to get creative about spending time together.

Gone are the lazy days of last summer and the long, blissful, hours we spent in his bed. Now our meetups are sporadic, last-minute, and often very late at night, which gives them an almost surreal quality. Sometimes I'll wake up in the morning, alone in my bed, and wonder if I imagined it all. A fever dream. Memories of our trysts flash through my mind like a movie trailer. Dex's mouth on me in the bathroom of our favorite little bistro. His hips against mine in the shower while his parents are hosting a game night downstairs. His hands on my breasts while I straddle his lap in a very small dressing room at the mall. His eyes, his smile, wispy and ethereal, fading into the next scene.

Apart from hooking up with my maybe-boyfriend, I see Mia about once a week, usually for lunch somewhere near the law office. But that's about all the time we get, because my nights are always reserved for Dex. Mia understands. Plus, she has Evan. Their summer schedules are perfectly aligned.

That's how summer flies by, in a febrile haze. And marking the end, this time, is Ben's wedding, which I've been looking forward to since spring, when Dex asked me to go with him. I was sure, by this point, he'd be calling me his girlfriend. But the wedding is today, and that still hasn't happened.

It's one of those relentlessly hot days—the kind where the heat soaks into your skin and stays there long after the sun goes down. While the rest of the bridal party are flushed and sweaty, and even a bit wilted after taking wedding photos outside, Dex is somehow impervious to the humidity and looks like an actual movie star in his tuxedo as he accompanies the bride's pre-teen cousin down the aisle. Every female in the room has some sort of reaction to him, from wide eyes, to giggles, to swoony sighs.

And when the bride walks in, blushing and radiant in her satin gown, I turn to glance at Ben catching sight of her from across the room. Instantly, my eyes fill with tears. And I know I'm not imagining things. The way he looks at her—it's the same way Dex looks at me…

But only when we're alone. And I don't know what that means.

Cocktail hour is outdoors at a beautiful winery, and the sun is just setting beneath the hills, bathing us in peachy pastel light. Dex comes from the bar with two glasses of champagne and hands one to me.

I still can't get over him in his tux. He could be the next James Bond.

For the first time in my life, I'm a little starstruck.

"To summer," he says as we clink glasses.

To summer, I think. *And what happens next?* It's late August, and summer will be over soon.

"You look so damn beautiful," he says as my mind begins to wander.

"Not too shiny?" I ask, wiping my brow.

He slowly shakes his head without taking his eyes off me. "You're radiant."

I smile and look down at my dress. I'm wearing a vintage silver embroidered piece I found in my mom's closet. She wore it in the seventies. It's sleeveless and floor-length, with a deep V-neck that makes me feel very glamorous. I usually opt for warmer tones, but I like the way the silver threads glint in the light.

Standing next to Dex, I can't help but feel insecure at times. But tonight, I know I'm beautiful.

We head inside for dinner and dancing. The dining room is dreamy and romantic, with gossamer drapes and wildflower centerpieces, tea candles gleaming in glass holders, and golden starburst chandeliers hanging from the vaulted wooden ceiling. We're seated at a table with Dex's parents, his Aunt Jane and Uncle Rich. The wine is flowing—Aunt Jane tells us she's enjoying a rare night away from her young kids, and she wants Dex's mom to join in her merriment. The two sisters laugh and reminisce while sipping glass after glass, mixing reds with whites and getting livelier as the night wears on. Despite being a little more effusive than usual, Mrs. Dexter is still mostly holding it together, but by the time dinner is served, Aunt Jane is three sheets to the wind and loving every minute of it.

Occasionally Dex looks over at me and gives me a secret wink, or rests his hand on my knee under the table where no one can see. Normally that would be enough to make my heart flutter with joy but, for some reason, tonight it's not.

Maybe it's because we're seated mere feet away from the newlyweds, kissing to the whoops and yells of friends and family. Not to mention the maid of honor, whose husband keeps lovingly rubbing her shoulder. And the bridesmaid seated to their left, whose boyfriend's arm rests casually on the back of her chair, as if to say, *This woman right here? I love the hell out of her. And I don't care who knows it.*

No, a surreptitious wink and a stolen squeeze, here and there, aren't enough for me tonight. They feel like consolation prizes. Like I've spent months waiting to be reunited with my soulmate but, instead of any grand gestures of love, all *I* get is felt up.

Or maybe, like Aunt Jane, I've had too much to drink (there's an open bar, and no one's carding) but the alcohol's having the opposite effect on me. And rather than feeling bubbly and carefree, I'm insecure and anxious.

After the main course, Uncle Rich asks his wife to dance, and Mr. Dexter excuses himself to find the restroom, leaving Dex and me with just his mom, who moves to sit beside me.

"Sunny, you are so beautiful," she says, squeezing my hand.

"Thanks," I say, squeezing hers back. "And *you* are gorgeous as always."

"Oh, honey," Mrs. Dexter says with a dismissive grin. But it's no secret that Dex got his stunning eyes and radiant smile from his mom. "Thank you," she says more seriously now, and I watch as those stunning eyes start to glisten, and that radiant smile begins to fade into a thin, straight line. She tilts her head and slowly exhales. "We just love you so much," she says, her eyes fixed on me. "I hope you know…you've always been like a daughter to us." Then she looks over at Dex, and I think I see her lips quiver.

"*Okay*, Mom," he says, reaching across me to grab her wine glass. "Time to get you some coffee, I think?" He chuckles and turns his gaze to me. "You know how it is—my mom always gets sappy when she's had too much to drink."

"Well, you can blame your Aunt Jane," she tells him, shaking her head and smiling at me as she wipes a single tear from her eye. "That baby sister of mine is always getting me into trouble," she jokes.

I laugh, my head spinning as Dex and his mom excuse themselves to find coffee, leaving me alone at the table. I have absolutely no clue what's happening, but it feels like Mrs. Dexter just broke up with me. Does she know something I don't? As far as I know, Dex *still* hasn't told his parents what's going on between us. But they're not idiots.

Suddenly, *I* feel like the fool. And the more time I spend alone at the table, the more self-conscious I become, so I get up to find the restroom.

I've just entered a stall when I hear the door to the ladies' room swing open followed by giggling and the loud clacking of high heels. Two women start talking. They sound like they're about my age.

"Can I borrow your lipstick?" one asks the other. "That's such a pretty shade."

"Yeah, go for it."

"Thanks. Oh my god—Ben's cousin is *the* hottest guy I have *ever* seen."

My heart leaps into my throat. I stand frozen in the stall and listen.

"Yeah, too bad he's here with a date."

"Oh, it's not like that—they're just friends."

My hand flies to my mouth.

"How do you know?"

"I overheard him say so."

My vision blurs.

"Besides," the same voice continues, "she's not pretty enough to be his girlfriend."

My ears are ringing.

The other girl scoffs. "Um, are we talking about the same person?

Silver dress? Banging body? And that *hair*? She's gorgeous!"

"You really think so?" asks the mean girl.

"Are you kidding me? I would *kill* for curls like hers. I wonder where she's from? You know…her ethnicity."

"When I was waiting at the bar during cocktail hour, I overheard someone ask her what she is. I didn't hear her answer, though."

"Seriously? Someone went up to her and said, '*What are you*?' That's rude."

I can practically hear the mean girl shrug. "Whatever. It probably happens all the time. I'm sure she's used to it."

I roll my eyes because it's true. Puzzled by my ethnically ambiguous features, people do often ask me this question. Needless to say, it infuriates me, and not only because it makes me feel subhuman. Because, without knowing more about my absentee father, the answer is, "I have no clue." He never cared to know me.

And now I'm in a relationship with a guy who won't acknowledge me. I really am on a roll.

"Well, I'm not asking her," the nice girl replies. "But my point is, she has beautiful features, and you're blind if you can't see that."

The mean girl sighs. "Well, maybe if that's your type. I just think that Ben's insanely hot cousin would look way better with someone more *conventionally* pretty."

"You mean a tall, skinny blonde with blue eyes, like *you*?" the nice one asks, clearly annoyed.

"Yup!" The bitch cackles.

"You really are a bitch, you know that?" says the nice one.

Great minds think alike.

"A bitch who's about to give him my phone number!"

I hear their heels clacking again, followed by the creak of the door as it swings open and shut, then nothing but the faint buzz of the lights overhead.

Maybe I'm in shock, but I don't cry when they leave.

Nothing the mean girl said is news to me.

It was eerie…like she'd read the pages of my nonexistent diary and quoted all the awful thoughts I've had about me and Dex.

When I walk back out into the hall, he's waiting for me.

"Hey, I've been looking for you everywhere! Come with me." He reaches for my hand, his eyes glimmering with excitement.

I let him lead me around two corners, my mind reeling. Finally, we reach a door at the end of a hall and, before he opens it, he looks back to make sure we're alone.

It's a staging room of sorts, with unused centerpieces and empty vases on one table, boxes of tea candles and a small stack of dinner menus on another. Various pairs of men's shoes, a sweatshirt, and a couple of duffel bags are piled messily in a corner. A black leather couch sits under a row of windows framing a bright full moon, which provides the only light in the otherwise dark room.

"I was in here earlier with the other groomsmen. The door locks," Dex says with a mischievous grin, and he gives the knob a quick turn left and right to double-check.

Then he walks toward me and slides his hands down my waist, pulling me close to him. I see something move out of the corner of my eye so I turn to look, but it's just our reflection in a mirror hanging on the wall. In the moonlight, my dress looks white. My breath catches in my throat.

Dex starts kissing my neck, because he knows I love that, and I close my eyes. His lips feel so nice on my skin. It's been ten days since he's kissed me like this. We were in the back row of an empty movie theater. We didn't watch one minute of the film. All I wanted that night was to go home with him. To spend the night in his bed and wake up in his arms.

Instead, we left the theater and had very cramped sex in my car.

I need more than that.

But I also need Dex to make this all go away—my doubts, my fears, and every wretched word that came out of that mean girl's mouth.

So I cave. I let my clutch fall from my fingers, and I grab his shirt collar and kiss him like my life depends on it. He throws his jacket onto the messy heap on the floor, then sweeps me off my feet—yes, like a groom carries his bride across the threshold, he takes me to the black leather couch beneath the windows and lays me down.

"I've been wanting to do this all night," he says as he kisses his way down my plunging neckline. I arch my body, the whisper of his lips drawing me closer and closer to him. He grips my ass and settles his hips between my thighs. He's wasting no time. I can feel him hard against me. I wrap my legs tightly around him. Hot blood pulses through my veins, desire rushes to the deepest part of me. Desire so thick it creeps into my chest and makes it hard for me to breathe. A longing so fierce it stings my eyes with burning tears. All I want is for Dex to make my pain go away—

But not like this. Not anymore. This is all I ever get from him.

He runs his hand up my thigh. His fingers find their way inside me.

I tense. He notices. He stops.

"Did I hurt you?" he asks me, concerned.

But I can't answer his question. "I don't think I can do this anymore," I say, the words so bitter I nearly choke on them. I sit up, my heart racing.

"What?" he asks, now seated beside me. He looks at me, confused.

"I don't think I can *do* this anymore." I stand. Tears spill from my eyes onto the silver threads of my dress. "The stolen kisses, the sneaking around—"

"Sunny, what are you talking about?" he says to me, stunned. "I thought we were having fun—"

"It was fun at the start, but it's not enough."

The mean girl was right. I'm not Dex's girlfriend.

He's hiding me. I'm his dirty little secret.

"What we have isn't real," I cry. "I've spent this entire year counting the days until summer. Counting the days until we could be together again. And now summer's almost over, and I feel like I only had you in bits and pieces. That's all I ever get. Just bits and pieces of you, Dex."

It's like I'm floating somewhere, outside myself. An out-of-body experience.

I watch as Dex just sits there in silence. Maybe *he's* the one who's left his body.

I honestly don't know if he heard what I said. "Where did you go? Please, Dex…say something!"

He continues staring straight ahead. Then he nods and says,

"I understand."

A dreadful sob escapes my chest, and I clutch my broken heart, trying to hold in the rest. I grab my purse and go for the doorknob, but it's locked. I forgot. I fumble to get it open, my tears getting in the way. I run down the hall to the restroom again and hide in the first empty stall I find. I cry silently until every muscle in my body aches. Until three separate groups of laughing ladies have come in and out. Then I open the stall door and make my way to the mirror.

I look at my décolletage, my fingers brushing the line where Dex just kissed me, and my tears threaten to fall again. I splash my face with cool water. I grab a paper towel and wipe the rogue mascara from underneath my eyes. Then I re-apply my lipstick and fix my hair. I'm starting to look like myself again.

Or is it *myself* I'm trying to hide?

I can see her so clearly when my eyes are closed. A little girl in a yellow dress. Tear-streaked cheeks. Heart ripped in half.

Just as I turn to leave, Dex's mom walks through the door.

"Oh Sunny, we've been looking for you guys! I think we're going to head home in twenty minutes or so. Is that okay with you kids?"

"Of course!" I say with a bright smile. "Thanks so much." Mrs. Dexter squeezes my shoulder as she moves past me into a stall. She mustn't have noticed that my heart is shattered.

I guess I'm a pretty good actor too.

The trip home is hell. Dex and I sit in the back of his mom's Jetta, and I look out the window the entire time. We're silent, but his dad's playing his Simon & Garfunkel CD, so no one notices. At one point I take in a raspy breath, and Dex reaches for my hand. I let him take it. He holds it in his lap for the rest of the car ride.

And I die, a little death. But it's so very different this time.

ten

DEX

I glance at the clock on my nightstand again. 4:23 a.m.

If I've slept at all, it's not for more than a minute here and there, in between panicking, and crying, and replaying the night over and over in my head. Wondering where the hell things went wrong at Ben's wedding. Trying my damnedest to make sense of Sunny's sea change.

Before we sat for dinner, everything was going great. Maybe my mom's weepy speech at the table altered the course of the evening. When she took Sunny's hand—told her she thought of her like a daughter—then started going on and on about how much we all love her.

It's true. We do *all* love her. But saying those words to Sunny? And *right there* in front of me, when I haven't yet told her myself? She started biting her lip. And her cheeks turned red. I could tell she was flustered. Embarrassed.

And I know my mom had the best of intentions. But the truth of the matter is, she just doesn't get it.

When I tell Sunny I love her, I want her to say it back, of

course. But what would her "I love you" mean if she doesn't know who I really am?

Sunny has no idea my mental health hangs by a thread. That I wake up sweating. Consumed by dread. It's the most awful thing about me. I can be Dex all day, but at night, sometimes, I'm still Ollie.

That's why I auditioned for community theater. I knew Sunny would be tied up at my dad's office this summer, and it's brutal spending long, lazy days without her.

Thank god I got cast in the role of Lysander. It's nice knowing he gets his happy ending. Better than nice—it feels freeing. What a goddamn relief to be him instead of me.

But under it all I feel like a fraud, and at some point I'm positive I'll break. It's bound to happen eventually, right? I'll have a panic attack on camera, or on stage. I can see it all playing out. Beads of sweat on my skin, shallow breath in my mic. My worst nightmare come to life. My darkest secret under a fucking spotlight. And who will I be then?

And will Sunny still love me if she sees me that way?

What is there to love about a guy who's Ollie by night and Dex by day?

But I can't tell my mom all of that. She's already suffered so much with every pregnancy loss, and I don't want to add to her struggles. I had to come up with *something* to say, though.

As soon as we left the table to find coffee, I knew she'd start firing questions at me.

"Dex, why haven't you told me you and Sunny are together? You're more than just friends…it's obvious, honey. So why not make it official? Your dad and I would be thrilled!"

More than just thrilled. It would be their biggest dream come true. Not only theirs—but mine as well.

For a minute I reconsidered.

But I could see myself crumbling under the pressure. How long could I keep up this act that I was perfect? Would I ever be the man that Sunny deserves? No—first I needed to get a handle on my anxiety. If I focused on acting and tried to ignore it, maybe at some point I'd finally outgrow it. Then I'd be worthy of Sunny's love.

"It's complicated, Mom, because of the distance. I don't think we can handle more than a casual relationship."

I definitely could have phrased that better. My mom looked disappointed in me.

"A *casual* relationship won't work with Sunny. If you don't tell her how you feel, you might lose her, Dex."

"She knows how I feel, Mom, we don't need to label it."

"Labels are important, honey. Just have the conversation. She loves you too, can't you see? It's written all over her face. The two of you are meant to be. You have nothing to be afraid of."

Afraid. I wish she'd used a different word. That one definitely struck a nerve.

"I should get back to Sunny," I said, squeezing my temples. I started to make my way back to the table. That's when I ran into Uncle Ted.

If only Sunny had heard me talking about her. My uncle was so happy to see us together. He couldn't remember when Sunny and I met, so I reminded him we'd been best friends since kindergarten. That's when my uncle took a step back and nearly knocked over a young woman standing behind him. She was tall, with blue eyes and blonde hair. And she was staring at me. She looked like trouble, that's all I'll say. Luckily, she spotted a friend and walked over to her.

"Well, you and Sunny make a stunning couple," Uncle Ted said after the blonde woman had gone. "You look like a pair of movie stars."

"*She's* the real star. Smart, kind, and gorgeous. I still can't believe how lucky I am. If I play my cards right, I'm hoping that could be us someday." I nodded toward Ben and his blushing new bride.

Had no clue at the time that my world was about to turn upside down.

"I can't do this anymore," Sunny told me. "What we have isn't real."

She may have said something else. But I could barely hear.

My vision went spotty—I was afraid I'd go blind.

To be honest, I was sure I was losing my mind.

Just say something. Anything! But what can I say?

She doesn't want to be with me.

Of course she doesn't want to be with me.

I'm a fake. A lie. A total sham.

So I nodded and said, "I understand."

I understand???

What the fuck was I thinking? That is far from the truth—I understand *nothing*. Like how the hell can two people share a love this intense and let it all go? It just doesn't make sense. But

I let my insecurities win. And letting Sunny go was a godawful sin. I can't believe I fucked up like that.

But I'll fight like hell to get her back.

I wait until sunrise, then I drive to Sunny's house. I'm going to tell her that I love her. Hell, I'll tell her about my panic attacks if I have to. I'll squash any doubt she has about us. I'm almost feeling confident when I step onto her lawn.

But as fucking luck would have it—I don't get very far.

"Dex? What are you doing here?"

It's her mom. She's dressed in hospital scrubs, heading toward her car. And she's scowling.

"I need to talk to Sunny," I say matter-of-factly.

But my heart is racing. My palms are sweaty.

"Honey, she's asleep. It's the crack of dawn! Why don't I have her call you later this morning?"

No, I can't turn back. I have to stay. "I'll sit and wait in my car," I say.

"You look like you've been crying. Did you and Sunny have a fight?"

She does her best to ask politely, but I'm well aware she doesn't like me.

"It was a misunderstanding, not a fight. I need to talk to her." *To make things right.*

"Dex, I don't know what your intentions are. But trust me when I say, this will *not* end well. Why don't you save us all the trouble and go home?"

I can hardly believe my ears. "I'm in love with your daughter. I have been for years."

I said it out loud—finally.

It's like the weight of the world lifts off my shoulders.

For a very brief moment, I feel free.

Until her mom's narrow eyes shoot daggers at me. "You know, it wasn't easy raising Sunny by myself. She missed out on something, I admit that. Two parents at home, and family dinners—that's why she was always with you. Now, you might think you know my daughter best, but all she wants is stability, honey. A family, a home, a stable career. *That's* what's most important to her."

My head is throbbing. My hands start to twitch. Where the *fuck* is she going with this? I want to ask her, but no words come out. I definitely don't feel like Dex right now.

"Dex, with your talent and good looks, you're destined for fame and fortune," she goes on. "If anyone can make it in show business, it's you."

She's not the first person to assume I picked this path for the celebrity. But the glitz and glamour mean fucking nothing to me. Acting is the only thing that calms my anxiety—besides her daughter, Sunny. If I tell her that, I know she'll judge me. I mean, who would want someone with such a horrible flaw to be their one and only son-in-law?

"Now, how many actors do you know with happy marriages?" she asks me. "There's a reason celebrity divorce rates are sky-high. You'll never be home. You'll be surrounded by temptation. Gorgeous models and actresses flinging themselves at you wherever you go. And even if you *are* faithful, there will be rumors. Your life will be tabloid fodder. And Sunny's too. Is that really what you want for her? It'll be damn-near impossible to maintain a successful relationship, much less give her the life she wants. The family she missed out on as a child. Think about it."

Fuck my life. Is she right? No! "You don't understand—I *love* her, though."

"If you love her, honey, you'll let her go."

Then she gets in her car and drives away.

And with the heaviest heart…

I do the same.

eleven

He didn't fight for me.

I spent the entire day after the wedding crying in my bed and waiting for Dex to ring the doorbell. To call me. Email me.

I would have settled for an AOL Instant Message.

But *nothing*.

I couldn't believe it, honestly. I know that I shouldn't have ended things with the expectation that he would make some grand declaration of love for me and everything would work out perfectly…

But I'd be lying if I said that's not exactly what I wished for.

When my mom came home from work later that evening, she found me still teary-eyed in bed.

"Sweetie, what's the matter?" she asked, her voice brimming with concern. She hurried to my side and felt my forehead first, then put her fingers on my wrist to check my pulse. When she was confident I wasn't dying, she asked me again. I couldn't find the words.

"Did something happen at the wedding last night?" She

sighed heavily as she rubbed my back. "This has to do with Dex, doesn't it."

I didn't say anything. I just wept in her arms.

I couldn't remember the last time I sought comfort from her. Since I met Dex, I've only ever wanted to cry on *his* shoulder. Now I couldn't. And it was torture.

"Oh sweetheart, I tried to warn you about him," my mom said tenderly, despite the biting nature of her words. I continued to sob. "You'll get over him," she added, like it was the easiest thing in the world.

At least she left for a work conference in Chicago the next morning, so I've been able to spend the past few days grieving in peace, without her judging me. But today is going to be rough; I'm meeting Mia to look at wedding dresses. She's been asking me all summer, and I kept putting it off. Now I have to go, when it's literally the last thing on Earth I want to do.

"Hey!" I say when I meet her at the bridal shop, giving her a massive hug. I figure if I take a page from her playbook and squeeze her extra-tight, she might believe I'm actually okay with this breakup—like I've tried to tell her on the phone already, twice. No. Three times. I didn't give her many details. All I said was that Dex and I called it quits because of the distance.

Mia pulls back to look at me. I'm wearing white shorts and a bright yellow halter top. It's the sunniest outfit I own. No broken hearts in *this* bridal store.

She opens her mouth to speak, but I beat her to it. If I take control of the conversation, maybe she won't ask me how I'm feeling.

"I thought your mom, or maybe one of your brothers might be with you," I say. Mia's the oldest of four, and the only girl in a big Italian family. I look around, but don't see any of her relatives.

Mia laughs sheepishly. "I'm driving them crazy. I dragged them to five or six shops already this summer, and I still haven't found a dress I love. My mom says I can keep looking, and if I find something good, to put it on hold."

"Got it," I say with a chuckle. "Have you settled on a style you like?"

Mia tilts her head. "I was thinking something fitted, that doesn't swallow me up."

"I agree," I say with a smile as I envision my beautiful friend walking down the aisle. Maybe this won't be so hard for me after all. Once Mia starts trying on gowns, it might actually be fun. I start browsing through a rack beside me. "What about this one?" I ask, pulling back a dress for her to see.

"Are you sure you're okay to do this?" Mia asks the minute I let my guard down. She looks so worried about me. Her hazel eyes are laced with pity.

"Believe me, I'm fine," I lie. "I knew things wouldn't work out with Dex. It's hard being long-distance. We're probably both a lot better off."

Ugh. Is there a bathroom in here? I feel like I might throw up.

Mia eyes me skeptically. "Have you talked to him at all since the wedding?"

I shrug. "There's nothing to say."

"Sunny, what if this is all some big misunderstanding? Don't you think you should at least call Dex before you go back to

Evanston? I remember this one time, Evan and I—"

She's always comparing our relationships. I really wish she would stop.

Thankfully, the store clerk joins us and cuts her off. "So, which one of you is the lucky lady getting married?" she asks.

Mia turns redder than her sports car.

"*She* is," I say, nodding toward her.

"Wonderful!" the clerk says, clapping. "Follow me to the back of the shop. Our petite collection is small, and it's selling out!"

Mia turns to look at me. "We really don't have to do this today, Sunny."

"Mia, I want to. You're my best friend. I can be happy for you and sad about Dex. Yes, it sucks that we broke up. But I'll be going back to school soon, and partying with my friends, and I'll forget all about him." *I need to quit while I'm ahead.* "Now let's find you the world's most perfect petite wedding dress!"

Mia laughs. I make sure I'm smiling as we head to the petite section.

Back at school a few weeks later, I tell Sam every heartbreaking detail I was too embarrassed to share with Mia. And Sam does *not* mince words.

"Well, fuck him!" she declares emphatically.

I look up at her, my eyebrows raised over the enormous mug of ashwagandha tea she made to help me "mellow out." We're seated on the couch in her new off-campus apartment, which is very bohemian chic, just like Sam. There are lush plants and spice-scented candles peppering the living room, a gorgeous Middle Eastern tapestry on the wall, and an expensive-looking Moroccan leather pouf that she insists I can rest my feet on. The room smells of incense—and maybe just a hint of weed. I don't smoke but, regardless, it's the perfect sanctuary.

"Well, don't actually *fuck* him. You know what I mean—just let him go," Sam clarifies before modeling a full inhale and a long exhale in a sweet attempt to help me.

I manage a shallow inhale followed by a dramatic sigh, and she continues. "I know it's hard. But you'll get over him. You deserve so much better," she says, squeezing my hand.

My eyes fill with tears. "There *isn't* anyone better for me than him, Sam. And I messed everything up. Instead of having a mature conversation with him about our relationship, I panicked. I let my insecurities get in the way and sabotaged the best thing I've ever had." I take in a deeper breath this time and exhale slowly.

Maybe Mia was right. I need to talk to Dex.

"I should call him," I tell Sam. "This is all my fault, and if I'd just been honest with him about how I feel—"

I can tell by the way she's wincing that I don't need to finish my sentence. "Sunny, you told him you needed more than casual sex, and all he said was, 'I understand.' I mean, that's barely even a response!"

"I know how it sounds," I say wiping my eyes. "But Dex wasn't acting like himself when he said that. It actually worried me. I mean, I've known him my whole life, and I've *never* seen him act that way. He was so distant, so withdrawn. It felt like he was…dissociating."

"Maybe," Sam says slowly with a furrowed brow. "But if something *had* been going on with him, don't you think he would have called you once he snapped out of it?"

I shrug. At a loss for words, I take another small sip of Sam's special tea and scrunch my nose. It tastes a little bit like dirt and, perhaps not entirely coincidentally, my eyes start watering even more.

"Look, actions speak louder than words," Sam goes on to say. "And you haven't heard from Dex at all in three weeks. I'm sorry, hon, but I think that's all you need to know."

I nod despite myself. "You're right," I agree, sniffling. "God, I'm surprised I still have tears left. I haven't stopped crying since the night of the wedding."

Sam grabs a tissue and hands it to me with a sympathetic frown. "I'm sorry, Sunny. I feel like an asshole. I've been told that I have a hard time sugar-coating things."

I laugh through my tears. "It's okay. I like that you have no filter."

She smiles with relief. "Okay, good. And don't worry. I'm sure there are plenty of other guys out there who can make you come so hard you—"

"Sam!" I shriek, setting my gigantic mug down on her coffee table and hiding behind my hands. She's quiet, so I peek at her through parted fingers.

"What?" she says with a devious smile.

"I'm never telling you anything again." I toss a mustard-colored throw pillow at her and we both laugh, and it feels so good that, before I know it, we're having a full-blown pillow fight. It's the happiest I've felt in weeks. We're giggling so much we don't even hear her roommate walk through the front door.

"Just so you know, this is very cliché," she says out of nowhere, which startles the hell out of me and Sam.

"Oh my god, Claire!" Sam exclaims, clutching her chest and resuming her laughing fit as she hops off the couch to give her roommate a hug. "Well, you just missed the pillow fight, but you're right on time for braiding each other's hair and prank-calling cute boys," she jokes as she joins me back on the couch. "Claire, this is my friend Sunny I've been telling you about."

Claire's deadpan expression shifts instantly, and she's beaming as she leans over to give me a hug. "I've heard so much about you, Sunny! I'm excited to finally meet you!"

"Same here!" I say, suddenly self-conscious about my tear-streaked cheeks. "I don't usually have mascara running down my face like this, but I'm kinda going through a breakup...or something," I explain with a wry laugh as I pat my eyes with a tissue.

"Hence the pillow fight," Sam chimes in.

"I'm so sorry," Claire says to me with a tilt of her head.

"Yeah, she's been hung up on a total player and deserves *way* better," Sam elaborates. Then she cranes her neck to see if I need more tea—I don't.

I frown. I worry that Sam is right, but I still don't want to believe it. I mean, the connection Dex and I had wasn't a figment of my imagination. Was it?

"Seriously," Sam says more gently this time, "I'm sorry about you and Dex. But if you want to come to this party with me and

Claire tonight, there will be tons of theater majors there. You'll have your pick of broody actor types to date."

"Thanks." I sigh. "But I think I need to take a break from guys."

And that's exactly what I do. As a junior and a resident assistant this year, I have a dorm room all to myself, which makes it easy to immerse myself in schoolwork. I shift my focus back to where it was always supposed to be, I guess—getting into Northwestern Law School.

I can't bear the possibility of running into Dex in Beachwood during breaks from school, so I tell my mom I have to stay on campus and study. She doesn't take the bait at first. She hates the idea that I won't be coming home, even though she'll very likely be at work. So I tell her the truth: I don't want to see Dex. Now *that* she understands. So instead of me coming home, she visits me for a weekend here and there, when she can.

At least now she won't accuse me of not "keeping my eye on the prize." I officially make it to April without so much as kissing a guy. My grades are impeccable, and my mom is thrilled, particularly when I tell her I was offered a job doing data entry for a legal research project on the Chicago campus.

"It's an interdepartmental study focusing on the mental health of children in the juvenile justice system," I explain to her over the phone.

"Oh Sunny, that's going to look great on your law school application! I'm so proud of you," she says while stifling a yawn. It's a Saturday morning and she just got home from the hospital. "See, I told you Dex was a distraction. Look how far you've come this year without him."

My stomach lurches. I'm silent.

My mom yawns more deliberately this time. "Well, I'm going to get some sleep, sweetie. Long shift last night. I'll talk to you soon. Enjoy your weekend," she says, then hangs up.

I put down the phone and just stare at it for a minute before I log onto my computer to check my email. I'm expecting some forms to fill out for my new job, but I only have one new message.

And because my mom's unsolicited comment about Dex hit me like a punch to the gut…

And the Universe apparently has a pretty twisted sense of humor…

That message happens to be from Dex's dad.

John Dexter.

My heart thumps wildly seeing his name in my inbox. The subject line reads, "Summer." I click open the message, my hands trembling.

We hope you're well, darling. Just a note to say that you're most welcome to intern at my office again this summer, if you think that would be a worthwhile opportunity for you. Wishing you the very best, always. John

I almost forgot that he used to call me darling. Instantly, the floodgates open, and I break down in tears.

I've spent the past six months trying my damnedest to repress, ignore, escape, *deny* the inconceivable pain of losing the one true love of my life, and in the ten seconds it takes me to read an innocuous email from his *dad*, I crumble to bits.

Sounds about right.

I call Sam right away. I don't know how much she even understands in between my heaving sobs, but she instructs me to pack a bag for the weekend and says she'll be outside my dorm in fifteen minutes to pick me up.

For the first hour I'm at their apartment, all I do is cry on the couch while Sam and Claire stand in the kitchen with their arms crossed, disagreeing over how to handle me in not-so-hushed whispers. Sam wins the coin toss, but when two mugs of her special tea don't do the trick, Claire, who was the last of us to turn twenty-one and is eager to get carded, leaves for the corner store with a triumphant grin and comes back with a bottle of tequila, which turns out to be much more effective. We sleep in on Sunday, get brunch, watch movies all afternoon and, before I leave, I use Sam's computer to respond to Mr. Dexter's email.

Thanks so much for thinking of me. I just got a job helping with a legal research project on the Chicago campus at Northwestern, so I'll likely stay here this summer. Hope all is well. Warmly, Sunny.

Then I go back to my dorm room and, feeling depleted both physically and mentally, I crawl into bed and pass out.

When I wake up the following morning, I have one new message from John Dexter.

Of course you did, darling. We're so very proud of you. Best of luck.

Tears start to form in my eyes again, but I take deep breaths like Sam taught me, and I'm able to will them away. There's no time for tears. I'm starting my new job today.

I finish getting dressed and catch the intercampus shuttle to downtown Chicago. It's a cold, gray day, which sums up the entirety of January through May in the Windy City. I walk past the law school and eye a group of first-year students heading to class with Civil Procedure treatises in one hand and large cups of takeout coffee in the other.

They look stressed.

I heave a sigh and continue toward my destination—an academic building just south of the law school. I find the office on the third floor. There's one person checking in ahead of me, so I wait by the windows. I'm gazing at the lake's choppy waves when I hear a voice from behind me.

"Sunny? Is that you?"

I whip my head around and am met by a mountain of a man—broad shoulders, prominent biceps and pecs under a soft knit sweater. Because he's so tall, it takes a few seconds before my eyes fly up to land on his, which are squinting at me through a pair of stylish Clark Kent glasses. It's not until I see his kind smile that I recognize him.

"Asher Abadie!" I exclaim. It's tall, thin-as-a-rake, Asher from middle school. But he isn't thin as a rake anymore.

He looks down at the clipboard in his hand, then back at me. "My boss gave me your CV about five minutes ago and told me I'd be training you. I wondered if you were the same Sunny from Beachwood and, as soon as I saw your curly hair, I knew."

I'm rattled. Those are the same words Dex once said to me. But now's not the time to think about him.

"I'm impressed you remember me," I tell Asher. "You only went to school with us for a couple of years, right?"

"Yeah, my dad was in the Air Force, so we moved around a lot. But you have one of those faces that's hard to forget," he says before clearing his throat and looking down at his shoes. "I remember you had that crush on…what was his name, again?" He looks back up. "Oh right, Dex. I'm surprised he's not some famous Hollywood actor yet. You still talk to him?"

"No. We're not in touch anymore." My heart aches saying the words. I hope Asher doesn't notice. "So, you go to Northwestern too?" I ask, desperate to change the subject.

"I do. Psychology major. And you're interested in—law?" he asks while flipping through my CV.

"I am." *I guess.*

My romance-writing dream is all but dead. I mean, how the heck am I supposed to write happy endings when my own love story is a tragedy? But, again, it's not the time to worry about that.

"Have you been working on this project for a while?" I ask, struggling to bring back my attention.

"Almost two full years now," Asher says as he combs his fingers through his hair. His sweater lifts, revealing a hint of his abs, and something flutters in my stomach.

Probably just nerves on my first day of work.

"Let me show you to your desk, and we can get started," he continues. We walk into an adjacent room where several people are working quietly on computers, most of them with headphones on. "So, this is you," he says, pulling a chair out for me. I take a seat, and he reaches across me to maneuver my mouse. I have to make a concerted effort not to stare at the rock-hard triceps barely hiding underneath his rolled-up sleeves.

Wow. Asher sure has changed since he was a gangly preteen. How did he get this ripped? He must work out a lot. Shit! Did he just ask me something?

"I'm sorry, what did you say?" I'm mortified.

Asher smiles. "I was just wondering if you've done data entry before."

"Oh," I say, hoping he can't feel the heat wafting off my face. "Actually, no."

"Well, it's very simple and, honestly…" His voice trails off as he looks around to make sure no one's within earshot. "It's a little boring," he continues with a smile. "But you'll get the hang of it quickly. So here's the database, and you're just going to use these documents over here"—he points to a stack on the table—"to fill in these charts over here," he says, now pointing at the computer screen. "And if you have any questions, I'll be right across the room, so feel free to grab me."

"Sounds good," I say, trying not to react to the fact that he just invited me to grab him.

Ugh, what's wrong with me?

"You haven't had sex in, like, a year—that's what's wrong with you," Sam explains later that night at her apartment. We're sitting cross-legged on her couch, and I'm praying that she doesn't offer me any tea.

"It hasn't been *that* long," I say with a bit of a scowl. "But almost."

"Well, I'm happy for you! This is the first time you've been attracted to a guy since…" Sam pauses. "You-know-who," she whispers, as though referring to Lord Voldemort. "This is big!"

She's right. It *is* big. Maybe I can move on from Dex after all. "Well, who knows if the attraction is mutual," I say with a sigh. "And even if it is…this time I want to take things slowly."

Sam is quiet for a second, and I imagine she'll come back with a snarky remark about how I need to get laid. But instead, she rubs my knee and says, "That sounds like a good plan."

twelve

It's a spring day in Chicago that's pleasantly surprising because it actually feels like spring. There's no biting chill in the air, only a warm breeze and the scent of flowers blooming. The kind of day that reminds you that life is full of new beginnings.

That no matter how broken your heart is, you can still smile, and laugh, and…find yourself attracted to someone else.

I have a crush on Asher Abadie.

It started out as something to bide the time. Because Asher was right—data entry *is* boring. Maybe I'm a welcome distraction for him too. We're the only two undergrads working on this project so, naturally, we've gravitated toward each other these past few weeks. And it's probably for the best because, in the absence of Asher's interest, I know exactly where my mind would wander. I'm not over Dex yet, but will I ever be? At this point, I'd settle for his perfect half-smile not being the first thing I think about when I wake up each morning.

But as I walk to the shuttle stop with Asher after our Friday afternoon shift, my only thought is whether or not he's going to ask me out. I've been getting vibes from him all week. The way his eyes linger on mine when we say hello and goodbye. The way I catch him stealing glances in my direction when he thinks I'm not paying attention. The way his hand keeps lightly brushing mine while we're walking.

He's going to ask me now. I feel it coming.

"Hey, I was thinking…I'd like to take you out to dinner sometime," he says as soon as we've run out of things to say about the unexpectedly perfect weather. He clears his throat. "If you'd be interested in that."

He's nervous. It's endearing. I've never seen Dex sweat about anything.

"I would definitely be interested in that," I say, smiling wider than I expected.

"Great!" Asher looks relieved. "Any chance you're free tonight?"

I didn't see *that* coming. I thought I'd have at least a day to mentally prepare myself. But maybe it's better this way. I won't have time to stress about my first date since Dex. "As a matter of fact, I am."

"Cool! How about we ditch the shuttle and have dinner downtown?"

"Sounds great!" I say. And when Asher smiles, my knees go weak.

We walk to The Cheesecake Factory. Asher orders a beer, and I have one of those fruity mixed drinks with an umbrella in it, and when the waiter asks for ID, I proudly show my real one, which still feels pretty thrilling, since I turned twenty-one less than two months ago. We eat all the bread in the bread basket.

Asher asks for the Cajun Chicken Littles, and I get the Navajo Chicken Sandwich on that deliciously puffy fry bread, and I don't even care that I sometimes have a little spiced mayo on my face. We split a tuxedo cheesecake, but I eat most of it. We have a really nice time.

We talk nonstop. Mostly about school, a little bit about work and plans for after graduation, typical first date stuff. But what surprises me most is how comfortable I feel with him. I didn't think I could feel this comfortable with a guy I haven't known since I was five.

We take a late shuttle back to campus, and he walks me back to my dorm. Not all the way to my room, just to the front door of the building.

"Can I kiss you, Sunny?" he asks me nervously.

I nod and smile.

And that's how it begins.

One month later, Asher and I are planning our fourth date. He offers to cook me dinner at his apartment off campus on Saturday evening. His roommate will be out of town the whole weekend.

"You're having sex tonight!" Sam squeals when we're hanging out that afternoon.

Claire laughs at her roommate's outburst, but must notice me biting my lip. "Okay, let's not jump to any conclusions, Sam. We don't even know if Sunny's ready to have sex with Asher yet." She turns to face me again. "*Are* you?"

"I'm not sure," I say as I take a seat at their kitchen table. We just got back from a yoga class, and Sam is making us lunch. "It's been nice taking things slowly."

"Do you feel like he's putting pressure on you?" Claire asks as Sam hands us each a plate with her signature tofu "egg" salad sandwich on sprouted whole grain bread.

"No, not at all. He's been such a gentleman," I say as I take a tentative bite of my sandwich. "Mmm, this is surprisingly good!" I exclaim before taking a bigger bite.

"*Surprisingly?*" says Sam.

"I guess I'm just scared," I continue, steering the conversation back to my dilemma. "It's been so easy and fun with Asher, and I'm afraid having sex might…complicate things."

"You're afraid you forgot how to do it?" Sam teases.

I laugh and shake my head. "I really like Asher. And I'm afraid that if we have sex, I'll just start comparing him…you know…to Dex.

And how could sex with anyone else ever *compare?*

Sam tilts her head. "Well, it *will* be different. But that doesn't mean it can't also be amazing. Plus, you'll never know unless you try."

"Just remember, there's no rush," Claire adds. "When you're ready, you'll know."

"Thanks, ladies," I say as I inhale the last bite of my sandwich. "Well, I hate to eat and run, but I want to squeeze in a nap before my date tonight. That should help settle my nerves."

Sam jumps up from the table. "Or you could meditate with

us!" she exclaims, pointing to the meditation space she recently created in a corner of their living room. "I just got some new cushions, want to try one?"

"Thanks, I'm good," I say, smiling as I hug her first, then Claire. They walk me to the door. "Wish me luck!" I shout as I start to head down the stairwell.

"Good luck getting laid!" I hear Sam yell from the doorframe, just as their eighty-year-old neighbor leaves her apartment and meets my sheepish grin with stern disapproval.

When I get back to my dorm room, I check my voicemail and listen to a new message from Mia. "Just calling to check in and say hi! I miss you. It's been awhile."

It's been four weeks. I haven't told her about Asher yet.

I can't fathom her reaction. She'll remember him from middle school. He was quiet, but nice. Tall and lanky. He's hot now. Sexy, even. Will she be happy for me? Will she ask me if I'm over Dex?

It's been 280 days since I last saw him. Not that anyone's counting.

I play out the conversation with Mia in my mind, and I get totally overwhelmed.

So instead of calling her back, I nap.

Asher knew exactly what he was doing when he invited me over for dinner. If I didn't already think he was incredibly sexy, tonight has sealed the deal. Tall, handsome, Asher—in an apron—making a delicious meal for *me*. It's intoxicating.

"The chicken smells amazing," I say, closing my eyes and inhaling the sultry scent of cumin, lime, and something spicy. "Can I help with anything?"

"Nah, I've got this," Asher says with a wink as he turns the heat down under the sizzling pan. "Here. Try a bite."

I smile as he brings a spoonful to my lips, his other hand hovering under my chin. I knew I would like it based on the smell of his kitchen alone, but as soon as the flavors hit my taste buds, my eyes widen in disbelief. "Oh my god, Asher…this might be the best chicken I've ever tasted! I'm worried you missed your calling. Are you absolutely *sure* you want to be a therapist?"

He laughs. "I'm glad you like it. I can't take all the credit, though. My mom's a chef *and* a great teacher. Unfortunately I'm way too into my psychology classes to even consider a different career."

I lean against the counter, my shoulders rounding. "That's incredible. I wish I felt that way about poli sci. Honestly, it's just a means to an end. I could have majored in pretty much anything, but I read that poli sci majors have high law school acceptance rates."

"Sounds like you have it all figured out," Asher says as he squeezes lime into two bottles of beer and hands one to me. "Do you know what kind of law you want to practice?"

"I'm not sure. Probably anything besides litigation." I laugh. "I can't see myself arguing in front of a judge and jury…too nerve-wracking. I'd much rather sit at a computer all day and do legal research and writing." I take a long sip. "I've always loved to write. Honestly, I think the reason I do so well in school is because I can write a killer essay on any topic you throw at me. I hope that doesn't make me sound conceited," I add, my cheeks heating up.

Asher turns to wrap his arms around my waist. "Hey, it's no secret how smart you are. That's only *one* of the things I like about you."

"Well, aren't you sweet," I say with a giddy grin before our lips meet. When he slowly pulls away, there are goosebumps on my skin.

"So, do you think you'll definitely stay in Chicago this summer?" he asks as he turns his attention to the peppers and onions in a cast iron skillet, all cut into beautiful thin strips. I can tell by his hopeful tone that he really wants me to say yes.

"It's official," I tell him excitedly. "I just worked out the details with Sam and Claire. They offered me their pull-out couch. It'll be cramped, but way more fun than living by myself downtown."

Asher gives the veggies a final stir. "Well, you're always welcome to hang out here. Justin is studying abroad this summer," he says, referring to his roommate.

"I might take you up on that," I say with a smile he doesn't see because he's garnishing the guacamole with radish and some sort of herb. Cilantro, maybe? I don't know. My cooking repertoire is limited to foods that come pre-packaged with instructions.

When Asher turns around, he pauses to look at me as he takes off his apron and tosses it onto the counter. He drags a hand down his chin. "You are so beautiful, Sunny."

"You're not so bad yourself," I say, stepping into him. He leans down to kiss me. I'm on my tiptoes with my arms wrapped around his neck, and he lifts me off the floor effortlessly. I'm kissing him in midair until he sets me back down ever-so-gently.

"You hungry?" he asks.

"Very," I say, my eyes still closed from our kiss. When I open them, he's smiling at me, his cheeks flushed.

We sit at the small dining table in his living room and enjoy the meal and each other's company. When I've taken the last bite of my dinner, he asks if I saved room for dessert.

"Always," I say, dabbing at my lips with a napkin.

"Good," he replies. "I remember how much you loved that tuxedo cheesecake…" he begins, his voice trailing off as he walks to the fridge. "So I drove to The Cheesecake Factory and picked up two slices."

While he's still in the kitchen, I get a bit misty-eyed. Asher's so sweet. So thoughtful.

It feels incredible to be treated this way. "That's really nice of you," I tell him.

He walks back to the table with two plates and two forks, and when he sets everything down, I pull him in for a kiss. He sits and we start eating.

"Two slices?" I ask, covering my mouth as I savor a bite of rich chocolate. "Last time, we split one."

"Well…" Asher hesitates. "You *did* kind of eat most of it." He looks up at me to gauge my reaction.

I feign a look of shock and playfully swat his arm. He laughs. "No, you're right," I concede. "I definitely ate most of it."

After dessert, we make our way to the living room. He asks me if I want to watch a movie and invites me to pick one from the DVD tower next to the TV. I search for one that I haven't already seen with Dex, but it's a struggle. I start at the top and scan each title, my finger sweeping over every DVD case as I go along. I make it all the way to the bottom before I find one. *Gladiator.* It was in theaters last summer, but Dex and I never got the chance to see it. He was too busy with rehearsals.

The movie's long, but I don't mind. I like being close to Asher. He sits with his arm around me, and I snuggle into him, resting my head on his chest. His other hand is on my knee. We shift around a bit from time to time but stay close, always touching. He draws soft circles on my shoulder with his fingertips. I lean my head into the crook of his neck. He kisses the top of my head. The movie's almost over, but I'm not nervous. Only curious about what will happen next.

When the credits start rolling, Asher turns to face me. "I know we've only been going out for a month, but I like you. *A lot*," he adds with a nervous laugh. "And I was thinking maybe we could make this thing official." He clears his throat. "I guess what I'm trying to say is—I'd like to be your boyfriend, Sunny. If you'll have me."

It's everything I once hoped to hear from Dex. And the way Asher's biting his lip in anticipation of my answer makes it clear how much I mean to him. This thoughtful, attractive man wants the world to know I'm his girlfriend. Why wouldn't I be all in?

"Yes," I answer, putting Asher out of his misery, and he

breathes a sigh of relief. Then his lips meet mine, but he pulls away almost immediately.

"I don't want you to feel any pressure. We can still take things as slowly as you want," he says.

I take off his sexy glasses, and I set them on the coffee table. Then I wrap my arms around his neck and kiss him. I lean back, pulling him on top of me. He's kissing my shoulder and my neck, and then I whisper in his ear. "I don't want to take things slowly anymore."

thirteen

DEX

It's been 281 days since my cousin Ben got married.

Which means it's been 281 days since I last saw Sunny.

I know this because it's the first thought in my head when I wake up every godforsaken morning.

I squeeze my eyes shut again before they fully open. It's bright in here. Brighter than usual. My head hurts. I feel a bit queasy too.

Last night was our final performance of *No Exit.* Afterward, the cast got together to celebrate. I played the role of Joseph Garcin, a man who's condemned to hell for all eternity. Needless to say, getting into character was pretty fucking easy for me.

Jesus, did I forget to close my blinds last night? I'm rubbing my forehead when I hear someone sigh right next to me.

That's when I remember. I'm not in my own bed. I'm in Brittney's.

She was one of my co-stars in the play. We talked for a while at the party last night, and she asked me to walk her home. When I open my eyes, she's smiling at me.

"Last night was amazing, Dex," she says. "If you're not busy this morning, we could do it again…"

"I wish I could," I say, smiling back as she runs her fingers over my chest. "But I've got an audition, unfortunately."

It's a lie, but I have to get out of here. Anxiety's stirring inside of me. It's always tough for me when a show I've been starring in ends. I'll have to book something for the summer soon, or I'll lose my mind not knowing what to do with myself.

"Too bad," she says coyly. Then I kiss her. I start to sit up when she reaches for my shoulder.

"Look, I remember what you said last night," Brittney begins. "You're not ready for a relationship because you're still getting over someone…"

I've said those words so many times this school year, I should probably get them printed on a t-shirt. It would make my life a hell of a lot easier.

"But if you ever wanna hook up again, no strings…" She shrugs. "I'm down for that."

"I'll call you," I say with a wink for effect.

Brittney nods and gives me a peck. I get out of bed, and she watches me dress.

She's sweet. Pretty. Talented. I'd be lucky to date her, under different circumstances. But it doesn't feel right, and I don't want to hurt her. I know she said no strings, but what if she develops feelings? Feelings I'll never reciprocate. It's not *her* fault—it's just my fate.

Brittney deserves better than a boyfriend whose heart belongs to someone else.

Someone I may never see again.

Never hold again.

Never kiss again.

Never stop loving.

God my head is aching.

Vision blurry.

Stomach churning.

I pause and take a deep breath.

Then Brittney asks, "You okay, Dex?"

I laugh. "I had a lot to drink last night. My head is pounding, and the sun's too bright. But after some coffee, I'll feel alright."

She giggles. "I don't know if you noticed…but everything you said just rhymed."

Fuck. My nerves are getting the better of me. In a minute or two, I'll be full-blown Ollie.

But I summon the strength to turn back into Dex.

You can do this. Stay focused. You're not unraveling—yet.

I opt for my half-smile, and I pull her in close. "Ha. I'm a poet, and I didn't even know it. I've been reading a lot of Keats lately. I guess he's rubbing off on me."

Brittney sighs. "That is…*incredibly* sexy." When she kisses me, I'm so relieved, my panic attack subsides. She gives me her number, and I leave.

When I get back to my apartment, I chug a glass of water. Then I take my new cell phone out of my pocket and stare at it for a good two minutes.

I call Seth first, and he gives me Evan's number. I pace around the kitchen while it rings—he doesn't answer. I try a few more times, but I never leave a message. On my fifth attempt at calling, a familiar voice finally answers.

"Who is this?" she asks.

"Mia! Thank god. Hey. It's Dex."

"Dex? Is everything okay? Evan's in the shower."

"I was actually hoping to get ahold of you, anyway. Mia…I need to talk to Sunny. All I have is the number to the dorm room she lived in last year, so I don't know how to reach her."

I can't live like this anymore. I mean, if Sunny's happy, I'll fuck off and leave her alone, but if she's as miserable as I am— hell, if she's half as miserable—then we need to reevaluate our lives. I know her mom wants what's best for her, but what if *I'm* what's best for Sunny? I'll do anything it takes to become the man she needs me to be.

I have no clue what I'd do for a living besides acting—but I can't worry about that now. I just need to talk to Sunny. We'll figure it out together.

Mia's silent on the other end of the line.

"Look, I know it's a lot to ask," I tell her. "And I'm sure you don't want to get in the middle—

"I'll do it," she says. "I'll give you her cell and the number to her dorm room."

"Oh my god, Mia. Thank you. Thank you so much."

"I'll always be rooting for the two of you, Dex. I'm a sucker when it comes to true love."

Knowing how to reach Sunny makes me happier than I've felt in 281 days.

I make myself something to eat. I take a shower. I nap. I need a clear head when I call her. By the time I do, it's already nighttime in Evanston. I try her dorm room first. I'd rather catch her there, so we can talk privately. If I call her cell and she's out with friends, it could be awkward.

Her line's ringing.

My heart hammers.

A guy answers. "Hello?"

"Oh," I say, stunned.

"You're calling for Sunny, right? Just a second, I'll get her."

"No," I say. "Sorry…I must have dialed the wrong number."

fourteen

I spent the entire summer at Asher's apartment. Sam and Claire didn't mind. They were happy for me. I'd never lived with a boyfriend before, so it was new, and exciting, and just distracting enough to ease my heartache over Dex.

Yes, *ease*—not erase.

One letter can make all the difference.

Sometimes I wonder where I'd be right now if I'd given Dex the love letter I wrote him in high school. I could have given it to him after the first time we slept together. Or after the last. If I'd known it would be the last time, maybe I would have. Whenever I think about him, a wave of grief washes over me. But I try my best to anchor myself back to the present. I have no other choice. Maybe soon I'll stop counting the days since I last heard from him.

Fall quarter's officially begun, and I just moved out of Asher's place and into the dorm where I'll be an RA again this year. But tonight I'm back at his apartment, making *him* dinner for a change. I don't have the first clue how to cook, but I'm hell-bent on reciprocating for every delicious meal he's made me. He offers to help, but I refuse.

"It can't be that hard," I say, rolling up my sleeves and twisting my long hair into a bun so he can tell I mean business. I hand him a glass of red wine and tell him to relax on the couch because I want the meal to be a surprise.

"Let me know if you need anything!" he says before kissing the top of my head. As he walks into the living room, I'm pretty sure I hear him chuckle.

I'm making spaghetti and meatballs because it's one of Asher's favorite meals and seems relatively simple to put together. The meatballs are pre-made and come frozen in a bag, so I dump them into a pan with jarred tomato sauce. I wait for my pot of water to boil, then toss in the spaghetti. That's when I notice a crackling sound.

Shit. I must have turned the heat too high on the meatballs, because they're all charred on the bottom. Most of the tomato sauce has evaporated too, and the remaining bits are thick and stuck to the bottom of the pan. I glance at the spaghetti. In my rush to check on the meatballs, I forgot to stir the pasta, and most of the strands are glued together. So I do what any self-respecting chef does when they manage to mess up a meal that a child could probably make. I cry.

Asher must hear me because he comes into the kitchen to survey the situation. "Oh no, what happened?" he asks, pulling me into a hug.

"Just look," I say, rubbing the tears from my eyes.

He lifts the lid on the meatballs and takes a peek at the spaghetti. Then he laughs and shakes his head. He's still looking at the food when he says it. "I love you, Sunny."

I look up at him, stunned.

Asher turns from the charred meatballs to me. "I love you," he says, looking into my eyes this time. "I've never felt this way about anyone before."

I press my head into his chest and wrap my arms around him. "I love you too," I say.

How could I not love Asher? What's not to love?

I bring Asher home with me for the holidays. Well, not home, exactly. I don't feel comfortable staying at my mom's with a boyfriend, so we get a hotel room in Cleveland instead. My mom doesn't resist as much as I'd anticipated. She's thrilled that I'll be introducing her to a boyfriend for the first time. She offers to take us to one of the best steakhouses in the city the night we arrive.

Asher's nervous, I can tell. He packed a suit and tie to wear to dinner. I told him he didn't have to, but he'd already made up his mind, so I decided to dress up too. I put on the little black dress I packed. It's long-sleeved and hits just above my knees, and I finish the look with black boots with very high heels, which means I won't have to stand on my tip-toes to kiss Asher tonight.

"Okay, I'm ready," I call out to him from the bathroom after I'm done with my makeup. I'm spritzing myself with perfume when he walks in.

"Wow," he says, dragging a hand down his clean-shaven face. He stands behind me with his arms wrapped around my waist and gazes at my reflection in the mirror. "What did I do to deserve you?" he says.

The way he's admiring me sends shivers up my spine. I turn to face him and let my eyes fall from his piercing gaze, to his chest, to the abs I know are hiding under the button-down shirt he just ironed. I brace my fingers against them. And suddenly we're kissing, and before I know it, Asher's lifting me onto the countertop and sliding off my underwear.

Thankfully we're not late for dinner, but my mom still manages to beat us. When Asher and I walk into the restaurant, she's already seated. She sees us and stands eagerly, a bright smile on her face.

"Sweetie, hi!" she says, reaching out to give me a warm hug. Then she takes a step back to get a good look at Asher. "Well, aren't you a handsome couple!" she tells us.

"It's so nice to finally meet you," Asher says, reaching out his hand.

We take our seats at the table—Asher and I on one side, my mom on the other. Then a man walks up to us. I assume he's there to welcome us to the restaurant. He's dressed impeccably and smells very nice.

He sits down next to my mom.

"Sweetheart," she says, as I look over at her curiously. "This is my friend, Luis."

I shift my gaze to Luis, then back to my mom again. Luis

reaches out his hand.

"I've heard so much about you," he says with a warm smile. He has a slight accent, and his voice has a soft rasp to it that's quite pleasing to the ear. "And you must be Asher," Luis continues, greeting him.

Have I assessed this situation correctly? Does my mom have a *boyfriend*? To my knowledge, she hasn't dated anyone seriously in years. She's so busy, after all. But people change, I guess. Maybe her priorities have shifted. Maybe she finally realized she *doesn't* want work to consume her life.

Maybe hell froze over.

"So nice to meet you!" I finally stammer.

"Luis and I met at a medical conference in Miami back in June. He's a surgeon, too," my mom explains as she gazes at him adoringly.

June? That was six months ago!

"General surgeon," Luis clarifies with a dismissive wave. " I do the easy stuff. Not like your brilliant mom, here." He gives her a sweet smile, and she blushes.

Yes—*my* hopelessly jaded mother is blushing. What in the *Twilight Zone* is going on here? In all the time I've known her, I've never seen her glow like this.

Frankly, it gives me hope where I'd all but lost it. Hope in happy endings.

I'm thrilled for my mom, but this is still a lot to process. Me, introducing a boyfriend to her for the first time. Her, introducing a boyfriend to me. There's a definite *Gilmore Girls* vibe at the table. What's more, I told my mom about Asher after we'd been dating for two months, and she waited *half a year* to tell me about Luis. But I guess I'm not surprised. She probably wanted to make sure he was in this for the long haul. After all, the last man she loved left when she got pregnant. I can't blame her for having trust issues. Still, she could have at least given me a heads up that she was bringing a date to dinner…especially since she knew Asher was coming. *I'm* usually the one keeping my relationships a secret. Now I know how Mia must feel.

Hmph.

I order a martini to take the edge off. But once the conversation starts flowing, the dynamic feels pretty natural. It helps that Luis and Asher are both so wonderful. I learn that Luis moved to Cleveland for work three years ago, after his late wife passed away from breast cancer. He has two grown daughters, one of whom is pre-med at Stanford, and the other, a fashion photographer in New York. "They love to make me travel," he jokes, pointing his fingers in opposite directions.

Asher tells my mom and Luis about growing up in a military family, and all the times he had to move and start at new schools. He talks about his plans to pursue a masters in social work, and his dream of opening a counseling center for veterans and their families.

"I'm really looking forward to that time in my life," he says with a smile. "Feeling settled in my career, owning my own home, having a family. I know I shouldn't take my youth for granted, but I moved around so much as a kid that I've always yearned for that kind of stability."

Out of the corner of my eye, I catch my mom beaming at me.

fifteen

SUNNY
FEBRUARY 2002

When Asher's younger brothers walk through the door, they're already drinking. It's 4:00 p.m. on a Friday, and they barrel into his apartment with duffel bags, ready for a weekend of partying. Eli, a sophomore at ASU, is carrying a case of beer in one hand and a flask in the other. Isaac, a senior in high school, is chugging a forty wrapped in a brown paper bag. Three hours later, we've polished off three large pizzas, and Eli's insisting that we check out a karaoke place his friend at ASU recommended, so we pile into a cab.

The bar is dark and lit entirely in electric blues and purples that remind me of the inside of a lava lamp. Since there are only four of us, the host combines us with a group of coworkers from a nearby dental office. They're mostly middle-aged. It's a random pairing but, within minutes of being shown to our karaoke room, Eli has already made introductions, memorized everyone's names, and somehow convinced the practice owner, Dr. Lee, to buy us all a round of shots. The waitress doesn't ask to see IDs.

The shots are clear and taste like fire. Seventeen-year-old Isaac, who's a hair shorter than Asher and could easily pass for a senior in college, gets an extra one because Mary, a reserved dental hygienist and grandmother of two, doesn't want hers. She needs to be "fresh" for bible study in the morning. Asher gives Isaac a disapproving look, but Isaac only shrugs.

"Let's get this party started!" Eli exclaims, grabbing the mic and appointing himself emcee of the evening's festivities. "Who's up first, any takers?"

Asher and I, both self-proclaimed introverts, have no interest in performing, so we sit back and watch while drinking beers. Catherine, the dental practice receptionist, volunteers to kick things off with an offbeat attempt at her favorite Celine Dion song. Dr. Lee follows with a Justin Timberlake number, and it turns out that he has an amazing and *very* unexpected falsetto. Asher and I are laughing harder than we ever have together. There are tears streaming down my face, and I almost drop my beer bottle, which makes us laugh even harder. Asher takes off his glasses and wipes his eyes.

Not to be outdone, Eli performs next and does an incredible impersonation of Eminem. The ladies in the room go wild. They're cheering almost as loudly as Isaac. But then, Mary grabs hold of that microphone. Quiet, unassuming Mary takes hold of that microphone and sings Tina Turner's version of "Proud Mary," and she absolutely *kills* it. Everyone is on their feet, clapping and screaming. Asher and I look on in shock, our jaws dropped, huge grins on our faces.

We're sure no one can top Mary's performance so, afterward, Asher and I leave the private room and sit at the bar, which is mostly empty. To be honest, I'm relieved to have a break from "M.C. Eli." He's a little too handsome. A little too charming. I'm also buzzed and want another beer. Asher orders me one, and a Maker's Mark for himself. As we sit and sip, he has his hand on my thigh, and he whispers in my ear that I look gorgeous, and he can't wait to take me home. I steal a sip of his whiskey and wink at him. "I can't wait either," I say.

It's true. I enjoy being in Asher's bed. To be quite honest, he's very skilled in that department.

It's still not the same as it was with Dex, though.

Sex with Oliver Dexter was a transcendental experience. Completely and utterly mind-blowing. Because the connection we had was special. I knew it then. I know it even more so now. I wonder if I'll ever feel that way again.

Don't go there, Sunny.

I must be getting drunk.

Asher and I lose track of time, drinking and kissing at the bar. When we get back to the karaoke room, Eli and Isaac are nowhere to be found. "I'm going to check the bathroom," Asher says with a furrowed brow. I follow him.

While I'm waiting outside the men's room, I hear angry voices but can't make out what they're saying because of the electronic dance music blaring over the speakers. Eli comes out first and, when he sees me, he smiles. I'm about to ask him if everything is okay when he puts his hand on my waist.

"Thanks for letting us stay with you guys this weekend," he says, leaning into me so I can hear him. "My brother's a lucky man."

Then he steps back enough for me to see his gaze travel from my eyes to my lips and back again. His hand is still on my waist, and he's so close that I can feel his breath on me, and his chest against mine.

And the worst part is—I don't mind.

When the bathroom door swings open again, I step back with a start. Eli casually turns to lean against the wall. Asher doesn't notice either one of us at first. Isaac is hanging off his shoulder like a wet noodle, his eyes half-open, a dopey smile on his face, and Asher is busy just trying to keep him upright.

"We have to get him home," Asher tells us. "Help me out, man," he instructs Eli.

We walk outside—well, three of us walk, and one of us attempts to. Asher tries to hail a taxi. "Dude, we can't put him in a cab like this, he's gonna puke," Eli keeps saying. "We have to get him some food." After minutes of back and forth on the subject, Asher finally concedes and we stop at a corner store, where he buys Isaac a Coke and some chips. We walk to a nearby park so Isaac can sit and eat.

It's almost two o'clock in the morning now, and Asher and I are fading. Eli and Isaac are having a ball. They're on the swings, singing Nickelback songs at the top of their lungs. Asher turns to me with an exhausted smile. "I'm sorry about them. Thanks for being a good sport."

"Anytime," I say, giving him a peck on the lips.

That's when we hear tires screeching behind us, and when we turn around, we see flashing lights. A police car just pulled over, and two officers are getting out.

"Everybody out of the park," the older of the two officers yells. He's so close to me, his voice so ear-splitting, that I nearly jump out of my skin. The younger cop says nothing.

Asher takes my hand and squeezes it. "It's okay," he whispers. "We're fine."

But I don't feel fine at all. My heart is racing, and my palms are sweating, and—I just applied to law school for goodness' sake! What if I get arrested? What will my mom say? Why am I drunk at a park with Asher and his brothers in the first place?

Suddenly I'm questioning everything.

"City parks close at 11:00 p.m., and it's 2:16 a.m.," the loud officer roars thunderously once we're all on the sidewalk.

"I'm so sorry, sir, we're not from here," Eli interjects with wide-eyed sincerity. I hold my breath.

"Is that right?" the older officer shouts. The younger one twiddles his thumbs.

Eli sighs. "Yeah, our dad was in the Air Force, so we moved around a lot."

The older officer looks up, and his face softens. A little bit. "Air Force, huh? My Grandpa Joe was in the Air Force. A fine man, he was," the officer continues with a faraway look in his eyes. "I bet your dad's a fine man too."

"Very fine, sir," Eli says with a solemn nod. "Very fine indeed." Asher gives Eli a look that could kill.

The loud officer is silent. He looks over at his partner, who just shrugs. "Alright," the older one says gruffly. "For your dad's sake, I'll let you go. But don't let me catch you out here again," he bellows as he and the younger officer start to turn away from us. I smile at Asher, and he gives me a huge hug.

And that's when Isaac throws up.

Eli, Asher and I all look at him, our eyes wide with horror, then turn to the officers. The loud one purses his lips angrily and is about to say something when Eli springs into action.

"You know, Isaac here is planning to enlist soon? He gets real nervous just thinking about it. He wants to make our dad proud, but he's afraid he isn't man enough." Eli glances down at the pool of vomit on the sidewalk and crinkles his nose. "It makes him sick to his stomach sometimes."

Isaac is staring straight ahead with vacant eyes while the loud officer looks him up and down. "Time to man up, son!" he finally hollers. He's so startlingly loud, I gasp.

The officers get in their car and drive off, leaving Isaac still staring into space and the rest of us completely dumbstruck. Then Isaac starts laughing.

"Well played, man," he says, patting Eli on the back. Eli takes a theatrical bow. Asher stares at them stonily, but I breathe a huge sigh of relief.

"Thank you," I mouth quietly to Eli when he meets my gaze. He winks at me.

We get home at three-thirty in the morning, and by the time we're in bed, it's four. Asher falls asleep right away, but I can't get my mind to stop racing, so I get up for a glass of water.

When I walk into the kitchen, Eli's there, wearing only boxers and eating leftover stir-fry he found in the fridge. "You okay?" he asks as I fill up a glass.

"I can't sleep. I still feel shaken up." Before I know it, tears are falling from my eyes.

Eli wraps his arms around me and holds me the way Dex used to when I was sad—with one hand on the small of my back, and the other on the back of my head.

And that's when I lose it. I bury my face in Eli's neck.

And I know it's not just our run-in with the cops that has me distraught.

It's the way Eli Abadie charmed every single person we met tonight. The way he had the audience in the palm of his hand when he was singing karaoke. Even the smell of his cologne. He smells just like Dex did, our very last time…

It's been 546 days since I've seen him. And I'm *still* not over him.

But kissing Asher's brother won't help.

So I wipe my tears and go back to my boyfriend's bed.

sixteen

SUNNY

MARCH 2002

Asher got his acceptance letter from the University of Chicago School of Social Work today. There was absolutely no doubt in my mind that he'd get in. I mean, it's *Asher*. Who in their right mind wouldn't want him?

I haven't heard from Northwestern yet. All of the law schools I've gotten into so far are out-of-state. I haven't given much thought to what will happen if Asher and I don't both end up in Chicago. Maybe I'm being overly optimistic, but I did really well on my LSAT, and I have a nearly perfect GPA. I'm sure I'll be getting good news from Northwestern any day now.

I bring a bottle of champagne to Asher's to celebrate, and we drink the entire thing while eating the delicious risotto he made us. Then we end up in his bed. Afterward, he holds me and kisses the top of my head over and over again while we watch the snow fall outside his window. I'm drifting off to sleep when I hear his voice.

"You know what I just realized? We've been together almost

a year, and you've never told me about your past relationships," Asher says.

The muscles in my stomach tighten like I'm bracing for a punch. I knew this would come up eventually. Asher's told me about girls he's dated in casual conversation, but I've been careful not to do the same because I *really* don't want to get into the details of what happened between me and Dex. I don't think I'm capable of discussing him without getting emotional. We have too much history. Plus, I've been through this before with Chris—he dumped me because I still had feelings for my ex—and I'm not ready for things to end with Asher. If there's anyone who can break this spell that Dex has over me, it's him. He's such an amazing boyfriend. What if all I need is a little more time?

"Well, I didn't date in high school, so my first relationship was freshman year of college. We weren't together long. Then I started dating someone I met at a party in Beachwood," I explain, fudging the details. "He goes to school in California, and we were on-and-off for about a year. And then there was you," I say smiling. I kiss him on the shoulder, hoping it will distract him and stave off further questioning.

Asher's quiet for several seconds, then clears his throat. "So, the long-distance one…is that why it ended? The distance?"

I squint at the ceiling, as if the answer were hiding somewhere between the cracks in the paint. "Maybe," I say with a shrug. "The distance definitely didn't help. It was tough. I wouldn't do it again."

I glance at the frosty window. At the snowflakes dancing outside. It takes a minute of silence before I realize the significance of what

I just said. And why Asher asked me in the first place.

He's worried about next year.

I feel terrible, but, before I get a chance to say anything, my cell phone rings.

It's my mom. Luis is moving in, and they're getting married.

"Oh my gosh!" I exclaim, turning to Asher. "My mom's engaged!" His eyes widen, and he smiles. I know he's genuinely happy for me and my family, because that's the kind of person he is. But I can also tell he's hurt. He doesn't say as much, but I see it in his eyes. When I get off the phone, he tells me he has a headache and turns off the light. Before long, he's asleep.

To add insult to injury, when Asher drops me off at my dorm the next morning, there's a letter from Northwestern waiting for me. It's in a small envelope—unlike the thick welcome packets I've received from every other law school I applied to.

"Do you think you and Asher will stay together?" Sam asks me. She and Claire are on their couch, and I'm sitting on a meditation cushion on the floor. We're having a girls' night, eating popcorn and watching primetime TV.

I decided a few weeks ago that I'll be attending Indiana University School of Law in Bloomington. As soon as I laid eyes on the campus, which is nestled in a charming college town, I was sold. I still can't believe I didn't get into Northwestern, though. What if this is the Universe telling me I shouldn't be going into law? That I picked the wrong career and should have studied creative writing instead? If I'd been true to myself, and not worried so much about what everyone *else* wants me to be, maybe I'd be in LA right now with Dex. Writing steamy romance novels and having steamy sex.

There I go again. I should *not* be thinking about steamy sex with Dex when I have a boyfriend. But that's a lot easier said than done.

I let out a deep sigh before I answer Sam's question about Asher. "I don't know what we're going to do about the distance. We haven't discussed logistics yet. I think we're both trying to ignore the problem until…we can't."

Asher hasn't brought up the long-distance issue since my completely thoughtless comment on that snowy winter day, and I'm grateful—especially now that I know we'll be apart. But I can't help also feeling anxious. My faux pas is palpable, like an irreparable snag in a favorite sweater. You know it's there, and you know you can't fix it, but you wear the sweater anyway because you need the comfort. Because you're not ready to toss it away. Deep down, I know we're delaying the inevitable. Eventually, one of us will pull the thread.

"I'm sorry, Sunny," Claire says with a hefty sigh. "I know exactly how you feel." Claire's boyfriend got into med school in Boston, and she'll be staying at Northwestern for business school. They found out a week ago, and she's been miserable.

"This is why I keep things casual," Sam says with a sympathetic frown. "I'm going to refill our popcorn. Want anything else? I made some hummus earlier today…"

Claire's eyes light up. "Are you *finally* letting your mom teach you how to make Middle Eastern food? I vote for falafel next!"

Sam aggressively shakes her head. "Absolutely not. My Lebanese mother would love nothing more than for me to quit school, find myself a husband, and spend all day cooking and cleaning for him and our litter of children," she says with a shudder. "*No* thank you. I only asked for her hummus recipe because chickpeas are cheap, and I'm broke."

Claire frowns. "Bummer. I *really* love falafel."

"So…no hummus?" Sam asks.

"I love hummus," I chime in. "I'll take some."

"Coming right up," Sam replies, hopping off the couch. With all the angst swirling inside me—feeling uncertain about law school, and where things are headed for Asher and me—I haven't been paying much attention to the TV. But while Sam is in the kitchen, something draws me in. It's a commercial for an acne-fighting cleanser. It cuts from one attractive young person to the next as they each pump the product into their palms and wash their faces in splashes of water that seem to appear from nowhere. Imagine my shock when I realize that one of the attractive young people is none other than Oliver Dexter.

He's looking right at me through the TV screen. The same, devastatingly handsome Dex I used to know, just a little bit older. His eyelashes are dripping wet, like the night we got caught in the rain. He grabs a towel and dries his face. Then he half-smiles.

And it destroys me.

The floor beneath me starts crumbling. The walls I've built are caving in. I break into a cold sweat. Every muscle in my body contracts, as though braced for cataclysmic danger. I look back at Claire, who's flipping through a magazine. How can she flip through a magazine at a time like this? The world is ending.

I need to get out of here.

I stand just as Sam comes back from the kitchen.

"You know what?" I say, shoving my shaky hands into my pockets. "I have terrible cramps. They just came on. I think I'm going to call it a night."

"Wait, are you sure?" Sam asks. "I have a great tea for menstrual cramps. Let me make you some."

"*This* tea actually tastes good," Claire reassures me.

"No, I'm fine. Thank you, though. I just need some rest." I attempt a smile, but I'm not sure it's convincing.

"Okay," Sam says, giving me a once-over.

"Call us if you need anything," says Claire, and they both give me a hug.

As soon as I get back to my dorm room, I reach for the phone.

I need to call him.

I need to talk to Dex.

But my fingers are frozen.

My mind is blank.

I don't know his phone number.

I don't know if he lives in a dorm, or off campus.

I don't know *him* anymore.

But I do know how to reach his parents. So I call them.

Mrs. Dexter answers. "H-hello?"

She sounds groggy.

Shit. I didn't even think about the time. Beachwood is an

hour ahead of Evanston. Of course they were asleep.

My thoughts are racing. I have no idea why I'm calling, or what to say. I could ask for Dex's number, but what for? I have a boyfriend. I'm not going to call Dex to shoot the shit about his acne commercial. And I'm sure he's moved on from me by now. He probably has some stunning model girlfriend. What if I call him, and she answers?

No. I can't do it. I never should have disturbed Dex's parents. I'm about to end the call, but something stops me.

I really want to hear Mrs. Dexter's voice one more time.

"Hello?" she says again.

In the background, I catch Mr. Dexter talking to his wife. "Who is it?" he asks through a yawn.

I hang up before I sob. Then I cry myself to sleep.

seventeen

SUNNY

APRIL 2002

I've been planning Asher's birthday surprise for weeks. The school year's almost over. We'll be graduating soon, and I'll be moving…so I want to make this night extra special. We still haven't discussed where our relationship is headed, but I'm okay with that. Right now, I'd rather focus on the present. On spending as much time with Asher as I can. Last weekend, we hardly left his bed. He was exceptionally attentive to my needs. Sometimes I think that's his way of trying to influence my decision about our future—with really good sex. While I appreciate his efforts tremendously, I wish he didn't need to convince me that we belong together. I should be thanking my lucky stars for him. But I have the perfect date planned for his birthday and, if all goes well, I'm hoping that any flicker of doubt I have about Asher will be extinguished.

We start the evening with dinner at a restaurant in Little Italy. When we walk in, Asher's face lights up at the sound of Sinatra's "Come Fly With Me" over the speakers. It's his favorite song. I called the hostess ahead of time and asked if they could play it at exactly 7:00 p.m.

We drink velvety red wine, and eat warm crusty bread dipped in herby olive oil, and enjoy proper spaghetti and meatballs that aren't cooked by me. I tell him to save room for dessert, and then I take him back to the Cheesecake Factory, where we had our first date. I order one tuxedo cheesecake, and I really do split it with him this time. Then I take him to the top of the John Hancock building for drinks, and we toast each other with miles of city lights twinkling around us like stars.

We go back to his place after that, but I tell him the night's not over yet. I pop *Gladiator* into the DVD player and we watch it in each other's arms. As soon as the credits roll, we're kissing. I straddle his lap, and he tightens his grip around me and carries me to bed. He strips everything off me slowly and kisses me even slower. Minutes turn into hours. Whispers turn into moans. And before we know it, it's 5:00 a.m.

But as I lie in his bed, there are nervous flutters in my stomach. I should be on top of the world right now. Our date was amazing. Everything went according to plan. Asher was surprised and happy with his birthday celebration. He even gave me multiple orgasms. For some reason, though, I feel restless. So I tell Asher we can't go to sleep just yet.

"What do you mean?" he asks, rubbing his eyes. "It's practically morning."

"I want to watch the sunrise with you," I tell him. Asher smiles and kisses me. I hand him his glasses from the nightstand, and we put on our clothes and walk to the rocks by the lake. We sit, and he holds me as the sun begins to appear above the horizon.

"I love you so much," he says, staring at the sky ahead. It's dark blue with murky wisps of coral.

"I love you too," I tell him. My pulse quickens because I know exactly what he's going to say next. And I dread it.

"We can do this, Sunny," he utters softly. "Bloomington is only four hours away, and we both have cars. It won't be hard."

My heart sinks.

He pulled the thread.

I have no choice but to face reality now.

I have the perfect boyfriend. We've been together for nearly a year, and he's treated me with nothing but love and respect. He's smart, and motivated. Not to mention, he's hot…he cooks… *and* he's great in bed.

And I *still* don't see a future with him.

I still don't love him as much as I love Oliver Dexter.

And I hate myself for it.

I hate myself for stringing him along—but I was sure I'd be over Dex by now.

Well, it's been nearly *two fucking years.*

Six hundred and eight days, to be exact.

I give up. I surrender.

But if I tell Asher the truth, it will shatter him. I don't want him to think he did anything wrong. He's the gold standard of what a man should be. It's not his fault that his girlfriend is irrevocably in love with someone else.

So I blame it on the distance.

"We'll be busy," I finally say. "Eight hours is a lot to drive in one weekend, especially with all the studying we'll have to do. We'll end up canceling, and postponing, and disappointing each other. And then we'll break up anyway, but during grad school, when there's so much more at stake."

The look on Asher's face devastates me. "So you'd rather give up before we even try? I *love* you, Sunny. I want to try."

I can't hold his gaze.

"But I guess you don't," he continues when I don't say anything. "So why did you do all this for me tonight? Just to break up with me?"

"Of course not," I say, my eyes filling with tears. "I just wanted to show you how much I appreciate you. How much I love you. I'm so sorry, Asher." I sob. "I didn't mean to break your heart."

Asher looks at me and nods. Then he says exactly what a perfect boyfriend would say. "I know you didn't."

I take his hand and hold it in my lap.

We sit in silence for a few minutes. Eventually, he lets out a resigned breath. "We should go," he says, quietly. When he helps me up, his fingers are still threaded through mine. "I'll walk you back to your dorm," he offers, which brings another round of tears to my eyes. He deserves so much better than a girlfriend whose heart belongs to her ex. When he meets the love of his life one day, he'll be happy I did this.

Before we leave, Asher turns to face the sky a final time. We watch hand-in-hand until the bright sun shines above the horizon.

That's when we let go.

eighteen

SUNNY
SUMMER OF 2002

It's the first time I've been back in Beachwood since Dex and I broke up. I can't imagine he'd be here now. He's a college graduate, like me, but he's probably busy in LA, auditioning for a movie role, or a TV show, or another commercial for acne products he'll never need because his skin is so goddamn perfect. Still, I took the long way to the grocery store yesterday so I didn't have to drive by his house. Even if Dex isn't home, running into his parents would be almost as painful.

I haven't seen Mia since I last left Beachwood either. There are butterflies in my stomach as I wait for her at our favorite high school coffee shop. And *not* the good kind of butterflies. Although Mia and I are still friends, we're definitely not as close as we once were. It's my fault, for pulling away. Through all the ups and downs with Dex, then Asher, I've found it nearly impossible to be myself around her. She deserves to be excited about her future with Evan. But if I tell her the truth about how *I'm* feeling, it's bound to kill the mood, and I don't want to feel like I'm bringing her down all the time.

When she walks through the door, though, Mia is beaming. "Sunny!" she squeals as she runs over to hug me. Her eyes are misty. "It's been too long," she says.

She's different. Taller, somehow. I look down and see a stylish pair of black pointed-toe heels on her feet. She's dressed in a pretty sleeveless blouse, tucked into a pencil skirt that hits right above her knees. Her long, dark hair is cut slightly shorter and looks perfectly sleek. In my Northwestern t-shirt and matching athletic shorts, I feel like a college freshman who just rolled out of bed. I put time into my hair and makeup, at least, but now I wish I'd worn something else.

Mia giggles. "I'm totally overdressed, I know. I just had an interview! It was at an engineering firm in Cleveland. It's literally my dream job, Sunny! I mean, for now, at least. I *really* hope I get it," she says as we take a seat at the table.

Mia's wanted to be an engineer since she was seven. Her dad loves to recall how she'd take apart her brothers' toys so she could rebuild them. Being the only girl among her siblings and cousins, Mia wasn't the least bit intimidated when she chose a major that was skewed male. She had a dream, and it's easy to see she's on her way to making it happen.

Gone are the days of Abercrombie-clad Mia, I guess. She looks so put-together. When we talked on the phone a couple of weeks ago, she told me she and Evan are looking for an apartment together. He has an accounting job lined up in Cleveland. Everything's falling into place for them.

"Congrats on your interview!" I tell Mia. "I'm sure you

knocked 'em dead. I ordered you a decaf cinnamon latte, by the way," I say, pushing the paper cup toward her. "Is that—"

"Still my favorite? Yes," she confirms before taking a sip. "Thanks, Sunny! So, how's your summer so far? You've only been back a week, right?"

I nod. "My mom got married last Friday."

"That's right!" Mia exclaims with wide eyes. "How was it?"

"It was sweet," I tell her before taking a sip of my coffee. "They had a small ceremony at the courthouse. Luis's daughters flew in for it. I really like them—Lily and Elena. They stayed at our house all week. We watched movies together, and drank wine, and went out to eat. It was a good distraction for me."

I said that last part sort of unwittingly. I didn't intend to take the conversation in this direction. But Mia pounces.

"How are you doing since breaking up with Asher?" she asks me, her dark eyebrows knit together. Maybe she's still in interview mode, but her hands are in her lap, and she looks a bit rigid as she leans forward, waiting for my answer.

I shrug. "I'm okay. I'm more concerned about him. He really wanted to stay together. But Asher's a catch. He'll make some lucky woman *extremely* happy one day." I sigh. "I hope he finds her soon."

Mia's gaze travels to her lap. "What about you?"

I don't understand. "What *about* me?"

Mia looks back up. "Have you…talked to Dex at all?"

It's like there's a fire raging inside me, and Mia lit the match. I close my eyes and exhale. "I haven't heard from Dex in years, Mia. Not since the night we broke up."

Why can't she let this go?

"Wait…are you serious?" she asks.

I open my eyes. "Of course I'm serious. Why?"

Mia looks away, shaking her head. "I gave Dex your number," she says in a near-whisper. She clears her throat before she continues. "He sounded desperate to talk to you, and I—"

"You did *what*? When?" My hands are trembling. I put down my coffee.

"It was a while ago. End of junior year. I tried to give you a heads-up—I kept calling and leaving messages—but you never called me back! So after a while…I just gave up. And the next time you called me, you were in a relationship with Asher, so I figured you and Dex had talked and—"

"We *didn't* talk," I say, my voice shaking. "You gave him my number—without asking me first, I might add—and he didn't even call." I choke back a sob. "I guess he decided it wasn't worth it." I hide my face in my hands, but it's obvious I'm crying.

"Oh, Sunny," Mia says. I feel her hand on my wrist. I let her sandwich my palm between hers. Her hazel eyes are glistening. When I look down at our hands on the table, I see something else shimmering. An actual engagement ring with a princess-cut diamond.

Mia pulls her hands back. No wonder she'd been sitting with them in her lap. She was hiding her ring from me.

I sniffle. "When did Evan propose?" I ask her softly.

She blinks at me through tears. "The day we graduated. I wanted to tell you when we talked on the phone but—"

"I'd just told you about my breakup with Asher." I finish for her. All this time I've been pulling away from Mia, she's been holding back too. I guess we really have drifted apart. "I hate that you feel the need to walk on eggshells around me."

Mia's cheeks redden. "Sunny, I—"

"And why did you think it was okay to give my phone number to my ex? I trusted you!"

"Sunny, I gave Dex your number because I want you guys to work things out. I want you to be happy, can't you see that? You're one of my closest friends, and—"

"One of your closest friends, who doesn't even know your boyfriend *proposed*? Mia…how are we supposed to be friends if you can't even share one of the happiest moments of your life with me?" I say, my lips quivering. "I feel like I barely know you anymore."

"Well, join the club," Mia says, wiping her eyes. "Because I've been feeling that way about you for as long as I remember."

Her words are like a shock of cold water, extinguishing my anger. Leaving me with nothing but flickering embers and the ashes of our friendship.

"I have to go," I say without meeting her teary gaze. "Best wishes to you and Evan."

I've been lying in bed for nearly an hour, but I can't sleep because the fight with Mia keeps replaying in my mind. Around 11:00 p.m., I give up and go down to the kitchen for ice cream. I put three generous scoops of rocky road in a bowl and eat it standing at the kitchen counter while looking at pictures on the side of the fridge. My mom has taken down every photo of me and Dex but one. We were about six years old, eating cotton candy at the zoo. I remember the day so vividly, because it was my mom who took us on one of her rare afternoons off from work. I pull the photo out from under its refrigerator magnet, and I'm holding it in my hand when she walks in.

"Hi, sweetheart," she says sleepily as she fills her water glass. She looks over my shoulder to see what I'm holding. My heart pounds like she caught me doing something wrong.

"You know," she says slowly, "John's been sick."

"What?" I ask, immediately turning toward her. "Mr. Dexter?" My chest tightens. I pray she's talking about someone else. Not Dex's dad. I love Dex's dad.

My mom nods. "Prostate cancer. I've been debating whether or not to tell you."

"*Debating*? What? Oh my god! Is he going to be okay?" My entire body is shaking.

"He's got the very best doctor in the city, I made sure of it," my mom says as she hands me a tissue. I didn't even know I was crying.

"I have to go over there," I say, which makes absolutely no sense, but it's the only thing I can think to do. The only thing I want to do.

My mom tries to reason with me. "Sunny, it's late! Just wait until morning."

I don't answer her. I'm too busy trying to find my keys. I thought I'd left them in the kitchen, but maybe they're on the front hall table.

"Sunny, are you listening to me? The Dexters are probably sleeping. You don't want to disturb them."

They're not on the front hall table. A jolt of panic surges through me. Now I'm sweating. *Where the hell did I put them?*

"Sunny!" my mom repeats angrily.

I must have left them in the pocket of my raincoat. I turn around to check.

"Found them," I say with a sigh of relief. I clutch my keys to my chest. "Mom, I know it's late, but I don't care. If Dex is there, he needs me. If I'm this distraught—and Mr. Dexter isn't even related to me—imagine how his son feels."

I leave without waiting for my mom's rebuttal. I drive to Dex's house with no plan except to drive there and park in the driveway and ring the doorbell. And that's what I do.

It takes a minute before someone opens the door. And for the first time in 664 days, there he is. Oliver Dexter. Standing in the doorway, looking at me as I look at him. We're mirror reflections of each other. Red-rimmed eyes, stunned faces. Sadness, disbelief, and relief—if I'm not mistaken. We take one step closer to each other. We look down, then we look up. We wrap our arms around each other, and the moment we touch, the entire world stops spinning. We're frozen in time. I hold him, and he holds me, and everything in between now and then disappears in space. We sigh. Eventually, we step back. I follow him inside the house and he closes the door. It's all wordless until we get upstairs.

We sit on the floor of his room with our backs against his bed.

"How's he doing?" I ask, reaching for Dex's hand.

"He's in the hospital," he says, and his voice sounds so small. He takes a deep breath. "He just had surgery," he continues, shakily, "and it went well—but then he got an infection."

Dex closes his eyes but the tears spill out and he sobs. I try to remember when I last saw him cry. We were kids, I think.

I want to take his pain away more than I've ever wanted anything in my life. I put my arm around him, and I kiss his hair, right above his ear. My lips just gravitate there before I realize what I'm doing. Dex looks at me and cries even harder then. "My mom told me to go home and get some sleep, but I'm so fucking scared," he says.

Then his hands start shaking.

As he's wringing them, his breathing gets shallow.

That's when he starts gasping for air.

His eyes are wild when I look at him.

"Hey," I say softly, kneeling in front of him. "I'm here. You're going to be okay, you have to breathe." I put my hand on his heart, and it's racing so fast, it terrifies me. But I don't let him see it. "Just breathe with me," I repeat calmly. I try a technique I learned from Sam, breathing in four counts and out for eight. I do it over and over until he does it with me. I keep my hand on his heart the entire time. Until it slows and beats in time with mine. Until he breathes a sigh of relief. Until he smiles, and he holds me, and we stay like that, on the floor by his bed for a while.

I've never seen Dex like that. So scared. So vulnerable. A mere mortal, like the rest of us. I've always had him up on a pedestal. But to see *this* side of him shakes me to my core. I didn't know it was possible to love him more than I already did.

"You should try to get some sleep," I whisper. "It's late."

He nods and gets up to sit on the edge of his bed. I stand and look for my keys. They're on the nightstand. As I reach for them, Dex grabs my hand.

"Will you stay?" he asks, looking up at me. "Just to sleep, I mean." Then he shakes his head. "Never mind—your boyfriend wouldn't like that."

I shake my head, confused. "I don't have a boyfriend," I tell him. I don't know why he thinks I do, but now's not the time to worry about it. All I want is for him to be okay. "I can stay."

I grab my phone and send my mom a text. She's already called me three times. Then I lie down next to Dex. He laces his fingers between mine, and I rest my head on his shoulder.

That's how we fall asleep.

We go to the hospital together the next morning. Dex's dad is feeling better and in good spirits. His parents are *thrilled* to see me. His mom hops out of her chair and throws her arms around me. "Sunny, you're back!" she says with a relieved sob. Then I start crying too.

I'm not sure what to say. "I'm so sorry I've been out of touch," is all I can come up with.

"Oh honey, stop," she replies as she hugs me even tighter.

"Nonsense," Mr. Dexter says. "You were busy with school. But we did miss you, darling," he adds, which makes me cry even harder.

They keep him in the hospital another week, but he's doing better every day. Still I don't leave Dex's side. I stay with him every night, and we sleep in his bed. We only sleep, and that's all, but we're together, and that's what matters.

My mom is furious. I come home one afternoon to grab some clothes, and she can hardly look at me. I'm in my room packing a duffel bag, and she stands in my doorway, talking to the window.

"I know you're upset about Asher," she begins.

I had told her *he* was the one who didn't want a long-distance relationship. I'd lied.

"But you can't fall back into this old pattern," she goes on. "You've spent most of your life chasing after that boy. Don't you have anything better to do with your time?"

"I'm not chasing after anyone, Mom. I'm being a friend."

"Friends your age don't have sleepovers, Sunny. You're not kids anymore."

I pause to gather my thoughts as my mom continues to stare out the window.

"You know what, Mom? You're right," I say, and she finally looks at me. "Dex isn't just a friend. He is so much more than that to me. He's my *family*. And you—of all people—should understand why."

I walk past her, out the door, and get in my car.

It's Saturday night, and Dex's mom calls with good news. His dad is being discharged, and they'll be home from the hospital in the morning. We stay up late watching movies and eating popcorn. Then we go upstairs to his bedroom and, as we've done every other night this week, we fall asleep side-by-side.

When I wake up, it's still dark. I'm warm. I can feel Dex's chest rising and falling against my back, his soft breath on my neck. His arm around my waist. His hand on my stomach. When I turn toward him, our lips are nearly touching. His eyes slowly flutter open.

Then he kisses me.

It all happens so fast. We're desperate for each other. We practically rip off each other's clothes. When he hooks his fingers inside me, I'm already wet, so he enters me and thrusts harder and faster than he ever has. We're not usually like this—clawing at each other like animals. I'm screaming his name, my hands traveling from the nape of his neck to his shoulders to his ass as he grinds into me. I'm seconds away from ecstasy, but I'm not ready for this to end…so I slow our rhythm. I lock eyes with him, and he nods because he understands. He wants this to last forever too.

Dex sits up in bed and pulls me onto his lap. I wrap myself around him—my legs around his waist, my arms around his shoulders. We're as close as two people can be. This is how we make up for the lost time. We find ourselves in each other's gaze. We revel in each other's pleasure. We kiss and rock slowly, then faster, then slowly again, over and over, until morning. It's been night for so damn long, but now it's bright, and we never look away, only deeper into each other's eyes until we come.

And the orgasm is…indescribable. Incomparable.

When we're lying next to each other again, Dex turns to me. "I've missed you so damn much," he says.

My eyes fill with tears. "You have?"

"*Of course* I have. My god—I was a wreck. I've *been* a wreck, these past two years."

"But…you didn't…fight for me, Dex."

He blows out a breath and shakes his head. His jaw tightens. "I wanted to, Sunny. Believe me, I wanted to. But—somehow I became convinced that letting you go was the right thing to do."

There's so much pain in his eyes, I have no doubt he's telling the truth. I nod, and Dex continues. "I did try calling you once."

My stomach clenches. "You did?"

"A guy answered," he explains, looking away. "I hung up."

"That's why you thought I had a boyfriend," I say, putting the pieces together. "I did, for a while. It was—"

Dex kisses my hand. "None of that matters now. No one else matters but us."

I smile, but my joy is tinged with guilt. "Mia told me she gave you my number, and I got *so* mad at her. But really, I was upset because I thought you didn't call. And I took it out on her. I feel awful."

Dex props himself on his elbow. "It was a misunderstanding. She'll forgive you, Sunny. Mia's a good friend, and she cares about you."

I shake my head. "I don't know if our friendship can come back from this. It's not just a misunderstanding. Mia and I have been growing apart for years. She's been so happy, and I was so miserable…we were on two different planes. I didn't even know she was engaged until I saw the ring on her finger."

Dex runs a hand over his hair. "I'm so sorry, Sunny. You were miserable because of *me*. I never should have let you leave that room the night of Ben's wedding. I should have pulled you into my arms and told you how much you mean to me." He blinks back tears. "I will never forgive myself for hurting you."

"It's my fault too," I tell him. "I should have been more clear with you about what I needed."

"None of this was your fault." Dex takes my face in his palms and kisses me once, twice, and a third time. Tenderly. Adoringly. "I never should have let you go. We're supposed to be together. I know it."

My heart swells with insurmountable joy as Dex half-smiles and holds me close to him. I haven't seen him this happy since the morning of his cousin's wedding, when he first laid eyes on me in my silver dress. That feels like ages ago. If you'd asked me last week, I could have told you the exact number of days that have passed since then—but I finally stopped counting. I don't have to anymore, because he's right here with me.

I'm on top of the world.

Until I remember I'm going to law school. "What are we going to do when I move to Indiana?" I ask Dex. "We've been long-distance before, and it was…a disaster."

"We'll do better this time. I'll visit you as much as I possibly can."

I nod, my spirits lifting. "I have some money saved up from

my data entry job. I'll visit you too."

"Just promise you'll tell me what's on your mind, okay? If something's bothering you, I want to fix it." Dex takes his hand to the side of my face. "I just want you to be happy, Sunny. That's all I will ever want."

"I'm happy now," I say, wiping my eyes.

"Happy tears?" he asks, sweeping his thumb across my cheek.

"Yes," I say with a growing smile. "They're happy tears."

When we wake up again, it's to the sounds of Dex's parents in the kitchen. It's 11:00 a.m. We get dressed and pad sleepily down the stairs. I'm still on cloud nine after the most incredible sex of my life, so it isn't until I see his parents' faces that I wonder what they'll think of me being here, walking in with their son from his bedroom upstairs. But they don't bat an eye.

"Good morning, honey," his mom says as she hugs me first, then Dex. His dad is sitting at the kitchen table with the newspaper, and we take turns giving him hugs.

"I was just getting breakfast ready," Mrs. Dexter says as she whisks pancake batter. "Join us, have a seat!" she adds cheerily, but she looks bone-tired, I can see it in her eyes.

"You must be exhausted," I tell her. "Why don't you sit, and we'll take it from here?"

Normally Mrs. Dexter would never dream of it, but today she smiles gratefully and agrees. Dex joins me at the kitchen counter, and that's when he puts his hands on my waist and gives me a kiss on the lips. A little one—but it's real—right here in the kitchen, with his parents sitting at the table. I don't know if they saw it but, either way, Dex doesn't seem to mind.

I can die right now, and die happy.

But we have a job to do. So instead, I get to whisking.

I'm still no whiz in the kitchen, but Mrs. Dexter has already prepared the batter, and I'm relatively confident I can make the pancakes without burning them. So I take care of the flipping while Dex slices strawberries and puts on a pot of coffee, and in no time we're seated at the table having breakfast. Dex inches his chair closer to me, and as we eat, he has his hand on my knee. When he's finished his last bite, he sips coffee with his arm around my shoulder. We sit there for an hour and enjoy each other's company.

It's everything I've ever wanted my whole life.

That's how it goes, the whole summer. Mr. Dexter rests and recovers. His health is improving, and the doctors are optimistic. But Dex stays home in Beachwood, to be sure. We spend our days together, the three of us, in the Dexters' living room, watching TV and doing crossword puzzles while Mrs. Dexter's working. Most days I make lunch and, when I do, I'll look over at Dex and his dad on the couch, the two men I love most in the world, and it's all I can do not to cry right there in the kitchen, over turkey cold cuts and cheese slices.

In the evenings, Dex helps me make dinner so his mom can relax when she gets home from work. Usually we'll eat on the patio and stay out there until his parents are ready for bed. It's what I used to dream about in high school. It's the same, lovely dinner with the Dexters, but better, because when Dex gets up to refill our drinks now, he kisses me before he leaves.

Everything is out in the open—Dex and me together—no secrets or sneaking around. He asked his parents, and they don't even mind me staying the night. "This will always be your home too," his mom says to me one Sunday morning while we're washing dishes.

We spend time at my house too, but not as much, of course. Though my mom is far from ecstatic about my relationship with Dex, I have Luis to thank for talking her off the ledge. When he and Dex met, they were instantly enamored with each other. I'm grateful to at least have *one* person at my house who's in our corner. My mom is still frosty, but she hasn't disowned me. Yet.

If I could live in an eternal summer, it would be this one.

But that's the thing about summers. They always come to an end.

Before I know it, Dex and I have only one day left together. He's with his dad this morning at a follow-up doctor's visit, so I'm back at my house, packing for my move to Bloomington. Preparing to start my new life as a law student.

Well, that's what I *should* be doing. Instead I'm sitting on my bed, poring over old photo albums. Reliving every precious childhood memory and making my way through an entire box of tissues.

I'm only halfway through sixth grade when I find the Polaroid picture of Dex and me that Evan took at his party, minutes before Dex first kissed me. Minutes before the course of my life changed forever. And now I'm at a turning point again.

I'm leaving for law school tomorrow. I'm willingly committing myself to three more years away from Dex. Why on *earth* am I doing this to myself? Why risk losing the love of my life for a career I'm not even sure I want? If I look back on this moment years from now, will I regret the path I chose?

I consider calling Mia for advice. About a week after our argument at the coffee shop, I reached out to her to apologize. She forgave me, like Dex said she would. But our friendship still feels strained. Besides, after what happened between us, I suspect she has no interest in getting involved in my relationship again.

I'm in the throes of an existential crisis, sobbing into my knees, when I hear a creaking sound. I look up and see my mom standing in my doorway. I must have been crying so hard I didn't hear her come home. I watch as she surveys the mess surrounding me—the albums, the stray photographs, the crumpled tissues. The corners of her lips turn down when her gaze meets my wet, puffy eyes.

"I can't do this," I tell her. "I'm going to move to LA."

My mom rolls her eyes. "Look. You had a fun summer. We've all been there. But vacations aren't real life, sweetie. Real life is what happens when you start law school in a few days. This is what you've been working so hard for, Sunny. You're not going to throw everything away for some boy."

"He's not just *some boy*," I snap.

My mom shrugs. "He's a fantasy. He's someone to have fun with, and nothing more. Just accept this fling for what it was and move on."

"You know what, Mom? I am *so goddamn* tired of you putting

him down all the time." I stand and walk toward her. "I don't know what you have against Dex, but I also don't give a shit. Because you're wrong about him. He is *not* a fling—he's the love of my life. And I'm moving to LA, whether you like it or not!"

I don't think I've ever seen someone turn so dark a shade of crimson. I've never spoken to her this way before. "Over… my…dead…body," she warns, her eyes practically bugging out of her head.

"I'm twenty-two years old, Mom! You can't tell me how to live my life."

"The hell I can't! Didn't I raise you to be smarter than this? Haven't you learned *anything* at all from our experience? Men leave, Sunny. You need to be able to support yourself. Do you know how hard it is to raise a child alone?"

I laugh bitterly. "Do *you* know how hard it is? Because you were hardly ever here to raise me!"

"Exactly! Don't you realize how guilty I feel because of that? How guilty I've *always* felt?"

"Because you chose your career over *me*?"

My mom scoffs. "Sweetie, I *had* no choice. We were completely on our own. We had no family, no safety net. It was terrifying. I worked as hard as I did to make sure you would never want for anything. That even under the most dire circumstances, I'd have enough saved up so that you would be okay. Better than okay. You have always been my top priority—and I'm sorry if it didn't feel that way. I'm sorry I drove you straight into that boy's arms, and that you're willing to uproot your entire life for *his* dream. What are you going to do in LA, anyway, huh? Wait tables? Or just wait at home for him?"

"There are law schools in LA, Mom. It doesn't have to be that way. I can still have a career and be with Dex."

"Oh yeah? And what happens when he moves to New York to be on Broadway? Or to London, for that matter. What are you going to do with your law degree then? When you're licensed to practice in California, and he's jet-setting to a different city every three months?"

"Then I'll write. I'll write romance novels like the ones I've been secretly devouring since I was sixteen. I'll pursue the dream I've been too scared to tell you about because I know you'll laugh at me. Because you'll tell me it's not a serious career. Well, guess what? I don't care if you like my dreams or not. This is *my* life. Not yours!"

I have every intention of slamming the door in my mom's face, when I hear a car pulling into our driveway. I run to the window.

It's Dex.

I bolt past my mom and down the stairs, and she's right on my heels, still yelling at me, but I don't register what she's saying. I have to get to Dex before she does. I swing open the door before he rings the bell. He looks alarmed.

I throw my arms around him and bury my face in his neck.

"I can't live like this anymore, Dex," I whisper. "I want to be with you."

nineteen

DEX

I have never seen Sunny's mom this mad in my entire life. And that's saying something. As Sunny clings to me, sobbing and shaking, my first instinct is to take her in my arms, put her in my car, and drive away while I'm still breathing. Her mom looks like she wants to kill me with her bare hands. But when Sunny pulls away, she threads her fingers through mine and leads me past her mom, into their house.

Fuck.

As soon as the door's closed, her mom starts screaming at me. "Did you put her up to this? Was this *your* brilliant idea, or—"

"Mom, this was *my* decision," Sunny interjects. "I haven't even told him yet."

"Told me what?" I ask. I keep my focus on Sunny's sweet, beautiful face because, if I catch a glimpse of her mom's bulging eyes one more time, there's a good chance I'll have a panic attack.

"She wants to move to *Los Angeles*," I hear her mom spit out. Sunny smiles at me through her tears.

She wants to move to LA with me.

My dad got a clean bill of health today—and now *this*. It's the best goddamn day of my life.

"But what about law school?" I ask Sunny as soon as it occurs to me.

"There are law schools in LA. But honestly, I think I'd be happier writing. I could get an MFA—"

"Sunny, did you really graduate with honors in political science so you could write smutty love stories?" her mom snorts. "This is a joke! Writing romance is for bored housewives. You're way too smart for that. And why do *you* have to be the one to make sacrifices for *him*?" she continues, pointing a shaky finger at me. I'm still looking away from her, but I can see it out of the corner of my eye. "Why doesn't *he* move to Indiana? Give up *his* career?"

"That doesn't make sense, Mom," Sunny says. "Dex has dreamed of being an actor since he was a kid." She faces me. "I'd never want you to give up that dream for me."

Before I have a chance to respond, Sunny turns back to her mom. "Dex was born to be a star. You've seen him perform—you know his talent is rare. Acting is his craft, and he'd be doing the world a disservice by not sharing it. Not to mention, he loves it. Nothing makes him happier."

It's the truth. Nothing else makes me as happy—except Sunny. But I can't rely on her to be my only source of joy. It wouldn't be fair.

"Besides," Sunny continues. "Don't I deserve to be happy too?"

"Happiness is fleeting," her mom yells. "You have to be practical, Sunny. Exactly how do you plan to pay for an MFA?

Because I sure as hell won't be helping."

Sunny's bottom lip quivers, but she holds her ground. "I'll get a loan," she says.

Her mom crosses her arms and laugh. "And be in debt for the rest of your life? Writers don't make money, sweetie. How will you pay it back?"

This is where I come in. "We'll be fine, Sunny. I'll start auditioning as soon as we get to LA. I'll take any roles I get. We'll save some money. And one day, I'll make it big. I promise you, I won't give up until it happens."

I regret the words as soon as they come out of my mouth. How can I promise that I'll be a successful actor? Entertainment is the most fickle business there is. Even if I bust my ass, there's only so much I can control. Whether or not I get my big break could simply boil down to luck.

Sunny slowly turns her gaze from me to her mom, who takes the opportunity to lay into her again. "Is that really what you want to do, Sunny? Wait for your actor boyfriend to become rich and famous so he can pay off your debt?"

She makes us sound pathetic. And Sunny's so pragmatic. There's no way she'll go through with this.

Will she?

I never dared to dream that Sunny would come back to LA with me—but she *wants* to. Is she really going to let her mom get in the way?

I look over at Sunny, hoping she'll say something to put my mind at ease. But her mom's not done quite yet.

"If you go to California, Sunny, I will not pay your way.

But if you attend Indiana University—like we planned—you won't have to worry about a thing. I'll cover your tuition, your apartment, your food…all of it. It's only three years. He can wait. If he cares enough about you, he'll *let you go.*"

Her mom's words are so pointed, I know exactly what she's doing. That was the same phrase she used to shoo me off her lawn two years ago.

If you love her, honey, you'll let her go.

I never told Sunny what her mother did, and I don't plan to. I wish I could be more spiteful. If Sunny knew the truth about her mom's meddling, she'd definitely come to LA with me. But at what cost? Sunny only has one blood relative in her life. No matter how shaky their relationship is, I can't take that away from her. If I did, I'd be no better than her mom. And as meddlesome as she is, at the end of the day, she's only trying to protect her daughter. Because she loves her.

I cannot fucking fault her for that.

I watch Sunny waver. And I don't want to make her decision any harder than it already is, so I jump in. "Your mom's right. I'll wait as long as I have to. You decide what you want to do, and I'll support you. No matter what," I say, with a pointed glance at her mom, who smirks at me.

For a moment, there's silence. Then Sunny takes a ragged breath. "I want to sleep on it," she says.

She doesn't want to let me down in front of her mom. She won't give her the satisfaction.

But my heart is broken, regardless. For about thirty seconds today, one of my biggest dreams came true.

Then I lost it.

We were up half the night packing her things. By the time we'd finished loading her car, it was three in the morning. I asked her if she wanted to come home with me and sleep in my bed. She said she couldn't, because she'd never want to leave. She promised she'd stop by in the morning to say goodbye.

And here we are.

She looks so broken. I'd sell my soul to make her feel whole again. That's how much I love her.

I should tell her.

She hasn't said a word since she got out of her car. She has her arms wrapped around me, and she's trying not to cry. Now she's turning away.

Is this it? Is she really going to leave without saying *anything*?

"Sunny—wait."

I'm going to tell her I love her. I can do it now. She saw me endure the worst panic attack of my life—helped me through it, in fact—and she didn't judge me. She didn't run away from me, or reject me. No, she loved me.

She loves me.

I take her hand in mine. "There's something I've been wanting to say to you for years," I tell her. "And I can't keep the words in any longer. I just—I want you to know that—"

"Don't." Sunny touches her finger to my lips.

My palms start sweating.

"I know what you're going to say and, trust me, Dex, if you finish that sentence…there's no chance I'm getting in my car and driving to Indiana."

I nod.

I didn't think my heart could hurt any worse than it already did. I was wrong.

"I can't hear those words coupled with goodbye," Sunny goes on with teary eyes. "So, do me a favor, please? Save them for when we can *really* be together. When we aren't separated by thousands of miles, and infinite uncertainties. When the stars align. Okay? That's when I want you to tell me."

twenty

SUNNY

It's the first day of kindergarten all over again.

I'm anxious. Overwhelmed. Astounded that every other student in the room seems happy to be here except me. There's a bit of nervous excitement in the air, of course. That's to be expected on the first day of law school. But I don't see anyone else freaking out like I am. I'm sitting on the edge of my seat. My right leg is bouncing up and down at high speed. My hands are braced against my desk. I must look like I'm about to make a run for it. Maybe I should. I don't belong here. I belong in LA with Dex.

But if I drop out of law school, or even defer my enrollment, my mom will disown me. Truthfully, I don't care the slightest bit about her money. But supporting me financially is the only way she's ever shown me love. She never played with me, or baked with me, or made art with me when I was a kid. But she's always worked hard to clothe me, and feed me, and put a roof over my head. So what will it mean if she decides to cut me off?

"Did we have reading for this class?" someone asks me.

I practically jump out of my seat. I'd been so lost in my

thoughts that I hadn't noticed anyone sit down.

"Oh…um, yeah," I respond, looking to my left. He's busy pulling books out of his backpack, so luckily I don't think he saw me flinch. "We were supposed to read chapters one and two." I bite my lip. "It was kind of a lot."

"Got it. Thanks," he says, totally unperturbed as he turns to me. "Jeremy, by the way." He reaches out his hand.

"I'm Sunny."

"Sunny," he says. "I like that."

I'm about to thank him when he asks a follow-up question. "Is there a story behind it?"

I crinkle my brow. "Do you really want to know?"

Jeremy shrugs. "Yeah. That's why I asked."

I sit back in my seat. "Okay…well, my mom had no idea what to name me. So she decided to wait until I was born. As soon as she was admitted to the hospital, this awful storm took hold, and for seven straight hours she labored through the sound of howling wind, and rain, and thunder…"

She worried it was ominous. A sign that she was in over her head. How would she manage to raise me without a family? She never said as much, but I'm sure she wondered if she'd made the right choice.

"But the minute I was born, the sun came out." I smile.

That's when she knew we'd be okay.

Jeremy nods. "See? That's a good story. And I never would have known unless I asked. 'The important thing is never to stop questioning.' That's an Einstein quote," he adds. "For the record."

"Let me guess. You want to be a litigator, right?" I'm a little more relaxed now. At least my leg isn't shaking anymore.

He laughs. "Wow. You've known me for three minutes, and you already have me pegged. I'm inquisitive, yes. I got kicked out of the main library yesterday for asking the reference librarian too many questions. Not the first time that's happened to me, actually. At least they let me check out the book I wanted. Really good primer on astrophysics. I was up half the night reading it."

"*Astrophysics?* You read *that* instead of our law homework? Why?"

He shakes his head. "I dunno. It was interesting?"

I'm still looking at him with a furrowed brow when our professor walks in. He's easily in his seventies, and wearing a tweed sport coat with a sweater vest and slacks. His bifocals are sitting on the tip of his nose, and his white hair is sticking out in every direction. He looks like someone you'd cast to play a law professor in a movie. Unfortunately, this is very real. My right leg starts bouncing again.

There's a low rumble of voices around the classroom as our professor holds the class roster at arm's length and peruses it carefully. "Now. Who shall be my first victim?" he asks, rubbing his chin. He's going to pick a student to call on, to engage in a discussion and ask questions about our homework assignment. The Socratic method, they call it. My worst nightmare. I'm terrified he'll call on me.

Thankfully he doesn't. But it's a near miss, because he calls on Jeremy. What are the chances? I feel sorry for him. I wonder if the professor will get mad at him for not doing the assignment.

The pages of Jeremy's untouched law treatise are still stiff when he cracks them open. He sets the book down in his lap. I guess he's going to try to wing it. My heart is racing on his behalf. I look around the room, and all eyes are on him.

Then something incredible happens. The professor spends nearly thirty minutes grilling Jeremy about the chapters he didn't read and, somehow, he manages to answer every single question correctly. Effortlessly. I read each chapter twice and *still* wouldn't have been able to give such thoughtful answers. Is Jeremy a genius? Or am I out of my depth?

When the interrogation's over and the professor moves on to someone else (not me, thankfully) I realize that I've been clenching my teeth. I was obviously much more unnerved by the experience than Jeremy, who leans back in his chair, totally relaxed.

"How did you *do* that?" I whisper to him after class. "You didn't even read the assignment."

Jeremy's lips curl ever so slightly. "I just scanned the pages real quick while he was talking," he says, nodding toward our professor. "Tried to figure out what he was going to ask next. No big deal."

Well, this guy obviously belongs here. But what about me?

The jury's still out.

"You have Torts next?" Jeremy asks as we pack up our things. I nod.

"Cool," he says, looking at his cell phone. "I have to call my girlfriend first, so I'll meet you in there. Save me a seat?"

"Sure," I say as he turns to leave.

He has a girlfriend. I'm relieved. I haven't made any friends here yet, and he seems like a nice guy. Now I don't have to worry about him hitting on me.

When I get back to my apartment later that afternoon, there's a bouquet of bright yellow sunflowers outside my door. My eyes well up with tears. I call Dex right away.

"Thank you so much," I say when he picks up.

"Congrats on your first day of law school," he says with a smile in his voice. "How did it go?"

I take a breath. "You know what? It wasn't that bad. I actually kind of enjoyed it. But…I really miss you."

He sighs. "I know. You won't have to miss me much longer, though."

I wipe my eyes with the backs of my fingers. "What do you mean? Are you coming to visit already? You just got back to LA a couple of days ago."

He lets out a little laugh. "Yeah. I booked a flight to Indianapolis and rented a car."

I'm grinning ear to ear. "Oh my god, Dex! When do you get in?"

"Uh—let me look at my flight info again. I get in…two hours ago."

I shake my head. "What?"

"Come downstairs."

I run over to the window and, sure enough, Dex is standing outside my building on his cell.

I fling my phone onto the couch, grab my keys, and run down two flights of stairs. When I make it outside, I jump into his arms and wrap my legs around him. I'm so happy, I'm shaking. And crying. He kisses my tears.

"I promised you I'd visit," he says with his half-smile.

I squeeze him even tighter. "What about your auditions?" I say into his ear. "I hope you didn't cancel anything."

I feel him shake his head. "I had one yesterday, and my next one's on Friday. I want to spend the days in between with you. We're going to make this work, Sunny."

I meet his gaze and kiss him. Then I let my feet fall back to the ground. I grab his hand and lead him upstairs to my apartment.

And I get none of tomorrow's reading done.

After Dex leaves, I use the weekend to catch up on my assignments and, by Monday, I'm back on track. Which is a good thing, because as soon as our Civil Procedure professor walks into class, something in my gut tells me she's about to call my name. And I'm right.

But once I get going, the Socratic method isn't nearly as bad as I anticipated. I'm pretty pleased with myself, in fact. I'm prepared, and I give intelligent answers. I come across as confident, even though my palms are sweating. When it's over, my entire body is buzzing from the thrill of it.

"Well played," Jeremy whispers from his seat next to me. He's looking straight ahead, his eyes on our professor, but I can tell by the hint of a smile on his face that he's impressed. Over the past week, Jeremy has gotten called on three times, and I think it's safe to say he's the smartest person in our class. So, coming from him, it's a true compliment.

"It's a rush, isn't it?" Jeremy says to me later, when we're packing up our things.

I smile. "I thought I'd hate the Socratic method. I'm not used to being the center of attention"—*that's always been Dex*—"but every time I came up with the right answer, I'd get this little endorphin boost, and by the end of it I felt…giddy."

"You're quick on your feet," he says. "I bet you'd like litigation if you gave it a chance."

I shake my head vehemently. "No way. It's one thing to get called on in class, but actually going in front of a judge? I'd be a nervous wreck."

Jeremy snorts. "Don't sell yourself short. You'll be bored out of your mind writing contracts all day. Come to the dark side with me."

"Not gonna happen," I say with a laugh. "My boyfriend's the performer. Not me."

"Oh, yeah?" Jeremy asks as we head out of the classroom and into the hallway. "What does he do?"

"He's an actor. A very talented one. He's done a lot of theater. One commercial so far. He just auditioned for another."

"So I assume he's not living here. I mean, Bloomington, Indiana isn't exactly the epicenter of the entertainment industry."

I giggle. "It certainly is *not*. No, he's in LA."

Jeremy sighs. "My girlfriend's in Chicago for med school. Sucks being long-distance."

I frown. "It's awful. I miss him so much."

Jeremy nods. "We can commiserate, at least. Well, I'm heading out," he says as he begins to turn away. "I'll catch you later."

"You're not going to class?"

He shakes his head. "I'm meeting with this professor in the philosophy department."

"Philosophy?" I ask, confused.

He shrugs. "Yeah, I'm reading this book about the paradox of idealism, and I just…really wanted to talk to someone about it, you know?"

I can't help but laugh. "So now you're reading *philosophy* instead of doing your law homework?"

Jeremy smiles, but not with his mouth so much as his eyes. "No, I'm caught up on all our schoolwork. I figure I won't miss much if I don't go to class today. It's all a little basic right now, don't you think?"

My eyes go wide. "You think this is *basic*," I repeat after him. "Why aren't you at Harvard Law…or some other Ivy League school?"

Jeremy runs a hand over the scruff on his face. "Well—I kinda dicked around a lot in college."

I laugh. "See you later," I say as I start to walk away.

"Hey, Sunny?" he calls out. I turn around.

"You wanna meet up later to study?"

I guess there's no harm in it. We're both in relationships. Jeremy's a friend. Plus, he's brilliant, so I could probably learn a lot from him.

I shrug. "Sure."

"Cool," he says with as close to a smile as Jeremy can muster. "I'll email you."

Dex calls me late that night.

"Oh my god, Sunny," he says right when I pick up. "You'll never believe it."

"Believe what?" I ask. He sounds so excited. But something in my gut tells me I won't like what I'm about to hear.

"I got a job," he says. "I'm going to be on *Passions*."

I shake my head. "*Passions*? Like…the soap opera?"

"Yes! Isn't that incredible? One of my professors hooked me up with a friend who works on the show. And it's a real part, Sunny. I'm going to be one of the main characters."

My hands are shaking. "Dex, oh my god! I'm so happy for you, I just—" I let out a breath. "I think I'm in shock."

My boyfriend is going to be a soap star.

I close my eyes and get a glimpse into the future: Oliver Dexter on the cover of *Soap Opera Digest*. Shirtless. Women lining up to meet him at soap opera conventions. Slipping him their phone numbers and flirting with him. His sexy co-stars kissing him. Touching him.

Falling in love with him.

I squeeze my eyes shut and will myself not to cry. Dex is over the moon. I can't ruin this for him.

"I'm in shock too," he says. "I want to fly you out here to celebrate, okay? I'm going to buy you a ticket as soon as I get my schedule."

I nod. "I would love that…thank you," I say with a hand over my hammering heart. "Um, I'm meeting with my TA early tomorrow morning, so I have to get some sleep. But I'll talk to you soon, okay? I'm *really* happy for you, Dex. You deserve this."

"Thanks," he says with a smile in his voice. The half-smile I love so much.

I hang up and stare at the wall for a while. I don't have an early meeting, I just didn't know how much longer I could pretend that I'm not terrified of what this means for our relationship.

I wish there were someone I could talk to. I haven't heard from Mia in weeks. Sam is taking a gap year to travel, and I'm pretty sure she's in Thailand. Claire and I haven't spoken much since we graduated. I obviously can't talk to my mom.

I've made small talk with a few women I've met so far in law school, but we're definitely not at the point where I feel comfortable talking to them about my love life. The closest friend I have in Bloomington is Jeremy.

I pick up my phone. I scroll to his number, which he added to my contacts earlier today, when we met up to study. My finger hovers over his name.

But I decide to go to sleep.

twenty-one

"How was your weekend?" Jeremy asks when he sits down next to me in Criminal Law.

"It was good," I tell him. "I flew to LA to visit my boyfriend."

Dex started his new job two weeks ago. And getting a glimpse at his life in LA was even harder than I expected. He took me to see the studio and the set. I met his co-stars, who are all insanely gorgeous. He introduced me to everyone as his girlfriend, but still, I couldn't help feeling threatened. I was a fish out of water among these impossibly beautiful people. But Dex wasn't. He fit in perfectly. And, more importantly, he looked so comfortable and happy. Meanwhile, it was everything I could do not to run away screaming. What does it mean for our future if I can't see myself in his world?

But when it was the two of us, alone…the fireworks…

I can't think about that now, though. Jeremy's nodding at me.

"The actor," he says. "How's he doing out there?"

"He's doing really well, actually. He's going to be on a soap opera."

Jeremy raises an eyebrow. "A *soap opera*," he repeats slowly. "You're joking, right?"

I shake my head. "It's true. He got a starring role on *Passions*."

Jeremy chuckles into his coffee tumbler, then takes a long sip. "A soap star, huh?" He clears his throat. "I bet he's a real dreamboat. Rock-hard abs? Smoldering eyes? Is he harboring a deep dark secret?"

I laugh. Jeremy has a pretty sarcastic sense of humor, so I'm not surprised by his response. "Pretty much," I reply. "Not the deep dark secret part. But the abs and the eyes? Definitely."

Jeremy smirks as our professor walks in and the din around the classroom settles to a hush.

About a month after I visit Dex in LA, his episodes begin airing on TV.

And right away, people start talking about him.

There are interviews on entertainment shows and in soap opera magazines. They call him things like "sexy newcomer" and "hunky soap star." No surprise there. But it does surprise me that they refer to him as "Dex Oliver."

"Yeah, my agent thought that Oliver Dexter sounded like an accountant," he says to me, laughing over the phone.

God, I wish he were an accountant. Like Evan. Mia's so lucky.

The next thing I know, I'm at the Starbucks in downtown Bloomington one morning, waiting to order a chai latte, when

I hear two undergrads in line ahead of me talking about Dex.

My Dex.

"So I have a new crush," one girl says to the other.

"Oh my god, the cute guy who sits next to you in Econ, right? I knew it!"

"Nope." She giggles. "Dex Oliver. He's so hot…I'd literally let him do *anything* to me."

"Oh my god, same. I read he has a girlfriend from back home, but I bet *that* won't last long…"

My stomach churns. I feel sick. I leave the shop without ordering.

When I get back to my apartment, I watch Dex's show for the first time. I have every episode recorded, but I've been too nervous to watch them before now. Too afraid they'll confirm what I already know is true. That Dex really is a star…

And it's only a matter of time before I lose him.

Ten minutes into the first episode, my heart sinks. Somehow he's even better than I expected. He stands out. And it's not only because he's shirtless half the time, which is so strange for me to see. *My* boyfriend's body on TV. The same abs and pecs I've brushed with my fingertips a million times, the neck I've bitten, the lips I've kissed—oh god. I turn off the show before I have to watch him kiss the hot blonde who's making eyes at him.

How will I ever get through this?

The only solution I can come up with right now is to pour myself into law school. I meet Jeremy at the library most nights. He's so smart, I doubt he even needs to be there, but he says he enjoys studying with me because I keep him disciplined. Apparently, if it weren't for me, he'd be out at the bars a lot more often, and then he'd start slacking off in school, which is what happened to him in college.

But the truth is, I like studying with him too. It's like having my own private tutor. People should be fighting to get him into their study groups, but Jeremy jokes that I'm the only person in our class who can put up with him.

I'll admit he's a troublemaker. Whenever he raises his hand to speak in class, students roll their eyes with a wry smile because they know what's coming. He's loud, argumentative and—infuriatingly—always right. He loves to start debates, play devil's advocate. Stir the pot. I don't think I'm exaggerating when I say that a fair number of our classmates truly despise him.

If law schools have bad boys, Jeremy is ours. Once, he got another student so riled up in class that our professor threw his hands up in defeat and dismissed us early. We also think he made a teacher's assistant cry one time—although she claimed her watery eyes were due to allergies.

Yes, Jeremy's an instigator. But it isn't just for show. He's so smart, you actually want to hear what he has to say and, by the end, you almost invariably agree. He finds every loophole. He makes us all better law students, I think. That's why I study with him. If I'm going to do this law school thing, I want to do it right. And Jeremy and I make a good team. He helps me tighten up my legal arguments, making sure no stone is left unturned. And I help him organize his writing, which is as untamed as he is.

Before I know it, my first semester's over. I won't get my grades back until after winter break, much to my mom's dismay.

But I don't have the energy to worry about her because *Dex is in town*. We spend the holidays in Beachwood. For the first time in years, our families celebrate together at his house. And this time, Luis, Lily, and Elena join the party.

It's a perfect evening. While we're at the table enjoying Mrs. Dexter's feast, Dex barely stops kissing me. A peck on the cheek, one on the hand, one on my ear. Several on my lips. My mom is seated on the other side of me, so we're safe from her glaring disapproval. Anyway, she's busy talking to Lily, who's in the first year of her neurosurgery residency. They're discussing surgical techniques, like two peas in a pod. After dinner, when everyone's distracted by football, Dex and I sneak upstairs to his bedroom and he has *me* for dessert. For a moment at least, everything is exactly as it was over the summer—with the exception of the photographers hanging out on Dex's front lawn.

One week later, our families toast the New Year with a catered meal at my mom's. As I sip my champagne with my boyfriend's arm draped around me, I can't help but reflect on everything that's changed in the past year.

I was with Asher last winter. Now I'm with Dex.

I started law school. He's becoming famous…

Nerves flutter in my stomach as I wonder what 2003 will bring.

Back at school in January, I get my first-semester grades. I'm stunned. I got As in all my classes. Studying with Jeremy definitely paid off. For the first time since I started law school,

I feel like I belong here. I raise my hand a lot more in class. I feel calm and prepared walking into exams. I do so well that, before the end of the school year, I'm offered a coveted spot as a summer associate at one of the best firms in Chicago.

Law school summers are when the firms wine and dine you, and give you a nice big paycheck in hopes that you'll sell them your soul after graduation. I'm not convinced I want to work for a big firm, but Jeremy, who's at the top of the class with me, thinks it's too good an opportunity to pass up. He'll be working in Chicago this summer too, at a different but equally prestigious firm. "Just give it a try," he says. "See how you like it."

Well, I do like it. Maybe because, for the first time in my budding career, I'm getting a taste of how it feels to be a VIP, like Dex. I don't pay for a thing the entire summer. *Everything* is on the firm. We eat dinner at all the new hot spots, enjoy drinks at the swankiest bars. We get premium seating at every sporting event—luxury suites and skyboxes wherever we go. I'm seduced by it all. And it's not just the recreation I find so exciting. The attorneys I work with are litigators, and they're cool, confident and fast on their feet. They're actors, essentially. It's thrilling.

Speaking of actors…Dex's career is really taking off. He's a soap opera "fan favorite," so they give him a bigger and better story line—an evil twin, of course—which means double the screentime and an opportunity for him to really show off his talent. He plays the brothers so distinctly, so convincingly, that they truly seem like two different people.

Between filming, and photoshoots, and interviews, Dex's free time is limited. He flies me out to LA a couple of times. He tries his best to make plans for us to see each other.

But he cancels on me. A lot.

I can tell it's the last thing he wants to do, so I try my best to hide my disappointment. After all, what did I expect? I always knew this would happen.

I just didn't think it would happen so fast.

twenty-two

SUNNY

SUMMER OF 2004

My second year of law school was pretty much a carbon copy of the first. I studied hard with Jeremy. I saw Dex whenever our schedules aligned. It definitely wasn't as often as we would have liked. He was supposed to spend the weekend with me in Bloomington after my finals, but he got stuck on the *Passions* set because his co-star's costume disappeared. By the time it was found and they finished filming, he'd missed his flight. Now I'm back in Chicago, working as a summer associate for the same firm as last year, and I have no idea when I'll see him.

Big things are happening for Dex. He's still taking the soap opera world by storm, but it seems like every channel I flip to, there he is guest-starring on a hit TV show. On sitcoms, where he plays the hot pizza delivery guy, or the hot fitness instructor, or the hot guy next door. On police dramas, where he's an unwitting victim, or a witness—or the incredible season finale of *Law & Order* that just aired, where it turns out he was the *killer*! I never saw it coming. Jeremy watched it with me. He's working in Chicago this summer again too. He said Dex was "pretty good," which is about as effusive as Jeremy gets.

But during the closing credits, Mia called, *shrieking*, to tell me what an amazing actor my boyfriend is. Jeremy could hear her through the phone. I love how excited she is about his acting career. I think it's brought us a little closer again. I feel awful I didn't go to her wedding, though. It was the weekend before my second semester final exams. Mia said she understood, and I'm grateful. If I'd really wanted to, I probably could have planned to get my studying done ahead of time. I considered it. But Dex wasn't able to go with me because of his work schedule, and I know I wouldn't have had fun at that wedding without him. As much as I hate to admit it, Mia and Evan's relationship is still too triggering.

The first two weeks of my summer in Chicago are so packed with law firm social events that I hardly have time to run errands. Finally, on a quiet Sunday morning, I drive to the grocery store with a long shopping list. I'm standing in the checkout line, minding my own business, when I see a picture of Dex on the cover of a tabloid magazine.

I flip through to find the article, and there are pictures of him at lunch with one of his soap opera co-stars. The sexy blonde he has the love scenes with. The scenes I can't watch. My chest tightens as I examine each photograph. Dex is sitting at a table, wearing a baseball cap, t-shirt, and shorts, none of which I've ever seen him in before. But the caption makes sure to mention that his shirt is Christian Dior—and the retail cost is double my monthly rent in Bloomington. His co-star is seated across from him in very large sunglasses and a very small dress. Also expensive. They're leaning toward each other. There's one photo where Dex has his hand on hers. The headline reads "Dex & Tess: Real-Life Lovers." My hands shake as I hold the pages.

My head starts throbbing. I'm dizzy and starting to wonder if I'm actually going to be sick when my cell phone rings. It's Dex. Like he knows, somehow, that I'm in a grocery store two thousand miles away, staring at pictures of him with another woman.

"It's not true," he says, the moment I answer the phone.

I let out a sob. I turn to leave the checkout line, and the woman standing behind me gives me a sympathetic frown as I walk away.

"Sunny, you *have* to believe me. Tess is gay. Her girlfriend broke up with her. I was trying to help her feel better."

"Dex," I sigh out. "What are we even doing?" My lip is quivering. "We haven't seen each other in months. I feel like I barely know you anymore. I mean—you're out to lunch wearing *Christian Dior*? Since when do you care about labels?"

"I don't. It was a gift. I'm a walking billboard," he explains. "People give me free shit because they know I'll get photographed wearing it. Look, Sunny, I can only imagine what you must be feeling right now. But I promise you have nothing to worry about. I just booked a flight to Chicago," he says. "I'll be there next weekend."

I nod and take in a breath. "Okay."

"Sunny, I need to know that you trust me."

I wipe the tears from my cheeks. Everyone who walks past me

down the cereal aisle is staring at me. I step to the side because a mom with an adorable curly-haired toddler needs Cheerios, and I'm standing in her way.

"I do," I tell Dex. "But that doesn't make this any easier."

The following weekend, Dex is in my apartment. He kisses me as soon as he walks through the door, and it's slow, sensual, his fingers traveling up the nape of my neck, into my hair, cradling the back of my head, like nothing has changed. Suddenly I have amnesia and forget all about how tough the last several months have been. About my fear of losing him. Or not being *enough* for him. About Tess, and the tabloids, and all of that shit. I can hardly remember my own name. All I can think about is how much I want him. So I pull him into my bedroom, and we make up for lost time again.

Afterward, we're sitting up in bed. I lean against his chest, and he wraps his arms around me.

"Are you excited for Paris?" he asks.

I recently decided to study abroad in the fall. It's something I've always wanted to do, but never got around to in college. I'm about to start my third and final year of law school, so this is my last chance. I wrestled with the decision, but Dex is becoming more famous by the second, and with each opportunity that comes knocking at his door, the threat of losing him becomes more real. I need Paris to distract me. But I do my best to hide my insecurity when I answer him.

"I'm *so* excited," I say. "I'm going to have coffee and croissants every morning, and walk down cobblestone streets with a tote full of baguettes, and drink wine with my friends while we pretend to study. My classes will be pass/fail, so I don't even have to worry about my GPA. It's going to be amazing."

"That's awesome," Dex says, hugging me. "Is, um, Jeremy, going?" As I'm leaning against him, I feel his heart rate pick up when he asks me.

"Oh," I say, adjusting myself to look at him. "No. He isn't."

This is the first time Dex has ever asked me about Jeremy. I hope I haven't given the impression that I'm remotely interested in him—because I'm not. Jeremy and I are just good friends. I could have sworn I told Dex that Jeremy was in a relationship. Maybe he forgot. "Um, did I tell you that Jeremy's girlfriend goes to med school here? I actually met her last week. She's nice."

The truth is, she was a bit prickly. Jeremy said she was tired from her obstetrics rotation, but I got the distinct impression she didn't like me.

Dex clears his throat. "That's cool. Well, Paris is going to be incredible. I'm happy for you."

"Thanks," I say, leaning against him again. His heart rate has slowed back down.

"I actually have some news," Dex says next after a brief pause. "I wanted to tell you in person."

I adjust myself again. "What's up?" I ask. Now *my* heart is racing.

Dex half-smiles. "I got cast in a movie," he nearly whispers.

I feel like the wind was just knocked out of me.

This is it.

He's going to be a movie star.

And I've never seen him happier in his life.

"It's an indie film, so the budget's smaller, but the director's amazing," he continues. "I've seen all of her work. Her last movie won the Audience Award at Sundance." Dex shakes his head in disbelief. "I think this could be big, Sunny."

I take in a breath. "That's amazing!" I exclaim as I pull him in for a hug. I close my eyes and squeeze him as tightly as I can.

Before I have to let go.

"I don't even know how my agent got me the audition," he says, still stunned. "I mean, I'm proud of the work I've done, but it doesn't really show my range. The director said she saw something in me, though."

"Of course she did," I say with a huge smile as I work hard to pull myself together to be supportive. To be a friend.

After all, long before we were lovers, Dex and I were friends. I have this sinking feeling that I'll be reprising that role again soon.

He's going to be an A-list celebrity. He'll be rubbing elbows with the most dazzling people in Hollywood. In the world, even. Why would he want to stay tethered to me? What could I possibly have to offer Dex Oliver, the movie star? I'd just be a burden.

My mom's vile words from years ago come barging back into my brain.

Is that really what you want, Sunny? To live in Dex's shadow like that? To abandon your own dreams and follow him around like a lovesick puppy? And hope, against all odds, that he'll come home to you every night?

Dex's voice pulls me out of the depths of my waking nightmare, and back into his arms. Then he gives me a morsel of hope.

"They're going to put my soap character in a coma. He'll get in a car accident, and the evil twin will disappear when the police start asking questions. That way they can write me back into the script if the movie tanks," he explains. "But the best part is—we'll be filming in London in the fall. I can visit you while you're in Paris."

Me and Dex, together, in the most romantic city in the world? Now, that's something to look forward to.

True to his word, Dex visits me in Paris in early October. The last time I saw him was in July, when he flew me out to LA for a weekend. It's been a few months, but I'm actually shocked at how much he's changed. He's a lot more muscular, for one thing. I wonder if they made him bulk up for the movie. He's wearing a dark gray cashmere sweater that fits tightly around his biceps. For the first time, he has a five o'clock shadow, which makes him look a little older. A little more rugged.

It's sexy. *He's* so damn sexy, I can barely breathe.

Dex must like what he sees too because, after a brief exchange of hellos and pleasantries, he has me pinned against the wall in the tiny foyer of my studio apartment. And his kisses feel different this time. There's an urgency to them, like if he doesn't have me right away, the world might end.

I like it.

I start to lift his sweater, and he pulls it over his head. "*Holy shit*," I say, as my gaze falls to his abs. He's always been fit, but now he has a fully defined six-pack—maybe even an eight-pack—not that it matters, but it'll be fun to count later. Right now, I'm too distracted. I kiss his neck and bite him, softly sucking his skin between my teeth. He smells incredible. Not just soap and CK One anymore, but something warm, woodsy and very masculine. Something expensive, like the sweater I couldn't wait for him to take off.

I'm not having sex with Oliver Dexter tonight. I'm having sex with Dex Oliver. The soap star. The soon-to-be movie star. And I'm completely captivated by him.

I unzip his jeans, get down on my knees and take him in my mouth until I know he's close. Then I lean against the wall again and pull him toward me by his belt loops. I put my arms around his neck and wrap a leg around him.

"Touch me," I whisper.

His hand goes up my inner thigh, and he moves my underwear aside. "*Fuck*, you're so wet," he says when his fingers are inside me.

I close my eyes and sigh. "See what you do to me, Dex?"

He kneels down and lifts my dress to pull off my thong. Then he kisses the soft, pillowy flesh of my inner thighs. I know he adores that part of me, and it makes me smile. He runs his hands up the backs of my legs and pulls me closer to him. Then he puts his mouth on me. He savors me like I'm the most delicious thing he's ever tasted. My hands are in his hair, and his tongue feels so good that the room starts spinning. But then he stands and, with his hands still gripping my ass, he carries me to the kitchenette and sets me down on the counter.

He peels the layers of my dress and bra away from my breast and takes my nipple in his mouth. He knows how much I love that. I brush my fingertips up and down the nape of his neck because I like the way it makes him shudder. Then I slide my fingertips down the ripples of his abs and reach for him. I grip him, and he braces his hands on the counter, leaving space between us, like he's trying to hold himself back from ravaging me.

But I don't want him to.

"Fuck me," I say under my breath. And he does. Right there, with pots and pans clattering next to me and crashing onto the floor. Then we move to the couch, where he teases me mercilessly with his tongue again and makes me beg for him. Finally, he throws me onto the bed, takes me in ways we've never tried before, and I'm screaming so loud my neighbor starts rapping on the wall.

But we're done now.

Dex and I lie next to each other on the bed, holding hands and recovering.

When our labored breaths start to steady, I turn to him, and he smiles as though the weight of the world just lifted off his shoulders. I feel his joy wrap around my core like a hug from the inside out.

Maybe *this* is the happiest I've seen him.

"Do you want to shower with me?" I ask. We're drenched in sweat.

Dex nods and kisses me.

Then he follows me to the bathroom. I turn on the shower,

and he gets in with me. I hand him my soap but, instead of washing himself, he lathers his hands and washes me. He even shampoos and conditions my long hair. He's so gentle, it doesn't hurt at all when he combs his fingers through my curls. I can't stop smiling. We've been in the shower together before, but never like this. The other times, we were having sex.

That was good. But this is better.

I take my turn washing him, and then we go to sleep.

The next day, we explore the city together. Dex wears a baseball cap to lessen the chances of him being recognized. It happens from time to time, but not as much since he's been in Europe. He hasn't quite reached international fame—yet. I'm used to people staring at Dex anyway, famous or not, so all in all, it's not much different than things have always been.

We take a slow walk through the Luxembourg Gardens with hot coffees warming our hands, a crisp fall breeze cooling the air. We visit Notre Dame and marvel at the vaulted ceilings and stained glass windows. We buy cheese, and baguettes, and a bottle of red wine, and eat lunch along the Seine. And that evening, as we stroll through Montmartre, Dex catches the eye of a street artist who insists on drawing us. Well, really, she wants to draw him.

"Sure," he says with a perfect smile. "Both of us," he adds as he grabs my hand. The artist nods in confirmation, inviting us to sit across from her on a set of metal folding chairs.

"Look at that jawline! So handsome," she says, peering at Dex through her glasses, which she wears low on her nose. Then she turns toward me. "Lucky girl!"

I smile self-consciously and fidget with a loose thread that dangles from my cardigan. My heart sinks. It's my favorite sweater. I wonder how it got snagged?

It feels ominous. I can't help but think of Asher and our unraveling relationship. Immediately, I let the thread go.

The artist draws Dex first. She isn't fluent in English but definitely knows enough to make ongoing commentary about how perfectly symmetrical his face is.

When her focus shifts to me, she's much quieter. I panic, imagining what she thinks of me. I picture the final product—Dex, a Disney prince, all muscles and jaw and big, gleaming eyes. And me with my wild curls, the Beast. I thought I'd become more confident about my looks in recent years, but it seems all my progress was blown to bits when I visited Dex on the set of his show, where all his female co-stars look like supermodels.

When the artist hands us her drawing, though, I breathe a sigh of relief. It's lovely. *I'm* lovely. Dex doesn't eclipse me like I feared. We look beautiful together. I see it again.

That night, we eat in the Latin Quarter—fluffy pita sandwiches stuffed with spiced lamb and thick, crispy French fries. Dex tells me his trainer is going to kill him for eating carbs, and I laugh, but it turns out he's completely serious.

After dinner, we walk for hours. Through crowded alleyways, along cobblestone streets, over wooden bridges where lovers hold hands and kiss. That's where he kisses me. It feels like a dream.

If only my joy weren't tainted by this sense of impending doom.

You'll never be able to hold on to a man like him.

I'm not worried about Oliver Dexter. I know I have his heart. But I'm helplessly watching as he turns into someone else. The abs. The facial hair. The expensive clothes. Yes, it's enticing. But it's terrifying too. The transformation is only physical now, but where does it end? How long will I be able to hold on to Dex Oliver?

When we get back to my apartment, he starts kissing me right away with the same intensity as last night. Maybe even more feverishly this time. We make our way to my bed. He's on top of me, frantically pulling off my clothes. His breathing is heavy. His heart is pounding wildly against my chest. I pull back to make sure he's okay.

I look into his eyes, but he's not there.

"Dex?" I ask.

He's fighting for breath.

"Dex, look at me," I say.

I see a flicker of recognition in his eyes before he rolls off me.

He's sitting up now, clutching his chest.

"I can't go through with this," he says.

twenty-three

DEX

It's like a scene out of a war movie.

There's an explosion—

Then nothing.

The audio cuts to silence. The screen goes white.

Then…*slowly*…the world starts to fade back in.

Your vision is clouded by smoke and dust, but you see pockets of light and shadow.

In the distance, you hear a faint ringing. It gets louder.

You begin to make out other sounds. But they're very far away.

"Dex?"

"Can you hear me?"

"Come back to me—please."

Her voice pulls me out of the rubble.

"Dex? Are you okay?"

It's Sunny.

And she isn't far away, she's right in front of me. On top of me. Straddling me. Her clothes half on and half off.

I've never seen her look so scared.

It takes me several seconds before I remember why. One minute I was kissing her, and the next—I was out of my mind.

Sometimes the panic's so bad that I leave my body for a while.

I should have gotten help for my anxiety a long time ago. But now? Someone will leak the story. I can see the headlines: "Dex Oliver: Insanely Hot or Just Insane?"

Fuck that.

I can't trust anyone to help me. I have no choice except to ride it out.

But I have to pull myself together now. I need Sunny to know the truth.

I can't live like this anymore.

I've been a mess since we started shooting this film. Not on set, of course. The acting part is going great. The problem is when we wrap for the night. The second I walk through the door of my apartment, I'm Ollie. Last night, in Sunny's bed, was the first time I've slept for more than a four-hour stretch in months.

I'd needed to see her so fucking badly. I was such a nervous wreck on the train ride from London that I actually walked into her apartment as Dex Oliver. I don't usually have to do that around her. I just haven't been myself in so goddamn long, I've practically forgotten what it's like. When I was kissing her in the foyer yesterday, I was convinced that if I didn't have her right away, the only genuine part of me might die. She's the antidote to everything that's wrong with me. All it takes is sharing the same air with her, and I breathe more deeply than I ever do when we're apart.

I was so happy today. Strolling the streets of Paris with the woman I've loved my whole life. I was myself again. There was no Ollie, no Dex. Just me and Sunny. The way it's supposed to be.

But then we got back to her place, and all I could think about was the fact that I'd have to leave her for London in the morning. And then what? I have no fucking clue when I'll see her again. I don't know what my life will look like after I make this film. All I know is that if I keep going down this road, I'm going to lose her.

It's already happening.

The more famous I get, the more I feel Sunny slipping away. And who can blame her? I cancel on her constantly. She has to go months without seeing me—unless, that is, she wants to turn on the TV and watch me all but fuck other women on screen. She claims it doesn't bother her, but I don't know if I believe it. It would destroy me to see Sunny with another man like that. Even if it weren't real.

Then there's the media. The paps. The tabloids.

Just being Dex was one thing—but I've created a monster.

How long will Sunny put up with me being Dex Oliver?

I've decided I don't want to know the answer.

"I'm lost without you," I tell her as I try to keep my breath steady. "I'm going to quit the movie. I'll move to Chicago, and we can be together after you graduate."

Sunny looks at me for several seconds, stunned. Then she shakes her head. "Dex, I know you're scared. You're on the cusp of something extraordinary. And your life's about to change. But you can't quit this movie—and *especially* not for me. You won't be happy doing anything else, and you'll regret it. You might even…resent me."

"I could never resent you, Sunny. You're my whole world," I plead. "I'm nothing without you."

Her eyes are glistening. "How do you think I'd feel if I let you give up the chance to be a movie star? You've been dreaming about this since you were a kid. And maybe you don't realize how spectacular you are, but most people who chase this dream never even come *close* to achieving it. You're so close, Dex… you're *so* close."

Maybe she has a point, but I don't care. My dream means nothing if I can't have her. "Sunny, if this movie is successful and my career takes off, how will it ever work between us? It's barely working now!"

She buries her face in her hands. I wrap my arms around her as she cries. "I know that you're hurting," I say into her beautiful hair. "I hear it in your voice whenever I have to cancel our plans. Or when it takes me forever to call you back, or when you see some bullshit story about me online. You're trying so hard not to show it, but I *know* you, Sunny. You're not happy. Let me fix this."

She pulls away, rolls off my lap, and sits facing me. Then she nods. "You're right. This *isn't* working. We're both miserable. Maybe we should take some time to focus on our careers…"

"Wait—what?" I stammer. "Are you serious? That's the exact opposite of what I'm suggesting!"

"What you're suggesting is preposterous, Dex! I cannot be the reason you give up your career. If you quit now, you'll never get a chance like this again. You'll be blacklisted. You committed to this movie, and you need to see it through. And I need to finish law school, and pass the bar exam, and…who knows, maybe in a year or two…"

She doesn't finish the sentence. She's trying to let me down easy, but I see what's happening.

She doesn't want me anymore.

I unraveled in front of her. I let her see what's underneath the act.

She's disgusted now. There's no way I'll get her back.

My eyes dart around the room, looking for something to ground me.

But all I can see is Sunny's life without me.

My hands are shaking. No, my entire body.

My heart, and soul, and the earth above me—

I know this feeling all too well.

There's *no exit* again, because I'm in hell.

I manage to get the words out, though I can hardly breathe.

"Sunny, tell me the truth—are you fucking Jeremy?"

Her eyes go wide. She gasps. "What? Dex, no! Jeremy's just a friend. There's *nothing* going on between us—"

"He's in love with you. He's gotta be. Every time I call you, you're with him. It's only a matter of time. If you don't already love him, you will. I know you will."

Sunny's practical. She'll choose Jeremy because he makes sense. They're going to be lawyers, living in the same city. They want the same things. It'll be so much easier for her to pick *him*.

"Dex…please," she sobs. "This has nothing to do with Jeremy.

You *have* to believe me."

I really wish I could.

I can't breathe.

But my mind keeps playing tricks on me.

I can't breathe.

I don't know what's real, and what's anxiety.

I can't breathe.

I can hardly make out what she's saying to me.

I can't breathe.

How many more times can I go through this before it kills me?

…

"Does this happen to you a lot?" she asks me when it's finally over.

I wipe the sweat off my brow and sigh. "Yeah," I tell her. "It does. Not as much when we're together. That's why I needed this weekend so badly, Sunny. I can only be my real self when I'm with you. When you're gone, I'm a disaster. I'm up all night panicking. You're my remedy Sunny. Or you *were*. But now I've lost you."

Her lip quivers. "I can't believe I didn't know. I remember you got upset like this when your dad was sick, but….I had no idea how much you've been suffering."

I shake my head. "I didn't want you to."

I didn't want her to see how fucked up I am and run away.

Exactly like she's doing now.

"Dex, I know you think I'm the solution to your anxiety, but I'm just a temporary fix. Have you…talked to anyone?" she asks me, wiping tears from her eyes. "Your doctor? Or a therapist?"

I look down at my lap. "When I was a kid. Not recently."

"You need to tell someone, Dex. You shouldn't have to live like this."

The pity on her face when she looks at me—it destroys any hope I've ever had that I can be the man she deserves.

I give up. Why try anymore? I'm pathetic.

I'm worse than pathetic—I'm Ollie. So I cry, like a child, in her arms.

She sobs with me. "Please promise me you'll get help," she says.

I know I won't. But I'd like to leave here with a shred of dignity, so I lie.

twenty-four

After nearly fourteen hours of travel from Paris Charles de Gaulle Airport—including a layover at JFK and an airport shuttle from Indianapolis—I'm finally back in Bloomington.

As luck would have it, Sam is in Indy for a friend's baby shower this weekend and called to see if I'd be up for a visitor. She said she'd be happy to drive an hour south to see me, especially considering it's the shortest distance we've been from one another since college. Shortly after we graduated, Sam left to tour Southeast Asia for the better part of a year, then moved to New York, where she's been working toward a PhD in philosophy at NYU.

Sam's phone call was a welcome surprise. My semester in Paris is over, and I've never felt so low in my life. I haven't seen Dex since we broke up three months ago. After he went back to London, I didn't leave my apartment for five whole days. I hardly left my bed. I barely ate. I slept to avoid the torture of being conscious, but then I'd dream of Dex kissing me, and holding me, and loving me, and I'd wake up sobbing. I told my professors I had the flu. I let myself have one week off from school to wallow, knowing full well that, afterward, I'd have to pick myself up and learn enough to pass the semester. Luckily I did. I already have a job offer from the firm where I summered—one of the best firms in Chicago—and I can't afford to lose it. My law career is the only thing I have going for me right now.

I've been looking forward to Sam's visit all day but, somehow, I managed to lose track of time in between watching old episodes of *Sex and the City* and eating cold leftover pizza. Now I'm scrambling to get out of my pajamas when she calls me from downstairs.

I buzz her into the building, throw on a sweater and a pair of jeans from my still-packed suitcase, and run to the door. I greet her with a huge smile on my face—which is mostly genuine since I'm excited to see her—but I dial it up a notch to make sure I don't look like I've been on the verge of tears all day.

Sam's eyes go wide when she sees me. "Oh my god, Sunny! You look so different!"

I run my fingers through my hair. "I know. I went to a salon in Paris and got it straightened before I left. I had them chop several inches off too."

Now, instead of curls cascading down my back, my hair is sleek and shoulder-length. I thought, maybe, if I came back to Indiana looking like a completely different person, it would help me see this chapter of my life as a fresh start. A new beginning, instead of a bitter ending. But, so far, my plan's fallen flat.

"Wow," she says as she reaches out to touch my silky hair. "It's beautiful. It'll take some time for my brain to adjust, because you don't look like Sunny without your curls, but you're gorgeous either way."

"Thanks," I say, smiling. I wrap my arms tightly around her. "I'm so happy you're here. It's been too long. Come in and have a seat. Do you want anything to drink? I have beer, wine—"

"Wine's great," she says as she sits on my couch. I pour two glasses of pinot noir and join her.

"I want to hear all about your PhD program," I tell her once we're settled.

Sam rolls her eyes. "Trust me, you don't. It'll bore you to tears. I mean, *I* absolutely love it—but if you're not a philosophy person, you probably won't want to hear about my research on metaphysical solipsism. It took a string of several bad first dates before I figured that out."

I laugh. "Okay, I'll take your word for it. I'm so happy you're enjoying it, though. You're going to be a kickass professor one day."

She smiles before taking a sip of her wine. "Thanks. What about *you*? How was Paris? Did you and Dex make love under the sparkling lights of the Eiffel Tower?" she teases while batting her eyelashes.

I bite my lip. "No, actually. We…broke up."

Her brows instantly knit together. She puts her glass down on the coffee table. "Oh, Sunny…" she says, placing her hand on my knee.

"He told me everything I was dying to hear, Sam. He said he'd quit the movie, give up his acting career, and move to

Chicago to be with me. But…I couldn't let him do it. I mean, he's dreamed of being a movie star his entire life."

She nods slowly. "I see your point. But why would he have to give up his career to be with you, anyway? Couldn't you take the California bar and find a job in LA? That way, even if he has to travel a lot, at least you'd have a homebase together."

I shake my head. "His schedule isn't the only thing that worries me. Fame changes people. It's already happening. The clothes he wears, the people he hangs out with. The regimented way he diets and exercises. He's not the Oliver Dexter I used to know."

And once the transformation is complete, he won't want me. He'll abandon me. Just like my father did. Like my mother, even, who was never around when I was growing up.

I can't sit around and watch Dex fall out of love with me. I'm already damaged as it is. *This* would break me. That's why I pulled the goddamn thread and broke us up.

"I'm so sorry," Sam says. "Are you guys still talking at all? How did you leave things?"

"I told him we should take some time to focus on our careers, and maybe in a year, or two…" I shrug. "I probably shouldn't have left things open like that, but I can't bear the thought of closing the door on us completely. I'd like to think there might be a chance for me and Dex down the road. Even if it's years from now."

She takes another drink of her wine when I realize I still haven't touched mine. I reach for my glass. "Anything's possible," she continues. "Maybe you'll reunite at a nursing home and have hot geriatric sex."

I almost spit out my pinot noir laughing. Sam's deadpan expression turns into a grin.

"I'm telling you, Sunny, my grandma's in a nursing home and she gets *plenty* of action. All the residents do. It's like being in college all over again, but better, because you can't get knocked up. STDs are rampant, though…" she adds with a frown.

I'm laughing so hard I'm crying. "Oh my gosh—Sam," I say, catching my breath. "I haven't laughed that much in a long time. I really needed that."

"That's what I'm here for," she says with a wink.

Just then, there's a knock at my door. I get off the couch, wiping tears from my eyes, my cheeks still warm from giggling. I look through the peephole.

It's Jeremy.

"Hey," I say as I swing open the door. "Long time no see."

He just stands there, in the doorframe, unsmiling and squinting his eyes at me.

"Um…Jeremy?" I ask, raising an eyebrow at him.

He shakes his head. "Hey. Hi. I—I barely recognized you."

"Oh." I run my fingers through my hair. "Yeah, I straightened it."

"Wow," he says, still serious. "Yeah, it's different." He blinks a few times. "Looks good." He presses his lips together and I try to determine if his expression is happy or neutral. It's hard to tell with Jeremy. I think I see a hint of an upward curl, but I'm not sure.

"Thanks," I say, tucking my hands into my back pockets.

I haven't seen Jeremy since before I left for Paris. We emailed all the time while I was abroad. Not about anything in particular, just little anecdotes back and forth about our days. I didn't tell him about my breakup, though. I probably would have—had I not witnessed the love of my life in a literal panic over my friendship with him. Now just being in the same room with Jeremy feels like a betrayal, regardless of the fact that Dex and I are no longer together.

"Well, welcome back," Jeremy says, giving me a hug.

For as much time as he and I have spent together over the past couple of years, you'd think we would have hugged before. But this is the first time.

"Hey," Sam says coming up behind me as Jeremy and I pull apart.

"Jeremy, this is my friend Sam, from college. Sam, this is Jeremy."

He briefly shifts his gaze to her. "Hey," he says, his micro-smile disappearing.

"Hey yourself," Sam replies in an unusually sweet tone. When I turn to look at her, she's flushed.

"I, um, sold some of my old law treatises to this first-year downstairs, so I was in the building," Jeremy explains as I turn to face him again. "Thought I'd stop by and see if you were back from Paris. And here you are."

"Here I am," I echo back. "Do you want to come in? Sam and I were just having some wine. You're welcome to join us."

I'd much prefer he didn't, under the circumstances. But it was nice of him to stop by, so I feel bad not asking. Plus, Jeremy's my closest friend in law school, and we study well together. I guess I'll have to get over this guilty feeling eventually.

He shakes his head. "I gotta get going, but thanks. I'll, um, see you in class? Monday?"

"Sounds good," I say as he waves goodbye.

As soon as I close the door, Sam grabs my shoulders and spins me to face her. "Sunny," she whispers. "What…the…fuck?"

I'm clueless. "Huh?"

She takes my hand and pulls me back to the couch. "*That's* Jeremy?" she asks when we're seated.

"Yes…" I respond slowly. I still have no idea where she's going with this.

She leans back against a throw pillow. "So you're telling me that's *the* Jeremy who's, like, a genius and stays up all night reading random textbooks?"

I chuckle. "That's him. Why?"

She shakes her head. "Because I was *not* prepared for him to look like that."

"What do you mean?" I ask.

"I mean, the way you described him—smartest guy in the class, lives at the library, studies *astronomy* for shits and giggles—I just figured he'd be a total nerd." She pauses. "I mean, we're all nerds, I suppose. But I thought he would *look* like a nerd."

I wait for her to continue, but she doesn't. "And? What does he look like?"

"Are you kidding me, Sunny? He's FUCKING HOT!"

I tilt my head. "*Jeremy?*"

"Oh my god." Sam buries her face in her hands and takes a deep breath before looking at me again. "Are you blind?" she asks, now laughing at me.

I give a sheepish shrug. "I just don't think about him that way, I guess."

"How is that even possible? He is sexy as *hell*. You must have had blinders on while you and Dex were together."

I frown. "Probably."

She takes a sip of wine. "And they *are* night and day different. Jeremy's more rugged. He looks like he has an edge to him. Like he'd bend you over a desk and—"

"Okay, Sam—I get it," I say, reaching for her hand. "I don't need that image in my mind."

She gives me a disapproving look. "What you *need* is to get over Dex. And you can do that by getting *under* Jeremy. I'm pretty sure I picked up on a vibe from him too."

"No," I say adamantly, searching for my wine glass. I find it on the floor, next to my feet, and take a sip. "There was no vibe. I think he was just thrown off by my straight hair. I'll admit he was acting a little weird…but we haven't seen each other in months. And Jeremy's not really known for his social graces." I laugh. "Most people in our class can't stand him—they think he's arrogant."

Sam smiles. "Well, it looks like he's got the goods to back it up. Just keep an open mind, Sunny, that's all I'm saying."

I breathe out heavily. "That's not going to happen. *Ever.* For one thing, I'm not attracted to him. For another, he has a girlfriend—"

She rolls her eyes. "Of course he does. They could break up, though…"

"But most importantly," I continue, ignoring her last thought,

"I couldn't do that to Dex. He felt threatened by my friendship with Jeremy. He even asked me if I was cheating on him."

Sam's eyes widen. "The plot thickens."

I take another sip of wine. "Yeah."

"Well, keep me posted. And if this love triangle ends with Jeremy and Dex dueling for the honor of your hand, please let me know so I can be there to watch."

I smirk. "Who would you root for?"

She scratches her head. "Hmm. *You*, of course! I'll always be rooting for you to be happy."

My eyes tear up. I give her a hug. "Thanks, Sam." When I pull away, I spot her empty wine glass. "Do you want a refill?"

She winces. "I shouldn't. I actually have to get some work done tonight. I know it's lame. I brought my laptop."

"Hey, I totally get it. This isn't college anymore. We're in the big leagues now. Do you want to work in my bedroom? You can sleep in my bed tonight too. I'll take the couch."

"Are you sure? I'm happy to stay out here."

"Don't worry about it. I fall asleep studying on this couch all the time. I'm used to it."

She laughs. "Thank you."

But long after she goes to sleep, I'm still lying awake, staring at the ceiling. Talking to Sam about Paris, and reliving that last night with Dex, has my mind spiraling.

Dex's panic attack terrified me. I was so worried about him.

I still am. It keeps me up at night, sometimes.

We may not be together anymore, but I will never not love him.

I need to know that he's okay.

I turn to face my cell phone, sitting on the coffee table. Then I pick it up and call him. He answers on the first ring.

"Hey," he says, surprised.

"Hi." I bite my lip. "I hope I'm not calling too late."

"It's fine. I was awake."

"Did you finish making the movie?"

I hear him smile. "Yeah. I did."

"How did it go?"

"I'm proud of it, Sunny. I'm glad I didn't quit. You were right. Thank you."

I nod silently.

Dex clears his throat. "I also wanted to say—I'm sorry."

I shake my head. "You have nothing to be sorry for."

"I didn't mean to scare you in Paris. I was just going through a hard time. But I got back to LA a couple of weeks ago and started therapy. I'm already feeling a lot better."

"Really?"

"Yeah. I'm getting help. Like I promised I would."

I sigh. "Good. I'm relieved to hear that. And…I'm always here for you, no matter what. I hope you know that."

"I do. Same here."

"Okay," I say softly. "Thank you."

"Are you back in Indiana?"

"Yeah. I start classes on Monday. I can't believe it's my last semester."

"Good luck. I know you'll knock 'em dead."

"Thanks, Dex."

For a moment, we're quiet. I close my eyes and revel in it. Just me and him, breathing.

"Thanks for calling, Sunny."

It's a less dramatic goodbye than the one we had in Paris.

But I still have trouble falling asleep.

twenty-five

SUNNY
JANUARY 2006

I slide into our usual booth in the back of the bar.

"Sorry I'm late. The new partner walked into my office at five o'clock and asked me to do some *quick* research for him," I say, using air quotes. "An hour tops, he promised me. It ended up taking three."

I pull off my knit hat and unwrap the blanket scarf I layer over my wool coat—which I decide to keep on since I'm chilled to the bone. I then unwind the thinner cashmere scarf I wear when the windchill hits below zero, and stuff all my winter accessories into my work tote. "Also, I *hate* Chicago in January. Why do we live here?"

Sitting across from me, Jeremy barely looks up from his legal pad as he's writing. "Because we graduated at the top of our class, and now we're litigation associates at the two best firms in the city, making six-figure salaries."

I roll my eyes. "I still can't believe I chose to be a litigator. Every research assignment I get has to be done *right away*, for some emergency motion the partner wants in his back pocket, but probably won't end up filing. Yet I have to drop everything to get it done, regardless."

"Litigation is a high-stakes game," he says, looking over his notes with a furrowed brow. "That's what makes it fun." Finally, he clicks his retractable pen and sets it down, then pushes a basket of French fries toward me. "Here—I ordered you some food. I know you get hangry when you work late. And your vodka soda is on its way."

I smile wide as I grab a fistful of fries. "You know me so well. Thanks, Jeremy."

"That's what friends are for," he says, putting his pen and pad into his briefcase.

"Are you going to sing to me now?" I tease before I happily bite into a fry.

He smirks.

"So how was *your* day? I ask.

"Pretty good, actually. Dave—you know—"

"Head of litigation?"

Jeremy nods. "Yeah. He asked me to be second chair for this trial he has coming up in a few weeks."

My eyes go wide. "No way! You're a first-year associate! You've only been at the firm, like, six months!"

"I know," he says after taking a sip of his beer. "I'll be working my ass off to prep for this thing. Dave said if I play my cards right, he might even let me do a cross-examination."

"Wow," I say, stunned. "Meanwhile, I *still* haven't set foot inside a courtroom. Not that I mind. I'd much rather do legal research and writing all day."

"That's what you excel at. We all have our strengths."

I dip a fry in ketchup. "Well, the head of *my* litigation department did call me a 'star researcher' last week. Best in the firm, he said."

"*Of course* you are," Jeremy responds, as if to say this isn't news to him.

"I guess that's why I keep getting slammed with assignments," I continue, sighing heavily.

"Well, it'll pay off in the long run. You'll be on the fast track to partner in no time."

I shrug. "We'll see."

I have to take this litigation job one day at a time so I don't get overwhelmed. So far I don't hate it—but I also spend most of my time behind a computer, which is my comfort zone. At some point, they're going to send me to court, and the mere idea makes me feel sick to my stomach.

"Here's your vodka soda," our waitress says as she places my drink in front of me. "Can I get you guys anything else right now?"

Jeremy and I exchange a glance.

"We're good," he says.

The waitress leaves and I take a sip of my drink.

That's when I see him—*Dex Oliver.*

On the TV screen behind Jeremy.

"Oh no, not again," I sigh out. I set my drink down and bury my forehead in my arms, which are crossed in front of me on the table. When I look up several seconds later, Jeremy's staring at the screen behind him.

He turns to face me. "Sunny," he says as gently as he's capable of. "It's been over a year."

I lean back against the squeaky vinyl and shake my head. "I know. But how am I supposed to get over him when he's literally *everywhere*? At the movies, on TV…on billboards, and magazines. He's the breakout star of last summer's highest-grossing movie, for fuck's sake."

Jeremy shifts forward in his seat. "And that's why you ended things with him. Because you don't want your life to be swallowed up by his fame."

I put my head in my hands. "I guess."

That, and the fact that I'm convinced I'm not good enough to be famous Dex Oliver's girlfriend.

"Remember what that partner at your firm said—you're a star too. You deserve much better than to live in someone else's shadow."

I bite my lip. "That's really sweet…thank you."

It's the nicest thing Jeremy's ever said to me.

I take another sip of my drink. "I know I have to move on. It's just a lot easier said than done. I mean, how would you like it if you saw *your* ex half-naked on the cover of every entertainment magazine?"

He considers my question for half a second. "I wouldn't care."

I roll my eyes. "That's bullshit. You and Anjali were together for years. Weren't you guys talking about getting married?"

"You mean *before* she fucked that cardiology resident?"

I wince. "I'm sorry she hurt you. I guess it's better to find out she's a cheater now than when you're married, though."

Jeremy sighs. "It was six months ago. I'm over it. And honestly?

I don't think we would have ended up getting married anyway."

"Really?"

"Nah. We weren't as compatible as we could be. It just took us longer to realize because we were long-distance."

I nod as I dip a pair of fries in ketchup.

Jeremy grabs a fry for himself. "You wanna know why you're not over Mr. Hollywood yet?"

I cross my arms over my chest and try not to roll my eyes again. "Sure. Enlighten me."

He finishes chewing. "It's because you haven't slept with anyone since him. You'll go on, like, two dates with a guy—*maybe* let him feel you up—then when he asks you for another date, you say you're busy with work, and he never hears from you again."

Suddenly, I'm sweating. I shrug off my wool coat and drain the dregs of my vodka soda. "I definitely need more liquor if we're having this conversation," I say, mostly to myself. I call over our waitress and ask for another.

"Make it two," says Jeremy.

"At least I'm putting myself out there," I tell him. "I've been on tons of dates since I moved to Chicago. It's not my fault there's never any chemistry."

"There's never any chemistry because you're meeting men online. You know what kind of men sign up for online dating? Men who have no game."

The waitress arrives with our drinks.

"Oh, thank god," I say and immediately swallow a third of mine.

"Sunny, you don't need to work that hard to get laid. Just find an attractive guy at a bar, go up and introduce yourself, and that's it. Your dry spell will be over before you know it."

I set my glass down on the table a bit more forcefully than I intended to. "Okay. If we're really going to talk about my sex life right now, then I should probably set the record straight. My dry spell is over…I slept with Sebastian last week."

Jeremy squints at me. "Who the fuck is Sebastian?"

I give an exasperated sigh. "That guy I met in the elevator at work, remember? Like, a month ago?"

"Oh yeah. The finance guy. He asked you out for drinks." Jeremy finishes his beer and starts sipping his vodka soda.

I nod. "We went out a few times, and he was nice. Good-looking…seemed to have his shit together. So I figured, why not?"

"And?"

"It was…hmm, how do I describe it? I want to make sure I do it justice." I pause to gulp down more of my drink. "*Mediocre.* That's it. It was mediocre."

Jeremy laughs hard at this—I knew he would. He's wiping tears from his eyes. "That bad, huh?" he says when he recovers.

"It was the worst sex of my life." I finish what's left of my drink and take a sip of Jeremy's. I look around to make sure Finance Guy's not here, then lower my voice to a whisper. "He couldn't…stay hard, you know? And he kept apologizing, and blaming it on the condom, but then he tried going down on me, and *that* was…" I shudder. "He had no idea what he was doing. Eventually I just told him to stop."

"Man. I'm sorry." Jeremy drags a hand down his chin. "I guess you have no choice but to get back on the horse and try again."

He stifles a laugh.

I ignore his pun and shake my head. "Absolutely not. This was a major setback for me. I waited over a year after my breakup to sleep with someone. And my first time back in the *saddle*"—Jeremy winks at me, pleased that I acknowledged his joke—"was awful. Do you know how depressing that is?" I sigh. "I don't think I'll ever connect with anyone the way I connected with Dex."

"You had intense feelings for him, Sunny. That's why the sex was so good. But one day, you'll have intense feelings for someone else." Jeremy runs a hand through his hair. "Dex isn't the be-all end-all. You'll find someone whose life is more compatible with yours, and you'll get your happily ever after. Like those sappy romance novels you love to read."

I crack a smile. "They're not sappy."

"Yes, they are."

"How would *you* know?" I ask, taking another sip of his drink.

He leans back in his booth. "I picked one up at the library the other day."

My jaw drops. "You're kidding, right?"

He shrugs. "I was curious."

"Which one did you get?" I ask, propping my elbows on the table and leaning toward him.

"I don't know, Sunny. Some…beach romance about two friends who end up fucking one summer, then their lives change forever."

I laugh. "That literally describes 75 percent of the books I've read."

"I feel sorry for you," he says with a raised eyebrow.

"Well, not everyone enjoys *astrophysics* the way you do," I tease.

Jeremy smirks. "You're never going to let me live that down."

"I mean—who brags about reading astrophysics for fun within five seconds of meeting someone?"

He smiles with his eyes. "I'm a pretentious asshole, I know. Yet, here you are three-and-a-half years later, so…you must see something underneath my stony exterior."

I shake my head. "You're not stony, Jeremy."

"But I'm not the sensitive, guitar-playing type from those terrible books you read, either."

"Most of them aren't terrible. You know…I used to dream of writing romance novels. Feels like a long time ago, now."

"You're a great writer, Sunny. You could probably write the next Great American Novel if you wanted to. Why limit yourself? Leave the romance-writing to the miserable trophy wives whose CEO husbands can't get it up."

I chortle. "You sound like my mom. And *please* don't joke about men who can't get it up."

He laughs. "Speaking of your mom, tell her I said hi."

I shake my head and smile. Jeremy and I have this running joke that my mom's obsessed with him—because she is. She's never met him, but they once had a lengthy phone conversation when he and I were celebrating after we passed the bar exam. I was several beers in and too tipsy to talk to her, so I handed him my phone, and they talked for no less than a half hour about some study he'd come across while reading the *New England Journal of Medicine*.

As I'm polishing off the last of my fries, a young woman comes up to our table and looks at me first, then Jeremy. "Um, hi," she says to him.

It takes a second before a wave of recognition washes over his face. "Hey, there. How's it going?"

She glances back at me, then at Jeremy again. "Good," she says, tucking a strand of hair behind her ear.

When she examines me a third time, I put the pieces together. "Hey, I'm Sunny," I tell her. "Jeremy's friend."

She instantly looks relieved. "Oh, great! Hi." Then she turns back to Jeremy. "I um, had fun hanging out the other week. We should do it again," she says.

He nods. "Yeah, definitely. I'll call you."

"Cool." She smiles at both of us, then walks away.

I try hard to suppress a smirk, but it's not working.

"What's so funny?"

"Come on, Jeremy. Is she even old enough to drink?"

He rolls his eyes. "She's a senior in college, thank you very much. Goes to…DePaul, maybe? I don't know. Somewhere local."

"Wow. You seem really into her," I joke. "What's she studying?"

"Communications?"

I snort. "Do you even know her name?"

"I'm almost positive it's Nicole."

"You really should go back to dating women your own age." I take one more sip of his vodka soda and pass it back to him. "Was the sex good, at least?"

He finishes his drink. "It wasn't mediocre."

I can't help but laugh. "That's a low blow."

"I'm sorry, I couldn't resist. But, hey—if you want to find someone more appropriate for me to date, be my guest. You can be my wingwoman the next time we go out."

"Why wait?" I say, looking around the bar. "I bet I can find someone for you right now."

He chuckles. "If you say so. Maybe I should tell you what I'm looking for first—"

"No need. I know your type," I say, turning back to him.

"Is that right?" He leans back with one arm stretched over the top of the booth.

I nod. "Pretty brunette with big, brown eyes. Thin…but also a little curvy."

Jeremy micro-smiles.

"What? I'm right, aren't I?"

"You're not wrong," he says with a gleam in his eye. "You also just described yourself."

My cheeks heat up, but I hold my ground. "More importantly, I described Anjali and *Nicole*, or whoever that girl was. Not to mention the woman who was leaving your apartment when I came over last Sunday, and the one who gave you her number at Millennium Park—"

"Okay, okay," he concedes. "Fair enough. So, do you see anyone here who fits the bill?"

I look around again. Obviously there are plenty of attractive brunettes in the bar.

But none of them look quite right for Jeremy.

"Sorry." I shrug. "Maybe next time."

He pulls his wallet out of his pocket and leaves a stack of bills on the table. "No worries. I have to be up early tomorrow for trial prep, anyway. You ready to go?"

I nod. "Yeah. Thanks for the drinks—and fries. My treat next time."

I bundle myself back up before we head outside. When we step onto the icy sidewalk, I hail an approaching cab.

Jeremy opens the door for me. "Text me when you get back to your apartment, okay?"

"I always do," I say. "See you tomorrow?"

He nods. "Same time and place." Before I get in the cab, he takes a step toward me and kisses me on the cheek.

He's never done that before.

twenty-six

DEX

I'm at a party at Leo's house when it happens: Ava Elwood spots me from across the room and smiles.

I'm six months into my new life, and it still feels surreal. Here I am inside the mansion of one of the finest actors of our generation—someone I've looked up to since I was a kid—and he's actually praising *my* acting skills. He says he sees a little of himself in me. These are the moments where I have to pinch myself to make sure I'm not dreaming.

When Ava walks up to us, she gives Leo a kiss on the cheek. I'm pretty sure they dated years ago. I remember seeing pictures of them in the tabloids. Not that it means much. I've been in this business a short time, but long enough to know that Hollywood relationships aren't always what they seem. In the past few months, my publicist, Wendy, has orchestrated a media frenzy of speculation over which A-list celebrity I'm dating. The truth is, I'm not seeing anyone. But every other week, Wendy will work out a deal with one of her publicist friends, where I get photographed with an actress doing something completely mundane, like going for a walk with coffee. It's a win-win situation for everyone involved, she tells me. Since I'm new to this industry, being linked to someone with an established career boosts my credibility. And the actress I'm spotted with automatically becomes sexier, supposedly, because she's caught the eye of the "new hot thing."

Yes, Wendy refers to me as a *thing*.

Ava turns from Leo to me, then takes my hand, which is surprising considering I've never met her. "Mind if I steal him for a few minutes?" she asks our host.

"Be my guest." He gives me a pat on the shoulder. "Call me next week. We'll have lunch."

When he walks away, Ava gently squeezes my fingers. "Come outside with me. It's too hot in here."

She leads me through the crowd of famous faces, through sliding doors, and out to the pool. It's January in LA, and the air is cool, so there aren't many people out here.

She reclines on a lounge chair, and I take the one next to her. I'm trying my best not to stare, but this is *Ava Elwood*—the supermodel known for her striking red hair and bright blue eyes. She's even more stunning in person.

"I have a confession to make," she says, pulling at the hem of her black mini dress, which covers almost nothing.

I raise an eyebrow. "Oh yeah? What's that."

Her cheeks turn pink. "I've had a crush on you since you were on *Passions*."

I look down at my shoes—brand-new designer shoes that I didn't pay a cent for—and laugh.

"It's true," she says. "I never missed an episode."

I meet her gaze. "That's very flattering. Thank you."

She giggles, her signature scarlet ponytail swinging behind her. "I'm sorry, I'm not very good at this…"

I tilt my head. "Good at what?"

"I can't remember the last time I asked a guy out. It's usually the other way around, but…" She bats her eyelashes at me. "Word on the street is, you play hard to get, Dex Oliver."

I sit up and bring my legs over the side of the lounge chair so I'm facing her. "Is that right?" I ask with a playful smile.

She laughs and crosses one red-soled snakeskin heel over the other. "I mean, you turned down a Victoria's Secret Angel. *Who* does that?"

I drag a hand down my chin. "Oh, man. She told you about that?"

Ava shakes her head and adjusts the diamond bracelet glittering on her wrist. It almost blinds me. "I don't know Caterina well. I heard it through the rumor mill. But it must be true, judging by your reaction."

I sigh. "I didn't mean to hurt her feelings. I had an early flight the next morning."

Truth is, there was no early flight. But I don't think Caterina would have believed me if I'd told her I'm waiting for the goddamn stars to align so I can be with the woman I've loved since we were kids.

It's been over a year since Sunny broke up with me, and I'm just as hung up on her now as I was on the train back to London. I've slept with a fair number of women since then, but I don't see the point in letting things progress past casual sex. On the other hand, I don't know how many more notches I can add to my bedpost without developing a reputation—especially now that my career's taking off, and my social life makes for great headlines. That's why I told Caterina I couldn't go home with her.

Wendy says, the more women I screw, the better. She's blunt like that. She insists it'll only make me more desirable, which means more money for us both. But I don't want to be *that guy*. I'm not that guy. I want to be in a relationship more than anything on this earth. But the woman I want doesn't want me. She made that clear in Paris.

We call or text every now and then. But all we talk about is work. She asks me what it's like to be a movie star, and I tell her the truth, except for how goddamn lonely it is. And I ask about her life, and she tells me absolutely everything *except* what I really want to know—which is whether or not she's dating Jeremy. She doesn't mention him at all, which I'm pretty fucking sure means she's in love with him and would rather not tell me. In case I lose my shit again.

Sunny's the only woman in the world I want by my side.

And now I'm pretty much fucked no matter what I do. My choices are basically to be celibate, sleep around…or date someone knowing full well that I'll probably never fall in love with them. None of these options sound appealing.

I'm not going to tell Ava Elwood that, of course. But it's obvious she can see through my bullshit. She's looking at me with one perfectly waxed eyebrow raised.

"Early flights are the oldest excuse in the book," she says

with a laugh. "You're an amazing actor, Dex. I'm sure you can come up with a better lie for when you don't want to go to bed with someone."

I fix my eyes on hers and give her my sincerest smile. "It wasn't like that. I swear."

She sits up and faces me, crossing one infinitely long leg over the other. "So you wouldn't use that excuse on me if I asked you?"

I blink at her.

"Not to bed," she says, turning pink again. "I want to take you to dinner." She leans forward, her knees now gently resting against mine. "And we'll see where things go from there."

The way she's folding her arms to push her breasts together, I have a pretty clear picture of where she wants things to go.

I'm stuck. I don't think I can say no—not to Ava Elwood. No man in his right mind would reject her, so what would it say about me if *I* did? This is my world now, and I need to do my best to fit in. If I keep playing "hard to get," as Ava said, I might lose any edge I have by being labeled the "new hot thing" in this town.

"I'd be happy to have dinner with you," I say. From what I know about Ava, she has a short attention span. We'll probably go out a few times, then she'll move on to the next guy.

"Fantastic. Let's look at our calendars." She's beaming as she opens the app on her cell phone. "I'm leaving for Tokyo tomorrow, but I'll be back the following week. How about you?"

I check my phone. "I'm in New York that week. How about the following Friday?"

She smiles. "It's a date."

After we exchange numbers, she tells me she has to head home to pack for her trip to Japan.

But before she gets up to leave, she leans in and plants her ruby lips on me.

Three weeks later, Ava and I meet for dinner in the private room of a Michelin-starred sushi spot. We have *a lot* of sake and very little food. The chef prepares us a special low-carb meal, per Ava's request. I'm getting used to eating this way, but I still fucking hate it. It's also a lot harder to stick to this diet when I drink. I'm always tempted to order a pizza as soon as I get through my front door—something to soak up the alcohol.

But I doubt I'll be going back to my place tonight.

Ava Elwood wants me. She's been explicit about that since her first cup of sake.

And I have to admit, I'm having a good time with her. She's a lot smarter than people give her credit for. If she hadn't been discovered at a mall in her hometown of Lincoln, Nebraska when she was fifteen, she would have liked to be a doctor. Her parents only allowed her to start modeling if she agreed to finish high school and apply to college. She actually got into Princeton, but deferred admission because her career was heating up. Once she was offered a modeling contract with one of the top agencies in the world, she never looked back. Now she uses her smarts to parlay her fame into successful business ventures, like her fashion and cosmetics lines.

After dinner, she takes me home with her. Before I know it, she's lying on her bed naked, her fire-red hair splayed across her white silk pillowcase, like flames. I'm about to grab a condom from my wallet when she stops me.

"We can't use condoms," she says breathlessly. "I'm allergic to latex."

"Oh."

"But I'm on birth control," she adds, reaching into her nightstand. She pulls out a pack of pills to show me. "See? Today's Friday, and I took my pill this morning. I *never* miss a day. If I get pregnant right now, it'll kill my career."

I hesitate.

There's only one woman I've never *not* used condoms with. My heart aches thinking about how different it was with her. How right it felt being intertwined with her, like two puzzle pieces clicking together.

How meaningful it was. Not just a random physical act, but two hearts melding.

God, I'm a sap.

But I really fucking miss Sunny.

"Dex?"

Dammit. I haven't answered Ava yet.

"I'm sorry about this," she continues. "I know it's not ideal. But I got tested a few days ago, and everything came back negative. I have the results on my phone, so I can show you—"

"No, it's fine," I assure her with a smile. "But I should get tested too. Let's wait a few days."

Ava groans and covers her face with her palms, but I can still see her crimson lips, and she's smiling. "Okay, I'll be patient. I've been waiting for this moment since you were on the cover of *Soap Opera Digest*, so what's another few days?" She puts her arms around my neck and kisses me, then whispers, "I just want you so much."

"Well maybe there's something I can do about that," I say. Then I shift down the bed and start kissing her inner thighs.

Two months later, it's Ava's thirtieth birthday, and she invites me to Saint-Tropez for a long weekend to celebrate, just the two of us. It's still early, but I've decided to give this relationship a shot. Ava's bright and motivated. Beautiful, obviously. Maybe, with time, I could develop feelings for her. I know I'll never love anyone the way I love Sunny. But Ava and I might be a good match.

We have similar lifestyles, anyway. That's something.

Saint-Tropez is fun, and relaxing, and a welcome change from LA. But on our second day there, the paps catch us kissing on the balcony of our hotel suite. Ava's topless, her back turned to the camera. I'm wearing a towel around my waist, my arms wrapped around her. The press has a fucking field day. There've been rumors swirling about us for weeks, and now the world has the proof it's been waiting for. The pictures are everywhere. The news articles are salacious, with headlines like: "Ava and Dex have Steamy Sex in Saint-Tropez." They've branded us the world's sexiest couple. I can't help wondering what Sunny thinks about all this. Or if she even cares.

Ava, on the other hand, is thrilled. She's been feeling uneasy about what turning thirty means for her modeling career but, according to her, sleeping with a man who's four years younger is confirmation she's "still fuckable."

When we get back from our trip, she asks me to come home with her. She's leaving for New York in a few days and wants to spend as much time together as possible. We're both exhausted from the long flight and, after a quick shower, we crash on her bed. But in the middle of the night, she wakes me.

"Dex—something's wrong," she says.

I reach for the lamp on my nightstand and click on the light. When I turn to Ava, she's doubled over, wincing.

I sit up and shift closer to her in bed. "Where does it hurt?"

"My chest…my stomach. I've never experienced anything like this before." She shows me her trembling fingers. "The pain's so bad, I'm shaking."

"Let's get you to the hospital," I say, rubbing her back. Her skin is flushed, and her eyes are wide, and I can tell she's terrified. I've been there before—so many times.

She shakes her head. "I have someone who'll come to the house. His name is Dr. Keller." She clutches her stomach and winces again. "Can you call him?"

I nod.

"Just promise me you'll stay for the exam, okay? I really don't want to be alone right now."

"Of course, Ava. Don't worry, I'm not going anywhere."

She attempts a smile and hands me her phone.

I call Dr. Keller, and he arrives less than twenty minutes later.

When I bring him to Ava's room, he sits on the edge of the bed to examine her.

"Could you be pregnant?" he asks as he feels her abdomen.

Ava looks at me, and her eyes fill with tears. She bites her lip, worriedly.

I feel so bad for her. She must be in such terrible pain that she's panicking and can't think straight. Of course she isn't pregnant—she's on the pill.

Right?

"Ava?" I ask when she continues looking at me, avoiding her doctor's question.

Finally, she turns to him. "Um…I don't know," she says. "It's possible."

My heart picks up speed.

"When was your last menstrual period?" Dr. Keller asks her.

"Well…my periods are kind of all over the place," she says. "But I really think this is just an upset stomach. Food poisoning, maybe." She shifts her position in bed and gasps from the pain.

"Are you still taking hormonal birth control?" the doctor continues, looking at her chart.

Ava just blinks at him without answering. There are beads of sweat on her brow. She looks like she's going to be sick. "Excuse me," she says, covering her mouth. Then she runs to the bathroom and, seconds later, we hear her throw up.

"I'm going to look in on her," Dr. Keller says to me. When he enters the bathroom, Ava closes the door behind him. I hear them whispering, but I can't make out what they're saying.

I take deep breaths.

I pace the room.

What the fuck is going on? Could Ava really be pregnant?

I walk over to her nightstand, where she keeps her birth control pills. I find the pack and open it. Maybe I'm crazy, but it looks exactly the same as when she showed it to me after our first date. Half of the pills are taken, and the last one she took was on a Friday. Today's Tuesday. So the best case scenario is she's skipped a few days.

But the worst case…

I sit on the bed again and try to wait patiently. Try to ignore the fact that my vision's getting hazy.

Dr. Keller comes back into the room and suggests we give Ava a few minutes alone. Waiting for her to come out of the bathroom is torture. I'm convinced the doctor can hear my heart hammering from across the room, where he's writing notes in her chart.

Finally, the bathroom door creaks open, and Ava walks out.

She's holding a pregnancy test in her hand.

"It's negative," she tells me, mere seconds before I start hyperventilating.

She gets back in bed, and Dr. Keller completes his physical exam.

"I feel a lot better after throwing up," she says to him. "It must have been food poisoning." She turns and gives me a tentative smile, like she's trying to gauge how upset I am.

I honestly don't know what the fuck to feel—but I'm not having this conversation with Ava until we're alone. I can't react like a normal person would in this scenario, because I'm not a normal person. I'm *Dex Oliver*. My life isn't mine anymore. It's entertainment. This doctor might be the most trustworthy person on the planet—but one of Ava's staff could be listening outside the door, for all I know. She has twenty-four-seven security at her home after a disturbing experience with a stalker a couple of years ago.

No, there's no such thing as privacy when you're a celebrity. So I do what I do best. I act. I play the role of the devoted boyfriend who's taking everything in stride. *Not* the one who's fucking freaking out because the world-famous supermodel he's been sleeping with for two months tried to trick him into knocking her up.

"Based on the rapid onset of your symptoms, and the duration and location of the pain, I believe you had a gallbladder attack," Dr. Keller says. "Attacks are triggered by foods that are high in fat. Now, I know you keep a strict diet—"

"I cheated this weekend," Ava tells him. "We were in Saint-Tropez, and I ate cheese, and…" She looks over at me. "We had *ice cream*." She whispers the words with complete and utter shame, like she's confessing to a felony.

The doctor nods. "We'll do an ultrasound first thing in the morning to confirm. In the meantime, sticking to low-fat foods should prevent another attack. But call me if your symptoms return."

"Thank you, Dr. Keller," I say, standing up to walk him out.

When I get back to Ava's bedroom, her eyes are pleading. "Dex, let me explain. This isn't what you think, I promise."

I sit beside her on the edge of the bed, my body turned to face her. "What the fuck is going on, Ava?" I ask, my voice thin and raspy. I'm exhausted, and desperate for an answer that doesn't make her as diabolical as I fear.

"Nothing, Dex, I swear. Dr. Keller just freaked me out with all those questions about pregnancy. Birth control pills aren't 100 percent effective—even when you take them religiously—so my mind started spinning, and I thought maybe there was a slight chance, that's all. I keep some tests in my medicine cabinet and wanted to take one to be sure."

My heart sinks. I prop my elbows on my knees and let my forehead rest on my palms.

"What's the matter, Dex?"

I turn to her and sigh. "I found your birth control pills in your drawer, Ava. You haven't been taking them."

Her eyes widen. "No," she says, shaking her head. "No, Dex, you have it all wrong. That's an old prescription. I switched pills a while ago."

"Prove it," I say. "Where's the new pack?"

Ava coils her fiery hair on top of her head and secures it with an elastic band. I can tell by the way her eyes shift back and forth that she's thinking. Finally, she shrugs. "It must be in my luggage somewhere."

I turn to her packed suitcases, stacked in a corner of her bedroom. I walk toward them, then start to unzip the one on top.

"Dex, wait—"

When I look back at her, she's crying. I watch as she sweeps her long manicured fingers over her eyes, wiping tears from them. "Okay, fine. I lied. But…let me explain." She bites her lip. "I'm in love with you, Dex."

My fingers start tingling.

"We *belong* together," she continues. "Can't you see it? I mean, we're the two most beautiful people in the world. Would it be so terrible if we had a baby?"

The room's spinning. I sit in a chair across from her bed and close my eyes. "You tried to trick me into fathering a child," I say after a minute. "Don't you see how fucked up that is?" I pause for a beat, then shake my head. "You were insatiable, too. You were all over me, morning, noon, and night. Now it makes sense. You just wanted to get pregnant."

She sighs. "I think you're missing the point here, Dex. I *love* you."

My palms are sweating. I can't speak. All I can do is stare at her. Time starts to slow, and I don't know how long I'm silent for.

Her eyes narrow, and her expression hardens. "Dex, what the fuck? Why aren't you saying anything?"

My chest tightens.

I need to get out of here. At this point, I'll say anything to end this conversation, so I can go home. She's not going to listen to reason, anyway.

"Look, Ava," I tell her. "We haven't been together that long. You might think you love me, but…I don't think we're there yet."

"Are you fucking kidding me?" she snaps. "I tell you I love you and *that's* your response?"

I stand and start pacing the room again. My stomach's churning.

"Do you know how many men would *kill* to be in your shoes, Dex Oliver?" she hisses.

Shit. My hands are shaking. I shove them into the pockets of my $300 sweatpants and hope she doesn't see what's happening to me.

When I look back at Ava, I search her face for a hint of the woman I met at Leo's party that night. But I don't recognize her at all. She's morphed into a different being right before my eyes. Something vile, and poisonous.

"Look," she says, shaking her head. "I'm sorry I lied. I just really want a baby, Dex. And I can't have a baby with just *anyone*. I'm *Ava Elwood*, for fuck's sake."

I gaze at her, dumbstruck.

"And you have to admit, our kids would be gorgeous," she adds, her eyes softening again.

I'm barely breathing. "I've gotta go."

"Dex, no! *Please* stay." She slithers out of bed and across the room to where I'm standing. "Let's get a good night's sleep, and we can talk about this with clear heads in the morning."

I turn away from her. "Ava, there's nothing you can say that will make this right. I need to sleep in my own bed tonight."

Fuck. I'm rhyming.

I don't remember packing my things or putting my suitcase in my car. I barely remember driving myself home, but here I am.

The moment I lock the door behind me, I collapse.

That fiery hair...the way she hissed...and that venomous look in her eyes.

I've been pierced by a viper. It's not just anxiety this time.

I see the headlines: "Dex Oliver Dies of Stress-Induced Heart Attack."

Too bad I never got help for that.

I promised Sunny I was fine.

I told her I was seeing a therapist, but I lied.

And now I'm dying—

I'm dying.

I'm dying.

I'm dying.

…

I wake up in a heap by my front door. The sun's streaming in.

I guess I lived to see another day.

I peel myself off the floor and stand facing the mirror. My troubled eyes and quivering lips are a dead giveaway—

I'm a fucking mess.

I take my phone out of my pocket and open up my contacts. I consider calling Sunny. I consider calling my doctor, to finally ask for help.

But instead, I choose what I always do. I fix my mask.

I smile with my eyes, and I flash my movie-star grin.

I let Dex Oliver take it from here.

twenty-seven

SUNNY

MARCH 2006

"**A**va and Dex have Steamy Sex in Saint-Tropez."

It's a gloomy Monday morning and I'm at work, taking a quick break from legal research to browse news stories on my computer, when I see the headline.

I barely make it to the bathroom before I throw up.

I can't shake the image from my mind. Ava Elwood's long legs, wrapped around the love of my life, while he's fucking her.

I have no right to be upset—I know that.

I'm the one who broke up with him.

And now he's with the most beautiful woman in the world. I shouldn't be surprised. This is why I let him go. If he can have Ava Elwood, why the hell would he ever want me?

No, Ava and Dex belong together. She's the epitome of perfection, exactly like him. And who am I?

I'm just Sunny.

I know that I shouldn't compare myself to her, or put myself down. That I'm beautiful in my own unique way—blah, blah, blah.

I've read every self-help article I could find about knowing your worth and getting over your ex. Unfortunately, none of these tips are tailored to my particular situation. Maybe someday, I'll write a post myself: "Seven Ways To Keep Insecurity at Bay When Your Famous Ex is Screwing the Hottest Supermodel on the Planet."

Dex has been photographed with gorgeous women plenty of times before now, but always doing something pretty innocuous, like sipping coffee—which I could easily brush off as nothing more than a friendly meeting.

But the pictures with Ava are different. They're *kissing*. He has a *towel* wrapped around his waist. His arms wrapped around *her*. She's topless, for god's sake. There's no room for interpretation here.

They're sleeping together.

If there's any silver lining at all, I guess this means I don't have to feel guilty for spending so much time with Jeremy anymore.

Nothing's happened between us—yet.

But…I think he might love me.

He pretty much told me so, the other night.

We'd been out for drinks with his colleagues, and one of the junior partners ordered us several rounds of shots. Jeremy didn't want me taking a cab home alone in my condition, so we ended up crashing at my place.

We were both so drunk, we collapsed onto my bed, hoping that if we closed our eyes, the room would stop spinning. And before I fell asleep, I'm sure I heard him say something to me.

I know I did.

"Sunny?" he whispered. "I think I might love you."

When I opened my eyes and turned to him, he was passed out.

It's been three days, and I haven't brought it up. But there's definitely something happening between us.

It started two months ago, the night he kissed me on the cheek before I got in my cab. Since then, instead of meeting at our favorite bar after work most nights, we started going to his place or mine, instead. We order food, watch TV. He puts his arm around me. I lean on his shoulder. Let my knees fall against his. Sometimes he massages my neck, or combs his fingers through my hair while I run mine through his.

When we're hanging out at my place, he'll usually head home around midnight. But when we're at his, he always wants me to stay so he doesn't have to worry about me getting home okay. He offers me his room, and he sleeps on the couch. And while I'm wrapped in his sheets, I find myself thinking about the things he does with the women he brings to his bed.

And up until now, I've felt guilty. Guilty that I can no longer deny that there *is* something more than friendship between me and Jeremy.

I didn't want Dex to be right. I didn't want to have to tell him that our story ends the way he predicted—with me choosing Jeremy.

But none of that matters now. Dex is with Ava Elwood. They'll probably get married. Start a family.

They'll have the most *gorgeous* children.

Dex and Ava make sense.

Just like Jeremy and I do. We live in the same city. We have the same job. We want the same things out of life. He can't wait to save up enough money to buy a house. And the other day, he mentioned how much fun he thought it would be to take his kids to a baseball game. He's always saying things like that. We're a perfect match.

And from now on, I can spend all the time I want with him, guilt-free. Whatever happens between us, happens.

Jeremy's on a work trip this week, assisting a partner with depositions for a case in Wisconsin, so I have to wait until Friday to see him.

When I get to his apartment, I'm already two glasses of wine ahead of him because I needed to drink while getting dressed, to soothe my nerves. I'd left work at 6:00 p.m., earlier than I usually do, and gone home to wash and blow-dry my hair, which I've continued to wear straight since Paris. After my shower, I put on jeans—and a wrap sweater for easy access.

Just in case.

The wine must not have helped, though, because I'm still nervous as hell walking into Jeremy's place. My mind is swirling with what-ifs.

What if I sleep with him tonight?

What if the sex isn't good?

What if it is?

What if I'm delusional, and Jeremy doesn't actually want me at all?

What if Dex breaks up with Ava, and he comes begging for me?

What happens then?

"I wasn't sure if you'd want Mexican or Thai, so I ordered both," Jeremy says. "I know how much you love Middle Eastern, but we had it twice last week, so I figured you might be tired of it."

He can't see me because he's in the kitchen, opening bags of takeout while I take off my shoes by the door. So I close my eyes and take a deep breath in an attempt to clear my head before I join him.

"Well, I can never get enough Middle Eastern food," I say as I'm walking into the kitchen to survey the spread on his countertop. "But everything you ordered looks delicious. This is a *lot* of takeout, though."

Jeremy shrugs. "We'll have leftovers for tomorrow. Do you know what you want?"

I nod. "Thai."

"Good," he says, like there was only one right answer to his question. "Me too."

Jeremy pours us two glasses of Riesling as I fill our plates. Then we sit on his couch. He turns on the TV, and we decide on one of those home renovation shows. While we watch, we talk about our workweeks and eat our noodles, taking occasional sips of wine.

I only make it through half my meal. I hardly have an appetite, and my mind is still busy, so I put down my plate, hoping more wine will help drown out my thoughts.

"You okay?" Jeremy asks, nodding toward my leftover pad Thai. "You didn't eat much." He doesn't look at me, and I can tell something's weighing on him.

Just like it's weighing on me.

I take a sip from my glass, then turn to him. "Did you see the headlines this week?"

Jeremy sets his food down. "About Mr. Hollywood and his new girlfriend? Yeah," he says gruffly. "I figured you'd be pretty devastated."

His eyes are narrowed. His brow is furrowed. His jaw is clenched.

He's upset. He's reacted this way the last handful of times I've mentioned Dex.

I put my wine on the coffee table. "I'm not here to cry on your shoulder, Jeremy. I'm done with that. But I do want to explain why I haven't kissed you yet. Even though I *really* want to."

His eyes soften, but he's tight-lipped. He only nods.

I look down at my lap. "When Dex and I broke up, he asked me if I was…um, sleeping with you. He felt threatened by our relationship, even though he had nothing to worry about then. I honestly didn't see you as more than a friend at the time. But…I do now."

I glance over at Jeremy, who's got his elbows propped on his knees and his hands clasped together. He's looking down at the floor, just listening to me.

"In the past couple of months, you and I have gotten a lot closer," I continue. "We spend almost all our free time together. We do everything that couples do, except…well, you know." I take another sip of wine before I go on.

"I'm attracted to you, Jeremy. I didn't let myself act on it before, because I didn't want to hurt Dex." I sigh. "But I don't have to worry about that anymore."

Jeremy gives me a sideways glance. Then, after several seconds, he micro-smiles. "You want to know why Anjali slept with the cardiologist?" He sits back against the couch cushions and turns to me. "She was pissed at me—because she found out I had feelings for you."

My heart flutters. "Oh," I say, biting my lip. "How'd she find out?"

Jeremy drags a hand down his face. "I made an asinine request one night, when I was drunk." He looks down at the floor again. "I, um, suggested we invite you to join us. In bed." He looks back up at me. "I mean, maybe she didn't know I had *feelings* for you. But she definitely knew I wanted to sleep with you."

I lift my wine glass to my lips, my cheeks blazing hot. "Smooth," I tease before taking a sip. "But for the record…I'm not into that."

Jeremy laughs. "Noted."

I smile as I swirl my remaining Riesling. I feel bad for Anjali… but I can't say I'm not also flattered.

I put my glass back down. "You wanted me, even back then? That was…eight months ago."

Jeremy doesn't shy away from my gaze. "Sunny, I've wanted you *a lot* longer than that," he says as he reaches to put a hand on my knee. He traces slow circles on me with his thumb. "I knew I'd have to wait. But, I also knew it'd be worth it."

That's when our lips meet. Finally.

Me and Jeremy.

I can't believe what an amazing kisser he is. His lips are so soft, and his tongue expertly flirts with mine, and his hands are in my hair, and he smells really good, and before I know it, he's pulling me onto his lap to straddle him.

My brain feels warm and fizzy from the wine, but in the best way possible. I'm relaxed enough not to feel self-conscious, but also astutely aware of how incredible Jeremy's hands feel on my body.

He's wanted me for so long, and I sense it when he pulls me closer with every kiss and grips me with his fingers, kneading the flesh beneath my jeans.

Jeremy doesn't like *anyone*, but he likes me. He might even love me. He's waited for me all this time.

I can't believe it took me so long to realize how much I want this.

"This isn't just a rebound for me," I tell him while he's kissing my neck. "I think…we could be really good together."

Jeremy peels his lips off my skin and smiles with his eyes. "I'm not *at all* worried about being your rebound, Sunny," he says in the gratuitously smug way that only he can pull off and sound sexy.

I bite the smile emerging on my lips. "Is that so?"

"Yeah." He wraps his arms tight around me. "Because once I fuck you…you're not going to want anyone else."

With that said, Jeremy lifts me off the couch and carries me to his room, where he throws me onto the bed. Now I'm lying in the same spot where I've fallen asleep several times, wondering what it would be like if he took off my clothes—and it's actually happening. He pulls my jeans off first, then my underwear. He unwraps my sweater, then unhooks my bra. He flings my clothes off his bed, and they land in a heap on the floor. I'm naked now, and he's still fully clothed. Kneeling between my legs, he looks—and only looks—at every inch of my body, his eyes traveling slowly from my lips, to my breasts, to my navel, to the curve of my waist and hips. His breath is heavy, and my heart is hammering when he settles his gaze back on mine.

Then he pulls off his white crew-neck, and I see him shirtless for the first time. He's lean, but more muscular than I imagined. What surprises me more, though, is that he has several tattoos on his chest, from the top of his left pec to his right ribcage.

"I didn't know you had ink," I say with a smile.

Jeremy looks down to undo his belt. "There's a lot you don't know about me yet," he says before he leans over me, and we start kissing again. He's running one hand through my hair, while the other finds its way between my thighs. His fingers slide inside me easily.

"Are you on the pill?" he asks.

"Yes."

"I always use condoms with someone new," he tells me. "But I don't want to with you. Is that okay?"

"Yeah," I say. "It's okay."

This is *Jeremy*. I've known him for years. He's my best friend, now.

"Do you have any idea what you do to me?" he whispers. "You are sensual…and sultry…and so *fucking* sexy…" He sighs as he drags his hand up my body to massage my breast. Every stroke of his fingers is confident and self-assured, like he knows exactly what I need, even before I do. "I've never wanted anyone the way I want you, Sunny. You don't know how long I've waited for this."

I look into his eyes, and the intensity of his desire blows me away.

Jeremy, who's usually so controlled, looks like he might die if he doesn't have me immediately.

It really turns me on.

I wrap my legs around his waist to pull him even closer to me. "You don't have to wait anymore, Jeremy."

Seconds later, he's reaching for his zipper. Then he pushes inside me just a little.

I'm desperate for more, and I tell him so. But when he gives it to me, I'm shocked.

"Oh my god," I gasp. My muscles tighten around him.

He stops. "Are you okay?"

I let out a laugh. "Of all the things you brag about, you failed to mention *this*?"

He smirks. "I've found that anticipating it usually makes the situation worse. Just try to relax, and it'll start to feel good. Trust me."

He says these words sincerely, and I nod, taking a deep breath and letting my body soften. He moves slowly, and I dig my fingernails into his back so I have an outlet for my remaining tension. When I drive my nails up and down his shoulder blades, he groans. "Scratch me as hard as you want—I like it."

I watch the pleasure on his face as he leans into the pain, and I decide to do the same. We find a rhythm together, and I soon discover Jeremy was right. It does start to feel good. No, better than that.

It's fucking amazing.

Once Jeremy sees I'm comfortable, it unleashes something in him. He's wild and unbridled in a way I've never experienced before. All I can think about is *him* and the things he's doing to my body. Every unexpected touch is an adrenaline rush that leaves me craving more. More sucking. More scratching. More hair-pulling. More biting. He sinks his teeth into my neck like a fucking vampire, making the *Twilight* fantasies I know he'd chide me for come true.

Finally, he pins my wrists to the bed, and he thrusts so deep, it makes me shudder with pleasure. He does this over and over until I'm about to come, and then he flips me onto my stomach. He puts all his weight on top of me and pushes into me while he whispers in my ear.

He tells me exactly how long he's wanted this.

He tells me about all the times he's imagined this.

About the times he's pictured me naked and come in his hand.

About the times he's pictured *me* while coming inside someone else.

His words get dirtier, and my heart beats harder, and my orgasm sends shockwaves through my entire body.

A few minutes later, he finishes.

We lie side by side in his bed and—I can't help it—I start giggling.

Jeremy raises an eyebrow at me.

"No wonder you're such a massive prick," I say, smiling at him.

He laughs and pulls me toward him, into his arms. "I love you," he says softly. "You know that?"

Since Jeremy's whispered confession the other night, I've spent hours wondering what I'd say if he told me he loved me again—outside of a drunken stupor. But I couldn't come up with an answer, so I decided to wait and see how I felt in the moment.

Now I know. Jeremy and I have had the friendship thing down pat for years. But tonight I found out that our physical chemistry is off the charts. Our connection was electric. Explosive. Jeremy was rough with me, and dominated me, and I never thought I would enjoy that—but I did. It was just as intense as being intimate with Dex but, at the same time, wildly different. Which is a good thing. My feelings for Dex and Jeremy are wildly different too. But there is a common denominator. When friendship and passion mix like this, what else could it possibly mean?

I nod. "I love you, too, Jeremy."

twenty-eight

SUNNY

MARCH 2007

Jeremy *loves* morning sex.

More often than not, he'll wake up first and, while I'm curled up on my side, still deeply asleep or dreaming, he'll wrap his arms around me and spoon me. Then he'll start kissing my neck, and my back, and my shoulders. When I begin to stir, I'll notice how hard he is, pressed against my ass, and I'll reach for him. Then he'll slide his hand between my thighs and, when I'm wet, he'll push my underwear to the side and thrust into me.

It's not a bad way to wake up.

Unfortunately, there's no time for that this morning.

I have my first solo court appearance today.

I've been to court a few times since I started at the firm nearly two years ago, but only with a more senior attorney, and mostly to observe. But today I'll be appearing on my own to argue a simple motion in an employment discrimination case. All I have to do is ask the judge for a one-month extension of our next court date so we can review newly discovered evidence. In the litigation world, this is a pretty basic endeavor, and something that Jeremy wouldn't even bat an eye at.

Yet I'm so nervous, I could hardly sleep last night.

I wake up before Jeremy does and jump in the shower. Afterward, I grab my new designer pantsuit and sleeveless silk shell from his closet. This outfit alone costs more than all the clothes I packed when I moved to Chicago *combined*—but Jeremy insisted on gifting it to me for my first day as, what he calls, a "real" litigator. He loves surprising me with lavish presents. While I certainly appreciate it, I've never been the type to indulge in expensive trends. My favorite outfit is a pair of worn-in jeans I've had forever, a slouchy cable-knit sweater that can't help but fall off my right shoulder, and sneakers. I want to be able to move in my clothes. I want to eat a hearty meal without worrying about my waistband digging into my stomach afterward. I want to wear shoes I can feel my toes in. According to my litigator boyfriend, that was fine for law school, but it's not the world we live in anymore. I guess he has a point.

Once I'm dressed, with hair and makeup done, I eye my reflection in the mirror.

Sometimes, I barely recognize myself.

My work clothes feel like a straitjacket.

I've started to miss my curly hair.

My curves have all but disappeared too. At my firm, taking an actual lunch break is frowned upon, especially when you're still a relatively new associate. I'm practically chained to my desk and, while the breakroom is stocked with snacks and ample leftovers from client meetings, I'm always so busy fielding urgent requests for research that I often forget to eat until I'm shaking from low blood sugar. As a result, I've lost several pounds.

Jeremy loves my willowy physique, although I don't think he realizes it's the product of work stress. I try not to complain too much, because I want to give this job a fair chance. I worked really hard to get here, and I'm still hoping that, with time, litigation will begin to feel more natural. Until then, I'm doing my best to grin and bear it, knowing that, at the end of the day, I get to spend the night with Jeremy.

I love how attracted he is to me. I love that he has to have me first thing in the morning, like most people need a cup of strong coffee. He tells me all the time that I'm the best sex he's ever had. That's the sentiment, at least. What he *actually* says is much lewder, and makes my cheeks turn bright red.

We've been practically living together at his place since we first had sex a year ago. Things moved quickly between us, but Jeremy said that's what happens when you find the person you're meant to be with. At first, those kinds of comments gave me pause. I always thought I was meant to be with Dex and, suddenly, there I was in a very serious relationship with another man—already discussing our future.

But if any doubts about Jeremy crept in, I'd remind myself that I'm safe with him. Jeremy won't abandon me for a starring role in a Broadway show or, worse yet, for a Hollywood starlet. He says I'm the best thing that's ever happened to him, and he'll never let me go. And I believe him. He's hardly left my side at all since we've been together.

He's the stability I've always wanted—and I'm all in.

I haven't told Dex about me and Jeremy. I actually haven't spoken to him on the phone since I found out he was dating Ava Elwood. I couldn't bear the thought of calling him while he was with her. I could so easily picture her laughing at my expense—saying something to Dex, like, "I can't believe you still accept phone calls from *commoners*." And then she'd straddle his lap and start kissing him.

It's ironic. Reading the headlines about Ava and Dex is essentially what drove me into Jeremy's arms and, less than a week later, they were broken up. Their reps issued a press release which, if I remember it correctly, went something like this:

"Although the pair enjoyed their time together, Ava and Dex have decided to part amicably due to conflicting work schedules."

I wonder what *really* happened between them.

Ava seems to have moved on quickly. Just last month, she announced her marriage to a Brazilian football player who's nearly as attractive as she is. It must have been a shotgun wedding, because rumors are circulating that she's also pregnant with their first child.

Dex, meanwhile, has been linked to half a dozen impossibly gorgeous women since his split with Ava. But nothing seems to stick. I don't know how he could possibly maintain a relationship even if he wanted to, considering how busy he is. Since his debut, he's made two more films that were also met with rave reviews. He's one of the most sought-after actors in the business now. It's like everything he touches turns to gold.

The only time I hear from him is when he texts to tell me he's changed his cell phone number, because of a stalker, or something. And when he does reach out, we'll message back and forth a little bit. But we only ever chat about work, and nothing personal.

Dex Oliver is larger than life now, but it's nice to know he still thinks of me sometimes.

I know I'll always think of him.

Jeremy says he doesn't feel threatened by my famous ex at all, but I'm not sure I believe him. If Dex and I saw each other in person, or talked on the phone, or even texted more than we do, I'm sure Jeremy would ask me to step back. Not that I'd blame him. I wouldn't be happy if he were friends with Anjali—not that she'd entertain the idea, considering how they ended.

But as long as Dex Oliver is a picture on a billboard or an image projected onto a screen, Jeremy has no qualms whatsoever about him. He even suggested we see Dex's newest movie together. To Jeremy, life's a competition and, as far as he's concerned, he's won. He has *me*.

I have to admit, seeing Dex on screen always sends me on an emotional rollercoaster ride. I'm happy for him. And I'm incredibly proud of him…

I also still miss him. I don't think I'll ever stop.

But watching him act is, if nothing else, a confirmation that this is exactly what he's supposed to be doing with his life. He was meant to be a star.

He's phenomenal.

"Want me to make you a smoothie?" Jeremy asks from bed.

I look back at him and shake my head. "I'm way too nervous to eat."

He gets up and walks to where I'm standing in front of the mirror next to his dresser. Then he wraps his arms around my waist and lets me lean against his chest. "You're going to do great today," he says as he gazes at our reflection. "You'll be in front of the judge for less than five minutes. This is a good way to ease you into going to court." He kisses the side of my head. "Plus—you look so damn hot, there's no way Jim could possibly say no to you."

I raise an eyebrow at him. "You're on a first name basis with the *judge* now?"

Jeremy gives me a self-satisfied look. "I'm in his courtroom a lot. He actually invited me to play golf with him next Sunday. His law clerks tell me he usually only asks partners. I guess he made an exception for me, though."

I roll my eyes at him while attempting to suppress a smile. "You know, Jeremy, you really are—"

"Wait…let me guess," he says, squeezing me tighter. "Charming? Handsome?" He watches me shake my head. "Well-endowed?" he suggests.

I can't help but laugh. "Those were *not* the words I had in mind."

"Hmm." He kisses my neck and starts feeling me up. "Are you sure? *None* of them?"

I have to work very hard to ignore my body's response to his touch because, if I don't, I'll end up back in bed with him and miss my court appearance.

"Let's pick this up later," I say, freeing myself from his embrace. "I don't want my suit to get wrinkled. Are you sure I look okay?"

Jeremy smirks. "What do *you* think? I can't keep my hands off you."

"Thanks, babe," I say as I comb my fingers through my hair to fix the pieces that got mussed up when he was kissing me. "You know…I've been missing my curls lately. I'm thinking about bringing them back."

Jeremy squints at me. "Don't you think this style looks more—I don't know, polished?" He watches my forehead crease, then adds, "For court, I mean."

I frown. "*Polished*? Really, Jeremy?"

He shrugs. "Maybe that's not the right word. *Professional.* Is that better?"

I shake my head. "No. It's not. It's offensive."

Jeremy scoffs. "How is that offensive?"

"Well, I'm sure I get my curly hair from…whatever ethnicity I partially am, so what you're really saying is that the hair I was born with doesn't look professional. It's the same bullshit reason companies use to justify firing an employee with dreadlocks, or—"

He starts nodding. "I see your point. But that's not how I meant it. Litigation is all theatrics, babe. Actors change their hair all the time, depending on the role, right? You have to look the part. When you're dressing for court, you want to keep it simple. If you walk in there with cascading curls like a Botticelli painting, that's all anyone's going to pay attention to, and they won't hear a word you're saying. Trust me—I'm in court all the time. You'll fit in perfectly like this." He gives me another tight squeeze and, when he finally gets a smile out of me, he goes to sit on the edge of the bed.

After a beat, I hear him sigh while I'm putting in my earrings. "Sunny, I know you don't like talking about your biological father. Not that there's much to talk about. He's a piece of shit for never wanting to know you, and I understand why you don't want to know anything about *him*. But…"

Every muscle in my body braces. As if I weren't already tense enough this morning.

He's right—I do hate talking about the guy who contributed half of my genetic material and didn't care enough to stick around. Whenever Jeremy's asked me questions, I've answered them to the best of my ability, but I've never once brought up the subject. So why the hell is he choosing to discuss this now, before I set foot in a courtroom by myself for the first time?

I turn around with my hands on my hips and glare at him. "*But?*"

Jeremy tilts his head. "Well, it's just that I was reading this article about genetics the other day—"

Of course he was.

"—and it got me thinking about when you and I have babies," he says.

My gaze softens and, before I know it, I'm smiling. I walk to the bed and sit next to him. "You've already started thinking about us having babies?"

He nods. "Not now, of course, but down the road, yeah. And I think it might be good to know what your ethnic background is. They've come a long way with prenatal genetic testing, and if there are conditions that you or the baby are at risk for, it would be helpful to know before we start trying."

My eyes well up. Jeremy has this way of making me feel so special. I mean, he has the most discriminating taste in the world, and he wants *me* to be the mother of his children.

He puts an arm around my shoulder. "I'm sorry. I didn't mean to make you emotional before court."

I shake my head and smile. "No, it's okay. What you're saying makes sense. Maybe I should start by asking my mom what she knows about his background and medical history, but…I'm a little scared, honestly. She's always refused to talk about him." I wince. "I had to do one of those family tree projects in school when I was a kid, and when I asked her for a picture of him, she said she'd ripped them all to shreds."

He takes my hand in his. "Don't worry. I'll be there with you. We'll handle it together."

I let out a little laugh. "She'll probably be a lot more receptive if *you* ask her. Her *beloved* Jeremy."

"Women have a hard time resisting my charm," he teases. Then he pulls me in for a kiss.

Once we get started, it's hard to stop, but eventually we do.

"I'm going to get in the shower," he says when we pull apart. "Do *not* worry about court, okay? You're spectacular, Sunny. Most people never make it to the big firms, but here you are. Here *we* are. We're a team, remember? Just like in law school. And if we do the grunt work now, it's going to pay off big-time when we make partner."

Jeremy's parents are both partners at big law firms in Manhattan. I haven't met them yet, but from what he's described, it sounds like they're not the warmest people. The only time they ever paid Jeremy much attention growing up was when he impressed them with an academic achievement. It's no wonder making partner means so much to him.

"We'll have everything we ever wanted," he continues. "We can send our kids to the best private school in Chicago. We'll have a big house in Lincoln Park with a two-car garage…and maybe a place in Michigan too. We'll retire there, and you can read as many sappy romance novels as you want while I'm drooling in front of the TV."

I giggle.

"Doesn't that sound nice?" he asks.

I nod. "It does. It sounds wonderful."

"Good." Jeremy stands and kisses the top of my head. "Hey," he says, tilting my chin up to look me in the eye. "You know I think you're beautiful no matter how you wear your hair, right? You could shave it off, for all I care. But…I can't say I don't find this particular style incredibly sexy on you."

He runs his fingers through my hair and gives it a little pull, like he does when we're in bed sometimes. Then he kisses me. "I love you."

"I love you, too."

Once he's in the bathroom, I walk to the front door where my Italian leather briefcase and Jimmy Choo stilettos—both gifts from Jeremy as well—are waiting for me. I step into my heels and give myself a final once-over in the front hall mirror before I leave.

Maybe Jeremy's right. My hair *does* look good straight.

I guess it wouldn't hurt to keep it like this a while longer.

twenty-nine

SUNNY

It's five o'clock on Friday, and I can't get out of the office fast enough.

Work has been an absolute nightmare since my first court appearance two weeks ago. You would think it had gone terribly, judging by what a nervous wreck I've been. But quite the opposite.

I did well. *Extremely* well—or that's what I'm told, at least.

One of the junior partners at my firm happened to be in the courtroom for a status hearing on another case and said I was a natural in front of the judge. I believe "poised and confident" were the exact words he used, but I can't be sure because, while he was complimenting me, I was still so keyed up from my five minutes in the spotlight that I could barely register what he was saying. But back at the office that afternoon, he told our *entire department* during a lunch meeting that I was born to be in a courtroom.

Which means that now, in addition to the heaps of legal research requests that land on my desk every day, partners are sending me to court for them on a regular basis as well. In the past two weeks, I've gone five times.

I thought I knew what work stress was before last week. Now all I want to do is call in sick and read romance novels to escape whichever circle of Dante's *Inferno* is reserved for lawyers.

On the bright side, Jeremy's *supremely* proud of me. He says I'm the one-in-a-million litigation associate who's just as stellar at making oral arguments as she is written ones. The fact that he's this impressed by me—especially when he's so quick to point out how completely inept most people are—makes me feel high as a kite.

I wish I didn't find his validation so intoxicating. All I can hope for is that my extraordinary courtroom skills are a sign that I actually do belong there, but my nervous system is just slow to catch on. When it does, maybe I won't feel like I'm trying to shove a square peg into a round hole all the time. And I won't need Jeremy's validation this much.

My boyfriend would never dream of being the first associate to leave the office like I am today. He insists on putting in face time, and refuses to call it a day until the majority of partners are well on their way home. He's often encouraged me to do the same, but he has no idea that I'm barely treading water right now. If I don't set *some* boundaries at work, I'm not sure how long I'll be able to put up with this job before it breaks me. For the time being, I tell him that I have a reputation at my office for being exceptionally efficient, and that I don't need to worry about staying late as much as the next associate. By the grace of the litigation gods, this explanation seems to satisfy him.

When I make it back to his apartment—which I'll officially

move into once my lease is up this summer—I take a steaming hot shower in an unsuccessful attempt to melt the week's tension off my body. Afterward, I put on my pajamas and start packing for our weekend trip to Beachwood.

We're leaving first thing tomorrow morning, and I'm anxious. Odds are, I'm finally going to learn the truth about the man who fathered me. And why—as far as my mom's concerned—he's dead to us. Although I definitely see the value in asking these questions, I'm still not sure I want to know the answers.

When I'm finished packing, I plop down onto the couch and turn on the TV. I must pass out mere seconds later because, when Jeremy walks through the front door, my favorite house flipping show is nearly over, and I don't remember watching any of it.

"Hey, sleepyhead," he says, kneeling to kiss me. "You feeling okay?"

I nod through a yawn. "Just wiped out from work. How was your day?"

"Pretty damn good," he says with a rare gleam of excitement in his eyes. "I have news."

"Wait, wait—don't tell me," I say, perking up a bit. "You made partner. And you're the first attorney in history to do it in less than two years."

He smirks. "Very funny."

"No? Let me try again. The President called. He wants you to be his Chief of Staff."

Jeremy rolls his eyes. "You're something else, you know that?"

"Okay, I've got it this time. You read an obscure book on

virology last night and figured out how to cure the common cold!"

He laughs. "Is there a two-drink minimum for this little comedy routine of yours? Maybe I should I take a seat—it seems like you're on a roll."

I giggle. "Nah, don't worry. Show's over." I grab him by the collar and pull him close so his lips are hovering over mine. "I missed you this morning," I say.

Jeremy had to go into the office at an ungodly hour today, so he didn't wake me up in the way I've become accustomed to.

"I missed you more." He closes the gap between our lips, and his kiss is so good it makes me moan. "You can't get enough of me, can you…" he says.

All I can do is shake my head. I have no clever retort, because it's the truth. Being intimate with Jeremy is far and away the highlight of my day. And it's the perfect stress release from the immense pressure of my job. Needless to say, I've been *very* stressed lately, and I think my boyfriend's picking up on the fact that I'm a little bit addicted to him. Of course, he doesn't mind.

"Quick, tell me this news of yours before I get distracted again," I tease.

"Well, I hope you had a nice catnap, because we're going out," he says. Then after a beat, he adds, "Go get dressed," apparently surprised that I haven't hopped off the couch yet.

But my tired limbs remain glued to the soft leather beneath them as I raise one exhausted eyebrow at Jeremy. "Out? Where? And, more importantly…*why?*"

"Well, it just so happens I'm among a very small group of attorneys who were cherry-picked by our newest partner to have dinner with a prospective client tonight. If we reel in this business, it means big money for the firm, and I'll be part of the team that made it happen."

"Wow," I exclaim, my eyes wide. I'm happy for Jeremy, but I'm also sleepy, and I hear it in my voice. I don't sound as impressed with him as I am—and he notices.

"What's the problem?" he asks with a furrowed brow.

I shake my head. "No, nothing. I'm really happy for you, babe—I'm just tired from work. I was hoping to get to bed early tonight since we're leaving for Beachwood first thing tomorrow morning."

He rolls his eyes. "Come on, Sunny. It's just dinner. We have to eat anyway, right?"

I let out a little groan. "Can't you go without me? I'm already in my pajamas."

Normally, when I'm lying on the couch like this, Jeremy sits close to me and puts my feet in his lap. But he doesn't do that now. He gets up from where he was kneeling beside me and sits in an armchair. I have to shift upright so I can see him. I watch as he drags his fingers through his hair and clenches his jaw.

"Babe, everyone on the team is married, and they're all bringing their spouses," he says. "I'm already the youngest associate of the group, which puts me at a disadvantage. If I show up alone, I'm going to look like the kid who just graduated from law school, and the client won't give two shits about my opinion on how we can best defend their case. I need to stand out for my intellect, Sunny, not my age. If I can dazzle this client with a great defense strategy and help seal this deal for the firm, I'm bound to be selected as second chair again if we go to trial."

As is often the case when I'm talking to my boyfriend, I'm smiling despite myself. "You and your obsession with being second chair. Can't you let anyone else have a turn?"

Jeremy doesn't see the humor in my joke. "No," he says flatly.

I let out a sound that's halfway between a whimper and a sigh. "These dinners always go on endlessly, you know that. We have to make our way through a million courses, and the wine pairings, and dessert—and that's only the beginning. Somebody *always* suggests going for drinks afterward, and then we're out until two in the morning. I really can't do that tonight, babe. Besides, you're brilliant, and your words speak for themselves. You don't need me on your arm for people to take you seriously."

His nostrils flare, and he's quiet for several seconds before he says, "Fine."

When he gets up and goes to the bar cart behind me to pour himself a glass of whiskey, my gut clenches.

Jeremy can be moody sometimes. I didn't notice it as much when we were just friends. It was mostly witty banter between us back in those days. I wonder if he used to come home from studying with me at the library and get gruff like this on the phone with Anjali.

I wonder if it bothered her the way it bothers me.

The vast majority of the time, he's showering me with love and affection so, when he *isn't*, it knocks the wind out of me.

I get up from the couch and walk over to him. "Are you mad?" I ask, my heart rate picking up.

Jeremy shakes his head but doesn't look me in the eye. And

he doesn't say anything. He downs his whiskey then stalks into the bedroom.

I follow him. "I know we were planning to take your car to Beachwood, but I can drive if you want. That way, you can stay out as late as you need to tonight and sleep in the car tomorrow," I suggest, hoping he'll come around.

When he finally looks at me, his gaze is glacial. "I think you should sleep at your place tonight. I can drop you off in a cab on my way to dinner. You're tired, and I don't want to wake you when I get home."

His words are like a punch to the gut. I honestly don't know whether I want to give him a piece of my mind or burst into tears.

I settle for both. "Are you serious, Jeremy? I haven't slept at my place in months. Are you really going to send me away because I'm drained from working my ass off and need a night in?" My eyes are stinging and I wipe at them with shaking fingers. "I feel like you're punishing me for trying to take care of myself."

He's looking through his closet for something to wear and doesn't turn to face me. "Don't be ridiculous, Sunny. I'm not punishing you, I'm being considerate." His tone is icy and sends shivers down my spine.

"Do you even hear yourself?" I ask him, my voice quavering. "Do you realize how cold you sound? It's like a switch flips, and you turn from Jekyll into Hyde sometimes."

He's silent.

Now I'm just pissed. "You know what? I *am* going to go back to my place tonight."

I start gathering some things I need from the bathroom when

I feel his hands on my waist. He turns me to him.

His brow's still furrowed, but the ice caps in his eyes have melted, and now his gaze is soft and warm. He's back—the Jeremy who looks at me like I'm his entire world. Who makes me feel safe and loved. I'm so relieved to see him that I allow myself to melt too, into his arms.

"Forgive me," he says into my ear. Then he kisses my tear-streaked cheek. "Work has me on edge. I shouldn't have taken it out on you. I promise I'll do better."

I sigh and look into his eyes. "Why are you so stressed?" The high-stakes world of litigation is where Jeremy thrives, unlike me. Work doesn't usually get to him at all.

He looks down at the floor. "I fucked something up earlier this week," he says, squinting his eyes shut and pinching the bridge of his nose. "I got lazy doing some legal research—something I'm well aware *you* would never do, which is why you're a much better lawyer than I'll ever be—but I missed something big that could have been a disaster for us in court. Luckily the senior associate who gave me the assignment knew enough to catch my mistake before it was too late." He lets out a heaving breath. "I'm just so fucking mad at myself. I feel like I'm walking on eggshells at work right now. That's why tonight's such a big deal for me."

I've never heard Jeremy admit to making a mistake at work before. But as attracted as I am to his confidence, it's actually a relief to see him this vulnerable. Considering his strained relationship with his parents, Jeremy doesn't trust easily. I know he wouldn't dare show me this side of him if he didn't really fucking love me.

✦   299   ✦

It feels good to be reminded of that. When he's cold and withdrawn, I sometimes question it.

"I'll go with you," I say.

He shakes his head. "No, babe, you're tired…and I was being an asshole. I don't want you to feel obligated to go. I never should have cut corners on that assignment—this is my mess to clean up." He gives me a sweet, gentle kiss on the lips. "Please forget what I said. You stay here and get some rest. If I get home late, I'll sleep on the couch."

I bite my lip. A wave of guilt pours over me. If I'd known this dinner was so important to Jeremy, I would've said yes from the beginning.

I probably should've said yes, regardless. I mean, here's this wildly intelligent, broodingly sexy man who believes he looks better with *me* by his side. Who's chosen *me* as his partner to take on the world. How could I say no to that?

"I'm going with you," I tell him. "You don't have to do this alone. We're a team, just like you always say."

Jeremy lets out a sigh of relief and gives me a tight squeeze. "God, I love you," he says. "Thank you. I'll make it up to you, I swear."

He takes my face in his palms and plants a kiss on my forehead. With Jeremy's resting expression being pretty firmly rooted in snark, it's not often I see him look this happy.

As he heads into the bathroom to freshen up, I'm still kicking myself for upsetting him.

"Do you know what you're wearing yet?" Through the cracked-open bathroom door, I hear Jeremy gargle mouthwash and spit in the sink. "Dress sharp," he tells me.

When I wake up the following morning, Jeremy's not in bed. I rub my eyes and sit up, yawning. The smell of coffee hits my nose. I hear the clinking of plates, and the opening and shutting of kitchen cabinets. A minute later, he walks in with a tray.

He's brought me breakfast in bed. There are scrambled eggs, toast, berries, and yogurt—all of my favorite things. He even put a fresh rose in a bud vase I didn't know he had. Not to mention, he brewed espresso in his exorbitantly expensive coffee maker that we never use because it's gratuitously complicated, and a bitch to clean.

"What's all this?" I ask, beaming at him.

"You were tired, so I let you sleep in. We have to hit the road soon, but this is my way of saying thank you for coming with me last night."

He's practically ebullient. The dinner was a success, and Jeremy's firm gained a new client. Not only that, my boyfriend stole the show. He'd done his research earlier in the day and knew everything there was to know about the client's business. He laid out defense strategies as clearly and concisely as a law professor, but with the confident swagger that makes Jeremy irresistibly sexy. By the time we were onto our third course, I was buzzed from all the wine we'd drunk and hardly felt tired anymore. I sat and listened to my brilliant boyfriend in awe, as he waxed eloquent about property easements. I was so incredibly turned on that I had to have him the second we got home.

Jeremy's not typically a big breakfast guy, so he makes himself a smoothie while I eat and, forty-five minutes later, we're on the road to Beachwood. It usually takes me a little over five hours to get there from Chicago, but Jeremy makes it in record time because he's a born and bred New Yorker, and drives like one. It reminds me a little bit of Mia, whom I haven't talked to in a while now.

She and Evan have been married about two-and-a-half years. Last summer, they welcomed their first child—a beautiful baby girl named Avery. I haven't met her yet, but Mia sends me pictures every now and then, when we email. In December, she sent a Christmas card addressed to me *and* Jeremy, which was thoughtful of her. It was a photo of baby Avery, sobbing on Santa's lap, while Mia and Evan made silly faces from the sidelines in an attempt to calm her. I thought it was adorable and showed Jeremy as soon as he got home from work. Maybe he was tired from a long day, but he had the audacity to call the picture "tacky," then said he didn't know which was worse on a holiday greeting—crying babies or matching pajamas.

I didn't have the energy to flip over the card and show him the snapshot of Mia, Evan, and Avery in identical buffalo plaid onesies.

I didn't want to add fuel to the fire, particularly because I was about to take him home for the holidays to meet my mom and Luis for the first time. But Jeremy charmed them both, and my mom was so thrilled that she was actually pleasant to be around, so I couldn't stay mad at him for long.

This is our first time back in Beachwood since then. When my mom opens the door to greet us, she wraps her arms around Jeremy first. Naturally.

We're here to celebrate Luis's sixty-fifth birthday. His daughters couldn't make it, sadly. Elena, the fashion photographer, is on a shoot in Milan that she couldn't get out of. And her sister, Lily, the doctor, is eight months pregnant and restricted from flying. The three of them agreed to celebrate together after the baby's born but, in the meantime, Jeremy and I wanted to be here for the occasion.

We have a lovely meal at Luis's favorite Italian restaurant, and Jeremy surprises us by footing the bill. He must have given his credit card to our waitress when he left the table to use the restroom because, when my mom asks for the check, she's told that everything has already been taken care of.

"This is on us," Jeremy says, and he puts his arm around me even though I had no clue he'd planned to pay.

When we get back home, Luis tells us he has a "belly full of spaghetti" and is going to call it a night. He is such a treasure, I honestly don't know how he ended up with my mom. He brings out the best in her, certainly—she's never as surly with him as she is around me, but she still has her moments. I guess they balance each other out. She's brilliant and beautiful, so she does have *that* going for her. I suppose what attracts Luis to my mom isn't so different than what attracts me to Jeremy.

While Luis makes his way upstairs, Jeremy suggests that the rest of us have a nightcap. When my mom agrees, he squeezes my hand and nods encouragingly.

This is it. Our chance to ask my mom about the man who fathered me.

We sit in the living room—Jeremy and I next to each other on the couch, and my mom in the armchair opposite us. I wait until she's halfway through her glass of sherry, hoping that will loosen her up a bit. I myself am so anxious, I've already downed my very generous pour of wine. And that's *on top* of the two glasses I had with dinner.

Finally, I work up the nerve to steer the conversation away from the riveting topic of my mom's fruitless search for an "adequate" landscaper. "While we're here, Mom…Jeremy and I were hoping to ask you a few questions," I say. "About my biological father."

My mom's gaze shifts between the two of us, her face expressionless. "Oh?" she asks, taking another sip of her drink.

I look to Jeremy for guidance.

"I'm very serious about your daughter," he tells my mom. "I see a bright future together—marriage, and children. And to that end, I've been thinking about the fact that Sunny doesn't know about the other half of her DNA. From a medical perspective, I'm wondering if there are any genetic concerns we need to be aware of down the road, when we're ready to start a family."

My god, he's good.

My mom looks impressed too. She's nearly smiling—at Jeremy, of course. "Well, that *is* a valid question," she concedes with a tilt of her head. "But I don't recall there being anything concerning in his family history." She turns to me. "He was half-French on his mother's side, and half-Lebanese on his father's. When you do prenatal genetic testing, they'll ask about your religious background. He was Catholic."

She's acting like she's reading notes off a patient's medical chart—like it's just another day at work—but every word she says feels like a knife going through my heart.

And the way she phrased things…

He *was*…he *was*…

"He *was*?" I ask.

Now my mom looks nervous. She bites her lip. Her gaze shifts down to the floor first, before she answers me. Then she looks into my eyes. "He died, Sunny."

I feel Jeremy's arm around my shoulder, but I must be in shock. It's like the world around me goes wavy all of a sudden. My vision's blurry, and my hearing's muffled, like I'm underwater.

I think Jeremy's asking me if I'm okay. I don't answer him.

I look at my mom instead. "When?" I ask her.

"Three years ago," she says. "I looked him up online and found an obituary. It didn't mention anything about surviving family members. As far as I know, he was an only child. His parents must be long gone. He was ten years older than me, which made him seventy-four when he died. A little young, but he was a smoker for decades. I suspect that's what caused it."

I don't remember doing this, but I must have turned to Jeremy, because my face is buried in his neck, and I'm sobbing. He's stroking my back and kissing the top of my head.

"Sunny, I'm sorry," I hear my mom say, although she sounds miles away.

My head whips in her direction. "You're *sorry*? *Now* you want to tell me you're sorry? All the years he was alive…you kept him from me! That was your choice to make when I was a kid, but as soon as I turned eighteen, the choice should have been mine. You robbed me of that, Mom."

She frowns. "I'll tell you anything you want to know about him, sweetheart—"

"I don't want to hear *anything* about him from you. I would have liked to hear it from him. But he's dead now, and it's too late."

My mom sits forward in her chair. "Sunny, I was protecting you from a cold, heartless man. Don't you think I tried reaching out to him? I *did.* By the time you'd turned one, I'd survived a year of being a single working parent—but I missed him. I wanted him to see what a beautiful child he'd fathered, and I was sure that if he did, he'd change his mind.

"You look exactly like him. Same coloring, same hair…same stunning features. I figured something biological would have to kick in when he saw you, and he'd want us to be a family. So I sent him pictures—the professional photographs of you and me together on your first birthday—and I wrote a letter to go along with them. I told him I still loved him. That his daughter needed her father. And that we'd welcome him with open arms whenever he was ready. Do you want to know what he wrote back?" She sighs. "He told me I looked good, Sunny. And he wished us well. That was it."

I turn back to cry on Jeremy's shoulder, and he wraps his arms around me. At some point, I feel my mom's hand on my back, and there's a little exchange between her and Jeremy, but I'm not listening. I'm releasing twenty-seven years' worth of tears over a man who never wanted me.

When my tears finally dry up, Jeremy shepherds me upstairs to my bedroom. He changes me out of my dress and puts me in pajamas. He takes me to the bathroom and squeezes toothpaste on my toothbrush while I pee. And when we get in bed, he holds me.

"I'll never leave you, Sunny," he says. "You never have to worry about that. I love you more than anything in this world."

Poor Luis and Jeremy work overtime the next day to ease the tension between my mom and me. They start by making a nice breakfast, because they know firsthand that my mom and I aren't our best selves when we're hungry.

After a quiet meal of pancakes and bacon, in which I catch Jeremy and Luis exchanging the occasional hopeful nod, we linger at the table for a second round of coffee. That's when Luis uses the mediation skills he must have acquired as a father of two daughters, and helps my mom and me express our feelings to each other.

I tell her I understand that she was trying to protect me. But I don't like how she handled things over the years—refusing to speak about him, and keeping me in the dark about my heritage. Watching me question my curly-haired reflection in the mirror as a kid, and walking past me without saying a word.

She tells me she understands why I'm upset, and that she's sorry. She says she knows it's hard to see sometimes, but everything she does for me is out of love. She explains that avoidance is her coping mechanism for anxiety. She avoids the risks. Avoids the triggers. Avoids the difficult conversations. She admits she's been considering therapy. She hasn't made an appointment yet, but she's saying it out loud now, to hold herself accountable.

I don't want to get my hopes up prematurely. But if my mom were to actually work on her issues, maybe we could have the relationship I've always longed for. One that's not rife with dishonesty.

Maybe that's why I've gravitated toward Jeremy since the moment we met. He may be brutally honest…but at least I can trust that when he says something, he means it.

Finally, my mom and I hug.

Then Luis treats us all to ice cream.

We end the visit on a high note, with a dinner of chicken and rice we make from scratch—the four of us—while Luis plays his favorite Spanish guitar album over the kitchen speakers. It's the kind of night I always dreamed of having in this house. With family.

But while Jeremy's driving us back to Chicago the following day, my thoughts turn on me, like the dark storm clouds in the sky, brooding over us.

I always knew my father never wanted me. But now I know that he rejected me more than once. The first time, it was just the idea of me, before I was born. But the second time, it was one-year-old Sunny from the photographs I used to love. The adorable little cherub with rosy cheeks and thigh rolls, smiling on her mother's lap.

He got a glimpse of me, and he left this world without ever

wanting to know me. My mom gave him an open invitation to join us when he was ready, but he never did. He never changed his mind—not even when he was dying.

And the pain of knowing this truth feels…insurmountable.

When we get back to Jeremy's apartment late that night, he suggests a drink on the rooftop to unwind before bed. The sky is clear in Chicago, and it's unseasonably warm, so I agree.

He grabs a bottle of champagne that was in the fridge. We haven't been grocery shopping in days, and it's the only alcohol we have. Then we walk up three flights of stairs to the roof.

Jeremy holds the door open for me and lets me through.

The entire rooftop is decorated with string lights, and candles, and vases full of white peonies. Pachelbel's *Canon* is playing over speakers. It's like a scene out of a movie.

Or a romance novel.

There's no one up here, but I figure we must have crashed someone's party. Maybe they're still setting up. They'll probably be back any minute.

I turn around to tell Jeremy we should leave, but he isn't standing behind me anymore.

He's down on one knee.

It feels like I'm dreaming.

I lift my hands to cover my mouth, tears welling in my eyes. "How did you do all this?" I ask him. "We were out of town…"

He shrugs and smiles. A *real*, full smile, like I've never seen on him before. He's so unbelievably handsome. "I have friends," he says.

I laugh and sniffle at the same time. "You *do?*"

He goes back to his signature smirk. "I paid the maintenance guy, okay? You're the only friend I need."

I giggle and wipe my eyes.

Jeremy swallows. "I've had this planned for a while now—long before this weekend. And I wasn't sure, given what happened in Beachwood, if this was still the right time. But then I realized, why not choose today to tell you that I want to spend the rest of my life with you. I knew it from the first time we kissed. I'd spent years waiting for just a *shot* at loving you, and when you gave it to me, I swore I'd never take it for granted. Because loving you is a privilege."

He pulls a velvet box from the pocket of his jacket. When he opens it, all I see through my tears are a million sparkles glinting under the string lights overhead.

And then he makes me a promise. "I vow to love you forever, Sunny. I will never, ever, stray."

These words echo so powerfully in my heart that I almost miss what he says next.

Almost.

"Will you do me the incredible honor of marrying me?" he asks.

If there's one thing I know for certain, it's that the man asking for my hand is unapologetically himself. And when he says he'll never leave me, I believe him.

He won't abandon me like my heartless dad. Or my mom, who's let decades of lies drive a wedge between us—however well-meaning her intentions.

No, Jeremy's different. I can count on him to be honest with me.

I'm not even sure I can say that about Dex. He's an actor, after all. And it's not like he's never lied about his feelings before. He's admitted to it. Like freshman year of college, when I told him I was dating Chris, and he pretended to be happy for me when he was actually a wreck.

Or all the years he kept the severity of his anxiety from me, not trusting me with the truth.

What happens the next time he's struggling? Even if he got help for his anxiety like he claims, life is full of ups and downs. The next time the going gets tough, will he confide in me? Or will he cover it up?

I know without a doubt that I will always love Dex.

But sometimes love isn't enough.

There has to be trust.

Now the answer to Jeremy's question is clear.

I take in a breath. "Yes."

thirty

DEX

I'm back in LA after spending the last three months in Vancouver shooting my latest film, a Hitchcockian thriller set in the 1950s. This might be my favorite movie I've made so far. Not so much because I enjoyed putting in the work, but because I fucking *needed* to.

After everything that went down with Ava a year ago, I was having a lot of trouble staying…well, sane. My anxiety was at an all-time high, and that's really saying something. I felt used, and objectified, and all I wanted to do was run into the arms of someone—anyone—who actually *saw* me and *loved* me.

But you know what? I came up empty.

My own mom doesn't even know the real me. It's not her fault, though. I still can't bear to tell her the truth about this wretched disorder that fucks with my head and threatens my sanity.

I showed Sunny who I am in Paris, but she rejected me. Of all the people in the world, I thought she would be the one to love me despite my imperfections.

I was wrong.

I wonder if she's with Jeremy now.

I Googled him the summer after they graduated law school. Sunny had mentioned the name of his firm in Chicago so, once his bio was up on their website, I found him easily.

He went to fucking Yale for undergrad. Graduated from law school with highest honors, just like Sunny. I already knew he was smart from what she'd told me about him—but the picture on his bio is what came as a shock to me.

He's handsome. He has this smug look I'd love to wipe off his face, but there's no denying he's attractive, even by Hollywood standards. In a movie, he'd play the villain so smoldering hot, he makes you question which side you're on.

There was a villain like that in the film I just made. But I never get cast in those roles. For better or worse, I'm always the hero. And as soon as I got to Vancouver and donned my metaphorical cape, it was like a switch flipped, and I was free. After months of panic attacks, and nightmares about venomous Ava and her fiery hair, being in character had never felt so good.

But Vancouver's a memory now, and I have to figure out a way to keep my shit together until my next project starts in a month. *Fuck.*

After a restless night of sleep, I'm having a cup of coffee in the kitchen of my multimillion-dollar Hollywood Hills mansion—a relatively new purchase that still feels nothing like home to me—when my cell phone rings.

Holy shit.

It's Sunny.

The last time we talked on the phone was…

My god, I don't even know. More than a year ago. Before Ava. Whatever she's calling about must be…significant.

I stare at the phone vibrating in my hand, and I'm so fucking scared, I almost don't answer it.

But what if she's changed her mind about me?

"Hello?" It's the first word I've spoken this morning, and it comes out raspy. I clear my throat.

"Hey," she says softly. "Did I wake you? I know it's pretty early in LA. Is that…is that where you are right now? LA?"

"Um, yeah," I stammer. "I, uh, just got back yesterday. I was in Vancouver. Shooting something."

It's like there's a complete disconnect between my brain and mouth, and I can hardly get the words out.

"How are you?" she asks me.

"Good. Good," I lie. "You know, just busy and tired. The usual." I really need to get the focus off me. "How are *you* doing, Sunny?"

I hear her swallow. "I'm good, Dex. I mean…I sort of hate my job. I'm sure lots of lawyers do. But other than that…"

She's silent for several seconds. She takes a deep breath.

I close my eyes and brace myself for it.

"I've been so afraid to tell you this," she begins. "While you and I were together, I promise you, I never had feelings for *anyone* else—"

"Jeremy," I say right away. Because that name has been seared into my mind since the day she first mentioned him to me. I knew back then exactly how this would end.

She sniffles. "I'm *so* sorry."

I dial into Dex Oliver—and crank it up a notch. Several notches, actually. "Sunny, you have *nothing* to feel sorry about. I understand. Our lives are not…compatible." I have to pause to swallow the bile in my throat. "And you and Jeremy…you make sense."

She's crying.

"Does he make you happy?" I ask, trying to control my breath. "Because all I want is for you to be happy."

It's true.

"Yes," she says in between heaving sobs. "I'm happy."

"You sound happy," I tease.

She laughs. And cries. Then she gets quiet again. "This is really hard for me, Dex. You'll always mean so much to me… and I don't want to hurt you. But I know that news travels fast around Beachwood, so I wanted to tell you myself"—she sniffs—"before you heard it from anyone else. Um…Jeremy proposed to me last night. And I said yes."

I mute the phone.

"*Fuck!*" I yell so loudly, it echoes in the vast emptiness of this stupid fucking palace I live in all alone.

Then I unmute. "Sunny, I'm so happy for you," I tell her. "That's great news."

She's quiet for a beat. "Thank you. I really appreciate it."

We exchange a few more pleasantries about work and family before we hang up.

Then I throw my $200 Hermès coffee cup across the room and watch it shatter into as many pieces as my heart.

Eventually, I clean the mess of splattered coffee and broken glass off the floor, then force myself to drink a protein shake—even though I feel like I'm going to be sick. I lace up my sneakers and go for a ten-mile run to ward off what I know *very* well is coming. There's no escaping Ollie, after all. The best I can do is postpone the inevitable.

When I get back home, I lift weights for an hour.

Then I swim laps in my Olympic-sized pool until I'm so exhausted I feel faint.

But I can't stop moving, and I *definitely* can't take a nap because if I do, I'll wake up sweating and panting and—

I don't even want to think about it.

So I choke down another protein shake and go to fucking Home Depot to buy paint, and brushes, and rollers for no other reason than I need something to keep my hands busy so they don't start shaking. I spend hours repainting my bedroom and, if I'm being honest, it looks like complete shit. I've never painted a room before, and it shows.

But I'm done now. I'm lying still on my bed, in my quiet room, and all I can hear is the storm brewing inside me.

I can't be alone tonight.

So I meet some actor friends at a celebrity hot spot—a place to see and be seen.

I do this because it means there will be eyes everywhere, watching me, and I'll have no choice but to put on a show.

Dex Oliver will save me. He always does.

And so far, he's doing a damn fine job. I'm eating and drinking. Cracking jokes and laughing. There are a dozen of us sitting around a long table in the corner of a crowded restaurant, and my audience is on the edge of their seats. I'm telling them about the elaborate prank my costars pulled during my first week on the set of *Passions*. I'm just getting to the part that involves a hungry orangutan and an obscene amount of bananas delivered to my dressing room, when I look up and see a familiar face eyeing me from the bar.

Could it be?

Her cheeks flush, and she waves at me.

"Will you excuse me a moment?" I say to my friends as I stand to make my way to the bar.

She smiles when I take the seat next to her.

"Well, I'll be damned," I say.

She scrunches her nose. "You *actually* remember me?"

I tilt my head. "Are you kidding? There's no way I'd forget you, Jenna Andersen."

It's been about nine years, but she looks exactly like I remember her from high school. Petite, fit. Tanned skin. Shoulder-length blonde hair. Olive green eyes. The same perfectly white smile.

I'd almost forgotten how pretty she is.

She takes a sip of her wine. Then another. She looks back at me and giggles. "I'm *so* incredibly nervous right now," she says.

My brow furrows. "Nervous? Why?"

Her green eyes widen. "*Why?* Because you're *Dex Oliver*, that's why. The biggest movie star on the planet."

I shake my head. "It's just me, Jenna. I'm still the same person underneath it all."

Ain't that the truth.

She finishes what's left in her glass and raises an eyebrow at me. "So fame hasn't changed you one single bit?"

I pause for a beat to think about it. "Well...I *do* wax my chest hair now."

She bursts into laughter. "That's all, huh?"

"Pretty much."

"You know, I came to this restaurant because I read it was a good place to see celebrities? I never thought I'd actually get to *talk* to one." She smiles. "How are you not getting mauled by rabid fans right now?"

"That doesn't usually happen at places like this," I explain. "People are pretty respectful. But I do get mauled plenty, out in the wild."

She looks around the room. "Do you ever get used to people staring at you so much?"

"For the most part." I scratch my head. "So, do you live in LA, or—"

She nods. "I do now. I just moved here from Pittsburgh, actually. I needed a fresh start." She lets out a long sigh. "I went through a bad breakup recently. Which I guess is why I'm sitting here, drinking alone."

"I'm sorry to hear that," I tell her. "But you're not alone now, you're with me." I point to her empty glass. "Want another?"

Her eyes light up. "*Please.*"

I motion for the bartender to bring us two more glasses.

"So what do you do in LA when you're not seeking out celebrities?" I tease.

She giggles. "I used to flip houses back in Pittsburgh, but the market isn't as good for that here, so now I'm doing interior design."

I nod. "Do you like it?"

She shrugs. "It pays the bills. So…how about you? I mean, I already know what you do for a living, obviously. But how's life otherwise? Are you dating anyone?"

"No, not at the moment," I tell her.

She swivels in her seat to face me and flips her hair, her eyes gleaming. "Can I ask you something?" she half-whispers.

I nod.

"Is it true you had a thing with Lola Piper? She's my absolute favorite singer in the world. I'm a *diehard* Pipette," she nearly squeals. "Did she really write the song 'Rolodex' about you?"

I look down and laugh. When I meet Jenna's gaze, I give her a slight wink.

She gets it.

"Wow," she says, shaking her head and beaming. "You're like, the luckiest guy in the world."

I drag a hand over my hair and sigh. "Honestly, Jenna? It sure doesn't feel that way right now."

Her forehead crinkles. "Why not? What's the matter?"

The bartender returns with our wine and I take a sip. "Do you remember Sunny?" I ask after a beat.

Jenna nods. "Yeah, of course. You guys were thick as thieves back when we were in school. Honestly…I always sorta thought you were in love with her."

I let out a wry laugh. "Yeah, well, that's the problem. I still am."

Even as I say the words, I'm surprised I'm talking to Jenna about this. But it's so rare that I'm around someone who knew me before I was famous. Not to mention, we lost our virginity to each other. There's a certain level of comfort between us, I guess. At least on my end.

"What happened?" she asks. "Were you guys together?"

I squeeze my temples. "We were on and off for years. But this morning, she called to tell me she's engaged."

"That sucks," Jenna says with a pout. "You're as miserable as I am."

"I'll drink to that," I say, lifting my glass.

She clinks mine, then takes a giant sip from her own. "I'm done with love," she says, wiping her mouth with the back of her hand. "I've been burned too many times."

"Do you want to talk about it?" I ask.

She looks down at her lap. "No...I don't." Then she smiles with her eyes. "But, thanks for offering."

"Anytime."

"What you *can* do is give me pointers on casual dating because, so far, it's *not* going well for me." She takes another drink. "I mean, I thought it would be easy. What guy wouldn't be happy to just hook up, right? But every man I've been out with in LA wants us to be exclusive." She rolls her eyes.

I laugh. "It's the downside of being an attractive woman, I guess."

She looks up at me with a playful smile. "What about *you*? You're pretty easy on the eyes...do you have this problem too?"

"Yeah, I've been there," I tell her. "You're basically screwed."

She giggles. "Good to know—thanks." She finishes her last bit of wine right as I'm finishing mine. "I'm *so* not used to being single," she says, her smile fading. "I was always a relationship girl, and now…I get lonely a lot."

I recognize the look in her eyes, and it crushes me. It's like seeing my own dejected reflection in the mirror every night before I go to bed.

I lean in to whisper in her ear. "Why don't you come home with me?"

When I pull back, she blinks a few times before answering. "Are you serious?"

I shrug. "Why not? You're lonely, I'm lonely. We're both brokenhearted, it would seem."

She bites the emerging smile on her lip. "You *do* have a point…"

"I mean, we've already slept together—once. And we made out a lot more than that—"

She laughs. "That was a long time ago. Speaking of which…I feel like I owe you an apology."

"*Apology*? For what?"

"For saying 'I love you' after we had sex," she says, bringing her palm to her forehead. "I was young, and naïve. I didn't even know what love was, yet. But I feel bad for putting you on the spot like that. And then, as soon as I got to college, I started dating someone else. I'm sorry."

"Hey—don't sweat it. Like you said, it was a long time ago."

"Thanks," she says with a sheepish grin. "It feels good to get that off my chest, though. So…are we really doing this?"

I smile. "It's up to you. The offer's out there."

She flips her hair again. "And it stays casual, right? No strings attached? No feelings?"

I nod. "Casual is really all I can do for now."

She puts her hand on my knee. "Then let's get out of here."

thirty-one

I let my briefcase fall to the floor and breathe a sigh of relief.

Kicking off the Louboutin heels Jeremy bought for my birthday in March, I grin the moment my bare feet hit the floor. Then I toss my tailored suit jacket onto his leather armchair. Well, I suppose it's my chair now too. My lease ended three weeks ago, and I've officially moved in.

I take my gaze toward the kitchen. I can't remember the last time I ate today. At this point, I'll just wait until Jeremy gets home, and we order dinner. I'm far too exhausted to make myself anything.

It's only Monday, and this workweek is *killing* me.

But come to think of it, every week feels like this.

I've been an associate at this firm two years now, and I've come to dread every single thing about my job. The court hearings where my stomach is in knots. The contentious calls from opposing counsel that give me an instant migraine. The endless stream of research and writing assignments that force me to skip lunch. The unwelcome knocks at my door from partners who insist I cancel plans because *every fucking thing has to be done right away.*

The worst part is, I'm scared to tell my own fiancé how miserable I am.

Because Jeremy is very invested in this dream of us both being high-powered attorneys. And when things don't go his way, he's pretty unpleasant to be around.

But after finally meeting his parents at their posh Manhattan brownstone a week ago, I honestly don't think I can blame him for his mood swings. And now I understand why he's put off introducing us the last three months since our engagement.

Jeremy's parents are *cold.*

Neither of them cracked a smile the entire time we were there. I suppose that shouldn't have surprised me, considering my fiancé is far from jovial himself, but at least Jeremy has a sense of humor. The first thing his dad said upon meeting me was that he was surprised his son had found someone who met his impossible standards. And he was *not* joking. Then his mom lamented that it would have been nice to have a doctor in the family, presumably referring to Anjali.

When we gave them the perfectly nice bottle of cabernet we'd bought at Whole Foods, both parents eyed it skeptically and agreed to open something "good" from their wine cellar instead.

Over dinner, his mother made sure to let me know that the "gratuitously expensive" ring their son bought for me was *not* the family heirloom she would have preferred me to wear. Then his father went on to tell me that, if Jeremy had put *any* effort at all into the four years he spent at Yale, he would have gotten into a much more impressive law school than the one we graduated from.

I was on the verge of tears and shell-shocked when we left. The moment we reached the bottom of the steps in front of their brownstone, Jeremy looked at me with the saddest eyes. I wrapped my arms around him, and kissed him, and told him how much I loved him. Then we walked quietly, hand-in-hand, to the Plaza. He'd insisted on booking a room there rather than stay with his parents—for obvious reasons.

Before we checked out of the hotel, he surprised me by telling me he'd put down a deposit for us to get married there exactly a year from now, in June 2008. I was shocked he booked it without talking to me first. I've always dreamed of a wedding in Beachwood.

Never mind that I always imagined getting married in the Dexters' backyard.

But my mom's house has nearly an acre of land that would be perfect for a reception as well. After the hard time Jeremy's parents gave him over dinner, though, I figured the least I could do was let him pick the venue.

My heart aches for him. I can't believe *that's* the home he grew up in.

Maybe, eventually, my love can help repair some of the damage his parents have done. He'll feel secure. Happy. And I won't have to walk on eggshells around him so much anymore.

That's my hope, at least.

After replacing my oppressive silk blouse and woefully

binding pencil skirt with a soft tank and knit shorts, I head to the living room and plop down on the couch to call Sam. Although she's still working toward her PhD in New York, we missed seeing her last weekend because she was visiting family in Berkeley.

I could really use her comic relief right now.

Jeremy's been moodier than ever since we got back from visiting his parents. For the past eight days, he's been stalking around the apartment, high-strung and even more argumentative than usual.

To make matters worse, we haven't had sex since before our trip to New York. Ten days without physical intimacy is far from the end of the world for most couples, but for me and Jeremy it's unheard of. And considering how moody he's been, this dry spell between us is making me feel lonely, stressed, and anxious.

Over the phone, I tell Sam all about the icy reception I got from Jeremy's parents.

"Yikes," she says. "No wonder your fiancé's so broodingly sexy."

I laugh. "Sam, I'm *engaged* to him now. You really don't need to keep telling me how sexy he is—I'm well aware."

"Maybe I'm afraid you'll go blind again," she teases. "I still can't believe you didn't see it before. I guess it's a testament to how strong your feelings were for Dex. The only time I was ever that blindly in love was with my second-grade boyfriend, Eric. But that was only because he used to give me his Twinkies at lunch. Once his mom stopped buying them, poor Eric didn't stand a chance." She sighs. "I was a fickle child."

I chuckle, although my pulse quickens. And it's not only because Sam brought up Dex.

It's the fact that she put my feelings for him in the past tense. And the truth is, they're very much still present.

I've learned to live with them, because it's all I *can* do.

But in New York this past weekend, I couldn't stop thinking about him. And it's not like we'd ever been there together. For some reason, though, while roaming the streets of the city, I felt haunted by his ghost. I suppose he travels there a lot for work. Maybe subconsciously, I hoped I'd run into him. It would have been the first time I'd seen him in over two-and-a-half years, since Paris.

Then again, if I *had* seen him, I would have been with Jeremy. And the thought of the two of them meeting makes me shudder. I imagine it would cause some catastrophic shift in air pressure—the kind that makes animals run for cover. And the moment they shook hands, the world would implode.

"Sunny? Did you hear me?"

"Sorry, Sam…I must have lost signal for a second," I lie. "What were you saying?"

"I was asking if you told Dex you're engaged yet."

"Oh. Yeah…I told him the next day. I was so afraid of his reaction, I was eager to get it over with but…he actually handled it really well. He seemed completely fine, honestly."

"Well, that's a relief," she replies.

I guess you could say that. It made me sad that Dex was so nonchalant but, at the same time, it confirms that I made the right choice to be with Jeremy.

As I'm having that thought, my fiancé walks through the front door.

With a scowl on his face.

Great.

"I should probably jump off," I tell Sam. "Jeremy just got home, and we need to figure out what we're doing for dinner."

She scoffs. "Dinner? Yeah right. I bet you're about to jump his bones. At least that's what *I'd* be doing if I hadn't just sworn off all men."

"Sworn off men? Since when? Weren't you dating that guy, Andrew? In your program?"

She sighs. "That fizzled."

"Did he stop bringing you Twinkies?" I joke.

"No…he actually gave his *Twinkie* to the *other* hot chick in our program."

I frown. "Oh, Sam, I'm so sorry."

"That's okay. Honestly, his Twinkie was getting pretty stale. And now I have more time to focus on my dissertation. I'll just have to live vicariously through you—so go have wild sex, and report back to me with details."

If only it were that simple. Judging by his narrowed eyes and clenched fists, it's probably safe to say Jeremy's not in the mood. It's like a cold front just blew into the apartment—I can feel the chill in the air.

But I laugh at Sam's joke anyway. "I will do no such thing," I tell her.

"You mean you won't have wild sex? Or you won't report back to me with details…"

"No details, of course." I chew on my lip as my fiancé cracks open a beer with a furrowed brow, then stomps into our bedroom.

"So you guys *do* have wild sex…I knew it! One look at Jeremy and I could tell he was a tiger in bed. Well played, Sunny. I'm happy for you."

As she says the words, I hear Jeremy slam a dresser drawer shut. I giggle despite the nervous flutter in my stomach. "Goodnight, Sam."

"Night."

When I hang up, guilt washes over me. I wasn't being myself on the phone with Sam—I was acting. Playing the role of the happy bride-to-be, all while my fiancé's stomping around the apartment, slamming drawers and scowling. He's so unapologetically himself, he can't be bothered to regulate his moods for five minutes while I'm talking to my friend—yet here I am, hiding things on his behalf?

The irony isn't lost on me.

I get up from the couch and take a deep breath before I walk into the bedroom. When I do, I find Jeremy changing out of his suit. His pants are still on, but his belt's undone, and he's shirtless.

God, he looks good.

I wish I could jump him like Sam assumed I was going to. I'm desperate to feel that close to him again.

It's strange to miss someone when they're three feet away from you.

Jeremy takes a seat on the edge of the bed and acknowledges me with a nod as I inch toward him.

"What's the matter?" I ask softly when I'm sitting next to him.

He sighs and rubs his forehead with the heel of his hand. "They made another associate second chair for this new client's case—the one *I* helped reel in. Can you fucking believe that? After all the goddamn work I put in, they give it to that fucker, Mike." He rolls his eyes, then mutters under his breath. "Went to Harvard Law and thinks he's better than everyone else."

Good lord, I hate when he gets like this.

My stomach clenches as I wonder what I can possibly say to help him feel better. Then it occurs to me that Mike has been at the firm a hell of a lot longer than Jeremy has.

"I'm really sorry, babe. But…Mike's a senior associate, right? About to make partner? Maybe they weren't even considering younger associates for this case."

Jeremy glares at me. "They'll pick whoever they think will do the best job, Sunny."

My pulse quickens.

"It has nothing to do with seniority," he continues, shaking his head. "We were in a meeting with the client this morning, and my tone was a little…*gruff*…according to the partner. I was trying to explain that if we don't file a motion to exclude expert testimony before trial, we're gonna get fucked later—and apparently that didn't go over well."

I guess I'm not the only one Jeremy's been gruff with lately.

"Well…you have been a little tense these days," I say, shifting to kneel behind him on the bed. I begin to rub his shoulders. "Maybe this will help."

Jeremy exhales deeply. "Now I feel like I have to watch every word I say so they don't fucking fire me."

"They're not going to fire you, babe," I say as I continue to knead the tight muscles in his back. "You are such an asset to the firm.

You're a brilliant litigator—not to mention they've practically had you on a pedestal since you helped snag this new client. I really don't think you have to worry about your job security."

He smirks. "Thanks—but I don't need advice on how to keep my job from the associate who's first to leave the office every day."

My fingers freeze over his shoulder blades for a few seconds before I drop my hands to my sides. "That was harsh. I'm trying to help you feel better, and you're attacking me?"

He turns to face me. "You weren't trying to make me feel better, Sunny. You were trying to get laid. Since when do you give massages anyway? All you want from me these days is sex."

My heart is hammering. "You can't be serious. I give my fiancé a back rub because he's stressed, and now I'm a sex fiend?"

His gaze is steely. "You're being needy. And it's not a good look on you."

I blink back tears. "Are you fucking kidding me? This coming from the guy who—until recently—had his hands all over me every morning while I was still dreaming? Who treated me like his daily dose of caffeine, without a second thought about whether *I* needed more sleep?"

He scoffs. Then he stands and starts pacing the room. "You *love* the way I wake you up, Sunny. You tell me all the time that it's your favorite goddamn part of the day—"

"Yeah, well, maybe *I* would like to be the one in charge of when I wake up for once. You take my body when you want it…and you make me yours…and I used to think it was so hot. But now I see it for what it really is. It's selfish."

He drags his hand through his hair. "That's bullshit, and you know it. On the days I go into the office early, you're always telling me how much you missed me. You don't really miss *me*, Sunny—you miss getting fucked."

Tears roll down my cheeks. "Yeah, you know why? Because sex is the only time I feel connected to you, Jeremy!" I grab tissues from the nightstand and wipe my eyes. "Why do you do this to me? One minute you look at me like I'm the only woman in the world who matters, and the next…you make me feel like shit about myself. Your mood swings are giving me whiplash."

Jeremy closes his eyes and squeezes the bridge of his nose. Then he finds his dress shirt, slung over the back of a chair. "I'm going out," he says, jamming his arms into the sleeves.

He leaves the room and, a minute later, the front door slams shut.

This is the bed I made for myself—and now I'm lying in it. Alone, and devastated.

I think back to the way things were at the beginning. Witty banter, and great sex, and the lovestruck look in Jeremy's eyes that made me feel safer than I'd ever felt before. But where's that sense of safety now, when he's hot and cold, and pulls the rug out from under me whenever the hell he feels like it?

Is safety knowing for a fact that he'll come home drunk tonight, and say he's sorry, because it's what he always does? Or is it his insistence that I'm the only person who understands him…the only one who could match his wit and intelligence… and we were tailor-made for each other?

Maybe it's the three-carat diamond ring on my nightstand, and the promise it represents. But what fucking promise is that, exactly? A vow to stay true in sickness and in health? Or a vow to keep me walking on eggshells for all eternity?

Dex would never treat me this way. And yet…

I broke up with him.

The front door opens and shuts. I glance at the clock. It's 2:00 a.m.

Jeremy walks into the room, takes off his clothes, and crawls into bed with me. His eyes glisten in the darkness. "I'm so sorry, babe," he whispers, stroking my hair.

A tear falls from his cheek and I wipe it away with my thumb.

When he kisses me, he tastes like whiskey. "I'm so sorry," he whispers again.

In between every kiss, he apologizes, and cries, and tells me how much he loves me. Just like he always does. And I come to the same conclusion I always do after a night like this:

I let go of the love of my life. And I chose *this* man. If this relationship doesn't work, then nothing in my life makes sense. So I forgive him.

Again.

thirty-two

DEX

It's a perfect summer day in Manhattan. I've been here the last six weeks shooting my latest film, and we wrap today. But I don't feel as angsty as I normally do when a project ends. Because when I fly back to LA tomorrow, I'll be picking up where things left off with Jenna.

After leaving the restaurant together that night in late March, we hung out practically all of April before I had to leave for New York. I guess a month goes by pretty quickly when you're spending so much of it in bed.

But true to our agreement, our relationship has remained casual. We don't talk about feelings. We don't worry what the other person is up to when we're not around. We don't define or label anything, although I guess it's pretty clear we're friends with benefits. Ultimately, we're both just grateful to have someone around when we don't want to be alone.

It's been a much-needed distraction for me, that's for sure. After Sunny told me she was engaged, I was convinced I'd fall apart. But being with Jenna has tempered my anxiety enough that it's settled to a low hum that's constantly in the background, rather than the raging riot I expected to annihilate me.

After we wrap filming, I decide I'd like to stay in costume for a few hours and just wander around the city like a regular person. This is the first movie I've done that's required me to wear a considerable amount of makeup and prosthetics. I played a detective in his late forties who—how should I put this—isn't quite as attractive as I am. I'm unrecognizable for the first time in years, and I'd like to take advantage of it. My makeup artists are fine with it and tell me to call whenever I'm ready for them to peel everything off.

I go to Times Square first and join one of those double decker bus tours. I overhear the couple seated in front of me talk about how wonderful my last movie was, and I smile. When I hop off the bus, I take a long walk through bustling city streets, then get myself an everything bagel with lox and scallion cream cheese (knowing full well I'll have to add an extra workout tonight to make up for it), and I eat on a bench in Central Park while I people-watch. I round out the day with a trip to Whole Foods, just for the hell of it.

I'm strolling through the store, completely unperturbed, when I make it to the wine section. That's when I see a face I recognize at the opposite end of the aisle.

It takes me several seconds to place him, but when I do, a jolt of adrenaline sets off a fight-or-flight reaction in my body.

Jeremy.

And he's with a woman who *isn't* Sunny.

At first, they're only looking at bottles of cabernet. Innocent enough.

But then he puts an arm around her shoulder.

After a minute, his hand drops to her waist.

Then he pulls her close to him.

And he kisses her.

I'm going to fucking kill him.

My muscles brace and I take a step in their direction.

But then the woman spins around to look at the bottles behind her.

And that's when I see her face.

Jesus Christ.

It's Sunny—but it's *not.*

Her hair is stick-straight.

Her clothes are tailored. Expensive. She's wearing Christian Louboutin heels.

She's so, *so* thin. It makes my heart break.

Why isn't she eating?

Is she sick? Is she stressed? Is it…him?

I want to run to the bakery counter and buy her a croissant.

I want to take her out for pasta, and ice cream, and feed her, and kiss her, and make sure she's okay.

I want to steal her away from him.

But she's smiling.

Now she's laughing.

She's wrapping her arms around his neck and kissing him.

They choose a bottle.

And walk away.

All I can think is—*what the fuck are they doing in New York?*—but then I remember Sunny mentioning he's from here.

When they're out of sight, my anxiety turns down slightly,

but it's not the low hum I've become accustomed to either.

It's louder.

I walk back to the apartment where I've been staying and, as soon as I lock the door behind me, I take deep breaths in and out. Still, when I look at my reflection in the front hall mirror, my heart jolts from the shock of what's staring back at me.

It's just makeup. Chill the fuck out.

But what if it's not just makeup? What if this is my future? A forehead creased by stress…eyelids drooping from grief…the corners of my mouth turned down in chronic disappointment…

This is my life without Sunny.

Beads of sweat form under the layers of silicone glued to my skin. My face starts to tingle.

I need to get this shit off me—now.

I call my makeup artists, Cheryl and Delia, and they arrive what feels like seconds later. Maybe I'm losing track of time.

Maybe I'm losing my mind.

"Dex, are you okay?" Delia asks, staring at my hands.

I look down: my knuckles are white from gripping the armrests of the chair I'm sitting in while they strip my face clean.

FUCK!

I clear my throat. "I'm good. It's just been a long day."

Delia looks skeptical—I think. Like she doesn't believe me. Or does she?

Maybe I'm imagining things.

Maybe I'm unraveling.

I keep waiting for Dex Oliver to kick in and crack a joke or two. But he's abandoned me when I need him the most.

Oh god no, my hands are trembling.

"How much longer before you're done?" I ask, clasping them together in my lap. "I haven't eaten in a while. I think my blood sugar's low."

"Oh, you poor thing!" Cheryl exclaims. "No wonder you're shaking like a leaf. Delia, go get him something from the fridge."

Holy shit, I can't see.

Just breathe, just breathe, just breathe, just breathe—

Just keep it together until they leave.

"Here you go, hon," Delia says, handing me a green juice.

I force it to my lips.

"Should be done in about five minutes," Cheryl says.

Thank you, lord.

My heart slows just enough to get me through until they're finished.

As soon as they're gone, I crawl in bed and hide under the blankets.

My ears are ringing—

I'm losing my hearing!

My vision is blurry—

I'm losing my sight!

My throat is tingling—

I'm losing my mind!

And there's no escape this time…

I kick off the covers and run to the mirror, desperate to see some version of Dex I recognize—but I'm face-to-face with Ollie.

I touch my cheek—he touches his.

I say his name—he moves his lips.

It's like a funhouse mirror in a haunted house—

But I'm trapped in here, and I can't get out.

I can't get out!

I can't get out!

I need Sunny. She's here. She can save me.

Of course, seeing her triggered this panic attack in the first place, but I don't care about that now. All I care about is feeling her arms around me. Hearing her say I'll be okay.

Breathing.

I pick up my phone to call her.

But what if Jeremy answers? What if he turns to the love of my life and says, "It's a good thing you're with me, Sunny. This Dex Oliver character is a fucking whack job!"

No, I've lost her…it's true…and not just to Jeremy.

The Sunny I knew is gone. A distant memory.

The world is dark, there's no sun in the sky.

My lungs…can't breathe…I'M GOING TO DIE!

I look down at the phone in my hand, my finger tracing the numbers: 911.

I have to call. I need to call.

But the media. I can't. This will be front page news!

I gasp for air

I gasp for air

I gasp for air

I—

…

I've lost time. I must have passed out—or worse. I have no idea.

All I know is, I can't live like this anymore.

I reach for my phone, which has fallen next to me, in the corner of the bedroom where I'm huddled.

Before I can second-guess myself or make any more excuses, I dial.

"Mom?" I cry when she picks up the phone. "I'm scared… and I need help."

thirty-three

I'm late.

Ten days late, to be exact.

I've been on the pill for the past nine years, and my periods have always come like clockwork—until now.

I could have taken a test days ago, but I chose to wait instead.

I think that was my first clue that I'm not ready for this to be happening.

I just don't understand how that's possible, when I've orchestrated my entire life to get me to *this* precise moment.

I'm a successful attorney…if you measure success in dollars, not passion.

I'm engaged to a brilliant, handsome man who wants to build a home and a family with me.

We might even be having the baby I've always wanted.

So why the hell am I so scared?

I glance at Jeremy, sleeping beside me in bed. Things have been good between us lately.

I mean, it's not like he *never* gets moody. But work's been going well for him, and that helps. Also, he set some boundaries with his mom recently, which seems to have made him less stressed. He finally got so fed up with her taking control of our wedding plans and inviting distant relatives he "couldn't care less about," that he cancelled the reservation he made at The Plaza. Which means that now, we can have the Beachwood wedding I've always wanted.

It's nice being on the same page.

After our disastrous trip to New York over the summer, it took three weeks of no sex and countless arguments for him to realize what an ass he was being. I suspect my telling him I wanted to go home to my mom's for a weekend and "think about things" was a major wake-up call for him.

Suddenly, he was the Jeremy I fell in love with again. Funny. Thoughtful. Adoring. He sent roses to my office. He went online and ordered the latest romance novels from all of my favorite authors. He bought me expensive lingerie, and left me without a doubt in my mind about his burning desire for me.

I didn't need the gifts. I only wanted him to defrost, which he did. And then some.

Now things are steamy between us again—obviously.

That's why I need to buy a pregnancy test.

I stop at the pharmacy on my way to work. My plan is to take the test as soon as I get home, since I'm always back from the office much earlier than Jeremy. That way, I'll have time to process my feelings about the outcome—whatever it may be—before I tell him.

But now that I have the kit in my work tote, I can't wait any longer.

As soon as I get to the office, I head into the bathroom. I've never had to take a pregnancy test before, so I read the instructions with shaky fingers, even though it's pretty obvious what I need to do.

Then I do it. And I start a timer on my phone for three minutes.

While I wait, I'm consumed with worry.

Yes, Jeremy's back to being sweet and warm with me again… but is it only a matter of time before he gets chilly?

As much as I want to believe he's changed once and for all… so far, the evidence isn't in my favor.

And do I really want to raise a child with a man I have to walk on eggshells around?

God, I feel like I'm going to throw up.

I must be pregnant.

This is morning sickness.

I've never felt this nauseated in my life.

My phone dings. Time's up.

I pick up the stick, which I'd put face down on top of the toilet paper dispenser.

It's negative.

I nearly cry with relief.

It's been a week, and I haven't told Jeremy I thought I was pregnant. I'm not sure I'm going to. I *still* haven't gotten my period, and right now that's my biggest concern.

I wonder what's wrong with me.

I consider asking my mom, but her mind will immediately jump to something catastrophic, like cancer, so I don't.

I'm having a hard enough time not catastrophizing as it is.

I call my doctor, and she tells me to come in for blood tests. When the results are back two days later, I go in to see her.

Her brow furrows with concern as soon as she takes one look at me. Quietly, she examines my chart. I wipe my sweaty palms on my hospital gown as I wait for her to speak.

"Well, you've lost twenty pounds since I last saw you, Sunny. And you were already thin to begin with." She scoots her chair toward me with a sympathetic frown. "What's going on? Aren't you eating?"

I bite my lip. "It's this *job*. I wake up filled with dread every morning because I hate it so much, and I can barely stomach breakfast. And while I'm working, I'm so busy, I almost always skip lunch. I guess the only meal I regularly eat is dinner."

It's not until I say the words out loud that I realize the extent of the problem. I always loved food—I never would have dreamed of skipping a meal before I became a lawyer.

That's when it dawns on me. I've become so used to being miserable that it doesn't even register anymore. Not even when my stomach is churning from being so empty.

My doctor sighs. "Look, I know you're in a stressful profession—I get it. But this job is doing a real number on you. Your blood pressure's through the roof. And your blood tests show you're anemic too. Have you noticed feeling more tired than usual lately?"

I shrug. "I'm always tired. When I get home from work, all I want to do is nap on the couch."

She nods. "And you're not eating nearly enough. That's why your periods have stopped."

A tear falls down my cheek and, before I know it, I'm sobbing. "I can't live like this," I tell her.

"I know you can't," she says.

She prescribes me an iron supplement and three weeks off from work, at which point she wants to re-check my blood pressure.

I don't give a shit what the partners will think about my medical leave.

But I'm pretty fucking scared to tell Jeremy.

I can already see the disappointment on his face when I tell him I despise being a lawyer so damn much, it's actually killing me.

As soon as I leave the doctor's office, I stop at Whole Foods for a croissant. But I'm still starving, so I decide to sit for lunch at an Italian restaurant. I order lobster ravioli and clean my plate—as well as half a loaf of bread, which I dip in olive oil and parmesan. I'd all but forgotten how delicious and decadent a meal can be. Both my body *and* soul are satiated in a way I haven't experienced in ages. Even though I'm stuffed to the gills, on the walk back to the apartment, I stop and buy a pint of rocky road for later.

When Jeremy gets home, I don't tell him about my doctor's visit yet—I'll save that conversation for tomorrow evening. I need a clear head for what I want to do when I wake up in the morning.

As soon as he leaves for work, I get up and shower. But I don't flat-iron my hair. I let it air dry and enjoy the beachy waves that appear. While I was sitting alone at lunch yesterday, I decided to stop chemically straightening it. In time, I'll get my natural curls back.

And that's only the first step in my journey back to myself. I made another significant decision yesterday. I have a three-week break from work, and I know precisely how I want to spend it.

I finish my breakfast of scrambled eggs and toast, then open my laptop. My heart's racing. But for the first time in far too long, it's not because I'm anxious.

I'm excited.

I navigate to Northwestern's graduate admissions page and find the link for their MFA program. I need a writing sample in the genre of popular fiction for my application—and I haven't written anything unrelated to law in years. But as soon as my fingers hit the keyboard, I'm in my zone.

I know exactly what story I want to tell. It's about a boy and a girl who meet when they're young, and later fall in love.

Five hours later, I have a rough draft. And I'm smiling so wide my cheeks hurt.

thirty-four

DEX

When the Oscar nominations were announced last month, I didn't think I stood a chance, considering the seasoned actors I was up against. Hell, it's been less than three years since my first movie came out, which makes me a relative newbie in this industry. But in the weeks leading up to tonight, all the media outlets have called me a shoo-in for this award. They say I've got it in the bag.

Still—when Helen Mirren herself opens the envelope for Best Actor, and with a beaming smile, says, "Dex Oliver," I can't believe what I'm hearing. I look at my beautiful mother first— after all, she's my date for the evening—and she bursts into tears. When I hug her, she whispers in my ear.

"I've been proud of you *every* single step of the way," she says.

Everyone in the Kodak Theatre is on their feet, cheering, and clapping, and reaching out to pat me on the back or shake my hand as I make my way to the stage. It's not until I'm actually up there with the statue in my hand, expressing my gratitude as thunderous applause fills the room, that I'm overcome with joy.

And it's not because I won. I honestly couldn't care less about that.

It's because here, on this stage, the entire world is my audience. And there's something very important I want to get off my chest.

When the noise dies down, I begin.

"The day we wrapped this movie, I had a panic attack. It wasn't my first. Not even my tenth. Probably not my hundredth, either. I was only five years old the first time it happened. My parents took me to see a psychologist, and I felt better for a while. But when I was in middle school, I was bullied. And the panic attacks started again.

"I was too embarrassed to ask for help. Too ashamed. I felt like there was something wrong with me. That I was broken. Or worse—crazy. So I suffered alone for years. In all honesty, I hated myself. I was desperate to be *anyone* else, so I chose a career where I could do exactly that.

"But what I learned is that there's no outrunning anxiety. It'll catch up to you at some point. And on the day we wrapped this movie, it caught up to me. I had the worst panic attack of my life, and I couldn't snap out of it. I was alone and terrified, and convinced I was going to die. Finally, I called my mom crying. And I did the hardest thing I've ever done. I told her I needed help."

I pause to look around the theater. I know I'm probably over the allotted time for my acceptance speech, but they haven't started playing the exit music yet. It's so quiet, you could hear a pin drop. Every pair of eyes is fixed on me, waiting for me to continue.

"I went home to Beachwood, Ohio, and I let my parents take care of me. A twenty-seven year-old man who makes a living playing the hero, could barely brush his own teeth. I was a wreck. I had to delay my next project. I told my agent and the director that I was dealing with a family emergency, and that's when I received inpatient treatment. I spent weeks talking to a therapist daily. I worked with a psychiatrist and started medication. It didn't help much at first, so after a month, we tweaked the dose.

"But finally—*finally*—I found relief. I haven't had a panic attack since the meds began working. This is the best I've felt in my life. And now that my anxiety's under control, I'm not ashamed of it anymore. That's why I'm sharing my story with you today.

"If you've ever woken up in the middle of the night sweating, and shaking, and gasping for air—your heart hammering so hard you're convinced you're going to die—I want you to know that I've been there. You're not broken. You're not crazy. You're not alone. You're human. Just like me. And there is help. All you have to do is ask.

"Thank you."

Now the crowd is on their feet again. But this time, they have tears in their eyes and tissues in their hands, some biting their quivering lips, others nodding slowly. *Knowingly.*

When my gaze meets my mom's, she winks at me. I rehearsed the speech in front of her and my dad probably a hundred times this week. I wasn't scared, so much as eager—because this message is so deeply important to me. I wanted to make sure I delivered it effectively. Well, the moment I see my mom's face, I know.

I nailed it.

The reaction to my confession is staggering. Not only in the Kodak Theatre, but around the world. My speech makes news everywhere—and it's not the negative press I lived in fear of for so long. Instead, the headlines look like this: "How Dex Oliver is Boldly Breaking the Stigma of Mental Illness," and, "Just Like Us! Superstar Dex Oliver Tells Anxiety Sufferers, 'You Are Not Alone.'"

I get countless letters from fans—some of whom are barely old enough to write—telling me how brave I am to share my story; how much it means to hear a celebrity speak openly about mental illness; how grateful they are that I'm raising awareness for this important cause. Many say I inspired them to finally seek treatment.

I've always thought of my anxiety as a curse. But today, I consider it a gift. Because knowing that my experience can help someone else who's suffering?

That makes it all worth it.

The following weekend, Jenna comes over to spend the night.

It's hard to believe we've been hanging out for almost a year now—minus the time I spent in treatment for my anxiety. When I got back to LA, I told her the real reason I'd been in Beachwood. She's one of the few people I admitted the truth to right away. And just like I expected, she was supportive, and kind, and made me promise to let her know if I started having symptoms again.

She and I have become close friends. I keep wondering how long we can maintain this friendship, while also sleeping together, before things start getting complicated. But so far, they haven't been complicated at all. Quite the contrary, it's been easy.

What hasn't been so easy is processing my feelings about Sunny in therapy. When I first started sessions, I wondered if my undying love for her was actually a product of my anxiety—a defense mechanism to keep me from getting close to anyone else, for fear they'd find out about my panic disorder and reject me.

But now I know that's not true. My anxiety's well-managed, and I love Sunny as much as I ever have. If not more. I don't *need* her to be the antidote to my anxiety.

I just want her.

And I simply don't know how to get over her.

My therapist says to be patient with myself.

But in three short months, Sunny will be married to Jeremy.

When she texted me after my Oscar speech to tell me how proud she is of me, I found the courage to ask when her wedding is, and she told me. Since then, I've had plenty of fantasies about crashing it. And in every single one, Sunny takes one look at me and runs down the aisle and into my arms.

It's a nice thought. Better than nice—incredible. And I wish, more than anything, that I still had a chance with her.

But I know Sunny. And I *really* don't think she'd be getting married if she weren't happy. Yes, she's pragmatic. But she's a romantic at heart. That's why she loves romance novels so much.

No matter what, I just want her to get her happy ending.

And as for me? I guess that remains to be seen.

For now, I still have this arrangement with Jenna to distract me.

After she spends the entire weekend at my place, we wake up late on Monday since neither of us has anywhere to be.

We're sipping coffee in bed when she turns to me. "Can we talk about something, Dex?"

"Of course." I place my cup on the nightstand and turn to her. In moments like these, I sometimes still expect to feel the familiar flood of panic in my veins. But my breath is even, and my hands are steady. All I feel is calm.

And grateful that I finally got the help I needed.

"This whole friends-with-benefits thing…" Jenna begins. "It's been fun. And I think we're lucky it hasn't blown up in our faces yet. But obviously this won't work long-term. At some point, I think we either stop sleeping together…or we actually try out a real relationship. And I've been giving both options some thought."

I nod, listening.

"I never told you why I swore off love," she continues. "And I'm still not ready to go into the details. But…remember how I started dating someone as soon as I got to college?"

"Yeah, I remember."

"Well…I fell head over heels for him. And, um—" She swallows. "It didn't end well."

She looks down at her lap quietly for several seconds. After taking her last sip of coffee, she puts her mug down, then goes on.

"I don't think I'll ever love anyone like that again, Dex. And, from what you've told me, I don't think you'll ever love anyone the way you love Sunny." She lets out a heavy sigh. "But…what if that makes us perfect for each other? I mean, I don't want to spend the rest of my life alone. And I also don't want to hurt anyone knowing I'll never love them the way they deserve."

Her cheeks flush as she meets my gaze. "So…what if we tried turning what we have into a real relationship? And, who knows? Maybe over time, we'd grow to love each other. It wouldn't be the same love we had for our exes, but…it would be *something*."

For a moment, I'm quiet.

She makes a good point. And what she's suggesting isn't totally unreasonable.

But…

She bites her lip as she eyes what I can only guess is a look of concern on my face. "You're not on board, are you," she says.

I sigh. "Part of me is tempted to say yes. I mean, we're obviously attracted to each other, and we get along so well—it would be easy. A hell of a lot easier than actually putting myself out there and trying to find real love again. I don't know if I'm capable of it either, Jenna. But I think I owe it to myself to try. I've spent so many years avoiding anything I thought would trigger my anxiety, and now that I've done the work to manage it, I don't want to act from a place of fear anymore. From here on out…I want to live authentically. And I think you deserve that, too."

Her eyes well with tears, but she cracks a smile. "So you're telling me I can't bury my head in the sand my entire life?"

I chuckle and take her hand.

I'm sad for Jenna. Whatever happened with her ex seems to have robbed her of the lightheartedness I remember so well from high school.

"I know you're right," she continues. "I can't avoid my triggers forever either. All the hard work you did to manage your anxiety, and the courage it took to share your story—it's really inspiring. I hope I can be that brave one day. I just…I don't think I'm there yet."

I wrap my arms around her. "It'll happen, Jenna. You have your whole life ahead of you. Don't give up yet."

She nods and smiles, wiping her tears. "Thanks, Dex. I *really* needed to hear that."

thirty-five

SUNNY
MARCH 2008

I should have known today would be a special day.

As soon as I stepped outside, I was met with bright, warm sunshine. It's not quite spring yet, and Chicago's been gray and gloomy for weeks. But this morning, it's sunny, just like the day I was born—exactly twenty-eight years ago.

It's the perfect birthday gift.

The change in weather would have been enough to please me, but when I get to work and check my email, I have a message from Northwestern's graduate admissions office.

I got in.

I've been accepted to their MFA program, which begins in the fall.

I'm on cloud nine. This is something I've wanted for years, but I let my mom talk me out of it, and I chose to go to law school out of fear rather than passion.

Knowing that I'm *finally* going to pursue my dream is the best feeling in the world.

Now all I have to do is tell my fiancé that I'll be quitting my job—well, switching careers, more accurately—and going back to graduate school.

He doesn't even know I applied. I decided it would be best to wait and see if I was admitted to the program before rocking the boat.

I never told him I thought I was pregnant either.

Because I wasn't pregnant—I was unwittingly starving myself. And my periods stopping was the wake-up call I needed to make some necessary changes in my life.

Maybe the reason I was so scared at the idea of having a baby back then was because I'd completely lost sight of who I was. Who I *am*. And I don't want to bring a child into this world until I can answer that question without hesitation.

Over the past five months since my doctor's visit, I've been working on that.

For one thing, I look like myself again.

I've been growing out my hair and wearing it curly, despite Jeremy dropping not-so-subtle hints—like gift cards to my salon for straightening treatments—to let me know where he stands on the matter. Since he's decided to be passive-aggressive, I thank him for the certificates and quietly exchange them for conditioning treatments. Thanks to Jeremy, my curls have never looked better.

I've been eating three meals a day, plus snacks—work be damned. If a partner has to wait ten minutes for me to finish a sandwich, then so be it. None of my expensive tailored suits fit me anymore, and I couldn't be happier. I bought myself new clothes that look good on me *and* are comfortable. I walk to work in sneakers and leave my Jimmy Choos in my office now.

Best of all, my blood pressure is back to normal. Not because I hate my job any less, but because I'm not desperately trying to be someone I'm not anymore.

For the past five months, since I started my graduate school application, I've felt like there's a light at the end of the tunnel. I don't let work get to me as much, because now I know this job is temporary. As soon as I applied to Northwestern, it was like a switch flipped in my head. Regardless of whether or not I got into the program, I'd made up my mind that I was going to quit law. And I've never felt better.

I've spent nearly three miserable years as a lawyer. But the silver lining is that I saved enough money to pay for the MFA program myself.

This time, no one can stop me.

Not my mom.

Not even Jeremy. Although I'm certain he'll try.

I know he's stubborn, but if he loves me as much as he says, he should at least understand that I need to prioritize my health.

Although I must admit…when my doctor put me on medical leave for my blood pressure in the fall, Jeremy's initial reaction wasn't concern.

He was angry. As if my body's stress response made me weak— or a failure.

"Are you *kidding* me, Sunny?" he said with a look of total disappointment on his face. "You let yourself get worked up over nothing, and it's going to kill your goddamn career. What a fucking waste of talent."

I felt like a good kid being scolded for a bad grade in school.

But when I told him that yelling at me definitely wasn't helping my blood pressure, he mellowed out a bit.

It was a rough three weeks for us while I was on medical leave, but I was so excited about secretly working on my writing sample that I didn't care as much about his moods.

In any event, when I returned to work a much calmer and happier version of Sunny than he'd seen in a while, he pulled a 180 and became sweet Jeremy again. Maybe he figured a short break from work was all I needed to get back on track as a litigator.

Whatever he was thinking, I guess I'll find out tonight.

Jeremy wants to take me to an upscale sushi restaurant to celebrate my birthday. The maki rolls and sashimi are delicious, as are the fancy cocktails, and my fiancé is in a great mood. We're laughing and flirting—and for a minute, I consider telling him about Northwestern right here and now.

Maybe he won't react so badly if we're out in public, I think to myself.

But if I'm to be my authentic self, then I need to know the man I'm marrying as well. *All of him.* Not just the performance he puts on when it suits him.

I learned that from Dex.

When I watched his Oscar speech the other week, I sobbed.

Thank goodness I was home alone. Jeremy was at the office prepping for trial.

For one thing, my heart broke because Dex told me he'd gotten help for his anxiety years ago—and I chose to believe him. I mean, he's an incredible actor, obviously. But I think, deep down, I knew he wasn't being honest. It was just easier to take his word for it, because I'd broken up with him, and we were miles apart. I wasn't in a position to help him.

I'm wracked with guilt over it. And I'm so sad he suffered in silence for as long as he did.

But the impact he's making on the world is nothing short of heroic. The media's reporting that therapists are experiencing a boom in business—particularly those who work with men and boys, who are less likely to seek help than their female counterparts.

And what I find most inspiring is that Dex isn't hiding under a mask and a cape to make the world a better place. He's doing it by being *himself*.

I keep that in mind when Jeremy and I get home from dinner, and he's leading me to the bedroom.

"There's something I need to talk to you about first," I say as soon as he turns to kiss me.

"Okay," he says pulling back. He goes to sit on the bed, and I follow him.

"When I was on medical leave for my blood pressure…I decided to apply to Northwestern's MFA program," I tell him. "Today, I found out I got in."

His brow is furrowed. He inches away from me on the bed. "You did *what?*" he asks. "*Why?*"

"Jeremy, I picked the wrong career. Law isn't for me. I put in three years, and the high-stress nature of the job made me sick. I don't want to find out what happens if I stick it out any longer.

It's no one's fault…it's just a fact. Being an attorney is not the right fit for me."

He scoffs. "It's no one's fault? Wow, Sunny, way to shirk any responsibility for your life. *Our* life. We're getting married in three months, for fuck's sake! And you're going to sit here and tell me you're changing careers—to something completely fucking impractical, by the way—and you want me to, what… *support* this harebrained decision? Bankroll you, so you can play in never-never land, while I bust my ass with a real job?"

I expected him to be argumentative, and I'm prepared to hold my ground. "I don't need your money, Jeremy. I have enough saved up to pay for grad school myself. But I *do* need your support. This career made me physically ill. Is that really the life you want for me?"

He stands and paces back and forth in front of me. "So you hate litigation—fine. Pick a different area of law, then. Write contracts or some shit. I don't care—"

"You said it yourself in law school—that would bore me to tears. I don't *want* to write contracts, Jeremy. I want to write *novels*. Beautiful, sweeping love stories that make people laugh, and cry… and maybe even inspire them to live a more authentic life."

He smirks. "You want to write *romance*, Sunny. People won't get anything out of your books but a cheap thrill. It's fucking embarrassing. How am I supposed to introduce you to people now? When we're at work events, should I say, 'Hey, this is my extremely intelligent and talented wife who used to be a successful attorney, but gave it all up to be the next Danielle Steel?'"

"Do *not* talk shit about Danielle Steel," I warn. "And why is keeping up appearances more important to you than the health and well-being of the woman you love?"

He stops pacing and faces me. "The woman I *love* isn't here anymore, Sunny!" he yells, his hands in the air. "Don't you see? The woman I fell for was at the top of her class in law school. A star legal researcher and writer. Someone who cared about her fucking appearance—"

"What the hell is that supposed to mean?"

Jeremy stands with his hands on his hips. "How much weight have you put on these last few months, Sunny?"

My palm flies to my gut, as though he really punched me.

"*Fuck* you," I say, my voice shaking.

I've never said those words to anyone.

I stand and walk to the other side of the room, putting as much distance between us as possible. "I was anemic…my periods stopped…I was barely a hundred pounds." My eyes fill with tears. "But…that's what you want, isn't it? You want me to be small. You want me to be meek. You belittle me, and criticize me when I don't live up to your expectations…you *prey* on my insecurities, so you can *control* me—"

"You're fucking crazy, you know that?"

"And now you're gaslighting me! I can't believe I didn't see it before…"

"See what?" he says, lunging toward me. My back is to the wall and he's an inch away from my face.

"You're a goddamn narcissist," I tell him, my chest heaving against his. "I'm just grateful you showed me who you really are before I married you."

I take off my enormous diamond ring and put it on top of the dresser beside me. His icy gaze follows my hand, then works its way back to my face.

"What the fuck do you think you're doing?" he hisses.

"You never loved *me*, Jeremy. You loved the fantasy of being with this straight-haired, stick-thin, high-powered litigator in designer clothes, because it fed your ego. But that's not the real me. I will never live up to your fantasy—nor do I want to."

"You really think you're going to leave me?" He grinds his teeth. "You have nowhere to go, Sunny. No friends. Who took you to go pick out your wedding dress, huh? *Me.* Who do you spend every fucking minute of your life with? *Me.* You have *nothing* without me."

Shit. He's not wrong. I've been living in Chicago nearly three years and don't have a single friend here. I'll have to go to a hotel tonight.

"Was that part of your grand plan too?" I ask him. "To isolate me so I had no one to run to when I saw your true colors? Or to keep me away from anyone who could help me see what a fucking asshole you are?"

I look into his cold, hard eyes, and I don't recognize the person staring back at me. There's no trace of anything familiar on his face. He isn't Jekyll, or Hyde—or even Jeremy. The man I thought I knew is gone.

I shiver when he leans in to whisper in my ear. "I've got news for you, Sunny. I hope you're not thinking of running back to Mr. Hollywood, because you're going to be shit out of luck if you do…"

Then he says something so lewd, so vile…I want to wipe my memory clean of it. But the gist of it was this—first, he tried to humiliate me by body-shaming me. Then he reminded me that Dex can have any woman he wants, including Ava Elwood. And I'd be lucky if he gave me the time of day anymore, much less touch me ever again.

I want to slap him.

But I don't—because he'll enjoy it. He'll love the fact that he got under my skin, and it'll only make that smug grin of his even wider.

So I finish this chapter of my life with the truth instead. "I'm not leaving you for Dex," I say calmly. "I'm leaving you for *myself.* Because I deserve so much better."

A giant weight lifts off my shoulders as I push past him and throw some of my things into a duffel.

I don't acknowledge him when he yells at me.

I don't respond when he changes his tune and begs me to forgive him.

I pack what I need as quickly as I can.

I tell him I'll send someone to pick up the rest.

And then I leave.

thirty-six

SUNNY

JUNE 2008

My palms are sweaty against the steering wheel as I make a left turn past Beachwood High School. The closer I get to my destination, the more jittery I feel.

Maybe I should have gone to my mom's place first. But she and Luis are both at work, so I made other plans. There's a conversation I need to have that's been a long time coming, and I don't want to avoid it anymore.

Although now, as I pull into the driveway of this house I haven't been to in years, I'm kicking myself for not stopping to shower or change my outfit. I just drove over five hours from Chicago, after all.

I hope I don't smell.

I do a quick check to make sure my deodorant's working, then step out of my car and walk slowly up the front steps to ring the doorbell.

After several seconds, the door swings open, but before I can say a word, Mia hands me a very happy baby wearing footie pajamas.

"Hold this!" she says, and darts back into her parents' house yelling after Avery, who's giggling so loudly I can hear her from the porch.

"Well, you must be James," I say to the six-month-old smiling at me. "Nice to meet you. I'm Sunny."

James laughs as though I'd just told the funniest joke in the world, and my heart swells to at least twice its size. Then Mia comes back outside with two-year-old Avery on her hip. She's covered head-to-toe in what I imagine is fingerpaint.

"I'm so sorry, Sunny!" she says, nodding toward her daughter. "If I turn my back for one second, this one starts doing something she *knows* she shouldn't. But I can give her a bath later. Come on in! I see you've made friends with James!"

"He's been smiling at me nonstop," I say. "I even made him laugh."

"He's *such* a flirt," Mia jokes, giving him a kiss on his big bald head. James squeals with delight and starts kicking his feet.

I follow her into her parents' home, which looks as cozy and inviting as I remember it. Not much has changed in the decade since I've been here—with the exception of Avery and James's toys strewn about the living room. When we get to the kitchen, she puts Avery down on the floor to play with blocks, then moves her son from my arms into a bouncer.

"They're both precious, Mia," I tell her. "I'm so happy for you."

"Thanks! It's sheer chaos most of the time…especially since I got promoted. I work longer hours, and I'm not getting nearly enough sleep. And this little guy's been teething and keeping us up all night!" she says, pointing to a beaming, bouncing James.

"That's why Evan's napping upstairs. But as crazy as our life is, I wouldn't trade it for the world," she says with a grin.

Then she moves a tray to the center of the table. "My mom made us strawberry lemonade. She remembers how much you used to love it. She and my dad just left for the grocery store, but they'll be back in a bit."

"That's really thoughtful," I say as Mia pours me a glass. "Thank you. And thanks for coming to Beachwood to see me. I know it's not as short a trip now that you guys are back in Columbus."

She shakes her head. "Are you kidding? It's barely two hours! Well, maybe a little longer—I drive *way* slower with the kids in the car." She laughs. "Either way, it's no problem at all. We were going to be here this weekend anyway, for—"

She stops herself.

"For my wedding," I say, nodding. "It's okay, Mia. We can talk about it."

Her eyebrows knit together. "How are you doing?" she asks.

I sigh. "Honestly…I'm fine. And I mean it, this time. I really dodged a bullet. I would have been miserable if I'd married Jeremy. I'm sure we would have ended up divorced anyway. And what if we had children? It would have been a mess. I think he spared me a lot of pain by showing me what an asshole he is *now* rather than later."

Mia's hazel eyes are teary. "I'm so sorry you had to go through that, Sunny. But I'm proud of you for leaving. That must have been hard. Has he tried contacting you?"

I roll my eyes. "He called and texted me for weeks afterward, even though I never answered. And his messages were as hot and cold as he was. First he would tell me how much he cherishes me and how incredible I am; then an hour later he'd say that I'll never find another man to love me. I eventually blocked his number."

"That's awful. Where did you stay after you broke up with him?"

"I found an apartment to sublet for a few months. I could have come back here, but I decided to work at the firm until summer so I could make more money to put toward school."

"I can't believe you're going to be a writer," she says with a smile. "I don't usually read romance novels, but you better believe I'm going to read yours." When Mia pauses, her grin starts to fade. "Until you told me you were switching careers, I had no idea you considered getting an MFA instead of going to law school."

I look down at the table before I meet her gaze. "That's actually part of why I'm here. I mean, I wanted to see you and finally meet your beautiful kids, of course. But…I also came to apologize.

"I wasn't always the greatest friend. I kept so much of myself hidden, because I was afraid to show you who I really was. Not only you—most people. I had this notion in my head that I had to be this perfect lawyer, with a perfect house, and a perfect family. But if I've learned anything in the past ten years, it's that nothing's perfect. *No one's* perfect. And I don't want to spend my life trying to please others. The best I can do is stay true to myself and the people I love." I look at her through tears. "I love you, Mia. And I'm sorry."

Tears roll down her cheeks. "I love you too, Sunny. And I'm so glad you don't feel like you have to hide anymore. The real you seems pretty wonderful."

We lean forward in our chairs and hug, both of us crying. When we pull apart, Avery and James are staring up at us with curious looks on their faces.

"I hope they're not worried about us," I say with a frown.

Mia shakes her head as she wipes her eyes. "They're fine. I try not to hide my emotions from them too much. I want them to know we're all human—even grownups—and it's okay to have feelings."

I nod, still sniffling. "Well, they may not know it now, but they are *so* lucky to have you as their mom. And if they ever forget when they're older…Aunt Sunny will remind them."

The next morning, I wake up to the smell of coffee brewing. I open my suitcase, grab the sundress sitting on top of my stack of clothes, and throw it on. Then I head downstairs to the kitchen and find my mom sitting at the table in her robe.

When she sees me walking in, she smiles.

All in all, my mom handled the news of my called-off wedding a lot better than I expected her to. Once I explained what Jeremy was really like behind closed doors, she actually cried. It's not often my mom shows her vulnerable side. But she's changed quite a bit since starting therapy.

It took about a year for her to book a session after she first mentioned it. I'd completely given up hope. But this past March, she finally got a referral from her doctor and started going weekly. It was perfect timing, seeing as I'd just broken up with my fiancé and decided to change careers.

My mom still wasn't thrilled when I told her about the MFA program. Maybe no amount of therapy will get her there. At least she knows better now than to try to talk me out of it. She even offered to help me financially, but I told her I didn't need her to.

Overall, our relationship is much-improved—and I'm grateful for it.

"How are you feeling?" she asks, tilting her head as I sit down with my coffee.

"Not too bad, considering today was supposed to be my wedding day."

My mom looks down at her cup. "Sweetheart, there's something I've been wanting to tell you." She bites her lip. "It's…about Dex."

My heart leaps into my throat. "Dex? What about Dex?" I can barely croak out the words.

I haven't talked to him in months. I have no idea what he's been up to since the Oscars. I haven't heard any rumblings about a new film. Haven't seen any paparazzi photos of him with models, or actresses. He could be engaged—or married—for all I know.

Is *that* what my mom wants to tell me? *Oh god.* I hold my breath.

"I was never supportive of your relationship with him, Sunny…and I want to explain why. I've been working on this with my therapist, but it's still so hard to admit. You see…Dex reminded me of your father. In many ways." She pauses and meets my gaze. "Is it okay if I tell you more?"

My pulse quickens, but I nod.

My mom takes a deep breath before beginning. "Your father was charming. Devastatingly handsome. He had a brilliant smile too, just like a movie star. He was an airline pilot, and I met him on a flight to Rome. You know how I loved to travel before you were born. Well, the moment I laid eyes on him, Sunny…I was a goner. I figured I had nothing to lose, so I asked him out for a drink after we landed. And it was…instant chemistry, just like you and Dex."

She sighs. "But he was never around, Sunny. He was always busy, flying across the world. He didn't want to settle down. Never wanted a family. He only wanted to travel and have fun. So that's what we did. I'd meet him in Paris for a weekend, or London. It was *thrilling*, and romantic, and—I couldn't help myself—I fell head over heels for him. And, well…you know what happens next. I never imagined I'd get pregnant. But I also never imagined he wouldn't want anything to do with me afterward."

She pauses to wipe her eyes as I blink back my own tears.

"When I saw you falling in love with Dex—I saw myself, sweetheart. And I was scared. *Terrified.* I would have done anything to spare you from falling in love with a man who would sweep you off your feet with his dazzling smile and exciting life, then leave you."

She looks at me, her cheeks flushed with shame. "I said awful things to you about Dex. But that's not all of it. I…"

"What, Mom?"

"The morning after his cousin's wedding, Dex came here

to talk to you. He said you'd had a misunderstanding, and he wanted to explain. And…I wouldn't allow it. I sent him away."

My hand gravitates to my aching heart.

My first instinct is to sob. To yell. To tell my mom I'll never forgive her.

To ask her if she knows how much pain her meddling caused me.

But…what's the point?

That was eight years ago. Dex and I got back together two years later, and we broke up again anyway.

I broke up with him. Because *I* thought I wasn't good enough.

Even if my mom had never meddled…the outcome would have been the same.

I just…I can't believe…

"He never told me," I say. "I was so mad at him because I thought he didn't fight for me. And he never said it was because you stopped him."

My mom shakes her head, crying. "He's a far better person than I am, Sunny. A far better man than I ever gave him credit for. And not only that…" She exhales deeply. "His Oscar speech? It inspired me. He's the reason I finally went to therapy."

I take in a ragged breath. "His speech gave me the courage to break up with Jeremy."

My mom brings her palms to her cheeks. "Oh Sunny, I feel awful. I drove you away from Dex and into the arms of a narcissist. Is there anything I can do to fix this? I haven't seen the Dexters in years, but I could call them if you want me to."

I laugh through my tears. "I think you've done quite enough

already, Mom."

She laughs first, then sobs. "I'm so sorry, Sunny. I wouldn't blame you if you hated me."

"I don't hate you, Mom. And you're *not* a bad person. You lost your parents when you were seventeen. You had no other family. And when you finally fell in love, he left you pregnant and alone. You suffered a lot of trauma—*of course* it affected you. I'm just happy you're getting help now."

My mom gets up from her chair and kneels down to hug me, then says in my ear, "I hope things work out between you and Dex, sweetie. I was blind to it before—but you really do belong together."

My smile is wistful. "I guess that remains to be seen." When I push my chair back, we both stand. "I'm going to go for a drive to clear my head," I tell her.

After one more hug, my mom releases me. I grab my keys and head outside.

Then I drive. Just like the times Dex used to pick me up in his dad's car, and I'd loop around Beachwood with no agenda, deciding where to turn on a whim.

So much has changed since then and yet—here I am—still driving in circles around my hometown, longing for him.

Loving him with every piece of my heart and soul.

If he were in this car right now, what would I say?

I glance at the passenger seat, half-expecting to see him.

Like that weekend in New York, I'm haunted by his ghost again. Every time I stop at a red light and look out my window, he's there.

Outside the elementary school where we met in kindergarten.

In line to buy movie tickets at the theater we used to go to.

At the park where we almost kissed in the rain.

I guess this ride isn't so aimless after all.

If it wasn't clear before, it's clear to me now.

I need to talk to Dex.

To get things off my chest, the way I did with Mia.

But when? And how? I'd prefer to speak in person, but I have no idea where he is.

I guess I could ask his parents.

Seeing as I'm parked in front of their house.

I turn into their driveway.

The lights are off. The house is quiet. It doesn't look like anyone's here. I get out of my car anyway.

Then I sit on the Dexters' porch swing. And I cry.

I cry because, after all these years, and after everything I've been through, this house still feels more like home to me than anywhere I've ever actually *lived*. And I know exactly why. It's because Oliver Dexter is my home. But as luck would have it, I don't know when I'll ever see him again.

When the Dexters get back, I'll ask them where he is—and I'll fly there. I'll meet him in LA, or New York. I'll travel across the world if I have to.

I take a deep breath as relief washes over me. I have a plan now. All I have to do is wait for his parents.

Not two minutes later, I'm blinded by headlights.

Mr. and Mrs. Dexter are back.

I stand, not bothering to wipe my tears. There's no use

pretending I'm not still hopelessly in love with their son. And if Dex has moved on, and he's happy, they'll let me know and spare me the heartache of hearing it from him.

The driver's side door swings open.

But it's not one of the elder Dexters getting out of the car.

It's their son.

thirty-seven

DEX

When I pull into my parents' driveway and see Sunny sitting on the porch swing, I'm convinced I'm hallucinating.

Because it's not the same Sunny I saw with Jeremy in Manhattan—straight-haired and whisper-thin.

This Sunny is radiant. Healthy, and glowing. Her long hair cascades past her shoulders in perfect ringlets. And she isn't wearing couture, either. She's in a simple yellow sundress that accentuates her curves.

Jesus.

I've never seen a more beautiful woman in my entire life.

But she can't be real, right? Bright, beautiful Sunny in her yellow dress—just like the day I met her?

This must be a dream.

I step out of the car and she stands, her eyes wet with tears. She lifts her hand to her perfect pink lips, like she can't believe she's seeing me either.

I walk slowly up the steps, half-expecting her to disappear when I get closer, like a mirage.

But I'm standing in front of her, and she's still here.

"Hi," she says softly as a smile forms through her tears.

I sweep her cheek with my thumb.

She's real.

"What happened?" I ask her. "Are you okay?"

She laughs, then cries.

I take her hand and we sit on the porch swing—just like we used to do when we were kids.

"I broke up with Jeremy," she says, looking into my eyes.

I don't hide my relief. I let out a breath it feels like I've been holding for the last three-and-a-half years—since Paris.

My reaction makes her cheeks flush pink as she smiles at me. She's so goddamn gorgeous, it's all I can do not to take her in my arms and kiss her.

But I don't want to be presumptuous. She looks like she has more to say.

"I also quit my job. Quit my *career*, actually. I got into Northwestern's MFA program. I'll be starting in September."

My eyes go wide. "Sunny, that's incredible. I'm really proud of you." I pause for several seconds, taking her in. "So…you're happy? I mean, I did find you crying here…"

She giggles, then takes a deep breath. "It's been a rough few years. I was miserable being a lawyer. I was miserable with Jeremy. I was so stressed, I could barely eat."

My brow furrows. Now I understand.

"I also found out what a jerk my biological father was." She sighs. "I'll tell you the whole story later, but…on the bright side, I know more about who I am now. I'm a quarter Lebanese and a quarter French. It explains a lot."

I grin. "That's why you always wanted to study in Paris."

She nods. "And why Sam and I gravitated toward each other. She's half Lebanese. She said she suspected all along, because I love Middle Eastern food so much. I actually bought a Lebanese cookbook recently." She bites her lip. "I decided I can't let my feelings about the man who fathered me keep me from learning about my culture."

I take her hand in mine. "I'm really happy for you, Sunny. You're such an amazing woman. You always have been. But…I think you finally know it now."

Her eyes well with tears again. "You're right, I do. And I have *you* to thank for that, Dex. Your Oscar speech gave me the courage to let go of everything that wasn't working in my life. You made me want to be my best self." She chuckles. "You also helped me get into grad school."

I tilt my head. "Oh yeah? How did I do that?"

"You were the inspiration for my writing sample." She looks down at her lap, and when she takes her gaze to mine, her cheeks flush again. "I wrote about us. I wrote…*our story.*"

My heart's racing, but not because I'm anxious. It's because I'm about to get an answer I've been waiting an entire lifetime for. "How does it end, Sunny?"

She takes her hand away from mine and unzips her purse.

Then she pulls out a folded-up piece of notebook paper and gives it to me. "It ends like this," she says.

thirty-eight

SUNNY

As soon as I hand Dex the letter, I yank it back with trembling fingers.

"Sorry," I stammer. "I probably should have asked you this before, but…you're not secretly married, are you? Or engaged? Or—"

"No. I'm not in a relationship." Dex half-smiles, and it's all I can do not to wrap my arms around him and kiss the hell out of him for all eternity.

But first, I need to give him this letter. Just like Summer gives her letter to Rex at the end of the story I wrote.

With a sigh of relief, I hand it back to him. He takes care in opening it, like he knows he's holding a piece of my heart, and I watch as his eyes skate across every line of my confession. What begins as a half-smile on his lips becomes a full one—and I'm filled with a sense of hope, like I've never felt before.

When he's done reading, Dex meets my gaze, the corners of his eyes crinkling as he takes my hand and threads his fingers through mine. I turn to face him, eagerly awaiting his response.

But he says nothing.

My mind starts to race.

Yes, he's single—but what if he's gotten over me?

Yes, he's smiling—but what if he's trying to think of a way to let me down gently?

Yes, his eyes are gleaming—but what if the look I see isn't love so much as nostalgia?

When Dex finally opens his mouth to speak, it occurs to me that my letter doesn't tell the whole story. Only a fraction of it. And he deserves to know everything.

I'm done holding back the truth.

"Wait—" I tell him. "Before you say anything, I want to explain. I wrote you this love letter ten years ago, when we were seniors in high school. I never gave it to you because… the timing wasn't right…but I've carried it with me ever since. I took it to college. To law school. To Paris, and Chicago. On my first day going to court by myself, I had it tucked inside my briefcase. See, I tucked my feelings away, Dex, but they've always been here. No matter how hard I tried to hide it, or fight it, I have always loved you. And I always will."

Dex lets go of my hand and looks down at the letter again.

My chest tightens.

"Did you *really* quote Savage Garden?" he says, still staring at the crinkled piece of paper.

I laugh despite my nerves. "Give me a break, okay? It was 1998."

But when he doesn't say more, my gut clenches as I brace myself for the worst.

After several seconds, during which my entire life flashes

before my eyes, Dex folds the ten-year-old piece of notebook paper along its original creases and stands to put it in his pocket. Then he walks from the porch swing to the top of the steps. I follow his gaze up to the sky.

"What are you looking at?" I ask, my breathing shallow.

His eyes are now on mine. "I think the goddamn stars finally aligned," he says, grinning.

My mind travels back to our tearful goodbye before I left for law school. We were right here on the Dexters' front lawn when Dex tried to tell me he loved me—but I wouldn't let him. I told him to wait until the stars align.

I felt like I was carrying the weight of the world on my shoulders that day—leaving my soulmate behind for a career I was certain wouldn't be a good fit. But that career is in my rearview mirror now. And my soulmate is in front of me, offering me his heart.

All at once, the tension in my body melts, and I can breathe deeply again.

I giggle as I look back up at the clear blue, sunny sky. "You're right. I see it too."

"So…" he says, wrapping his arms around my waist. "Does that mean you'll *finally* let me say it?"

I take a step back and bite my lip. "Just one last thing—" I tell him.

He half-smiles and shakes his head. "Seriously, Sunny? How long are you going to make me wait?"

I chuckle, but my brow furrows. "I need to get this off my chest first. I want to tell you how sorry I am for breaking up with you in Paris." My eyes fill with tears. "You were so vulnerable with me about your anxiety. You told me you needed my help, and I abandoned you because I was convinced I wasn't good enough for you." I sob. "I don't know if I can ever forgive myself. But if you let me…I'll spend the rest of my life trying to make it up to you."

Dex takes me in his arms again. "Sunny, you don't have to apologize. You did the right thing. I put this huge burden on you to fix my problems—and that wasn't your job. I don't know that I ever would have gotten the help I needed if you didn't break up with me in Paris. You did me the biggest favor of my life."

"Really?" I ask, wiping my tears.

"Really," he says.

This time I know he's being sincere.

I smile so wide my cheeks hurt. "Okay…*now* you can say it."

Dex takes my face in his hands. "I love you, Sunny. I always have, and I always will," he says.

And then we kiss.

We kiss, and kiss, and kiss, right there on the front porch— and we only stop when we hear the clicking sound of camera shutters.

There are two photographers on the Dexters' lawn. When we spot them, they yell, "Thanks, Dex!" before running to their parked cars and driving off with screeching tires.

Dex shakes his head. "Welcome to my world," he says. "Although it might not be my world much longer."

My brow crinkles. "What do you mean?"

He half-smiles. "After the Oscars, I turned down a couple

of roles. I've never done that before. I always felt like I needed to work, because if I didn't, well—I'd fall apart. But I don't feel that way anymore. I don't *need* acting the way I used to. So I was thinking of taking a break for a while to focus on a different project."

"What kind of project?" I ask, my eyes widening. The excitement in his grin is contagious.

"I want to work with kids, Sunny. Kids who have anxiety. I was thinking of developing a program that infuses the arts into mental health treatment. So kids would be getting the care they need from a therapist, while also learning how to use the arts to manage their symptoms. And maybe once or twice a year, we'd put on an original show. Some of the kids could write the script, some could act. Some could paint the sets, or play music." He shrugs, but his eyes are glimmering. "That's all I've got so far."

I blink back tears. "That sounds incredible, Dex. Where will you do it?"

"That's the thing," he says raising an eyebrow. "I can do it anywhere. Chicago, maybe?"

I wrap my arms around his neck and start kissing him. But before we get carried away, I pull back. "We probably should head inside before more photographers show up. By the way, I forgot to ask—what are you doing in Beachwood?"

Dex laughs and runs a hand over his hair. "I, um—I came here to stop your wedding."

My jaw drops before I belly laugh. "*What?* Seriously?"

He nods. "I had it all planned out. A final grand gesture to win you back. It was going to be very dramatic," he says, kissing me again. "But I like this ending a lot better."

"This isn't the end. It's only the beginning," I remind him, repeating the words he said to me under the stars, the last time we went camping.

With one arm wrapped around my waist, Dex threads the other under my knees and scoops me up.

"Where are we going?" I ask with a smile.

"I'm taking you home," he says. "Well, to my parents' home."

"Where are they, by the way?"

"Visiting my Aunt Jane and Uncle Rich in Maryland. They won't be back for a week. I'm sure you and I will be *really* busy making up for lost time…but at some point we'll have to call and tell them we're back together. I think they've been waiting for this day as long as I have."

"Did they know about your plan to derail my wedding?" I ask with a smile.

Dex laughs. "Are you kidding? It was practically their idea."

I heave a deep sigh. "I love them so much. And I love you."

"I adore you, Sunny."

After he pauses to grab my purse from the porch swing, the man I've always loved carries me across the threshold of the home I've always loved. He kicks the door shut behind us, then takes me upstairs to his bed, where we kiss each other endlessly, like teenagers again.

When we pause to take a breath, I sweep my thumb across his cheek.

Oliver Dexter smiles at me. "They're happy tears."

epilogue

SUNNY

JUNE 2010

I haven't been back to Beachwood High School since I graduated twelve years ago.

There was a ten-year reunion party here in the fall of 2008, but it was the same weekend Dex and I moved to Chicago. Before we left, on our last night in Beachwood, we went camping at our favorite childhood spot—and he proposed to me under a starlit sky. He gave me his maternal grandmother's ring, which he'd only just found out his mom had been saving for me for years.

Apparently Dex's cousin Ben had asked for it nearly a decade earlier, and it caused a minor squabble between Mrs. Dexter and her brother Ted. Finally, she convinced him the ring was meant for me. There's no denying it...with its yellow gold band and round center stone surrounded by an array of diamonds, you can't look at it without seeing a bright, shining sun.

Mrs. Dexter always believed her son would give me that ring one day.

She was right.

While I took classes toward my MFA at Northwestern, Dex developed a pilot program, using the dramatic arts as a tool to help kids with anxiety. He named it the Dramatic Hearts Academy, and last year they had a successful launch at a school on Chicago's North Side. Now he's working to expand the program across the country.

Even though he hasn't made a movie in over two years, he's still famous as ever. But now it's as the face of a nationwide campaign to break the stigma of mental illness. In addition to working with kids, he's already booked a year out for speaking engagements. His Ted Talk got so much online traffic, it nearly broke the Internet.

Now that I've graduated and we're back in Beachwood permanently, Dex will be working with kids at our high school. To drum up excitement for the initiative, he offered the students in his Chicago pilot program an all-expenses-paid vacation to exciting Beachwood, Ohio—in exchange for performing their show.

It's the opening night of a three-day run, and literally everyone and their mother is here. Including mine, of course, with Luis by her side. Last year, after much good-humored prodding from her husband, she joined him in retirement. It was a bumpy beginning for my former-workaholic mother, but she's come to love it. In addition to traveling with Luis, she enjoys swimming, gardening—and reading *romance* novels, of all things. Turns out she found an old stash I'd hidden in my closet and couldn't resist the temptation.

"Hello, my sweethearts," she says, wrapping her arms around both me and Dex. We're standing at the door to the auditorium greeting guests, and there's a line of people a mile long, eyeing *the* Dex Oliver and waiting for their chance to meet him.

"Hey, Mom," Dex says, winking at her.

I still can't believe they're this close.

Last summer, Dex and I got married in the Dexters' backyard, like I always dreamed. With our family and friends—and a handful of A-list celebrities. My mom was positively beaming when she walked me down the aisle.

As soon as Dex and I got back together, she took it upon herself to write him a long letter of apology. And Dex, being the most empathetic and compassionate person I know, accepted it readily.

Needless to say, my mom and I get along better than ever. Between writing letters to Dex and reading romance novels, she and I have a lot more in common than I thought possible.

After she and Luis enter the auditorium to take their seats, we greet Mr. and Mrs. Dexter.

"Hi, Mom. Hi, Dad," I tell the best in-laws I could hope for. They're a major part of the reason Dex and I decided to move back here. When we have kids, we want them to grow up enjoying Sunday morning pancakes at their house. And telling ghost stories around the firepit in their backyard.

"Hello, *Mrs. Dexter*," my mother-in-law says to me with a wink.

I've been Mrs. Dexter for a year, and I still feel giddy anytime someone calls me that. I'm so glad my husband never legally changed his name to Dex Oliver. Mrs. Oliver just doesn't have the same ring to it.

"Long time no see, darling," my father-in-law says to me with a laugh.

It's funny because we live with them—just for now—while our house is being built. Our new home will be ready by the end of this summer. It's only a ten-minute drive from the Dexters, and even closer to my mom's, making it the perfect spot for the family gatherings I always dreamed of.

As the Dexters make their way into the auditorium, I see a familiar face smiling at me.

"Sam!" I squeal, wrapping my arms around her. "I can't believe you're actually here in Beachwood!"

Sam visited me and Dex in Chicago a few times, but wasn't able to come to our wedding because her brother got married the same weekend. When she told me she would've much preferred celebrating with us, I knew she wasn't lying, given the complicated relationship she has with her family. Apparently her mom spent the better part of the wedding weekend crying because Sam has no marriage prospects. And her Lebanese grandmother has now taken to calling her a "spinster."

She hugs me back, then pulls away and gives us a pointed look. "And *I* can't believe you guys moved back here when I just got a teaching position at Northwestern!" She sighs. "At least Chicago's driving distance, so I can come harass you two in your love nest."

Dex laughs. "You're welcome anytime. And Sunny and I will come visit you too. I love Chicago—it's a great city."

"It is," Sam admits. "It just sucks that everyone I know is in New York or California. Or *Beachwood*," she adds, playfully rolling her eyes. "This Northwestern gig better be worth moving back to the Midwest for."

"Of course it'll be worth it, Sam—or should I say, *Dr. Sam?* I'm so proud of you for making your career dreams come true."

"Thank you," she says, beaming. "Speaking of dreams, how's the romance writing going? If I remember our conversations in college—which I do in *great* detail—your husband is giving you some excellent material."

I turn to see Dex half-smile. "The writing's going well," I redirect as my face warms. "I've been working on a series of books that I'm planning to self-publish next year."

"That's so exciting! I can't wait to read them. Just promise you'll put in detailed instructions on how Dex does that thing— you know—the one that made you scream so loud—"

"Sam!" I shriek, grabbing her shoulders as Dex chuckles. "First of all, *please* keep your voice down before this ends up on Page Six," I say with an eye on the crowd. "Second of all, I don't write sex manuals—I write *romance* novels. And third of all…I'm literally *never* telling you anything again."

Sam looks to Dex and shakes her head. "She *always* says that."

I turn to my husband, who is thoroughly amused. "Normally, I don't kiss and tell. But I was really hung up on you in college and ended up giving Sam way too many details about our relationship which, unfortunately, she refuses to forget."

"All I'm saying is, the more details in your books the better. I'll buy several copies and hand them out as a public service to every guy I slept with who couldn't find my—"

"Sam! There's a *child* right behind you!" I say, bringing my palm to my face. The kid and her dad are facing away from us, but still.

She winces. "Yikes! I didn't realize. Well, I'm going to take a seat inside before Sunny's face turns any redder," she says, kissing my cheek.

I smile as she waves goodbye to us.

"She's hilarious," Dex says to me. "Great comedic timing."

I shake my head, laughing as the child and father who'd been standing behind Sam turn in our direction. "Sunny D!" the father exclaims when he sees us.

It's Evan Chen. My stomach flips, wondering if he overheard our conversation with Sam. I'd be mortified.

"Sunny D! Sunny D!" four-year-old Avery repeats, tugging at her dad's hand. She's so much bigger than when we saw her in Beachwood over the holidays, I can hardly believe my eyes. She looks exactly like a mini version of Mia—and hearing her call Dex and me by our high school nickname floods me with overwhelming joy. Back then, we were joined at the hip as friends. Now we're joined in marriage.

After we all hug, Evan turns to look back at the front door again. "Mia should be here any second," he says with a furrowed brow.

Right on cue, his wife comes barreling into the school at high speed, with two-year-old James barely keeping up. She's got an enormous diaper bag slung over her shoulder, and she's carrying something weighty in the crook of her right arm, which I can't make out until she reaches us.

"Hold this!" she says, handing me a swaddled baby girl. She bends down, lifts two-year-old James onto her hip, and exchanges an exasperated laugh with Evan, whose arm is being pulled in every direction by their eldest daughter.

"You must be Maeve," I say to the sleeping baby in my arms. I rock her back and forth as Mia wipes jam off a giggling James's face.

Dex leans toward me to whisper in my ear. "That's a good look for you," he says.

My cheeks heat up as I smile at him.

"We're so sorry!" Mia says breathlessly. "The babysitter canceled, my parents picked up the cold Avery had last week, and Evan's are in Hong Kong." She sighs deeply and blows a strand of hair off her face. "Are we even allowed to bring kids to this thing?"

"Of course. We're very kid-friendly," my husband reassures them.

"Great! Evan will take 'em outside if they're too noisy. We'll see you guys after the show!" Mia says with an eager grin as she puts James down on the floor and takes Maeve from me.

"Bye, Aunt Sunny!" Avery sings as she frees herself from her dad's grip and darts into the auditorium. Mia runs after her with Maeve and James, while Evan hangs back.

"Be right there, honey!" he calls after his wife. Then he leans toward Dex. "By the way…I couldn't help but overhear." He looks around before he continues, his voice nearly a whisper. "What is this thing you do that has Sunny screaming so loud?"

"I'll explain later," Dex tells him as I hide behind my hands.

Through parted fingers, I watch the two men fist-bump.

When everyone's seated, Dex walks onstage to raucous applause and gives a brief introduction about tonight's performance. Then, as the lights dim, he comes back to sit with me, our family and friends, in the front row.

The show is incredible. Even better than the Chicago performances, because the kids are more comfortable in front of an audience now. When it's over, Dex goes back onstage to thank everyone for coming, then tells them more about The Dramatic Hearts Academy.

While my husband is speaking, I wait for him in the wings. My mind flashes back to eighteen-year-old Sunny, who stood heartbroken at the bottom of the stairs behind me, after witnessing Jenna Andersen kiss him.

It's funny how much has changed since then. I used to see Jenna as an ideal I could never live up to. The Homecoming Queen. The Head Cheerleader. The Most Popular Girl in School. Now I know that I don't need to be anyone but my perfectly imperfect self. I also realize that, like my husband, Jenna's just as human as I am.

After I confessed to Dex that she was the reason I didn't give him my love letter in high school, he told me that he ran into her in LA. That she was as heartbroken over her ex as Dex was over me. That they commiserated about the lost loves of their lives, and became involved again, but decided to remain friends.

I know Jenna believes she isn't capable of loving anyone the way she loved her ex, but I hope she's wrong. I hope she gets her happy ending, just like I did.

If I could, I'd go back in time and give eighteen-year-old Sunny a hug, then wipe away her tears. I'd tell her not to worry, because all her dreams come true—eventually.

But life isn't that easy. We can never predict what's around the next corner.

If we could, would we take it all for granted?

All I know is that standing here, after every tear I've shed, I'm the happiest I've ever been. Soon, I'll be a published author. I'm married to the love of my life. And I'm about to tell him we're going to be parents.

Everything I went through led me to this moment. And it was worth it.

I watch as my husband walks offstage. When he meets my gaze, he smiles.

Then he kisses me.

THANK YOU!

As an independent author, your support means the world to me. If you enjoyed *If the Stars Align*, please consider leaving a review. Not only does your thoughtful feedback make my day, it helps put my books in more readers' hands. Just scan the QR Code below!

Want more Sunny and Dex?

If you're anything like me, you're not ready to part ways with the new Mr. and Mrs. Dexter yet. Scan the QR Code below for a Bonus Epilogue, and find out where Sunny takes her husband after the Dramatic Hearts Academy performance…and why.

ACKNOWLEDGMENTS

On a hot summer night in July 2022, I was on the verge of falling asleep when a line popped into my head: "I want you to know that I have always loved you." I have no idea where it came from or what it meant. But that's how this book began.

My first draft of this novel was in the form of a letter from Sunny to Dex, and it didn't fit neatly in any genre. It was an admirable first attempt, but the truth of the matter is that I didn't know how to write a book back then. I didn't even know *what I didn't know*. Enter Emily Colin. I've said it before, and I'll say it again: I'm convinced the stars aligned when I registered for your online writing course. That class changed my life, setting me on the path to the writer I am today. I am infinitely grateful for everything you've taught me as my editor and book coach. Thank you for supporting me, believing in me, and convincing me to completely rewrite my novel. Had it not been for you, poor Sunny and Dex would have suffered many more years of being apart.

To everyone who read my novel in its various stages of development—my husband, Dominique, my mom, Claudette Collins, my high school English teacher, Bonnie Seebold, my friends Parissa Andideh, Gaby Choi, Emily Giger, Amy Goff, Sarah Kooperman, and Kayla Negohosian—thank you so much for taking time out of your busy lives to read my book and give me feedback. Your encouragement means the world to me. And to my friends Puja Kapadia and Jane Kenyon, thanks for your invaluable emotional support, and for cheering me on throughout every step of this journey.

Thank you to my dad, Arnie Collins, for instilling in me a love of reading, writing, and storytelling. I cherish the original bedtime stories you made up for me on the fly, and I still remember how much I looked forward to a new installment every night. You dreamed of writing a novel, and I hope you know this accomplishment is as much yours as it is mine. You were taken from us too soon, but now you live on in John Dexter. Your darling daughter will always love you.

Thank you, Mom, for your unconditional love and support. Seeing how much you enjoyed this book, particularly since you're not typically a reader of romance novels, was such a joy for me. I'm honored to be your favorite writer. Thank you for always being proud of me—and not judging me for the steamy scenes.

Thank you to my children for putting up with a mom who can't always get the snacks *rightthissecond* because she's in the middle of writing a scene. You've been (more or less) patient with this process, but most of all, your excitement is the fuel I need to keep me going when I'm up half the night writing. Believe it or not, I'm doing this for you, because I want to show you it's possible to make your dreams come true if you work hard enough. I love you both beyond words. Also—please don't read this book until you're eighteen.

And last, but certainly not least, a heartfelt thank-you to my readers. I hope you enjoyed reading Sunny and Dex's love story as much as I enjoyed writing it. As a therapist, one of the most common misperceptions I hear is something along the lines of,

"Everyone has their shit together except me." My motivation for writing this particular story was, in part, to shatter this myth. No one is perfect. Everyone's fighting some sort of battle.

If you've ever woken up in the middle of the night sweating, and shaking, and gasping for air—your heart hammering so hard you're convinced you're going to die—I want you to know that I've been there. You're not broken. You're not crazy. You're not alone. You're human. Just like me. And there is help. All you have to do is ask.

ABOUT THE AUTHOR

Nathalie Theodore is the IPPY award-winning, Amazon bestselling author of *If the Stars Align*, *If My Wishes Came True*, and *If We Play Fair*, the first three novels in her Dramatic Hearts Club series. A lawyer-turned-therapist and novelist, she writes love stories that dive deep into the psychology of her characters, using her background in mental health to create beautifully flawed, true-to-life protagonists. In addition to writing, she enjoys spending time with her family in their hometown of Chicago. More often than not, you'll find her at a coffee shop, a bookstore, or a baseball game.

CONNECT ONLINE

NathalieTheodore.com
Facebook @DramaticHeartsClub
Instagram @NathalieTheodoreWrites
Substack @NathalieTheodoreWrites

ALSO BY
NATHALIE THEODORE

THE DRAMATIC HEARTS CLUB SERIES

If the Stars Align
A standalone friends-to-lovers romance that spans a decade

(Sunny & Dex)

If My Wishes Came True
A standalone love-at-first-sight romance with a plot twist

(Jenna & Charlie)

If We Play Fair
A standalone enemies-to-lovers fake-dating baseball romance

(Christy & Holden)

SCAN THE QR CODE TO READ MORE

9 781966 472001